SW

SHADOW OF THE CORPS

SHADOW OF THE CORPS

JAMES M. DUPONT

PEGASUS CRIME

NEW YORK LONDON

SHADOW OF THE CORPS

Pegasus Books LLC
80 Broad Street, 5th Floor
New York, NY 10004

First Pegasus Books hardcover edition July 2013

Interior design by Maria Fernandez

Library of Congress Cataloging-in-Publication Data is available.

ISBN: 978-1-60598-462-9

10 9 8 7 6 5 4 3 2 1

Printed in the United States of America
Distributed by W. W. Norton & Company, Inc.

For my wife, Andrea

PROLOGUE

The yellow cab rolled to a stop just after 4:00 P.M. This was good. The banks would still be open.

The passenger tossed a duffel bag in back and hopped in after it.

"The First Citizens Bank on Front Street," he said, "and step on it."

The cabbie put the car in gear. "You got it, buddy." Pulling away, he checked his rearview mirror. There, he saw a tough guy like all the others that he had picked up here from time to time. All of them shifty-eyed and in a god-awful hurry. Forgoing hello, they'd toss in their bags and make their demands, always to the banks, hotels, or brothels on the outskirts of town. If it was the brothels, they would hand him a five and tell him to wait—it shouldn't take long. Typically, it didn't. Those who did say hello went on and on with their sad-sack stories, tales of how they had been screwed over by the system, the younger ones eager to begin life anew, the older ones with lost and rheumy eyes. Many, the cabbie knew, would find themselves back inside before long. Human waste, the lot of them.

The passenger glanced up. "What the hell you looking at?"

The cabbie cast his eyes down the road. "Nothing, buddy. Just traffic." He knew enough to pass judgment with his mouth shut.

He readjusted the rearview mirror and decided to take the scenic route to town. Einstein in back would never know the difference.

With a suspicious eye on the cabbie, the passenger pulled out his wallet and, from this, a slip of paper. Penned in ink were four names, which he studied. He closed his eyes and tested himself. He did this several times. When his head began to hurt, he considered eating the scrap, destroying any trace. Sadly, however, he didn't trust his memory. There were mornings when he could barely remember his own name, the God's honest truth. Growing up, his mother had called him dim. The teachers were kinder and had labeled him below average. The kids just called him stupid. In the eighth grade, the name-calling ended when he broke the bones of a couple of kids who had been teasing him. Expulsions followed, and Einstein never returned. Years of trouble followed, until at eighteen an army recruiter assisted him with his GED (assisted, as in handed him the answers to the tests), and then had him sign the paperwork to complete his enlistment. It was time for Einstein to be all that he could be, and the rest, as they say, is history.

Entering the town proper, the passenger kicked back and relaxed.

Outside, the sidewalks were mostly deserted.

He rolled down the window.

The afternoon was crisp, the air freezing. Regardless, it felt terrific; it felt like . . . freedom. Yeah, freedom, baby, freedom, and he smiled for the first time in what felt like forever. Blissfully, he closed his steely eyes.

"Here we are, pal," said the cabbie. "The First Citizens Bank on Front Street. That'll be eighteen fifty."

The passenger handed him a twenty. "There's another one in it for ya if you wait for a sec."

Nervously, the cabbie laughed. "You ain't gonna rob that joint, are you, mister?" Once, many years ago, a pick-up from the same institution did just that, popped in, and popped out with guns a-blazing. The cabbie didn't stick around to collect what was rightfully owed to him. Later, he read about it in the newspapers: one wounded cop and one dead ex-con, no mention of the cabbie who had been stiffed.

"That's funny," the passenger replied. "Stick to driving."

Inside, the bank was warm and inviting. The passenger did his best to fit in, just another rich asshole doing some rich-asshole banking.

At guest services, he found a finicky young man with a nametag that read: Steve. He cleared his throat to get noticed.

Steve looked up from his computer and said, "Oh. Hello, sir. How may I assist you today?"

"My safe deposit box, Steve-ee-boy. And I ain't got all day." Yes, just another rich asshole with prison tattoos that disappeared up the sleeves and down the neck of a faded, dusty trench coat, a faux-diamond stud in his left earlobe, stubble on his chin.

"Of course," said Steve. "Right this way."

Along the way to this faraway room, the passenger counted six surveillance cameras. Six! Here inside the anteroom was lucky number seven, mounted high in the corner, watching. He was used to being watched. Still, when would it end?

Steve accessed a computer. "Your name?"

"Sean Fitzsimmons."

Steve entered the name. "Can I please see some identification, Mr. Fitzsimmons?"

Sean handed over his driver's license. "It's a bit outdated. But that's me there in the photograph. Gone bald since, but still a handsome sonofabitch, wouldn't you say?"

"As the Devil," added Steve, without looking up from his screen. "And the password, please?"

"The password?"

Now Steve did look up, his eyebrows raised. "You do realize that this box requires a password?"

"Oh, yeah. A password. Sure." On the back of the slip of paper, the boss man had penned the password. Once again he pulled this from his wallet. "Let's see. And the password is . . . Angel 12." He smiled to reveal a dentist's worst nightmare.

Steve, inputting the data, politely inquired, "So, would that be a one and a two, or should I spell out the number twelve?"

"One and two, Steve-ee-boy. Angel 12. I had a girlfriend named Angel once. Boy, what a piece of ass. And the legs on that broad." He kissed his fingertips Italian style.

Steve, unamused, said, "Yes. Very well. Okay. Everything matches. Follow me."

The two entered a deeper, darker room where literally hundreds of boxes lined opposite walls.

There must be a damn fortune in here, thought Sean, who then zeroed in on the back of Steve-ee-boy's head. A swift punch, and this room, these riches, would be all his. High on the far wall, however, was camera number eight, watching with an unblinking eye. Sean smiled at this, unclenched his fist, and waved hello.

Steve found the box and handed it over.

"I need a moment alone, Steve-ee-boy. Nothing personal."

"Of course. Right this way." Steve showed him to a closet. "Take your time, sir."

Sean shut himself in. Suspiciously, he glanced around and saw no cameras. He set the box atop a pedestal. Anxiously, he rubbed his hands, clueless to the fact that embedded in the ceiling was camera number nine. In black-and-white imagery it showed a thick, shaved head hovering over a safe deposit box, tattooed knuckles cracking the lid. The microphone picked up a staticky yet gleeful: *"Holy shit."*

Sean pulled out a fat wad of cash and a pistol, and stuffed these items inside various pockets. Next, he pulled out a cell phone and what appeared to be a clip of bullets.

Camera nine was motion-activated, the tapes maintained continuously and rarely checked. In fact, no one would bother unless the authorities came with questions, or thievery was suspected. In the case of Sean Fitzsimmons, the authorities wouldn't come until well into the summer. Security would dig through the archives and find the date in question. They would pull the tapes and watch Sean Fitzsimmons from the moment when he first entered the bank.

This, along with the other evidence, would lead the authorities back to the federal pen, back to the boss man himself. Until then, there was havoc to be had, and money to be made, plenty of opportunities for Sean to be all he could be.

Sean closed the lid and took a deep breath. He couldn't help his criminal mind, and actually thought about robbing the joint, just like the cabbie had said. He would approach the most vulnerable teller and in his best John Wayne voice tell her to empty them drawers, toots, and make it snappy. He loved them ole western movies, and would add that if she didn't hurry she'd be pushing up daisies. It was a vision that made him strangely happy. Currently, however, he had four names on a hit list, and as the boss man always said, first things first.

He opened the door, hooked his thumb over his shoulder, and used his best John Wayne (which was actually pretty horrible) on Steve. "Box is in there, pilgrim. Have yourself a mighty-fine day, whah, hah."

Back inside the taxicab, Sean slammed the door and slapped the seatback in front of him. "The *Enterprise Rent-A-Car* on Pollen Street, pal, and make it snappy!"

SHADOW OF THE CORPS

PART 1

JUSTICE WANTS WHAT JUSTICE IS OWED

"Justice is the means by which established injustices are sanctioned."

—Anatole France

PART I

JUSTICE WANTS WHAT JUSTICE IS OWED.

CHAPTER 1

The first snowflake drifted from a dark and moody sky, flitted down, and touched the silver bell.

A Marine in full dress-blue regalia stood sentry amid the tombstones. With white-gloved hands he lifted the silver trumpet, inhaled, and played Taps—the notes as crisp as the air, lingering across the vast, harsh field of the dead, resonating with those who stood and mourned.

Near the maw of the grave sat a relatively young woman. Veiled in black, her lamentations seemed as piercing as the trumpet. It was difficult to watch her, let alone to listen. She reached for the pine coffin, cried, collapsed time and time again. Two teenage boys stood nearest her, holding her, crying with her—her sons, no doubt, doing their best to remain strong in the company of death.

As for dad, well, dad was the man of the hour, wasn't he? The occupier of the pine casket. Its lid closed with resolute finality.

Dale Riley stood in the back of the dark-clad gathering, where he overheard someone whisper to another that nothing could be done to restore dad's face. This was precisely what Dale was afraid of; was, in fact, the reason he'd driven here from Charlotte. Two days ago, what would have been Wednesday morning, he'd sat at the kitchen table with his wife and son and parents, reading the newspaper and picking at a plate of soggy scrambled eggs. Being unemployed, leisurely breakfasts had become a bit of a hobby. A front-page article in the Raleigh *News and Observer*—one of two newspapers that his father religiously subscribed to, the other being the *Charlotte Observer*—reported a shooting in a prominent Raleigh neighborhood. One man shot and killed, suspect still at large. At first, Dale thought nothing of this. *A man shot and killed. Shit happens.* But then, after the funnies and a rather generic if not uninspiring horoscope, Dale happened upon the obituaries. One in particular keyed his interest. He reread it. For a brief moment he tried to convince himself that this was a different Alex Snead. Tragically, however, everything seemed to fit. The obit described a loving husband, caring father, and god-fearing Baptist. Furthermore, it went on to say that Alex had served eight years in the Marine Corps as a JAG officer, his most recent assignment Cherry Point, North Carolina. Details that left little doubt that this was, in fact, the same Alex Snead.

Sipping from his cup of coffee, he had the gut feeling that the front-page article and obit might be related. In other words, was Alex the same poor bastard who had taken a bullet in a prominent Raleigh neighborhood? The obit reported nothing as to the cause of death, as was evident on the third, if not fourth, reading.

"Everything okay?" his father inquired, peering above his reading glasses.

"Yeah, Dad. Everything is fine."

Unless, of course, you're Alex Snead.

"Are you sure?" Gina pressed. "You look as white as a ghost." Gina, on the other hand, looked beautiful; her dishwater-blond hair in a bun, cheeks and neck dusted lightly with freckles. Still in her pajamas, her taut, heavenly body lilted beneath the soft cotton flannel. She'd been feeding their six-month-old, Clint, goop from a glass container, and was currently wiping his mouth with a towel.

"It's just . . . I think I know this guy." He set the obit on the table nearest Gina.

She set aside the towel, picked up the newspaper, and read. "You know him from the Marine Corps?"

"Yeah. My days in the Corps." He left it at that; wasn't in the mood to go into specifics. "It says that the funeral is Friday morning. I think, you know, that maybe I should go."

"How well did you know this guy?"

"Well enough, I guess."

"You never mentioned him."

"You sure?"

She shrugged. "I don't think so."

"Well, there are a lot of guys I knew that I've never mentioned."

A different argument came to the fore. "Dale," she began, embarrassed to be bringing this up in front of his parents, "your unemployment check doesn't come until next Friday. We barely have enough money to buy food for Clint."

Anticipating this, he said, "There's a couple hundred on the Visa. I just need to fill up the tank. I mean . . . it shouldn't be that expensive."

Gina might have persisted if not for the sour expression on Ellen's face, who sat at the far end of the table, knitting.

Dad pulled out his wallet, reached in, and threw a few twenties on the table.

Gina shook her head. "We can't. You guys are doing so much for us already."

"Nonsense," dad replied. "And it's good to pay your respects to old departed friends. Go to the funeral, son. It's the right thing to do."

Ellen eyed the twenties with malice. To dad's kindness and generosity, mom was equally mean and stingy. In this instance, however, Ellen held her tongue, her eyes darting back to her knitting.

Dale scooped up the cash. "Thanks, Dad. Mom. I'll pay you back, okay, promise."

"When you can," dad replied. "No rush."

Early Friday morning, the morning of the funeral, Dale stuffed himself inside a tired three-piece suit that he had resurrected from the basement. Without the jacket he appeared as fat as a rhino. His girth spilled over the waistband. He was painfully aware that he had put on some weight, but this was ridiculous. The jacket helped, or so he told himself. He kissed his sleeping wife and son good-bye, and then, as quiet as a two-hundred-and-fifty-pound church mouse, sneaked downstairs.

The month was February; the promise was snow.

He grabbed his father's overcoat and threw it on.

Outside, frost blanketed the lawn, thin patches of ice along the walkway.

The door to his faded-blue Honda Civic opened with the sound of cracking ice.

"Okay, Old Betsy," he said with frosty breath, "don't leave me hanging." With nearly 250,000 miles on the odometer, she had every right to do just that. She had suffered years of both physical and mental abuse: physical with how he had driven her; and mental with the names he had called her—Old Betsy today when just yesterday she was *The Whore*, or *The Bitch*. However, Dale was a father now, trying to change his ways.

Prayerfully, he keyed the ignition.

The cabin lights dimmed.

The engine whirred and whirred.

"Goddamn it," he exclaimed, and then pounded *The Bitch's* steering wheel.

He took a deep breath.

Okay.

He tried her again.

"Please, baby. *Please!*"

At last she sputtered to life.

He goosed the gas.

"Atta girl. You can do it, baby."

He patted the dash and thanked her profusely.

With Raleigh a good three hours away, he unbuttoned his slacks. His gut spilled out and would have sparked another round of disgust had he not been preoccupied with worry.

CHAPTER 2

Dale intended to hit the 9:00 A.M. service at the Pullen Baptist Church, Raleigh. There, finding just the right moment and a sympathetic soul, he would ask a few well-phrased questions. Since reading the obit, he had grown increasingly worried. His relationship with Alex had been professional and rather brief, so emotionally he was fine. What troubled him were the specifics of Alex's death. *Heart attack, or shot? Aneurism, or shot? Rabid dog, or shot?* Either way, he had to know.

East of Greensboro he encountered a road construction crew, the traffic at a standstill.

On the radio—*KROK 99.1*—*DJ Savage Jack* was saying, *"Better grease up them sleds and toboggans, little kiddies, and dig out a scarf for Ole Frosty, 'cause the big one is coming. That's right, it's high time for a little wintertime fun, and for you commuters out there, well, I'd hightail it for home if I was you. Unless, of course, you got yourself a pair of them there snow skis in the trunk. And speaking of snow skis, here's a shout-out to our sponsors at—"*

Dale glanced skyward. Hightailing it for home simply wasn't an option. He had to know.

When at last eastbound traffic flowed, two knuckleheads ahead of him, late for work or wherever, jockeyed for the left-hand lane and collided. The white SUV veered left and onto the grassy median, where the tires sank into the muddy earth. The black Buick canted, flipped, and came to rest upside down and in the middle of the Interstate. Adding insult to injury, a red pickup truck smashed the rear panel of the Buick and sent it spinning like a top. Traffic collided like an accordion. Fortunately, Dale had been far enough back to avoid any damage. He did, however, get ensnared in the net of twisted metal, at which point he banged *The Bitch's* steering wheel and cursed a small storm of his own.

Good Samaritans (Dale included, although it took him a few seconds to cool down) assisted the victims. Thankfully, no one had been seriously injured. The driver of the Buick, a middle-aged man in a suit, crawled out through a shattered window, blood trickling along the side of his face. Another suit in a Mercedes offered this man refuge from the cold. The man in the white SUV, screaming into his cell phone, welcomed both young and old with a firm middle finger.

And for the second time that morning, Interstate 40 eastbound turned into a parking lot.

This was about the time when DJ Savage Jack had a brilliant idea: that although Christmastime was over, why not, with the promise of snow, resurrect the festive mood? The first hit song he played was *Winter (freaking) Wonderland*, followed soon thereafter by *Frosty the (goddamn) Snowman*. And all the while, Dale was doing his best to be that better man, to be patient in the face of adversity, to breathe and relax, and to not allow the entirety of the situation to send him spinning like the Buick. He sat there with the others, watching the cops come and go, the tow truck, everyone so goddamn leisurely about their duties. Throughout all of this, he refused to pound *The Bitch's* steering wheel. He wouldn't do it, no way. Instead, he inhaled to a count of five, exhaled to a count of ten—something he'd read about in a men's fitness magazine, how to achieve Zen in sixty seconds. He actually found himself enjoying the shitty Christmas tunes, just a wee bit frustrated that he could find no other radio station.

At 9:02 the cops started waving people through, Raleigh still an hour away. But that's okay. So he was late, big deal. Funerals tend to go on forever, don't they? And they can last, it seems, a lifetime.

He arrived as the hearse was exiting the church's parking lot, followed by two black limos and thirty, forty cars.

He became the procession's caboose and cranked down Savage Jack (*A Holly Jolly Christmas* just didn't seem a fitting tune).

At the cemetery, the vehicles flowed in through the wrought-iron gates. A warmly dressed cop directed traffic, parking cars on both sides of the cemetery road.

Dale killed the engine and immediately regretted doing so. What if Old Betsy had given him her very last mile? A fitting place to call it quits, sure, but hardly the time for Dale to find himself alone without wheels. But for the dearly departed, he wouldn't know a soul. That, and he hadn't a cell phone from which to call for assistance. Worst case, he'd ask a fellow mourner for a jump-start. Failing that, he'd beg a ride. To where, he wasn't sure. Certainly he couldn't ask for a ride three hours back to Charlotte.

Outside, he glanced around self-consciously, sucked in his gut, and buttoned up his slacks.

Pallbearers exited the second limo, pulled the flag-draped coffin from the hearse, and carried Alex Snead toward the open gravesite.

The minister followed with a bible held high.

A black sea of family and friends engulfed the widow and escorted her over to the gravesite, to that cold and lonely metal chair.

Quickly, the final rite was staged—the pine coffin suspended on straps atop the gaping maw, flowers here and there, a widow, her two sons, a single Marine in dress blues and white gloves, holding a silver trumpet, the sterling tint of which contrasted greatly with the weather, and more so with the mood.

With the mourners gathered, the minister cracked his bible and began with a reading from Psalms: *You hear, oh Lord, the hopes of the helpless. . . .*

The widow cried. Jesus, how she suffered. Not a praying man, Dale bowed his head and said a prayer, that God might ease her suffering.

Two elderly ladies quietly chatted, lamented the closed casket, his disfigured face, that they hadn't had the opportunity here or at the church to see him one last time, for closure, to offer their good-byes.

When the minister closed his bible, the pallbearers lowered the coffin.

Mourners came with fistfuls of dirt, tossed pebbles and clumps that bounced off the lid and echoed. In passing, the minister reminded each and all that we are dust and unto dust we shall return.

Snow began to fall.

The Marine trumpeter lifted his trumpet and played his mournful tune.

When all that remained belonged to the gravediggers, the two young men assisted their mother back toward the limo. The entourage followed her, the Marine, and the minister.

As the widow drew near, Dale wondered if she might not spot him in the back of the crowd, if she might not point a finger. Ridiculous, of course, as the two had never met. Still, what if somehow she recognized him? What if she cried out: *My husband is dead and it's all your fault. I hate you. I HATE you*! He lowered his head so as not to be recognized.

The widow passed by, lost in sorrow, barely able to carry her own weight.

The sea of black filtered toward their vehicles.

Politely, Dale tapped one of the elderly ladies on the shoulder. Quietly, he whispered, "Excuse me, ma'am." Quietly, yes, although his heart was thumping quite loudly.

She turned. "Yes?" She had kind blue eyes and soft white hair, was probably in her seventies.

He'd been thinking about how to phrase the question. The best he could come up with was this: "I'm an old friend of Alex's, ma'am. I read about his death in the newspapers. I'm wondering, well, I'm wondering how it happened. I'm wondering if you know what happened to Alex Snead? How he . . . died?"

Shuffling toward the vehicles, the ladies shared a woeful, puzzled look. The one with the kind blue eyes sidled up next to him. She took his right arm. Perhaps this wasn't the time or place, but the young man seemed sincere if not confused. There was something else. Fear, perhaps. Quietly, she replied, "You honestly don't know what happened, dear?"

"No, ma'am."

"It's such a tragedy." With a tissue she dabbed the corners of her eyes.

"A tragedy, ma'am?"

"It's awful. The poor thing."

"How awful?"

The second lady corralled Dale's other elbow. "Oh, for heaven's sake, Mandy, just tell this young man what happened."

Mandy leaned in. He could feel the warmth of her breath when she whispered to him: "The poor dear . . . *he was shot.*"

The pounding in Dale's chest seemed to have stopped. He didn't, or couldn't, speak. He stared at her with wide and frightened eyes, the collar of his father's overcoat flipped up against the cold.

"I'm sorry," Mandy said. "I'm so sorry. It's terrible, isn't it? It's horrible."

Suddenly, Dale felt like running. Like sprinting through the cold and stark tombstones, sprinting just to get away, as if he could run from reality, from the dead body of Alex Snead, as if he could run away from his past. Instead, he stood as rigid as a tuning fork, vibrating as though he had been struck by a hammer. Around him the mass flowed by like lava. He didn't even hear himself when he said, "Jesus. He was *shot?*"

"I'm so sorry," Mandy said. "Were you two very close?"

Dale didn't answer her. He didn't know what to say. He stood in disbelief.

Shot, the poor dear. Shot!

The lady on his left whispered: "Wendy is lucky to be alive. She and her two boys. They had just sat down for dinner when it happened. When a gunman opened fire from outside their dining room window. Can you imagine?" She, too, dabbed her eyes with a tissue.

No, Dale couldn't imagine. It was all a bit much, really, the funeral, the widow, and even the snowfall. And now, two years after the threats, enter a gunman. Two full years since the court-martial that had forever changed Dale's life and the life of Alex Snead. Two years of troubled times, and now this.

Mandy, seemingly smaller than before, and more distant though she hadn't moved, said, "I'm so sorry for your loss, young man. I'm sorry." She released his elbow and motioned for her friend to come with her and follow.

Standing alone, Dale called out after them: "Did they catch him? The gunman? Did they at least catch the shooter?" People looked his way. He hardly noticed.

Mandy turned. "No, dear. Nothing. I'm sorry." She then folded in with the others.

The mass thinned into their cars.

Exhaust plumed amid the gloomy morn.

Gravediggers emerged from the shadows with shovels.

Snowfall coated the earth and tombstones white.

Dale found himself inside Old Betsy, gave little thought to the fact that she started after the third attempt. He watched the other vehicles meander down the winding road, and then he glanced to the shadows cast by trees and by tombstones. He wondered if the gunman was out there, hiding, watching, waiting for an opportunity.

That instant the sky turned white with snowflakes. Behind the wheel, Dale sensed that the snow would never end, that indeed it would last forever.

CHAPTER 3

On the eighth anniversary of September 11, in the early morning hours just past midnight, the Devil descended from the heavens and blew fire upon the earth. That's how a village elder saw things. That's how he explained it to the investigating officer, Lieutenant Colonel Brandt. As Dale Riley drove through the snow, creeping along Interstate 40 for home, this is what he thought about. He kept DJ Savage Jack low, remembering the eighty-three people that had been killed that night in a war zone: seventy-eight Afghan civilians, and five United States Marines.

From Lieutenant Colonel Brandt's JAG investigation, Dale knew that the five Marines had been deployed to this village in an effort to gather intel on al Qaeda. Their leader was First Lieutenant Mark Tegee, an intelligence officer on his first assignment overseas. The mission demanded a certain amount of toughness and sensibility. By all accounts, First Lieutenant Tegee was the perfect Marine for the job.

Gunnery Sergeant Ahmad Bandani served as the interpreter, a first-generation American fluent in Farsi. The consummate Marine, Ahmad was professional and dedicated, tough, with a penchant for cheap cigars and top-shelf scotch.

Rounding out the quintet were corporals Chad Adams and Samuel Lynch, and Private First Class Jon Burch. These three were the muscle. They carried automatic weapons and hand grenades, a broadband UHF radio for air and artillery support. While First Lieutenant Tegee and Gunnery Sergeant Bandani schmoozed with the village elders, these three remained in the background with their heads on swivels and their fingers on their triggers. An ill-timed sneeze might have sent them rocking and rolling Rambo style, but no one sneezed, and none but a curious kid or two even dared to look their way.

They had set up camp on the eastern edge of the Sorubi village—some one hundred nautical miles south of the capital city, Kabul—where they could keep watch on the hardscrabble land in the event of malcontent violence. At night, these Marines would take turns patrolling, darkness till dawn. On the eve of the anniversary of 9/11, Corporal Lynch pulled up a chair just outside their tent. The night grew bitterly cold. Moonlight reflected off the nearby snowcapped mountains. He kept his rifle across his lap and his feet pressed warmly together. In his hands he held a pair of night-vision goggles, which he used to vigilantly scan the village. A sneak attack would be virtually impossible. A sniper round, however, was a different story altogether. This was, after all, a war zone where the Devil and his minions play gaily in fields of flesh and blood.

Approaching midnight, the temperature continued to plummet. Corporal Lynch found the expanse of sky nothing short of amazing. There were stars like he had never before seen in his entire lifetime. Having grown up in the mountains of Montana, he believed that no place on earth could beat the nighttime skies from his own back yard. But here on the other side of planet earth, it seemed as if he could reach up and come away with a fistful of diamonds. He set aside his night-vision goggles, and he tried to do just that. He reached up, but came away with only frosty air. He smiled. He pondered other life forms in galaxies far away. He imagined a kindred spirit somewhere up there in the infinite expanse, another Marine holding vigil of the night. He winked toward the heavens and said, "What's up?"

And then a single star fell, just one; a single star from the blanket of diamonds. What an Afghan elder would call the Devil, spreading his wings to breathe fire down upon them.

Perplexed, Corporal Lynch set aside his rifle. He stood. He watched the Devil come. The sound seemed familiar. He'd heard it before. He never called out to warn the others. It never actually occurred to him to do so, that in an instant there would be fire and chaos, that the flames would fan out from several points of origin, that fire would engulf adobe homes and consume warm flesh, the night alit with horrors.

In an instant the corporal was gone, obliterated, and the tent and the Marines inside it. Gone. KIA. Victims of warfare.

In the fire-lit chaos two mothers stumbled upon the charred remains of an infant. The grief they shared was unthinkable. When one moved to collect the infant, so did the other. What is it about motherhood that would spark such a sick and twisted game of wishbone? Imagine the horror when the infant's flesh tore apart like a thigh from the whole of the roast! The mothers pried apart from one another lest the Devil steal another.

Seventy-eight Afghans and five United States Marines died that night in the village. That was the official body count, eighty-three all told. In the JAG investigation, Lieutenant Colonel Brandt concluded that the bodies of the five young Marines had either been obliterated by the blast, or were unidentifiable amid the carnage. Either way, the mothers (and fathers, let's not forget about the fathers) of these Marines had nothing to bury but the memories, which all would greatly mourn when the nights drew long and weary with brilliant stars of no concern.

CHAPTER 4

On the third of April, 2010, nearly seven months after that fiery night at the Sorubi village, the United States military convened a court-martial.

The venue was a dusty courtroom aboard Marine Corps Air Station Cherry Point, North Carolina, a small stitch of land along the eastern seaboard with enough bombs and aircraft and Marines who fly them to obliterate a nation.

In the jury box sat lieutenant colonels and colonels, navy lieutenant commanders and commanders, six men and three women, each heavily decorated, each a card-carrying member of the Republican Party. Stereotypically, military jurors shoot first and ask questions later. This group was no different.

At the prosecutor's desk and on behalf of the United States Government sat Major Alex Snead, loving husband, caring father, and god-fearing Baptist. His eyes were the sharpest of blue, his hair short and blond. He had a thin frame coated lightly with muscle, and, most importantly, he had a perfect record. As lead prosecutor for six prior court-martials, he had secured a verdict of guilty in all six. Considering the government's evidence in this case, he anticipated lucky number seven. He sat with confidence and a legal clerk, organizing his materials, mentally preparing for opening statements.

The courtroom hummed.

The benches were filled to maximum capacity.

Bailiffs turned people away.

At precisely 0900 hours, the esteemed Colonel William T. Alberts entered the courtroom, wearing olive-green service *Alphas*—khaki shirt and tie, jungle-green jacket with ribbons, matching slacks with black polished shoes. At six feet tall and 230 pounds, he was a brute of a man with a short, caustic temper.

Sergeant Hernandez, the lead bailiff, bellowed out from the front of the courtroom: "All rise. The Honorable Judge Alberts presiding."

Judge Alberts knew intimately the details of the case. It had made national—and international—news. The brass at the Pentagon had sent a delegation of officers, all seated at various points in the courtroom. Nearby were interns from the North Carolina senators' offices in Raleigh, as well as members of the Senate Committee on Armed Services. Visas had been granted for three delegates from Afghanistan, one with a direct line to President Karzai. There were newspaper reporters with pens and pads (voice and video recorders disallowed), and a sketch artist with contracts with six different media outlets.

Captain Dale Riley, attorney for the defense, had entered a plea of not guilty. Having yet to face the adversities that oftentimes plague adulthood, he stood fit and trim with an optimist's smile.

"We will begin with opening statements," said Judge Alberts, who then looked at Major Snead and added: "You have sixty seconds, young man. Your time starts now." The days of leisure were over, gone with the days of his youth. Judge Alberts intended to get to the heart of the matter and to do so quickly. He punched the timer on his wristwatch.

Major Snead stood. "Sixty seconds, sir?"

Gruffly, Judge Alberts said, "Fifty-eight seconds and counting, Major Snead. Tick-tock."

Gathering his wits, the loving husband and caring father said, "All right. Well. Ladies and gentlemen of the jury, on or about the 11th of September, 2009, Captain Michael J. Ruffers, the defendant, violated eighty-three counts of Article 118 of the Uniform Code of Military Justice. In command of an AV-8B Harrier jet, Captain Ruffers did willfully bomb a village in northeastern Afghanistan. He did so unprovoked and out of hatred, killing seventy-eight Afghan noncombatants and five United States Marines. We the government of the United States of America will prove beyond a reasonable doubt that Captain Ruffers committed these crimes, and that he should pay with his life. We the—"

"Time's up," Judge Alberts interrupted. "Nice job." Of course he said nice job with a great deal of sarcasm, with contempt that was fair for a judge, but not so fair for those in his courtroom.

Dejectedly, Major Snead said, "Sir. In the name of justice, the government of the United States of America deserves more time. There are a lot of things I had intended to cover."

Judge Alberts plucked up his gavel and twirled it. "In the name of justice, huh?"

"Yes, sir."

"Let me be the first to inform you, young Major, that justice is nothing but a two-bit whore. Justice wants it hard and fast so that she can take what's owed to her and be on her way. You either nailed her brains out—*boom!*—or you didn't. Either way, she doesn't give a shit. Justice wants what's owed to her, and that's it!"

Major Snead threw down his paperwork and considered threatening the court with an appeal. However, the military appellate court is comprised mostly of retired military lawyers with big rubber stamps that say *DENIED*. His argument was reduced to a sigh. Dejectedly he took his seat.

Having had enough of one clown, Judge Alberts turned to the other. "Captain Riley, you're up. Your time starts . . . now." Again he punched his timer.

Having worked with Judge Alberts before, Captain Riley had spent countless hours preparing a sixty-second opening statement. Sixty seconds flat. Last night before bed he'd rehearsed it several times. In bed he'd rehearsed several more. He was ready. Almost couldn't wait. But that was last night. Today, he stood speechless. He glanced to the audience, to an ocean of military uniforms, where he found his boss—Colonel Christopher Thoms—sitting two rows back.

Before court, Colonel Thoms had sent for him. Anticipating some sort of pep talk, Dale entered the colonel's office in relatively good spirits. The office walls were rich with awards and photographs. A mahogany desk commanded the room, supporting a MacBook Pro, a wooden Rolodex, several expensive-looking pens, and a little glass house with a baseball inside signed by someone famous.

Behind his desk, Colonel Thoms chomped on an unlit cigar. His head was bald and pasty. Meaty. His neck thick. He gestured toward the two leather chairs. "Please, Captain Riley, have a seat."

Dale tried to appear at ease. He had been in here before, last year for his annual fitness report. Then, Colonel Thoms told him that he was doing a bang-up job, to keep up the good work. Ultimately, he gave Dale good marks and said that he was well on his way to promotion. Settling in now, Dale said, "Thanks for having me, sir. It's an honor."

"Big trial today. You nervous?"

"A little bit, sir."

"Well, don't be. You'll be fine." He spoke with the cigar in his mouth, so that his words came out muffled.

"Thanks, sir. I appreciate that."

An uncomfortable silence followed.

Chomping on the end of the cigar, eyeing his guest, the colonel said, "Tell me something, Captain Riley."

"What is it, sir?"

"You're up for promotion next year, right?"

"Yes, sir."

"Major Riley. Sounds nice, doesn't it, *Major* Riley? Has a certain ring, wouldn't you say?"

Dale smiled. "It does sound nice, sir." It sounds nice because the promotion comes with an annual bonus and jump in salary, a respectable, though manageable, increase in responsibilities.

"So tell me, *Major* Riley, when you look at your client, what do you see?"

Over the course of his two-year tenure here, Colonel Thoms had not once inquired as to the nature of Dale's casework, or clients. Strict legal guidelines precluded this. Commanding officers of local JAG Corps preside over both prosecuting—and defending—attorneys, and need an arm's-length distance to adhere to the principles of impartiality. This is not to suggest that mentoring isn't allowed, or that certain questions framed generically couldn't be entertained. Specifics, however, are to be avoided, and for good reason. History is replete with the corruptible. Prejudices alter the scales of justice.

When you look at your client, what do you see?

Where was he going with this?

Granting the colonel the benefit of the doubt, Dale said, "Well, to be perfectly honest, sir, when I look at my client I see a bit of a prick, sir. To be perfectly honest."

The colonel chuckled. After all, weren't they just two old pals sharing a casual conversation? "Yes. Of course. A bit of a prick. I like that." He removed the cigar and examined it. "But do you see a guilty prick, I wonder?"

"A guilty prick, sir?"

"Yes. A prick that bombed an Afghan village? A prick that killed all those people, those five Marines?"

"Well, I'm not so sure, sir. The JAG investigation has holes. Flaws. Lieutenant Colonel Brandt should have spent more time on it. It seems he grasped the first theory that presented itself and ran with it. I think I can win this one."

"Hm." Colonel Thoms placed the cigar adjacent to the MacBook Pro. "I read that piece-of-crap JAG investigation, and you're right. Lieutenant Colonel Brandt did a shitty job. But do you know what?"

"What's that, sir?"

"I want you to forget about that goddamn JAG investigation. It's a piece of crap, so forget about that. You've dealt with this monster quite extensively. So what is your *gut* telling you? Is your client guilty, or is he not?"

"I'm not sure, sir." *Where was he going with this?*

"Let me put this in a different light, if I may: what would be in the best interest of the Corps, in the best interest of your country, and in the best interest of your career, *Major* Riley?"

"Are you asking me—"

"You know what I see when I see your client? I see guilt. I see an arrogant prick, like you said, who killed all those people that night. I see a man who deserves to hang. That's what I see."

"Wait. What are you asking me to do, exactly?"

"Nothing. I'm not asking you to do a goddamn thing. But I can tell you this: with a good fitness report, come January of next year we'll be calling you Major Riley. And I could write that good fitness report for you. I could. No problem. I'm wondering, however, what you might do in return."

Yes. What might you do in return? What's it going to be, Captain Riley? Throw the prick, guilty or not, under the bus and pin on major, or roll up your sleeves, as a good defense attorney would, and fight? Throw in the towel, or go toe to toe? Tick-tock. Time's a-wasting. What might you do for the Corps, and for your country? What might you do to get that promotion?

It had been such a sly and calculated move, Colonel Thoms calling Dale in at the last moment, catching him off guard, allowing him little time to consider his options, hoping that he would cave in with the promise of promotion. Standing before Judge Alberts, Captain Dale Riley looked from his boss to his client. Yeah. He still saw a prick. No doubt about it. But a guilty prick? That, he didn't know. He wasn't sure. How many times had Captain Ruffers sworn his innocence? Hell, the prick had even cried. Moreover, Dale loathed the fact that he'd been put in this position in the first place. Something was wrong, but lord knows he couldn't figure it out in the next sixty seconds.

"Time's wasting," said Judge Alberts. "Tick-tock, Captain Riley. Tick-tock!"

Captain Riley cleared his throat. "Your honor. Ladies and gentlemen of the jury. My client didn't bomb that village that night.

He's innocent. And we'll prove it. Thank you all very much." And with that, he sat down.

Perplexed, Judge Alberts said, "You still have fifteen seconds, Captain Riley. Is that it? Is that all you got?" Rare was the attorney who finished in sixty seconds' time, and none had finished early, until today.

"Yes, sir. For now, anyway. Perhaps I'll nail her hard and fast next time, sir. Perhaps next time, boom, like you said."

Judge Alberts offered a rare smile, for at the very least the trial was moving along swiftly. "Okay. If you say so. Major Snead, call your first witness."

CHAPTER 5

The investigating officer, Lieutenant Colonel Brandt, assumed the witness box with a fresh high-and-tight haircut and a chest littered with medals and ribbons, several of which were of the combat variety. The bailiff swore him in.

Doing his best to put opening statements behind him, Major Alex Snead smiled. "Sir, please state for the court your name, rank, occupational specialty, and your relationship to this case."

"Certainly. I'm Lieutenant Colonel Anthony Brandt, ordnance officer, and I was assigned by Headquarters Marine Corps to conduct a JAG investigation into the circumstances surrounding an incident that had taken place on or about the 11th of September, 2009. Specifically, reports that coalition air forces bombed an Afghanistan village, resulting in the deaths of five United States Marines and seventy-eight innocent Afghan noncombatants." His diction was dry and even, void of emotion, and otherwise well rehearsed.

Major Snead approached the lectern, where he set down his notes. "Sir. What led you to the conclusion that Captain Michael J. Ruffers bombed the Sorubi village that night?" They had rehearsed this ad nauseum the day before, and while there was a ton of evidence that he intended to introduce, he had boiled his argument down to three major findings. Best to keep things simple.

On cue, Lieutenant Colonel Brandt held up a finger. "First, the bomb pattern suggested that this was the work of a coalition aircraft." He added another finger. "Second, lab tests showed that the primary compound of the bomb residue was H-6." Another finger. "And lastly, and most importantly, every coalition pilot who flew into Afghanistan airspace that night could account for their bombs, every pilot but Captain Ruffers." He withdrew his fingers down to one again, which he used to point at the accused. "Every pilot but him."

All eyes turned toward the defendant. They searched him for guilt, remorse, anything. What they found was a handsome young man with jet-black hair and crystal-blue eyes, devoid of any emotion. As instructed by his attorney, Mike Ruffers fixated on a point in space and didn't so much as blink. "Any attempt at remorse might come across as disingenuous," Dale had said. "So show nothing at all, got it? Sit like a stone and keep your smart mouth shut." So far; so good.

With enough flair to recapture the attention of the courtroom, Major Snead approached an easel near the jury box, where he flipped over an enlarged photograph. "Lieutenant Colonel Brandt, could you please explain this photograph to the courtroom?"

"Absolutely. That's an aerial photograph of the Sorubi village, taken the day after the bombing. The expert I consulted with concluded, and you can see for yourself by the blast pattern, the way the residue fans out to the east, that most likely an aircraft delivered the bombs on an easterly heading and at a very low altitude. From afar it would appear as if a single bomb had created this. Upon closer examination, however, the expert concluded that there could have been several bombs, upwards to six."

The photograph was of a barren stitch of earth with a lazy V-shaped scorch running from west to east. Adobe homes had been leveled, a few dots here and there that appeared to be villagers meandering about in the aftermath.

Major Snead returned to the lectern. "Now. In layman's terms, what is H-6?"

"H-6 is a highly explosive chemical compound used for military grade weaponry. It's also the primary active component in the mark-82 bombs that Captain Ruffers flew into theater that night."

"So the explosive that your lab discovered in the bomb residue"— Major Snead pointed toward the photograph—"is the same stuff that Captain Ruffers flew into theater that night?"

"Correct."

"Tell me: how many of these mark-82 bombs did Captain Ruffers fly into the combat zone?"

"Six. He took off from the USS *Wasp* with six bombs."

"And when he landed, how many bombs did he have?"

"He landed with zero bombs."

"Interesting."

"Very."

"Let's assume the best, shall we? Let's assume that Captain Michael J. Ruffers used these bombs in a manner of authorized warfare. After all, he flew into a war zone, did he not, and so perhaps he came under enemy attack?"

Lieutenant Colonel Brandt smiled. He'd spent seven months stitching this case together, and here, at last, was the fabric of justice. "Let me explain something, Major Snead: when Captain Ruffers took off from the ship, he did so as dash-two in a two-jet formation. In other words, he wasn't alone. Major McGuire was the lead aircraft that evening, call sign Angel 11. Captain Ruffers was his wingman, Angel 12. Together, they flew off for war. In theater, Captain Ruffers radioed Major McGuire and said that he had a fuel leak, and that he had just enough to make it back to the ship. Because Major McGuire was obligated to remain in theater to provide cover for the Marines on the ground, he had no choice but to send Captain Ruffers home. Alone. When Captain Ruffers departed the formation, he still had his bombs, all six of them. When he landed at the ship, zero bombs. Nowhere between the war zone and the ship did Captain Ruffers have authorization to utilize these bombs in a manner of warfare. Nowhere, and by no man."

"I'm confused," Major Snead confessed. "What happened to the bombs? I mean . . . where did they go? Did they just vanish into thin air?"

"You want to know what I think, or what the captain said?"

"Let's begin with what the captain said."

"He said he jettisoned them into the Arabian Sea. Said he wasn't sure if he had enough fuel to make the ship, that a lighter aircraft flies farther."

"A lighter aircraft flies farther. I'll buy that. Could you please tell the court where, exactly, the navy divers found these bombs?"

"They didn't. With sonar and magnetometers they searched the ocean floor for days, covering every inch of water from the shoreline to the ship. They didn't find a thing."

"Lieutenant Colonel Brandt, what do *you* think happened to the bombs?"

Lieutenant Colonel Brandt turned to address the members of the jury. "After exhaustive research, it is my conclusion that Captain Michael J. Ruffers utilized these bombs to obliterate the Sorubi village that night. That village"—he pointed toward the photograph—"was on the way home from their close-air-support track. The timeline was perfect. The blast pattern matches up with what one would expect from a Harrier jet. The bomb residue matches as well. It all fits neatly."

Major Snead moved once again to the easel, where he filed the aerial photograph behind another. This graphic showed a tangle of charcoaled limbs, two tiny skulls pressed cozily together, what appeared to be brain matter and seeping blood from several fissures. It was a horrific image, and someone in the audience gasped. "Eighty-three people killed that night, to include these young children, ages five and six." A morbid pall descended upon the courtroom, a sickening glower of horror. Major Snead, his eyes drawing away from the photograph, began to approach the defendant. Oh, he could have gone on and on about this evidence and that evidence, but let's face it: the jury, the courtroom, needed a show, and the major needed another conviction. Convictions were good for promotion, and Major Snead had rather big dreams. "You're going to pay for this, Captain Ruffers!"

Captain Riley shot up. "Objection, your honor. That statement suggests a finding of guilt. That statement—hell, that photograph—is gratuitous, your honor, and absurd."

Before the judge could make a ruling, however, Major Snead drew closer. "Do you know what happens when they pump your veins full of death, Captain Ruffers? Look at me! Do you?"

Deliberately, the defendant looked his way and seemed to be fighting an arrogant if not wicked smile.

"Your honor," Captain Riley yelled, "this is totally inappropriate."

Major Snead continued: "Your muscles stop working, and you can no longer breathe."

"Jesus," Captain Riley said to this god-fearing Baptist, "what in the hell are you doing?"

"You piss yourself," Major Snead added, doing what the hell he had planned on doing, "and you shit yourself, but your mind keeps humming along for six . . . painful . . . minutes. One minute for every bomb that you dropped on that village." He pointed toward the photograph. "It should be a minute for every man and woman, and two for every child!"

At last Judge Alberts clacked his gavel. "Okay, Major Snead. You've made your point. Move on."

But he hadn't made his point, not entirely. He glanced to the judge, and then to his wristwatch. "Six minutes, Captain Ruffers. Your time starts . . . now." Dramatically, mockingly, he punched the timer on his wristwatch in the same fashion that Judge Alberts had done during opening statements.

Unamused at this obvious show of contempt, Judge Alberts again clacked his gavel, much harder than before. "Major Snead! You are out of line."

Major Snead turned toward the bench and struggled with whether or not he should say what was on his mind. In the end his arrogance got the better of reason. He said, "Just giving it to her nice and hard, your honor. *Boom!* You either nailed her brains out, or you didn't. Isn't that what you said, sir? Aren't those the rules by which we are playing?"

Outraged by this defiance, Judge Alberts shot to his feet, his chair nearly tipping over. "Major Snead! My chambers. *NOW!*"

Someone in the courtroom said loud enough for the entire room to hear: "Holy shit."

Judge Alberts swept his gavel across the room, searching for the loudmouth, finding no one in particular, just a bunch of equally shocked faces. He had half a mind to clear the entire courtroom. He didn't. Instead, he hammered his gavel. "Fifteen-minute recess. Bailiffs, if anyone leaves, don't let them back inside. Major Snead, follow me."

CHAPTER 6

With the two away in chambers, Captain Mike Ruffers leaned over and whispered to his attorney: "You're not going to let him get away with that bullshit, are you? The way that Major Snead talked to me? About the six minutes and all? That's bullshit, man."

Captain Riley, massaging his temples, whispered back: "Take it easy, Mike. The jury is watching you."

"Can they read my lips? 'Cause if so, I want them to know that I will fucking beat that man. If I ever see him in public, I will put a fucking bullet in his head."

Shielding his client from the jury box, Captain Riley looked him dead in the eyes. "Shut your mouth, you hear me? Shut the fuck up!" Having worked with this creep for far too long, he was nearing the end of his patience. More than once he regretted taking this case, but no more so than today. What a freaking nightmare.

Bailiffs walked the aisle, reminding folks to keep it down.

The sketch artist had one eye on the defendant, the other on his pad.

Reporters jotted notes.

Lieutenant Colonel Eric Scholl walked up the aisle to Dale and took a knee. "Hey. Sorry I'm late."

Dale started. "Oh. Hey."

"I had this thing, with this guy. So how's it going?"

"I've had better days."

Lieutenant Colonel Eric Scholl was Dale's closest friend. He had average looks and average intelligence, and was of delightfully low humor. In the current matter, Eric had acted in the capacity of unofficial co-counsel. Over beers, the two of them had dissected the JAG investigation. They discovered errors in the logic, not many, but perhaps just enough. They strategized, and pieced together a game plan. Yesterday they closed the books and toasted with beer. They were ready. Actually, Dale was ready. It would be Dale's show. Eric would remain in the background to assist wherever he could.

Eric said, "So, what did I miss?"

"A bit of a massacre is all. Like I said, I've had better days."

Eric glanced over at the defendant and cringed. The defendant's aura was all wrong, creepy and sinister. Was it the eyes? The mannerisms? Was it the man's smile? Or was it simply a vibe, an energy? Whatever it was, Eric wouldn't have assisted in this case if Dale hadn't asked. "Yeah. I saw the last part there about the six minutes and all. And that photograph up there? Brutal. But you got this one. Your turn for cross, so get up there and kick that rat bastard Brandt in the nutsack."

"In the nutsack," muttered Dale. "Sure."

Taken aback by Dale's lackluster tone, Eric said, "Dude. Where's your moxie, man? Shit."

"Eh. I'll tell you later."

"You want me to sit with you? Pull up a chair and hand you paperwork or something? Give you a hand-job beneath the table? Keep you nice and relaxed?"

Dale smiled. "You're sick, you know that?"

"You're all stressed out, my friend. I'm just trying to help."

"Thanks. I think I'll be okay without it."

"Without what?" Mischievously, he glanced toward the jury box, several jurors looking their way.

Dale shook his head and fought back a smile.

"All right," said Eric. "Have it your way. I got a seat in the back. Fucking place is packed. Just snap your fingers, and I'll come running."

"Lucky me."

Major Snead reentered the courtroom, followed by Judge Alberts. With the characters back in play, the courtroom settled in.

Quietly, Judge Alberts clacked his gavel. "Okay. Now. Captain Riley. You may begin your cross-examination of the witness."

Where was that moxie? Dale searched for some as he carried his notes to the lectern and spread them out. The hesitation wasn't because he was nervous, because he wasn't. The hesitation was because he wasn't entirely sure what it was that he was going to say. He glanced toward his boss and cleared his throat. He turned toward the witness box. "Good morning, Lieutenant Colonel Brandt. How are you?"

Lieutenant Colonel Brandt smiled. "Fine, Captain. And you?"

"I'm okay." He drummed his fingers. "Sir, can you please tell the court what specifically led you to the conclusion that Captain Ruffers bombed the village that night?"

"I already told the court. Specifically. Were you not listening?"

Dale laughed. "Sometimes I'm a bit slow. So please, and try to be as specific as possible."

Impatiently, Lieutenant Colonel Brandt said, "Specifically, I contacted USCENTAF in Saudi Arabia and got a list of all the airplanes that flew into theater that night. Specifically, I traveled to each and every physical location of each and every squadron. I got my hands on their flight schedules, their logistics records, and specifically inventoried each and every one of their bombs. Of the squadrons that flew into theater that night, only one came up short: VMA-231, the Harrier squadron that employs Captain Mike Ruffers, your client. Specifically, I interviewed the squadron pilots, all of them, and narrowed my search down to Angel 11 and Angel 12, Major McGuire and Captain Ruffers, respectively. I listened to the whole story about how Captain Ruffers said he had a fuel problem, about how he said he had jettisoned his bombs in the Arabian Sea. I looked at his flight path in relation to the village, the timeline, the bomb residue, specifically, and everything matched . . . perfectly. Everything fit, specifically."

"Nice work," said Captain Riley.

Dryly, he replied, "I know."

"Now, you said in your JAG investigation and in earlier testimony that H-6 was the primary compound found in the bomb residue, correct?"

"That is a factual statement."

Dale wondered how far he should take this, figured he could continue without committing either way. "Sir. Is H-6 exclusive to mark-82 bombs?"

"Of course not."

"Could you please educate the court as to the other types of ordnance of which H-6 is the primary compound?"

"Lots of stuff."

"Mortar rounds?"

"Some mortar rounds, sure."

"Artillery rounds?"

"Absolutely."

"Why then, sir, did you focus on aviation assets? Perhaps a mortar squad did this, or an artillery battery."

"Witnesses said that it sounded as if a jet had swept in before the blast."

"Witnesses said that?"

"It's all in my report."

"Sir. I read the JAG investigation report. The witness, singular, didn't say that. The witness said that it sounded like the Devil spread his wings and breathed fire. He said nothing about a jet."

"That's what he meant."

"And the expert who examined the blast pattern from the aerial photographs that you provided to him said that he was only seventy percent certain that this might have been the work of a combat jet. Seventy percent certain: I don't know if that's enough to convict a man. What do you think?"

"What do I think?"

Dale nodded.

"I think you're a shithead."

"Excuse me?"

In an organization where rank excuses the vilest treatment of subordinates, Lieutenant Colonel Brandt added: "I think you're a slimy, scumbag lawyer. I think that you will say or do anything to get your killer of a client off the hook. I think that makes you complicit. And I think someday, young man, you will wake up and find yourself burning in Hell."

Judge Alberts reached for his gavel, but then thought otherwise. Why not allow this to play out? See how the young captain handles himself. Could be entertaining in a Gladiator-enters-the-Coliseum sort of way.

Had he not been so conflicted, Captain Dale Riley would have ripped this witness a new one. Sure, rank has its privileges, but this was Dale's domain, where in theory the law reigns supreme. At end, however, Dale held tight, and thus Lady Justice would get nailed neither hard nor fast. Certainly no boom. Impotently, void of moxie, Dale said, "I'm just not convinced that the contents of this investigation are enough for a conviction. I just don't know."

When the enemy is down, a Marine doesn't let up. There is no mercy. Lieutenant Colonel Brandt said, "He did it, young man. Your client is guilty! Wake the fuck up."

Dale said, "Perhaps he did do it, sir. Honestly, I don't know." He looked to Judge Alberts. "Sir. I think I'm finished for now."

Judge Alberts, familiar with Captain Riley and sensing that something might be amiss, said, "Is everything okay?"

"It's just . . . I need to look into something, sir." Indeed, Dale needed to look into his soul. Was he the sort of man who would trade his integrity for promotion? The idea of doing so seemed unseemly, enough to make his head hurt. More so than anything, he needed to go for a run, needed to clear his mind. Colonel Thoms had taken him completely off his game.

Judge Alberts said, "Very well. Lieutenant Colonel Brandt, you are excused for now. Don't go far. Your obligations to this court are not yet over. Okay. Major Snead. Who's next?"

CHAPTER 7

Major Duncan McGuire, pilot of Angel 11 on the night in question, was next to take the witness box. Ever since he had been a kid, he'd wanted to be a military pilot. Eventually, he discovered that it wouldn't be easy. Built like a linebacker, his mind was like squash. He had to work ten times harder than the next guy. At flight school his academics were barely enough to squeak by. He did, however, excel at such things as the obstacle course and the three-mile run, pumping out pushup after pushup, and hammering out situps. Aside from his physical prowess, he had an uncanny ability to read people. He used this to his advantage, ingratiating himself to those in power and expecting nothing less from men of lower rank. That Captain Mike Ruffers refused to play this game galled him to no end. Thusly, Captain Ruffers was a turd to the nth degree. In his expert opinion, Captain Ruffers was the killer. It would be his honor to testify against him.

After the preliminary how-dos, they got down to brass tacks.

"Before the mission that night," Major McGuire was saying, "ole Captain Ruffers over there said in the ready room that he'd like nothing more than to bag himself a couple of ragheads so that Allah could sort them out."

Major Snead, at the lectern, shook his head in question. "He said what?"

"In the ready room, before the mission, Captain Ruffers said that he'd love nothing more than to bomb a pocket of ragheads so that Allah could sort them out. He said that he'd been in theater six months and had yet to bag himself a raghead. He said that tonight would be his night. Hell, he even laughed about it, slapped his knee and yucked it up."

"Nice," said Major Snead.

"Said he wanted paybacks for September 11. His words, exactly."

"And you're certain of this?"

"I'm positive of this."

Having established intent, Major Snead said, "Major McGuire, can you tell the court what happened during the mission? After Captain Ruffers said that he wanted to bomb a pocket of ragheads so that Allah could sort them out? What happened next?"

"After we briefed the mission, we manned our jets. The sea was easy that night, the takeoff from the ship routine. As a section, we climbed out and flew north, toward bad-guy country. The skies were mostly clear. Coalition forces controlled the airspace. Once we received authorization from the AWACS jet to enter the boundaries, we switched our primary radios to the combat frequency. We waited on the call. On the deck, Marines were patrolling the countryside, would radio if they encountered enemy resistance that required heavy firepower. With their authorization, that's when we'd fly in and deliver our ordnance. So there we were, circling high above the rugged terrain, our night-vision goggles painting the earth green. That's when I received a radio transmission from Captain Ruffers, who was flying a combat-parade position behind me. He was talking on the secondary radio, his voice troubled. Said he had a fuel problem. Said his tanks were low. That if he didn't get moving right away, he wouldn't have enough gas to make the ship."

"So you let him go?"

"That's correct. I sent him back to the ship, alone. I had no other choice. The Marines on the deck were relying on us for close air support. I couldn't leave them hanging. So I let Mike go. It was a good thing I didn't escort him back to the ship, either, because as soon as Mike turned south I got a radio call from Striker, the forward air controller on the ground. Striker said that he and his Marines were in trouble, pinned down by enemy gunfire. They needed help like yesterday. So I jotted down the lat/long of the target, told Striker that I was five minutes out, and that I'd be coming in as a single ship."

"What happened next?"

"Flying toward the target, Striker calls and says that artillery is peppering the target. He swings me around west, brings me in on an easterly heading. The timing was perfect. After artillery had their way, Striker clears me hot. I came in low and delivered my bombs. Blew 'em up. It was perfect, man. Beautiful."

Major Snead said, "You're a brave man, Major McGuire."

He smiled. "There's a fine line between brave and stupid."

"Either way, thank you for your service. You're a real American hero."

Major McGuire, as much as he could, blushed.

Captain Riley fidgeted in his seat, searching that very soul of his.

Beside him, Ruffers seemed strangely at peace, lost in thought, perhaps, remembering the night.

"Now," said Major Snead, "could you please tell the court what happened when you got back to the ship and met up with Captain Ruffers?"

"After I landed and parked my jet, the duty officer came up to me, asked me what the hell happened. I told him what I just told you, about the fuel leak Captain Ruffers reported over the radio. That's when he informed me that Ruffers had landed without his bombs. We keep track of this shit, you know? It's a big freaking deal."

Major Snead rolled his fingers for McGuire to continue.

"Well, I hunted him down, found him in his stateroom, listening to music and dancing his toes. I pulled him off his rack and held him by the collar. I said to him: 'What the fuck, man? Where are your bombs, you dumbass?' I mean . . . I was pissed. I was the section lead that night, responsible for the integrity of the flight. In a way, it was my fault what happened out there."

"I wouldn't go that far," said Major Snead. "Now, let's get back to that conversation. What did Captain Ruffers say after you asked about the bombs?"

All worked up, Major McGuire said, "He had that stupid, arrogant smile on his mug. It took every ounce of strength not to punch him in the nose."

"Okay. Just tell the court what he said."

"He's telling me to relax, right, to take it easy, champ. He's getting all cozy, you know, said he jettisoned his bombs in the drink. Said he wasn't sure if he had enough fuel to make it to the ship. Told me that a lighter aircraft flies farther, as if I needed a lesson in aviation. So I said to him: 'Don't fuck with me, man. You and I both know that there are dozens of airfields in Pakistan at which we have landing rights. Why not land there? Why press it to the point of having to jettison your bombs to squeak out an extra mile or two?'" He regarded the defendant with a scowl. "The dick said he was just doing that pilot stuff, making shit happen. But it didn't make sense, you know. His story. So I had the maintenance guys check his jet to see if it was low on fuel. They confirmed Mike's story, that his tanks were nearly dry. But after running a few tests, they couldn't find a leak. Nothing. In my opinion, he dumped the fuel on purpose, setting the table nice and neat for his feast of fucking lies."

"Objection," Captain Riley said. "Conjecture."

"Sustained," Judge Alberts said dryly.

Major Snead said, "So the tanks were in fact empty, but there were no signs of mechanical failure. Is this correct?"

"That's correct."

"So what did you do?"

"Well, I'll tell you what I didn't do: I didn't beat the shit out of him. I wanted to. Believe me. But I didn't. The next day, when we heard about what happened out there, to the village and all, I drafted a formal letter to the wing commanding officer. I had my suspicions. I mean . . . before the mission he's talking all tough about killing ragheads, and the next day we got plenty of dead ones, don't we? Not long after that, I'm talking with Lieutenant Colonel Brandt over there. And here I am now, talking to you."

Major Snead, collecting his things, said, "Thank you, Major McGuire. Thank you for your testimony and for your service to your country. You're a hero, and you should be proud of your actions that night." He looked to the defense. "Wish I could say the same for everyone in the courtroom. Your honor, that's all I have for now. I might have more on redirect. We'll see."

"Very well," Judge Alberts said. "Captain Riley, dazzle me."

CHAPTER 8

Major Alex Snead had called Major McGuire a brave man, a
real American hero.

Isn't that why so many young men and women join the
military, because deep down inside they possess some element of
heroism? Or at least think they possess it? Or wish to possess it?

Isn't that why Dale Riley had raised his hand to take the oath?

His uncle was a Marine. As a kid, Dale had listened to the stories. They were exciting, and he couldn't get enough. He imagined
himself someday wearing the uniform, that he too would do heroic
things.

With a juris doctorate and academic honors from the University
of North Carolina School of Law, Dale Riley accepted an invitation to Officer Candidate School, Quantico, Virginia. He knew
it wouldn't be easy. The recruiters informed him that for every
hundred applicants, only one or two make it through. They fail
the physical or come up short academically. Some fail to clear
the obstacle course or the combat course. Others get homesick,
wake up one morning holding an M-16 rifle instead of momma.
They find themselves in a mock field of combat, covered in mud,
soaked to the bone in ice-cold rain with days before a warm
shower and dry clothes. One might think that lawyers would
be spared from this brutishness, but spared they are not. Every

Marine is a rifleman first, officers qualified with both rifle and pistol, familiar with hand grenades and Bangalore torpedoes and .50 caliber machine guns, experts on battlefield tactics, on theories of warfare. Officer candidates are held to the highest of standards. A commission comes with exceptional demands of mental and physical strength, and moral certitude. All of this, and here we have Captain Dale Riley, seriously considering Colonel Thoms's offer. Pathetic. Disgusting. And downright shameful. Regardless of his client's innocence or guilt, whether the guy to his left was a prick or a prince, he deserved, at the very least, a stringent defense. That's what Dale had signed up to do—his duty. That's what a hero would do. Naïve, perhaps, but what young hero isn't naïve?

Captain Riley approached the lectern and took a deep breath. At last he had found some moxie. Metaphorically speaking, it was time to remove the kid gloves, to rock 'em and sock 'em, robot style. "Sir. Let's begin with what happened after you and Captain Ruffers separated the flight."

Major McGuire sighed. Slowly, deliberately, somewhat sarcastically he replied, "I flew to the battle. Striker, remember him? Yeah. Sure you do. He gave me the lat/long of the target, and then he cleared me hot. You with me so far, Captain? You want I should go over it again? A little slower? Draw you some crayon pictures or something?"

Captain Riley chuckled. "No, sir. No pictures. You're doing great. Please continue."

"Right. So anyway, after Striker cleared me hot, I flew in and hit artillery's hits. Easy, cheesy, Japanesey."

"And then what happened?"

"Shit blew up, young Captain. Kaboom!" He smiled, and someone in the audience laughed.

Captain Riley said, "Kaboom, huh?"

"Ka . . . freaking . . . boom!"

"Major McGuire, how many bombs did you drop on the target? The one that went kaboom?"

For the first time since taking the witness box, Major McGuire seemed a bit caught off guard. Slow of wit, improvisation wasn't his thing. "Excuse me?"

"How many bombs did you drop on that target, the one given to you by Striker?"

"What the hell kind of question is that?"

"Please answer it."

"Six. Okay? I dropped six mark-82s on the target. I had six bombs on board, and I dropped all six."

"And you're sure of this?"

"I'm positive of this." An incredulous expression washed over him. "What the hell are you getting at?"

"And after you bombed the target, where did you go?"

"Where did I go? I flew back to the ship, like I said. My bombs were all gone. It was time to go home." He shifted in his seat, the smile long gone. Kaboom.

"Could you please explain to the court your flight path back to the ship?"

"What in the hell are you getting at?"

"Please answer the question. After you dropped your bombs, what was your flight path back to the ship?"

"I flew the standard checkpoints home, okay? There was a specific way in, and a specific way out. Keeps us pilots from running into each other. I flew the specific way out."

"So there were canned routes, kind of like highways in the sky?"

"Something like that, sure. Highways in the sky."

"The highway you took back to the ship, would this be the same highway that Captain Ruffers took?"

"More or less, I guess. Until he veered off and bombed the village."

Ignoring this, Captain Riley said, "Are you aware, sir, that the highway you flew home that night runs five miles east of the Sorubi village?"

"No. I was unaware of this. But it makes sense, doesn't it? On his way home, Captain Ruffers found that pocket of ragheads he was looking for. He swept in and bombed them. It makes perfect sense."

"Well, that's one theory. And you know what? Let's assume, for the moment, that it's true. That Captain Ruffers veered off the highway like you said, and bombed the Sorubi village. Records show that you were thirty minutes behind him; that you landed at the ship a full thirty minutes later. So if Captain Riley did this, if in fact he bombed the village like you said, I'm wondering what you saw down there while flying the highway home."

"What I saw?"

"Smoke, Major McGuire? Fire? Was there mayhem? Anything at all to suggest that Captain Riley had bombed that village?"

"What do you think, that I was on a sight-seeing cruise? That I was taking in the scenery with a cocktail in my freaking hand?"

With all this sarcasm and hostility, Captain Riley was feeling less guilty about what it was he was about to do. "No one is suggesting that it was a sight-seeing cruise, sir. I'm just wondering if you saw anything down there. Smoke or fire. Anything."

"I wasn't looking out my damn windows."

"Did you see anything?"

"No. Okay? The answer is no!"

Captain Riley turned to face the jury. "I'm not a pilot, but it would seem to me that should I find myself inside a theater of war, I'd notice mayhem nearby. A burning village just might catch my eye."

With this, Major McGuire leaned forward and clenched the rail, his forearms thick and running with veins.

"Major McGuire, have you ever used the word 'ragheads'?"

"*What?*"

"Ragheads. Have you ever used that term?"

"What the hell does that have to do with anything?"

"Please answer the question."

Major Snead shot up. "Objection, your honor. Relevance. Prejudicial. He's attempting to slander a highly decorated officer, your honor."

Calmly, Judge Alberts replied, "Major McGuire will answer the question."

"But it's a stupid question," said Major Snead. "What does it have to do with anything here?"

From his stack of notes, Captain Dale Riley pulled a slip of paper and held it up. "Major McGuire, I have an e-mail you sent to several officers in the squadron, one in which on no less than three occasions you did in fact, within the narrative of the text, use the term *raghead*." He addressed the judge. "Your honor, I would like to enter this into evidence as Exhibit 1a."

"Let me take a look."

Captain Riley approached the bench, handed the paper to the judge.

Quietly, Judge Alberts read the e-mail. "Sergeant Hernandez, please give this to Major McGuire."

Gruffly, Major McGuire took possession. With a furrowed brow he read, and for a very brief moment it seemed as if every ounce of pride deflated from his chest. "You bastard. You are not going to do this to me. I swear to God you will not get away with this. I promise you that. I fucking swear."

Judge Alberts, unfazed by profanity—indeed, cuss words littered the most casual of military conversations—said, "Major McGuire, is that e-mail authentic?"

Major McGuire, deaf to the judge, collected himself and said to Captain Riley: "I'll get you, you bastard. This is bullshit."

Louder this time, Judge Alberts said, "Major McGuire! Is that e-mail authentic?"

The major didn't answer, crumpled up the slip of paper with half a mind to throw it at the wiseass defense attorney.

Dale plucked up another copy and deliberately read: "'What in God's green earth are we doing giving aid to those fucking *ragheads* when we should be blowing those motherfuckers to hell and back?'" He held up the paper. The major could crumple all he wanted, this was not going away. "This e-mail contains a newspaper article about US-government aid to Saudi Arabia; an article forwarded by Major McGuire to the pilots in the squadron; to include his own hateful narrative about giving aid to what he himself called 'fucking ragheads.' It's all right here in black and white, Major McGuire. It's all right here, and it ain't going away."

Fuming, Major McGuire mumbled beneath his breath.

"I'm sorry," replied Dale, a hand to his ear, "what did you say?"

I will fucking kill you, would have been the answer, had the major been inclined to repeat himself.

"You know what?" said Dale. "Never mind. It's not important." Dale approached the lectern, taking his time. He gripped it and steadied himself. "Major McGuire. Could you please tell the court how many bombs you dropped on that target?"

"I told the court."

"Refresh my memory."

"Fuck you."

"One, Major McGuire? Two? And how many bombs did you drop on the fucking ragheads in the Sorubi village that night?" He hammered the lectern, papers jumping. "How many?" He stormed the witness box. "How many bombs did you drop on the village that night? How many, goddamn it? Answer the question!" There. He said it. He introduced the theory that Major McGuire had bombed the village that night. After all, both jets had returned to the ship without their ordnance. Striker might offer testimony that he'd seen Major McGuire drop several bombs on the target, but could Striker, in the heat of the battle, account for all six of these? Realistically, Dale didn't believe that he could. Therefore, it wasn't a bad defense theory, and one that he wasn't entirely sure that he would introduce. But introduce it he had, and damn if it didn't feel great to do so.

Major McGuire's window to the world went white. He would later have no recollection of his actions: that in a flash he hopped the railing and rushed the lawyer; that his tackle was textbook perfect (his high school football coach would have been proud), arms and legs akimbo to the ground.

Someone screamed.

Bailiffs entered the fray.

Major Snead came next, and then the benches cleared.

A full-blown melee ensued.

On the bottom of the pile, Major McGuire sank his teeth into the scumbag's shoulder.

Dale screamed.

One of the bailiffs brandished his Taser, aimed, and pulled the trigger.

The prongs hit Major Snead—loving husband, caring father—square in the buttocks. Alex flopped to the ground, convulsed, and wet his slacks.

On his feet now, Judge Alberts was banging his gavel, over and over again, louder than ever.

It took five men and a mean chokehold to disable Major McGuire.

Dale sat up with a bloody lip, the onset of a shiner, his shoulder bloody from the bite.

Slowly, the dust settled.

The sketch artist was also standing, getting a good view, drawing like mad and smiling his ass off.

They handcuffed the major and then jerked him to his feet.

Again, he lunged toward Dale. "I'll fucking kill you, you rat bastard. I swear to God. If it's the last thing I do, I will end you!"

Judge Alberts yelled out: "Remove this man right this second. Take him from my courtroom immediately."

The bailiffs hauled him away, down the aisle toward the back door, Major McGuire lunging all the while.

A medic pulled the probes from the flesh of Snead's buttocks.

Dale found his feet and straightened his uniform. Jesus, it had happened so fast.

Judge Alberts said, "Okay. All right. Let's everyone calm down. Captain Riley. Are you okay? Major Snead? Is everyone okay?"

Major Snead sat there on the floor, confused, wholly disheveled and wet in his uniform.

Dale, rotating his arm, said, "Yeah. I'm okay. I think."

Leaving his bench to assist, Judge Alberts said, "Let's get these two to the hospital. Come, people. Would someone call for help?"

Everyone was on their feet, scrambling about in the aftermath, even the members of the jury; everyone, that is, but one man.

Still rotating his arm, Dale glanced toward his desk. Sitting there just as casual as could be, in fact smiling at all of this, was the pilot of Angel 12, the defendant, Captain Michael J. Ruffers of the United States Marine Corps.

CHAPTER 9

That had all gone down two years ago. Two years. Dale could hardly believe that it had been that long. The bite to his shoulder had left a scar. The black eye had lasted for two weeks and had then turned yellow for three more. And it was more than just a swollen lip. The dentist had had to pull the upper left canine, which had been shattered to the root, and replace it with a porcelain dummy. In the light at the dentist's office the color seemed a decent match. Everywhere else, however, the tooth appeared darker, if not awkward looking. In two year's time he hardly noticed it anymore, just another one of life's unfortunate blemishes.

An hour west of Raleigh, the snowfall morphed into a blizzard.

Visibility diminished to a yard, and then to a foot, so that wrecks and abandoned vehicles began to clog up the Interstate.

Dale pulled into a rest station, where he rummaged through his trunk for the snow chains he had purchased several years ago when a forecast for ice and snow as far south as Georgia hadn't materialized. Ninety minutes later, his fingertips frozen, his nose bright and runny, he was on the road again, cursing the illiterate bastard who had written the instructions.

He wished for a cell phone to call home to Gina, but cell phones cost money. Moreover, he wished for a break in the snow, the wipers at full steam, the snow chains clanking rhythmically against the wheel wells.

Cars continued to pile up, emergency lights coming and going, and throughout all of this DJ Savage Jack was reportedly having the time of his life, sipping hot cocoa and playing ridiculous Christmas tunes, asking his listening audience to phone in and tell him just how much they were enjoying the snowfall. Another reason Dale wished he owned a cell phone.

Just east of Greensboro, he spent his last twenty bucks on gas, a diet soda, and a bag of greasy potato chips.

By the time he pulled into his parents' driveway, his nerves were shot. It was dark outside, and he thirsted for a beer, knowing full well that one would never do.

He killed the engine and rested his forehead against the steering wheel.

The engine cooled and ticked, and in his mind's ear he could hear the old lady at the cemetery, Mandy, leaning in to break the news.

You didn't hear? The poor dear . . . he was shot!

Shot!

Alex Snead, hired legal gun from Headquarters Marine Corps, tasered in the ass two years ago, shot in the head last Monday. *The poor dear.*

Dale peered outside, the snowfall hushing the neighborhood, collecting on lawns and in streets, the windows of his car.

The neighborhood hosted the middle class and was far from the zones of poverty. In other words, it was safe out there . . . right?

And it wasn't Mandy's voice speaking to him now, but his own, sharp and sarcastic: *Sure it's safe, chap, you bet. Just as safe as a prominent neighborhood in Raleigh; just as safe as that.*

Paranoia, like the now-encroaching cold, chilled him to the bone and he shivered.

Someone had left the porch light on, which shone yellow through the snowfall.

He searched the shadows, as far as his eye could see, wondering if there wasn't a gunman out there, anxious to pull the trigger.

Another closed casket . . . another mournful widow . . . and another Marine in full dress blues with white gloves to a silver trumpet.

Certainly, he had pissed off enough folks at the court-martial, hadn't he?

Last he'd heard, Major McGuire, due to his violent antics inside Judge Alberts's courtroom, had been asked to resign his commission. That, or face an administrative separation. Not long thereafter, Dale received a postcard from Hades, one of those jokey cards with the Devil and a pitchfork and liquid hot magma. The note on the back read: *See you here soon, you rat bastard, when I deliver you myself.* No return address or anything. Currently, the card was in the basement with his boxes of things. Why he kept it, he wasn't sure.

As for Colonel Thoms, well, what a nightmare that turned out to be. Certainly, Colonel Thoms was in no position to come packing heat. Not these days.

And Lieutenant Colonel Brandt, author of the JAG investigation, well, he didn't seem the vengeful type, did he? Although who's to say for certain?

There remained the possibility, of course, that Alex Snead had been the victim of a random shooting, although Dale didn't quite believe this. Anyone who had taken Criminal Law 101 knew that truly random murders were rare.

Thinking this through, he could hear the organ music from just inside the house, or, as Gina referred to it, the *goddamn* organ music. Mother turned it on for breakfast and off after dinner. Throughout the day it drove both him and his wife apeshit. However, the organ music, as loathsome as it was, was the least of his worries.

Outside, the coast was clear.

He hopped from the car and quickly through the snowfall.

He keyed the front lock.

Quietly, quickly, he slipped inside, locked the door, and took one last peek through the door's glass window.

His father's overcoat went with a shake on the rack, followed by his jacket. He then buttoned the top button of his slacks because he didn't want Gina to see him this way, as if she hadn't noticed that he had put on a few pounds. (That sharp and sarcastic voice again: "A few pounds? How's about sixty, tubbo, if not sixty-five? A few pounds? Pah-leeze!")

At the entrance to the kitchen he stood for a while, unnoticed.

Ellen, the one responsible for the goddamn organ music, was wearing a dressing gown of pastel pink, which she accessorized with a scowl. She sat at the far end of the table, knitting and humming along to something presumably by Bach.

Dad, his dinner plate pushed away, was still working the morning's crossword puzzle with concentration akin to that of a surgeon.

Gina was seated nearest the entranceway with her back to him. She held their son in her lap, where she offered him a bottle of warm breast milk. Even from behind she was beautiful. God, how he longed to have her. Tragically, however, their love life was like the economy—in a severe recession. Whenever he made a play for her, she said that she wasn't in the mood: the stress of unemployment; living with his parents; the future of their son, excuse after excuse. Dale, on the other hand, harbored no such reservations. He lusted for her, always had and always would, eyed her body as she sat at the kitchen table, an ass that had bounced back fabulously after birth. And oh, what an ass! When they first started dating he had joked that someday he'd pitch a tent on her ass and camp there for eternity. He'd cast his rod from there, and at night he'd watch the stars from there. In the morning he'd awake to the crack of dawn. She smiled when he said this: awake to the crack of dawn. He loved her smile as much as her ass, if not a little bit more. Nowadays, she offered neither, and he stood there in the doorway to the kitchen and sighed.

"Son. Come in. Grab some dinner." Rick set aside his crossword puzzle as he plucked his reading glasses from the bridge of his nose.

Dale smiled and entered. He kissed his wife on the cheek, his son, and pulled up a chair.

Rick turned toward his own bride. "Ellen, please, fix your son a plate. Can't you see he's had a long day?"

"He's old enough to fix his own plate, isn't he?" She offered her son a parsimonious smile that appeared more cruel than compassionate.

Rick, waving her off as though she were useless, moved as if to stand.

"That's all right, Dad. I can get it." Dale went to the stove and returned with a plate of meatloaf and steamed, soggy vegetables. He resisted the urge to snatch a cold beer from the fridge, figured he'd save it for later; didn't want Gina to give him that look.

At the table he dug in and washed it all down with water.

Rick, finding just the right moment, said, "So, how was the funeral?"

Dale wiped his mouth. "Depressing."

Ellen, without looking up from her knitting, said, "He was a young man, wasn't he? Didn't you say he was a young man?"

"Yeah. He was young." Dale smiled to his son, winked, and then grabbed his son's soft, little hand.

Rick said, "How did he die again, anyway? The papers didn't say."

Dale didn't answer, at least not yet, anyhow. He glanced to his wife, who appeared to be about as cold as the snow outside. Hell, she wouldn't even look at him—the silent treatment, still upset from the argument they had had the night before. She was slow to heat up, and even slower to cool down. He knew from experience that this could last for several days. He turned toward his father. "He, uh, well, I think he might have been shot. I don't know for sure. Someone just said." Again, he looked to his wife.

"Shot?" said Ellen.

"I don't know for certain. It might just be a rumor."

Gina was regarding him now, seemingly perplexed. She furrowed her brow and cocked her head, waiting for Dale to explain.

At this moment, however, Dale was more interested in offering up an apology than explaining whatever it was that he had gleaned at the funeral. He smiled at her, shrugged, and mouthed the words, *I'm sorry.* His eyes were white flags—*You win, okay? Whatever it was we were arguing about, you win.*

However, she was not in the mood for this apologetic bullshit. He'd been a royal jerk the night before and had penance yet to pay. She wiped her son's chin and tidied up around her. "Dad, thanks for dinner. It was good." It did not go unnoticed that she had offered no such thanks to dear mother.

Rick said, "You're welcome."

Ellen chimed in: "Yes, dear. You *are* welcome."

"We've had a long day. Clint needs a bath, and bed. Good night." And with that she turned and walked away.

Dale, helpless but to watch that magnificent ass of hers, called out: "I'll be up in a minute, okay?"

She didn't answer, kept walking, through the living room and up the stairs toward the bedroom.

Ellen, seemingly cruelly delighted by all of this, said, "Is everything okay, dear? Between you and your wife?"

Dale pushed away from the table. "Everything is perfect, Ma. Just perfect."

PART II

EYE OF THE STORM

To remain faithful throughout to the principles we have laid down for ourselves.

—Carl von Clausewitz

PART II

EYE OF THE STORM

CHAPTER 10

The *William Tell* Overture chirped loudly from the cell phone—a Motorola with limited minutes on a phantom account.

Only one man had the number.

Sean Fitzsimmons grabbed the cell off the passenger's seat of his rented Nissan Altima. He hit the talk button. Without haste, he said, "Number three's gone."

"Are you sure?" the voice inquired.

The signal was scratchy but okay.

They weren't to use names, and were to talk in code as much as possible; keep the conversation short and sweet.

Sean checked his rearview mirror, moved to the right-hand lane so the maniac in the SUV behind him could pass to the left.

It was snowing outside, sheets of the stuff. Snowplows had recently come through, the Nissan cutting effortlessly down the Interstate in their path.

He said, "Yeah, I'm sure."

In fact, the hit had been easier than imagined. Last Monday, he'd followed Alex Snead home from work. He parked a block away and slammed a few beers. In the rearview mirror he proffered a pep talk. This would be his first kill. Yeah, he was nervous. But he had a job to do, and he needed the money—twenty-five hundred bucks for popping a dude when a bullet cost two-ten, a fine return on investment.

He crushed the empty beer can on his forehead.

From beneath his seat he fished out the Ruger .45.

He chambered a round and entered the darkness.

The neighborhood had been quiet and cold with a biting northern wind. Snow had yet to come.

At the house where the target had pulled into the garage, he sneaked around back. No fence. No barking dogs. Sean was in luck.

In the army they teach the finer points of urban warfare, stay low, stay near, pop up every now and again and take a peek-see—*you're up, take a peek, and you're down again.* That's what he was doing now, poking his head in windows, ducking and shuffling along.

At last he found what he had come looking for.

Four of them had gathered around the dining room table, husband, wife, and two boys, holding hands and saying grace.

It was so damn cute that Sean Fitzsimmons wanted to puke his guts out.

The man of the house, the target, had his back to the bay window.

Sean had planned on one shot, one kill, like they had taught him in the army. A head shot, lethal.

Sean popped up, took aim, and slowly squeezed the trigger.

The window shattered and released the screams. And my, how they screamed and screamed and screamed, mom and the two boys scared out of their wits, scampering away on their hands and knees.

With a wild heart, Sean squeezed another round; he squeezed another and another, fuck it!

The target wasn't screaming. He was sliding off the table, taking dinner with him, glasses and dishes, the full salami. The target hit the floor like a rag doll; blood everywhere. There was no doubt about it: the target was dead. For good measure, Sean pumped him with another round. He then dashed away from the shattered glass and screams, consumed once again by the darkness.

One down and three to go.

A life of packing groceries for minimum wage just couldn't compete.

Now, he was traveling west on the snowy, icy Interstate, anticipating a few more hours before hitting Interstate 77 south. From there it would be but a hop, skip, and a jump to his next destination. This time he'd do that one shot, one kill thing. He was still new to this murder-for-hire racket. Practice makes perfect.

"Who's next?" the voice inquired.

"Well, looks like two. But first I'd like to meet Benjamin."

"Don't worry. You'll get what's coming. So why not one?"

"One. He's been hard to nail down. I'm working on it."

"Okay. We've said enough."

And with that, the line went dead.

Sean tossed the cell on the passenger's seat and cranked up the radio. CCR was singing "Fortunate Son." Sean sang along.

He was in a good mood.

Hell, he was in a *great* mood.

Life had taken a turn for the better.

And it was about damn time.

CHAPTER 11

With the dishes in the dishwasher, Dale Riley snatched two cold beers from the fridge, opened one, and stole away down the stairs to the basement. Gina was upstairs with their son, the water running in the tub. Dale would test those waters later, metaphorically speaking. For now, he wanted to decompress. It had been one hell of a day.

The walls down here were littered with memories—academic and athletic awards from high school; his law degree from Chapel Hill framed in gold; a commission from the United States Marine Corps; photographs with everyone happy and smiling. These basement walls, they mocked him. When he'd moved his family here two, three months ago, there were nights when he went frame by frame, reminiscing. As the nights multiplied, however, and as the memories grew familiar, they too became less friendly. Stuck up, if not snooty, too damn good for the man who had ginned them. Yes, the memories mocked him. Tsk'ed him. Asked what in the hell had happened to him? *You had the world by the balls, counselor, and now this? Jesus, man, take a look at yourself. Pathetic.*

Tonight, he ignored them; clicked on the television to drown them out; turned off the lights so that they couldn't be seen.

These mocking walls faded into darkness.

At the poker table, he dealt himself a hand of solitaire, the ever-changing glow from the television set barely reaching.

He drank from his bottle of beer.

He lost the game and dealt himself another.

Yesterday, on the telephone, he'd promised Eric Scholl, his co-counsel from two years ago, whom he still kept in slight touch with, that he'd call with news from the funeral. Finishing his first bottle, he popped the cap on the second. He turned down the volume on the TV, picked up the phone, and dialed Eric's number.

"Hello?"

"Eric. It's Dale."

"Dale. How's it going?"

"Okay. What are you up to?"

"Oh, you know, just standing around a seriously massive blood-stain in the bathroom of a five-star hotel. Same shit, different day." Not long after Eric retired from the Corps, he interviewed with the FBI. The FBI loves ex-military types with Top Secret clearances. They don't pay much, but there's a nice pension after twenty, and a nicer one after thirty. Lieutenant Colonel Eric Scholl was now Special Agent Eric Scholl. Therefore, it stood to reason that perhaps Eric really was standing around a seriously massive bloodstain in the middle of a five-star hotel. But knowing Eric, he could have just as easily been at home on the shitter, reading the *Daily News*.

Playing solitaire by the ever-changing glow of the TV, Dale said, "Sounds exciting."

"You have no idea."

"So. I went to the funeral today."

"Yeah?"

"Yeah."

"Funerals are the worst."

"Tell me about it." He pushed away from the table.

"Promise me something, okay?"

"What's that?"

"Promise me that when I die you'll freeze me, okay? No funerals. No crying, and no carrying on. Freeze me, and be done with it."

Dale laughed. "Freeze you? For what?"

"For later."

"What if you die by decapitation?"

"A good seamstress, and I'm as good as new."

"What if someone puts you through a wood chipper?"

"Why would anyone want to put me through a wood chipper?"

"Shit happens. What if you piss off the mafia?"

"Okay. If I go through a wood chipper, burn me, okay. Whatever you can scoop up, toss in the furnace."

Dale laughed. Eric still had it. "Deal."

Silence followed. Eric said, "So, what happened? With Alex? Did you find out how he died?"

All joking aside, Dale felt anxious again, worried. "He was shot. Can you believe it?"

"Shot? Jesus."

"Yeah. Jesus. An elderly lady at the cemetery said that someone shot him at the dinner table with his family."

"At a restaurant?"

"No. He was at home when it happened."

"Do the cops have any leads?"

"I don't know. The cops haven't made anything public. Not that I know of."

"Hey. Hold on a second, would ya?"

"Sure." He could hear his friend in a muffled conversation with another. He set aside the beer and glanced around, his eyes coming to rest on the basement window—the same window that he used to sneak out of in high school. The window was heavily packed with snow, which glowed from a nearby streetlamp. He sat and watched this, waited for a hand to reach down and clear away the snow, a pair of eyeballs searching for a victim.

Eric came back on the line. "Hey. I hate to cut you short, but I gotta get going. What are you doing tomorrow night for dinner?"

"No plans. Hanging here at home, I guess."

"How's about I take you out?"

"Are you here? In Charlotte?"

"Nope. Indianapolis. But we're scheduled to fly in tomorrow morning. Got a little work down there, another seriously massive bloodstain, so they tell me."

"Yeah. Dinner. Sounds great. What time you thinking of?"

"I'm not sure. We'll have to play it by ear. I'll call you in the afternoon, okay, and we'll go from there."

"Okay. Tomorrow it is. Sounds great."

"See you tomorrow, buddy, and take care."

"See you tomorrow."

It had been a while since Dale had seen his old friend, nearly eight months. He couldn't wait. He could tell Eric things that he couldn't tell his parents, or his wife, could discuss the court-martial, the outcome, and the threats that may or may not have led to the shooting death of Alex Snead. Perhaps it was all a bit of an exaggeration, this business of cold revenge, and if so, Eric, always the voice of reason, would rightly set him straight. He'd tell Dale not to worry, to relax and take it easy. Tell him that there isn't a gunman outside your basement window, clearing snow for a headshot.

Dale grabbed the remote, turned up the volume, and again glanced at the window.

What if Eric were to tell him something different, however? Tell him to head for the hills? Tell him to get his hands on a gun? To sleep with one eye open? When Dale had lost his job and then his money, he pawned his pistol and shotgun for a measly fifty bucks. What a fool. He'd pay twice that much to get them back. If only he had twice that much. If only he still had the fifty he'd pawned them for.

Suddenly, he thought he saw a shadow out there, out beyond the window.

He clicked off the television set.

Sitting in the darkness, he watched.

He listened.

He rose to his feet and crept toward the window. It would take a chair to reach it, and so he grabbed an old wooden one that sat against the wall. Slowly, he dragged it over.

The basement was nearly pitch black now, nothing but a faint glow from the window; shadows beyond.

He placed the chair and stepped up.

His heart raced, his nerves on edge.

Was this a smart thing to do? Put your face up to the window to look around? The faint glow from outside illuminated his frightened expression, his wide and worried eyes.

A loud crash shattered the tension.

He grabbed his chest, certain he'd had a heart attack.

From the kitchen he heard a scream.

Christ!

He hopped from the chair and tripped in the dark.

Scrambling to keep his feet, he searched the walls for the light switch, found it, and flooded the basement yellow.

He grabbed a baseball bat near the stairwell, took the stairs two, three at a time.

With the bat at the ready, he burst into the kitchen and yelled: "Who the hell's there?"

Again, his mother screamed. "Jesus. You scared the death out of me."

Lowering the bat, he said, "I scared you? What was that noise?" And then he saw it, on the floor at her feet, a stack of broken dishes.

She looked at these. "They slipped. This wouldn't have happened had you put them away like I asked."

He breathed a sigh of relief, knelt to pick up the pieces. "It's okay, Ma."

Dad came next. "What in the world is going on in here?"

"It's okay, Dad. Broken dishes, is all. I got it."

CHAPTER 12

After hanging up with his buddy Dale, Special Agent Eric Scholl reentered the bathroom.

Mostly, the hotel was immaculate.

Mostly.

A sign on the front door welcomed the guest to a five-star experience: sharply dressed bellmen hopping to; a fussy yet polite concierge with an encyclopedic knowledge of local cuisine and sights to see; floors of marble and trim of gold; violins from well-hidden speakers with which to charm the ear; a pleasant aroma of lilacs and hydrangeas.

Down in the basement, however, the sights and smells were far different.

Adjacent to the workout room were the bathrooms, the female in particular the origin of the stink. More so, the odor originated from the reduced pool of blood, nearly as black as motor oil.

Five stars upstairs, and hell down here.

The blood had once belonged to a young lady by the name of Eloise Saleem.

She had died here in this bathroom. Judging by the corpse, it had been a gruesome death.

They found her four nights ago. Actually, Jonny found her four nights ago. His real name was John Royston, a high school flunky

63

who worked as the night-shift janitor for his old man, the assistant manager.

"A J-O-B," Jonny bragged to all of his loser friends. *"Mo'money, mo'money, mo'money."*

Jonny was a white kid who wore his pants low and his hat sideways. And Jonny didn't take no shit from no-body, but for the occasional shit from his old man, and that from his immediate supervisor. Someday, Jonny would cut a rap album, buy this joint up, and fire all the pimps and their bitches, including his old man. Until then, he'd bide his time for eight bucks an hour, enough cash for cheap pot and hip clothes and cool sideways hats.

That evening, around 10:30 P.M., he rode the elevator down to the basement. He liked it down there. It was quiet, oftentimes abandoned, the perfect spot to smoke a joint and waste time with the television on in the workout room.

With earbuds plugged in, he stepped off the elevator, rapping along to his main man, Tupac.

He'd start with the bathrooms, check for leaky faucets and running toilets. Perhaps he'd jiggle a handle or two, change a few light bulbs.

He cracked the door to the women's restroom. "Hello? Anyone in the hizzy?"

No one answered; no one in the hizzy.

He set his clipboard on the sink, his cap, then noticed a stream of what at first he thought was rusty water running from a leaky pipe.

"Ah, shit, man. What a damn mess, yo."

This would require extensive work, much more than he could handle. He'd have to fill out a work order and get the plumber in here. In other words, no smoking a joint, and no killing time with the television on.

Only, wait a minute.

Upon closer examination, this stuff didn't really seem like rusty water, did it?

Wait a damn minute.

The stream was thick, and more crimson than rusty, running slowly down the drain. *Ploik!*

"Hello?"

A sense of dread washed over him as his eyes traced the path of the crimson stream, up to where it disappeared beyond the farthest bathroom stall, over near the showers.

"Helloooooo?"

No one answered but the stream running down the drain, hitting the sewers, *ploik!*

The gravity was fierce, drew him farther inside.

Slowly.

Ploik!

"Hellooo?" He glanced toward the door. "Ah, fuck!" He hesitated, ran a hand through his hair, almost felt like crying.

He was helpless, the way a motorist is helpless when bodies and twisted metal litter the landscape around them. Safe within the car, however, the driver can take a morbid peek and keep on trucking, enjoying a sense of voyeuristic anonymity. Here amid the crimson stream and the increasingly cloying smell, it was as if a sinister fog had engulfed him, welcomed him, pulling him farther inside.

"Goddamnit!" he cried, and then stepped farther in.

Ploik!

Another step, another hand through his hair.

Ploik!

He crested the corner of the farthest stall.

He saw her running shoes first, toes spread wide.

Ploik!

Then he saw her legs, dark, streaked with blood.

Not rusty water after all, huh?

Ploik!

How about blood, and tons of it, painting this hizzy red, yo!

Her white shorts were splattered red.

He swallowed; his eyes grew wide.

Ploik!

Another step, and the vision got worse.

His hands shot up to his mouth.

Later, he would hate himself for not moonwalking the fuck right out of there the second he saw the rusty water.

Ploik!

Sweet Jesus. Someone or something had been *at* her.

Her top had been ripped clean; her guts hanging loose like strings of bloody sausages.

There was a brilliant, gaping hole in her chest, much darker than the rest of her, perhaps the black hole that had pulled him farther inside.

Gruesome. He started to bawl.

Still, he took another step, and poked his head around the corner.

Seeing her face is what got him to screaming.

And my, how he screamed and screamed, how he groped at his chest as if he himself had been stabbed.

He pissed his corporate trousers.

And then he shit them.

Where were her vacant eyes? Where were her hollow cheeks, her gaping mouth?

Covering her face was a holy bible, splayed open, a passage circled in blood.

He screamed because he couldn't see her eyes, and so what if she wasn't dead? What if she was alive with guts like Medusa's hair? What if she might sit up and reach for him, grab him, and do unto him what had been done unto her?

Collapsing, he stepped away, planted his shoe in the stream of her blood, slipped, and landed nearly on top of her, his hands deep in the stream of her blood.

He had a lucid thought, his last for a very long while, that her blood was so warm. Not hot. Not cold, but just right, like Goldilocks's pudding.

Frantically, he jerked his hands free, studied them with wide, frightened eyes, his mouth gaping, snot running down from his nose. His hands were painted red, and dripping, only, this wasn't paint, was it?

No, this was not paint!

He opened his mouth farther, which seemed impossible, and released a terrible scream.

Jesus. She was on him now, a part of him now.

And then he thought he saw her stir.

Still screaming, he scampered away on his hands and knees, peering over his shoulder as he went, afraid she might be following him.

Across the marble floors and out into the hallway, smearing her blood along the way.

At the elevator, he slammed the button for up, over and over again, splattering it red with his bloodstained hands.

When the door opened with a ding, he scampered inside.

His shit had snuck past his boxers and had collected at his knees, which he mashed as he scampered; the piss had soaked through his trousers.

Inside, he punched the buttons, splattered them all red, fighting for his breath.

He crawled into a corner, wedged himself in tight, tighter, and lastly hugged his knees.

He watched as the doors slowly closed, expecting a hand to reach in at any moment. He shot his bloody hands up to his face, covered his eyes; uncovered them only to take a peek.

She'd come in after him, he was sure of this, a bloody hand followed by a grossly mangled body. Here, inside this elevator, he would dance his final dance.

The doors closed and he watched them through the split in his fingers, watched them kiss together, watched them until the doors opened up again, there before him the immaculate lobby. He spilled out whimpering, quite literally blubbering.

A young couple happened upon him. Who screamed loudest? The boy, or the girl?

Others gathered, gawked. Someone puked.

He crawled along the marble floor, and they gave him a very wide berth.

He made it as far as the lobby piano, crawled underneath it, and curled into a ball.

He popped his thumb inside his mouth. It was bloody. He didn't care. He sucked, closed his eyes, and begged for his mommy.

Soon the cops arrived, the medics.

They shot him with a tranquilizer, and at last he opened his eyes. He pointed toward hell, said, "She's down there. My God. She's down there."

The cops went down and found her.

Jonny went home. There, dear mommy showered him. He then locked himself inside his bedroom and didn't come out for several weeks. The rap album would never be cut, he would never buy the hizzy, and dad could rest easy knowing that his son would never fire him.

Now, Special Agent Eric Scholl stood in that bathroom. The place was still a disgusting mess, even without the body. Eric's partner, Special Agent Lionel McCarthy, held a photograph in his right hand, which he positioned to match the bloodstains.

"Sorry about that, boss. That was an old friend on the phone. Thought I should take the call."

Not to mention how refreshing it was to step away for some fresh air. The stench, Christ, it was horrible.

Lionel said, "No worries. Hey. Do me a favor. Grab the report over there on the sink. Read me that biblical passage again, the one that the killer circled with the victim's own blood." Lionel was a veteran on the force, had been with the FBI for a good twenty years. He was tall, black, and handsome, as smart as a whip, and a good partner for a rookie like Eric.

Eric grabbed the report, the cover of which read: *The SF Killer.* He thumbed through this until he found the passage in question. "Here we go. Okay. It says: 'Do not fret the evildoers, or be envious of those who do wrong, for like the grass they will soon wither, like green grass they will soon die.'" Eric closed the file. "What do you make of it?"

"Don't know. All we know for certain is that the killer stabs his victims with scissors, and then uses these scissors to snip the letters S and F into their bellies. He places a bible over their faces, opened to a passage circled in their blood. He's a religious nut. I hate the religious nuts."

"What do you think the S and F is all about?" The two were in the bathroom, alone, their voices echoing. A couple of local cops had let them in and were standing outside near the elevators.

"Don't know. S and F. Could be his initials, but I doubt it. Whatever it stands for, it means something to the killer. We'll find out. Trust me. Sooner or later. Anyway, we've seen enough here. C'mon. Let's get some dinner and a good night's sleep. Tomorrow morning, first thing, we fly to Charlotte." He looked at his partner. "You feeling all right?"

Actually, Eric was feeling like shit. It was the stink. It was awful. It got to Eric systemically, like the flu. Standing over the bloodstains, he felt like puking. His face was both ashen and green. He said, "I feel fine. Terrific."

Perhaps he oversold it, and Lionel wasn't buying.

Lionel glanced to the lakebed of blood, back to his partner. "This stink, it either bothers you or it doesn't. I've partnered up with guys who for years just couldn't get over the smell. They learned to cope, is all, but it takes time. As for me, I guess I'm one of the lucky ones. It has never bothered me much." He patted Eric on the shoulder. "C'mon. I'm starving. I know a great steak joint a few blocks from here. I like mine bloody." He looked to his partner and smiled.

CHAPTER 13

The next morning, a government-leased C-5 landed on runway 36-Right at the Charlotte Douglas International Airport. Throughout the night, snowplows ran the miles between takeoffs and landings, old and dirty snow now lining the runways. Countless flights had been canceled, countless more people stranded. It would take several days for things to get back to normal again.

The C-5 bypassed the main passenger terminal and taxied toward the Wilson Air Center FBO. Inside stood Roy Woodall, a Charlotte field agent assigned to escort his colleagues from WFO, the Washington, D.C. Field Office. He stood at the door to the flight line, tall, with a boxer's nose and shoulders, wearing the company suit and overcoat.

Watching the jet taxi in, Roy texted his ex-wife, Sheila: *Sorry. It'll never happen again.*

A moment later, his cell phone chirped. He read: *I leave Toby with you for 2 nights, 2, and he gets a 56 % on his math exam? Seriously? WTF????????*

His thumbs moved quickly: *I'll do better next time. Sorry.*

There might not be a next time. Do you have any clue how long and how hard it is going to be for him to get his grade up again?

I know. Sorry.

U don't know. If U did, U wouldn't have allowed this to happen!

We got carried away, lost track of time. I haven't seen him in forever.

U might never see him again. I'm meeting with my lawyer about this. BS!

If I saw him more often this wouldn't have happened.

If U saw him more often this would happen more often.

It won't. I promise.

UR promises mean nothing anymore. I'm pissed. U have no idea.

I'll make it up to you. I will!

Last time I heard that, I found out U were fucking around on me.

He stood, thinking. How do you come back from a low blow like that, albeit well deserved? With his cell running low on juice, and with the C-5 taxiing to a stop out front, he texted: *I'll text later, okay? We'll work this out. Please. No lawyers.* At three hundred bucks an hour, he still owed the lawyers (his *and* hers) nearly fifty grand.

She texted back: *Yeah. We'll see.*

He clipped the cell to his belt.

Fucking lawyers.

Outside, with the jet engines winding down, the passenger door fell open like a tongue.

Two suits stepped out: Special Agent McCarthy, followed by the newbie, Special Agent Scholl.

Cautiously, they picked their way through the ice and snow.

Roy held the door for them, welcomed them in with a smile.

Inside, they exchanged handshakes and hellos. Pick the three feds from the men in the lobby. Easy money.

On the way to the company car out back—a black Grand Marquis about as subtle as their overcoats—Roy said, "We went ahead and took the liberty to reserve two rooms at the same hotel. Figured you boys would be staying for the evening."

"Thanks," said Lionel, ducking into the passenger's seat.

The newbie climbed in back.

Roy keyed the ignition. "Not much to see at the crime scene, really. Lots of blood. I spoke with homicide detectives Polo and Perry. They said they'd meet us there around nine."

Lionel said, "Those the two who conducted the investigation?"

"Yep. Pieces of work, the both of 'em."

He glanced toward the driver. "They competent?"

Roy smiled. He hit the wipers to dust the recent snowfall. "Like I said, pieces of work, the both of 'em."

The hotel was a four-star Doubletree in a trendy south Charlotte neighborhood. Across the way within walking distance was the high-end Southpark mall, a myriad of restaurants and coffee shops and retail stores, plenty of opportunities to drop a fortune.

The Grand Marquis pulled in off Tyvola Road and parked near the entrance.

The crime scene was on the third floor, room 312.

The hotel manager keyed the door. "Have at it, boys. And please, stop by the front desk when you're finished."

Room 312.

When the manager opened the door, the stench rolled out like fog. It smelled like the Indianapolis restroom, only denser, more pungent.

Mecklenburg homicide detectives Richard Polo and Jim Perry swaggered in first as if they owned the joint.

Special agent Roy Woodall followed them in.

Lionel stood in the hallway with Eric. "You coming in?"

Eric gagged, pressed his forearm to his lips. He collected himself, straightened his tie. "Yeah. I'm coming in, sure."

Lionel offered a sympathetic look and then gestured for his partner to enter. Sooner or later, he'd have to get used to this. No time like the present.

Eric topped off his lungs and stepped into the fog.

Inside, the other men gathered around the massive bloodstain. They stood in a circle at the foot of the queen-sized bed, their hands on their hips.

Eric zipped past them toward the windows. He cracked one, frustrated that it would only give an inch. The other window wouldn't even open. Hints of fresh air sneaked in. He struggled with whether or not he should shove his face in the crack. Compromising, he placed his hands on his knees, stole as much fresh air as he could.

Detective Richard Polo saw this, offered a good-ole-boy chuckle. He set his briefcase on the queen-sized bed. Borderline obese, his dome meaty and pasty white, he popped the lid to the briefcase. He reached in and pulled out a stack of photographs. One by one he placed these on the unruffled comforter. When he was finished, he picked one out and coaxed it over toward the sickly one near the window. "Here. Take a look at this, boy."

Eric reached over, took it, returned his hands to his knees.

Polo said, "Her name was Aalia Khalil. Hell of a thing, she was only twenty-two years old."

Hesitantly, as if the slightest movement might be enough to get him puking, Eric studied the photograph. He did so with his hands still on his knees, his head still hanging low, and sweat dripping off his chin. In it, a young woman was dead on her back, her legs spread eagle. She had on silky pajama bottoms; her top ripped clean. Blood covered her torso, had soaked into the carpet, that spot right over there. Her dark-red guts (*Jesus*) drooped from the cuts to her belly, accessories to the afterlife, contrasting sickly with her silver, blood-spackled necklace and bracelets. He noticed an imperfect, gaping hole in her chest, right about where her heart ought to be. And, of course, there was the bible covering her face, King James Version, a passage circled in what forensics would discover to be her own blood. She looked similar to the victim in Indianapolis. Same M.O. Same killer.

Eric glanced toward the bloodstain, gagged, and turned his head toward the window.

Homicide Detective Jim Perry, bone-thin with a weak jaw, standing over the bloodstain with his hands on his hips, chewing on a toothpick, said, "The victim here lived alone in Newark, New Jersey. She was a pharmacy student up there at Rutgers, had come down for some course they was offering at UNC Charlotte. Wednesday morning she hopped a plane from Newark, rented a car from Avis, and checked in here early that afternoon." He paused, shook his head. "She checked out around 10:00 P.M." He looked around at the others. "Checked out as in died."

"Thanks for clearing that up," said Lionel, who had moved from the bloodstain to the bed and was now thumbing through the photographs.

Detective Perry continued with his rundown: "Her cell phone records showed a few calls back and forth to Jersey. Turned out to be her daddy. We contacted him that night. He was pretty upset."

"I wonder why," Lionel casually replied, still shuffling through the photographs.

Combatively, Perry replied: "'Cause his daughter was dead, that's why. What'cha got, shit for brains?"

Lionel and Roy exchanged a look.

Roy smiled and rolled his eyes—*pieces of work, the both of 'em.*

Perry said, "So anyway, as I was saying before you done interrupted me, is that after her daddy calmed down some, he said he last spoke with her around six P.M. Phone records back this up. Said he phoned again around ten-thirty, and ain't got nothing but voicemail then. Inside her purse there we found a credit card receipt from Maggianos, the Italian joint across the parking lot over there inside the mall. She had some of that there lasagna and two glasses of wine. Ate her grub at the bar. Closed her tab at 8:13 P.M., according to the receipt. The barkeep remembered her some, said she seemed happy and that she ate alone."

Lionel said, "Any surveillance cameras in the restaurant?"

Perry said, "Well I was getting to that now, wasn't I?" To his partner he said, "These damn feds don't let a man get a word in edgewise, do they?"

Polo chuckled. "Just tell these boys about the surveillance cameras, Jim. Put differences aside."

Perry switched the toothpick to the other side of his mouth and sarcastically replied, "No surveillance cameras in the restaurant, sir. We looked, like good little boys. Now you're going to ask me if there are cameras in this here hotel, right, sir? And my answer would be yes, sir. Absolutely. One caught her coming back from the restaurant around 8:30, up to the lobby door, alone. Another inside the lobby caught her as she went up to the elevators. Again, alone. Hell. These hicks ain't so stupid after all, is they?"

Again, Polo chuckled.

Perry continued: "No cameras in the damn hallways. We can only assume that after getting off the elevator, she entered her room here, died right here. Spilt a hell of a lot of blood." Staring at the bloodstain, he shook his head. "Sum-bitch."

Lionel addressed his next question to Polo: "Who discovered the body?"

Detective Polo said, "The night manager. Folks down the hallway called the front desk complaining of television noise. So, the night manager walks the hallways, and figures it's coming from this room here. Figured someone left their television on and went out for the night. Happens all the time, he says. He knocked. No one answered. He then used his universal key to come in. With the lights came the body." Another chuckle. "The boy's been out sick ever since." He glanced to the sick one near the window. "It's a hell-of-a-thing, all this blood. Gotta have a tough belly."

Eric glanced at him, wanted to say, *or a fat one*, but decided against it, afraid that if he opened his mouth, he would vomit.

"Did you guys find any fingerprints?" said Lionel. "Hair? Fibers? DNA? Anything?"

Detective Polo replied, "No fingerprints. No hair or fibers, and no DNA. We scoured every inch in here. The killer was as clean as a whistle. He left the scissors and the bible, and there was nothing but the victim's blood on either one."

"Any idea where the bible came from?" asked Roy. Standing next to Perry, his job was to merely play escort. That being said, he was still an agent with a brain.

Detective Perry said, "The bible came from the hotel here, has the imprint inside the jacket. The manager couldn't say for certain if it had come from this room or the lobby. Bibles are everywhere, he said, and come up missing all the time."

Okay, folks. All right. Valiantly, Eric had done his very best. Sweating buckets now, there just wasn't enough fresh air. The room was spinning, his heart like a jackhammer. He tossed the photograph on the bed with the others, and nearly sprinted to the bathroom. He heard Polo chuckle. He didn't care. At the toilet he dropped to his knees and opened the seat.

He made it just in time.

He flexed, and let her fly.

When he was finished, he grabbed a hand towel and wiped his face. He groaned. He still felt sicker than shit, but at least the overwhelming urge to vomit was gone. He wiped his eyes. He sat back on his heels and caught his breath.

Curiously, he examined the contents in the toilet. He hadn't eaten much for breakfast, a banana and yogurt and coffee. Dinner the night before had been a salad, while across from him Lionel chewed on a rare and bloody steak. Mostly, he saw bile in there, yellowish liquids. All of it very gross. Again he wiped his eyes, his face.

And then he saw something else.

Puzzled, he took a closer look.

In time, the U.S. Justice Department would hinge nearly their entire case on this one piece of physical evidence, something that tied the killer directly to the crime scene.

With a hoarse, post-vomit voice, he called out: "Hey, guys. Get in here. Check this out."

Lionel entered first. "What you got?"

Eric stood and pointed. "Take a look."

"Take a look where?"

"In the toilet bowl there."

"You want me to look in the toilet bowl? At your vomit?"

"Yes. I mean, no. I mean, forget about the vomit, okay, and look right there, stuck to the side of the toilet bowl, just below the lip. Go ahead."

Hesitantly (and the thought did occur to him that perhaps his new partner was some sort of sick prankster), Lionel leaned over. He saw what his partner was pointing at. He took a knee to get a better look. "Detective Polo, bring me a pair of tweezers, would you?"

Standing in the doorway to the bathroom, Detective Polo said, "What you got, good buddy?"

"Just, get me the tweezers, please."

"Okay. Okay. Calm your damn horses."

When the tweezers arrived, Lionel snatched the piece of evidence, stood, and held it up to the light. "Well, I'll be."

Roy wedged in past the others and took a gander. "Is that . . . what is that?"

"A contact lens," said Lionel. "A contact lens with blood on it. And look closely. In the blood, there's a fingerprint. I'll be damned, there's a fingerprint." He looked to his partner. "Excellent find, Agent Scholl."

The good feelings were short-lived, however, as once again Eric dropped to his knees.

Disgusted, the others retreated.

CHAPTER 14

Nightfall had come.

Dale stood at the front window, parting curtains.

A streetlamp shone down the block, twinkled off the snow-fall that had accumulated eight inches deep. It was still falling, though lighter than before.

Earlier, around four, his buddy Eric had phoned with plans for dinner. They agreed on seven, at an Asian restaurant north of the city called *eeZ Fusion & Sushi*.

And boy oh boy was Gina happy to hear the news, the fact that her husband would be going out to dinner while she sat at home with his parents, listening to goddamn organ music and eating leftover meatloaf.

It began well before this, actually, that morning in bed, when Dale rolled over and reached amorously for her hips.

Tenderly, she took his hand in hers, and placed it back across enemy lines.

Undeterred, he inched closer, whispered, "How's about a quickie, babe? Before Clint wakes up."

"I'm tired. Not in the mood."

"Didn't you sleep well?"

She rolled over, began to speak, stopped, thought for a moment, and then said: "I've been giving our situation a lot of thought, Dale."

Here we go again! "Yes? And?" Still hopeful for that ever-elusive quickie, he did his best to play it cool.

"And, well, maybe things would be better in Wilmington?"

"Gina. We've talked about this before. There aren't any jobs in Wilmington. I'll never find work there."

"Apparently there aren't any jobs in Charlotte, either."

"Hey. That's not fair. You know as well as I do that my odds are better here."

Quietly, she said, almost as a whisper, "No one is saying that you have to come with us."

He'd heard it countless times before, her wish to move to Wilmington, to be back with her parents instead of his, but he had yet to hear her suggest that she would be willing to go without him. He sat up in bed and clicked on the lamp. "Wait. What did you just say?"

She sat up with him. "Dale. I only need twelve more credits, and then I'll have my nursing degree. Twelve more credits. Think about it." She had dropped out of college when, while pregnant with Clint, she simply couldn't take it anymore. Morning sickness had overwhelmed her. She couldn't concentrate in class, and her grades had slipped to average. So, she dropped out and promised herself that she'd pick it back up again when things settled down. But nothing ever settled down, did it? Life only got more and more complicated.

Dale rubbed his face. In fact, Gina finishing her nursing degree wasn't such a bad idea. Nurses were in high demand. Lawyers nowadays, less so. But doing so without him, well, that was something else. "I don't know, babe. I just don't know."

"With a nursing degree I can get a job. They're hiring nurses everywhere these days. I can make some money for the family."

"Are we separating? Is that what this is all about?"

"No. Dale, I'm not leaving you." She glanced away, searched for conviction, found some, and firmed up. "I'm leaving your parents. I love you, but I can't take it here anymore. They're driving me crazy: the goddamn organ music, the constant complaining, the mood around here. Jesus. I fucking hate it."

"Gina. That's not fair to my parents. They took us in when we had *nothing.*"

"My parents offered to take us in as well. Why couldn't we have gone there, where it's not so damn oppressive?"

Her parents: Doctor Cole Finnigan and his socialite wife, Payton. Oh, sure, they were good people, the Finnigans, the community loved them, but wasn't it enough that Dale had to suffer his shortcomings with those who had seen him fall from his very first steps? Imagine this at the Finnigan table: Payton with her second glass of wine, regarding her son-in-law with the same nose she reserved for the wretched souls with whom she had little choice but to share this earth, and now a dinner table. Dale had never been good enough for their smart and lovely daughter. By all rights, Gina should have married a doctor. That's what nurses do in Payton's circle of family and friends: they marry doctors, and have little doctor babies if they're boys, and little nurse babies if they're girls. Lawyers, well, lawyers were okay if you needed a will or a power of attorney, but they make horrible husbands, slick little bastards who cheat on their wives and lie with abandon.

"Gina. Hang in there, okay? Just a little bit longer. Things are going to turn around. I can feel it. I'll find a job. We can get a place of our own. I promise."

Promises, promises. She had heard it all before. Well, it was time to mix things up, wasn't it? Time to try something new. Come hell or high water, she was going to go to Wilmington!

From the crib, Clint stirred and awoke with a shrill, hungry cry.

She turned away from the disagreement and reached for her son.

And that was that, the conversation was over, nothing resolved, and certainly no "quickie."

The day went downhill from there.

At seven P.M. a car pulled up in the driveway, headlights illuminating Old Betsy now covered in snow.

At the front window, still parting curtains, Dale called out, "Eric's here. I'll be back soon, okay?"

From the kitchen where they had gathered for dinner there came only silence.

He called out again: "I'll see you guys in a bit, okay?"

His father called out: "Be careful, son. The roads are terrible out there."

"Okay, Dad. Gina, I'll be back soon. Okay?"

Still nothing.

"All right. Good-bye."

He turned the doorknob and hesitated.

He hesitated because he wanted some sort of endorsement from Gina, the go-ahead to go out to dinner. Something he obviously wasn't going to get.

He hesitated because he worried that there might be a gunman out there, waiting for Dale to come out and play.

He hesitated because he worried for the safety of his family. Ultimately, he figured that they'd be safer here without him. The gunman, if there really was a gunman, would be coming for Dale, and Dale alone. He had left Snead's family alone; surely he would do the same for him.

He considered inviting Eric inside, despite the fact that he was certain that the social dynamic would be a disaster. Also, he wanted to talk with Eric about the shooting death of Alex Snead. There was no way that they could have this conversation in front of Gina and his parents.

So in the end, he figured it best to go out to dinner. He'd only be gone an hour or two. In that time, if the gunman came looking for him, disappointment would certainly send him away.

He exited the home, shut the door, checked the lock, and then hustled through the snowfall.

CHAPTER 15

Some friendships are such that no matter the time estranged, a handshake and hello make everything as right as rain again.

Inside the restaurant, the hostess seated them at a window table, where they flipped napkins to their laps and studied the menus.

A young waitress dropped by to go over the daily specials. She took their drink order—*a 2004 Trentino Pinot Grigio*—and said, "An excellent choice, sir. You gentlemen decide on dinner, and I'll be back in a bit with your wine."

With the waitress away, Eric said, "Dinner's on me. You can get me back later."

Honestly, it was a relief to hear this. In any event, Dale had an anemic Visa in his wallet just in case. "Thanks."

Everything on the menu looked delicious.

Eric debated between the Dragon roll with lobster tail, or the garlic chicken with brown rice. He was starving. He hadn't eaten since breakfast, and that he had vomited in the toilet bowl at the crime scene. Sadly, the stink from that room was still with him. On him. Whatever. Earlier at lunch, Lionel had recommended that he snort some lemon juice.

He shot Lionel an incredulous look. "Are you fucking with me?"

"No. It'll help. Trust me."

Reluctantly, he fished the lemon from the iced tea before him. He squeezed some juice into the palm of his hand. He pulled the straw. *What the hell.* He snorted first into his right nostril, and then quickly into his left. He coughed. Water squirted from his eyes.

Lionel burst into laughter and damn near choked on his sandwich.

For a while, however, it did seem to work. Maybe Lionel was right and not just fucking with him.

Now, sitting here reading the dinner menu, the stench had returned. Regardless, he was famished.

The waitress filled both glasses with wine, placed the bottle in a bucket of ice tableside, and went away with their dinner orders.

Eric lifted his glass. "To the good old days."

The crystal clinked softly.

"To the good old days."

They sipped and settled in.

Eric said, "So, how's the job market in Charlotte?"

Dale shrugged. "It sucks. The banks have laid off a gob of attorneys. The market is flooded. Perfect time to be out of work." He sipped wine. "How's the FBI?"

Despite the blood and the stink, Eric was happy to be there. He knew a ton of folks out of work, and so considered himself fortunate. In present company, however, he thought it best to downplay his good fortune. "It's okay. It's a job, right? You should apply. I hear we're going to be hiring something like a hundred and fifty agents this year. Submit an application."

Sipping wine, Dale smiled. "I did."

"No shit?"

"Mailed the application package off last week."

"Why didn't you tell me?"

"I don't know. I planned on telling you, I guess. It's just, nothing has been working out lately. I didn't want to get too excited about this."

"Yeah. But I can put a good word in for you. Get you in front of the line for an interview. Hell, if I can get hired, you can get hired."

"You don't mind? Putting in a good word for me?"

"Of course not. I'm telling you, you'd fit right in. Honestly, corporate law is for dweebs. This, my friend, tracking down the bad guys, this is where you belong."

Dale sipped more wine. When life has been pummeling the shit out of you, it's nearly impossible to get up from your stool, enter the ring, and land a few jabs of your own. And the FBI had never been his first choice. The pay was average, the hours long. Perhaps Eric was right, however, that ultimately the FBI is where he belonged. Still, he wasn't going to get too excited over this distant possibility.

They fell into a comfortable silence.

Eric smiled and mischievously said, "So. Living with mom and dad, huh?"

From anyone else this would have been an insult. From Eric, it was harmless, good ole fashion ball-busting. Dale shot him the finger, remembered that this was a family restaurant, and quickly withdrew it. "I'm living the dream, my friend. We get cookies and milk every afternoon. Three squares a day. For dessert there's even ice cream. And dad likes beer, keeps the fridge stocked."

Eric chuckled.

Dale said, "Seriously, though, Gina and I have got to get the hell out of there. Dad, he's been pretty good about all of this. Mom, on the other hand, it's just, I'm not sure if she thinks we're invading her space, or if it's old age, or what. She's not what one would call pleasant. It wasn't so bad at first, but lately? Oy vey!"

"Yeah, but cookies and milk. Every afternoon. Tell me, we talking Oreos the real deal, or those cheap imitations?"

"And Gina . . . she said she might leave me. Said she couldn't take it anymore."

"What?"

"Yeah. Said she wants to go home to Wilmington, live with her mom and dad, finish her nursing degree, without me."

Eric didn't know what to say. He'd been the best man at their wedding. And yet for everyone he knew out of work, he knew just as many who had gone through a divorce. "You sign a prenup?"

"Of course. What? You think I'm stupid?" He smiled. "Give up this lifestyle? Oreos that yes are the real fucking deal? A car on her very last leg? Give away half of my measly unemployment check? Never!"

With a more serious tone, Eric said, "Sorry to hear it, man. Really."

"If it's any consolation, it's nothing definitive. And even if she did decide to pick up and go, which I doubt, she said that the separation would only be temporary. Until she finishes her degree."

The waitress returned with their entrees. Dale's portion was huge. Later, he'd ask for a doggie bag, take some home to Gina as some sort of peace offering. For now, he dug in.

Eric did the same.

With some food in his belly, Dale wiped his mouth, said, "What are you doing in Charlotte, anyway? You never said."

Eric looked around as if someone might be eavesdropping. No one was. The closest table was a family of five, husband and wife and three hostile kids. "Can you keep a secret?"

Dale smiled. "It's me, baby. It's Dale."

Eric took a sip of wine and then leaned over the table. Quietly, he told Dale about the *SF Killer*, how he butchers his victims with scissors, snips the letters S and F into their bellies. How the killer leaves his victims with a bible covering their faces, a passage circled in their own blood. He confessed that the smell of blood sickens him; that he had puked in the toilet bowl.

"And you are never going to guess what I found in there."

"Found in where?"

"Inside the toilet bowl."

"Dude. I'm eating."

"A contact lens."

"That's what you found in the toilet bowl? See, I never would have guessed that."

"Yep. And not just any ole contact lens, either. There was blood on this one, imprinted with a fingerprint."

"Are you serious?"

"Yeah."

"The killer's fingerprint?"

"Maybe. My partner, Lionel McCarthy, took the lens up to the FBI forensics lab in Quantico. Wanted to get it there as soon as possible. He left me here with Special Agent Roy Woodall, asked me to collect the rest of the evidence from the local homicide detectives. Roy, he's a field agent here in Charlotte. Good guy. Funny. Marital problems; wouldn't shut up about his ex. Anyway, after we secured the evidence at the federal building uptown, he lent me his car. And here I am."

"So, what you're telling me is that there's a serial killer on the loose here in Charlotte?"

"I don't know. He seems to travel some. Earlier in the week he was up in Indianapolis."

Dale leaned back. "That's freaking crazy, dude."

"No shit, huh?"

Now that the topic had turned to killers, Dale said, "So what do you make of Alex? The fact that he was shot."

"I don't know. You sure he was shot?"

"No. Some old lady at the cemetery told me so. She seemed believable, however. I mean, why would she lie to me?"

"Okay. So Alex was shot."

"Right."

"Right."

"Well, do you think I have anything to worry about?"

Eric glanced outside, at the sidewalk, the snow, and back in again. "I don't know. Do you think you have anything to worry about?"

"What if it had something to do with the court-martial?"

Eric had taken a big bite, was chewing. He swallowed, wiped his mouth. "Dude. That happened like two years ago. Don't you think people would be over it by now?"

"Some people, maybe. But what about Major McGuire?"

"Why would he want to kill Alex?"

"I don't know. Perhaps he felt that Alex hadn't prepared him well for the witness stand. Perhaps after the administrative separation, he lost his marbles." He pointed to his fake tooth. "He did this, didn't he? And that's when he was supposedly sane. And if you think he was mad at Alex . . ."

"Do you have any idea what he's up to these days? Where he lives? Anything?"

"Aside from sending postcards from Hades, no clue."

"Postcards from Hades?"

"That's right. I got a postcard from Hell. No return address. A little note telling me that I'd be coming soon, or something to that effect."

"Maybe the Devil sent it?"

"I haven't ruled that out. Speaking of the Devil, what about Colonel Thoms?"

"Well, I don't know about Major McGuire, but Colonel Thoms is in no position to be gunning people down. Of that I'm quite certain."

Dale shrugged. "Maybe."

Eric poured the rest of the wine in both glasses. He drank, smacked his lips. "You got a gun?"

Dale shook his head. "No."

"Get one. Better to be safe than sorry."

Dale nodded, too ashamed to state the obvious: that a gun would cost money. "Yeah. A gun. That's a good idea."

CHAPTER 16

S mart phones nowadays, it is unbelievable what they can do. In the parking lot of a convenience mart, a cold beer in his hand, Sean Fitzsimmons utilized an application called *Google Earth.*

A blue dot flashed his precise location.

A red pin dropped from nowhere, landed on the address he'd punched in.

Between the two pins ran a blue line, the suggested route.

In wonderment he shook his head.

If only they'd had this technology when I was in Afghanistan . . .

He slammed the can of beer, crunched it in his fist, and then tossed it on the floorboard.

The cabin of the vehicle was a mess, scattered with countless beer cans—some full, most empty—newspapers and computer print-outs, old and filthy underwear. But it was a rental, so who gives a flying fuck? Hell, he'd shit in the back seat if it came to that, and wipe his ass with a floor mat.

From the convenience mart he followed the voice commands of his cell, navigating the roads.

He turned into a neighborhood, a sign reading: Birkdale. It should have read: Middleclass Heaven. Brick and clapboard homes lined the snowy blocks, one after the other, beautiful streetlamps on corners, a neighborhood pool that had been shuttered down for the winter.

Many of the homes were asleep, some with soft lights, others with smoke from the chimneys.

A few cars traveled slowly.

Sean followed the blue line on his cell, turned right, deeper inside the neighborhood.

Up ahead on the right was the location of the red pin.

He turned down the radio and slowed down.

At the house, he pulled up to the curb. He checked the points of the compass to see if the coast was clear. It was. He didn't see a soul.

He hopped out, over to the mailbox. With an ungloved hand he cleared the snow. The nearest streetlamp shone on the numbers. Yes, this was the house, a two-story brick, single-car garage.

He smiled, hopped back inside the rental.

At the end of the road, he flipped around in the cul-de-sac.

He parked a smart distance away, killed the engine, and watched.

Downstairs, the lights went out. Upstairs, they went back on again. Shadows moved. He couldn't tell if they were young or old, male or female. In time he'd know for certain.

From the floorboard he fished out a cold can of beer. Well past the point of intoxication, maintaining the buzz was his sole motivation.

With his sleeve he wiped his mouth, let out a loud, wet burp.

He blew his nose with his fingers and flicked the contents over toward the passenger's seat, a thick, green run of snot sticking to the window.

Upstairs, the lights went out.

He waited.

The lights stayed out for good this time, the folks going nighty-night.

From beneath the seat he pulled out the pistol and stuffed it down the front of his jeans.

From the glove box he pulled out a flashlight.

He'd give them fifteen minutes to settle in, and then he'd go to work.

Ten minutes later, he was outside, quietly closing the car door.

It was freezing out here, but a man sweating beer doesn't feel so much the cold.

He was a ghost in the night on a mission, a phantom, a veritable badass.

He sneaked across the street, crunching snow underfoot, over to the hedges that separated the property line.

That's when a pair of headlights turned the corner and came down the street.

Near the house, Sean crouched behind the hedges.

He remained very still and didn't dare to breathe.

The headlights swept across the lawn and the denuded bushes that he was hiding behind.

They pulled into the driveway behind what appeared to be a compact car that was literally buried in snow.

Shrouded in darkness, he let out his breath and grew nervous. What if a neighbor had seen him, had decided to phone the police?

Repositioning for a better look, the car very well could have been an unmarked cruiser—a black, four-door sedan, a big block beneath the hood.

Sean pulled the pistol and clicked off the safety. He wouldn't go easy this time. He'd rather die right here in the snow than spend another night in prison.

For motivation, to get psyched up for a possible shootout, with the heavy butt of the pistol he clacked himself on the forehead. It smarted like hell and sprang blood. In other words, he liked what he had done, but not so much that he gave himself another.

Car doors opened.

Two men exited.

Sean waited, wondered if they had even seen him. Wondered if they were even coppers.

As they walked toward the garage door, they activated a motion-sensing floodlight that had been mounted near the front door.

At the head of the walkway they stopped, chatted, and laughed.

Neither so much as glanced his way, and he figured that he was in the clear. He strained to hear what they were saying, but couldn't make out their words. However, since they were standing in the floodlight, he could see them very well.

Very well indeed, and he could not believe his eyes.

In his hip pocket were four printouts that he had pulled off the Internet at a public library in Tennessee, images of the four men he'd been contracted to kill, one of which was already dead.

Here at the head of the walkway, chatting, were two others, Dale Riley and Eric Scholl, number two and number four on the hit list, respectively. Having memorized their faces and names, Sean was certain of this. Both were older and one had put on considerable weight, but by God here they were. He'd come here expecting to kill the fat one, but hallelujah and amen, the Lord above had delivered another.

In the shadows Sean smiled, tightened his grip on the pistol.

Okay. So what now?

Perhaps he should crash through the bushes, guns a-blazing?

Or maybe he should sneak in for a cleaner, closer shot?

While Sean weighed the pros and cons, Eric turned and hustled back inside the sedan.

The door slammed shut, and the car backed away down the driveway.

The fat man was opening the front door.

Damn it!

Sean didn't know what to do.

Squatting there, his forehead dripping blood, he tried to think.

Think, Sean, think.

To adapt and overcome, like they had taught him in the army. Problem was, he'd never been much of a thinker, or a leader. Give him some marching orders, clear him a path, and he'd be good to go. Ask him to think outside the box, and a relatively simple task could take all day.

Fully aware of his shortcomings, he hunkered down and tried his best.

Okay, Sean. Okay. It boils down like this: pork chop over there isn't going anywhere but to bed. But Eric is going where, exactly?

Sean had no clue where Eric lived, or who he worked for. Pork chop had been relatively easy to hunt down, the Internet teeming with his personal data, right down to this physical address. Not so much for Eric Scholl. It was as if Eric's Internet profile had been wiped clean by someone or some agency.

So why not follow Eric, gun him down somewhere down the road, come back, and blast pork chop while he sleeps?

Growing up, the kids had called him stupid, but damn if this plan wasn't genius!

He smiled at his own ingenuity, licked the blood that had trickled from his forehead to his lips.

As soon as pork chop entered the house and closed the door, Sean sprinted across the street.

He hopped inside the rental, set the pistol on the passenger's seat, and keyed the ignition.

He put the car in gear.

The black sedan wasn't far down the road, had just turned the corner. Sean would trail behind him like in the movies, sneak up and blast him at a light or something, somewhere down the road. Come sunrise, he would be five grand richer, twenty-five hundred bucks a pop.

He slicked the blood from his forehead over his bald head, turned the corner, and anxiously followed.

CHAPTER 17

nside the black sedan, the preset radio stations had all been programmed to either country or bluegrass.

Eric didn't care for either genre.

On these dark and slippery roadways he scrolled through the radio frequencies, searching for something more his speed—*The Boss* or *Aerosmith* or even *Ozzy*.

The navigation system had him turn right onto Highway 73, and then told him to travel point eight miles for Interstate 77 south.

Highway 73, he soon discovered, was lonely and slick with a snowplow traveling west.

He passed a truck in the right-hand lane, up ahead the headlights of another car traveling the path that the snowplow had cleared.

It wasn't a good night to be out, and few people were. The temperature had plummeted below the freezing level, the snowfall like crystals.

He thought about calling home. It was challenging enough, however, to roll the dial on the radio, the steering wheel demanding both hands, the front wheels fitful in the ice and heavy snow. He figured he'd call them later from his hotel room. Now wasn't such a good time.

"Turn right now," the navigation system commanded.

Eric took the onramp for Interstate 77 south.

He didn't notice the headlights trailing behind him. Not just yet, anyhow.

On the Interstate, snowplows had cleared a somewhat decent path, although there remained significant patches of snow and ice.

The LED lights on the dash showed his speed at a breakneck 31 mph, the navigation system estimating fifty-two minutes until he reached his destination. He couldn't wait. He wanted a hot shower and a warm bed, to speak with his wife, Theresa, and maybe even his son, Mark, if the boy was still awake.

Driving along, he wondered if Lionel and the forensics guys at Quantico were having any luck with the contact lens. He thought about the victim, Aalia Khalil. After her dinner at Maggianos—lasagna and two glasses of wine—she had returned to her hotel room. The surveillance camera picked her up in the parking lot, and again when she entered the lobby. She entered the elevator, alone. That was the last recording of her. Studying the film, no one seemed to have followed her from the restaurant, and no one picked her up in the lobby. It could only be assumed then that after she got off the elevator on the third floor (no surveillance cameras up there) she entered her room alone. Which meant that either the killer had gained access while she was away at dinner, and was waiting inside her room for her, or she had let him in later. It was Eric's belief that most likely she had let him in later. She died in her pajama bottoms, her top ripped clean. She had entered her room and had changed, and sometime later a man came knocking on her door. What did he say? What did she see in the peephole that set her at ease so that she reached down, unlocked the door, and turned the knob? The man entered, and whatever he had promised, he had delivered violence instead. Eric recalled the photograph, Aalia Khalil spread eagle, her guts hanging loose like her jewelry, a bible covering her face. The *SF Killer* because, like with Eloise Saleem up in Indianapolis, he had snipped the letters S and F into her belly, none too careful with her guts. What a sick motherfucker. He tried not to think about it. About any of it. He turned up the radio and focused on the headlights as they illuminated the snowfall.

He traveled south past the city lights of what the locals called the *Queen City*. The way the city glowed reminded him of the Emerald City of Oz. Instead of a wicked witch, however, we have ourselves a serial killer, and nobody's clicking their heels to go home, certainly not Aalia Khalil.

At exit 5 he took the off-ramp. The snowplows had yet to clear the exits. Tire tracks ran deep in the snow. Eric had to travel slowly, cautiously, the tires spinning.

Behind him, a set of headlights followed off the Interstate. They'd been with him for a while now. Mostly, he had paid them little mind, but what were the odds that they would take the same exit?

The GPS had him turn east on Tyvola Road.

The headlights made the same turn.

Eric didn't like it. He didn't believe in coincidences.

Driving slowly, he shifted his eyes from the snow-heavy roadway to the rearview mirror, back and forth. He reached beneath his jacket and unsnapped the restraining strap of his holster. He gripped his Sig Sauer, gave it a tug to make sure that it wouldn't snag in the event that he would need it.

He had yet to fire his weapon outside of the FBI Academy, and the thought made him nervous.

He wished that his partner was here, but he wasn't. No ruby slippers, either.

At the entrance to the parking lot of the Doubletree Hotel he turned in, the tires slipping, spinning, his eyes on the rearview mirror.

The headlights turned and followed.

He found an empty spot about thirty yards from the front entrance. He killed the engine and watched through the rearview mirror.

Behind him, across the way, the headlights pulled into an empty spot and quickly went dark.

Nearby, streetlamps shed light, snow falling lightly around him. Otherwise, the parking lot was dark and quiet.

Eric took a deep breath. He wasn't the type to sit here all night and cower.

Fuck it, he said, and exited the vehicle.

Just because he was in the midst of a serial killer case does not mean that every living being harbors deadly intent. Therefore, who's to say that the car wasn't carrying a mother and her kids? That soon the occupants of the vehicle wouldn't be slipping in the snow toward the lobby, laughing, throwing snowballs?

Eric locked the door and stuffed his hands inside his overcoat pockets.

Playing it cool, he began toward the lobby.

The door to the other car opened.

And no, it wasn't a mother, and neither were there kids.

It was a man, who called out through the snow: "Excuse me, mister. Excuse me."

Eric stopped. The man was approximately twenty feet away. "Yes?" A streetlamp was behind him so that Eric couldn't see his eyes to judge his intentions. He couldn't see the blood leaking from the man's forehead where he had clacked himself with the pistol that he currently held in his right hand, concealed from view behind the car door.

"I'm lost, sir. I was wondering if you could tell me how to get to the airport."

"I'm not from around here," Eric said. "Sorry."

In a flash the man lifted his right arm and squeezed the trigger. *Clack!*

White-hot pain ripped through Eric's ribs and dropped him to his knees.

The gunman closed in. He fired again—*Clack!*—and again—*Clack!*

Bullets blasted the snowfall, the gunman missing by inches.

Eric unleashed his pistol, winced, and quickly returned fire. He wasn't interested in accuracy, not yet, anyhow. He simply wanted the gunman to stop his advance, to know that he was up against another armed man, and that it wouldn't be so easy.

The gunman zigged, zagged, squeezed the trigger but missed wildly.

Eric took aim and fired—*Clack!*

The gunman yelped and retreated to his vehicle. He slotted his wrist between the open door and the body of the vehicle. He continued to fire.

Puffs of snow exploded all around them, glass from car windows shattering.

A round hit Eric in the shoulder and spun him.

"Sonofabitch!" he cursed, and then squared himself and took aim yet again.

The gunman was concealed behind the door.

Eric aimed low, and squeezed another round—*Clack!*

Again the gunman yelped and cursed. He hopped inside his car and slammed the door.

As the car sped away Eric got off one final shot, shattering the glass on the driver's side door.

The car exited the parking lot and turned in the direction from which they had arrived.

Panting, his breath smoky, Eric reached for his shoulder, his hand coming away wet and warm with blood. *"Ah, fuck!"*

From the main lobby the bellhop dashed out. "Hey? What's going on out there? Who is that? You thugs go away, you hear? Go away."

Losing blood, feeling cold and lightheaded, Eric collapsed. "Help. I've been shot. Call for help. Shit!"

"Shot? Are you okay? Who is that?"

"I'm a cop. A federal agent. Call an ambulance. Hurry. Please."

CHAPTER 18

Dale put the leftover sushi in the fridge and then quietly climbed the stairs to their bedroom.

It was late, and he figured Gina and Clint would be asleep by now.

In the bathroom he brushed his teeth and threw on some pajamas.

Slowly, he crawled into bed.

"Dale?"

"Oh. I thought you were asleep." He was glad that she wasn't, he and his little friend.

Gina rolled onto her back. "We need to talk."

Clint was snoozing in the cradle, humming softly.

"What is it, babe?" The blinds had been pulled to ward off the streetlamps, the room pitch black.

"I'm going home for a while. I made up my mind, and I'm gonna go home." There. She'd said it, and it felt good, much more definite this time.

"I thought we agreed that we'd give it a little more time."

"No. *You* agreed. *I* want to go home." The tears welled up, but for now she held strong.

"Look, honey, everything is going to turn around. I can feel it. It's gonna get better, babe. I promise." He caressed her shoulder. The mood was uneasy, but God help him if he didn't also feel sexually aroused. Perhaps if they made love it would kill the tension. From her shoulder he slid his hand to her breast and wormed his body closer.

"It's just not right here."

"How about here?" he said, sliding his hand to her other breast. "Is it right here?"

"Stop it, Dale. This isn't funny."

Frustrated, he jerked his hand away. "I wasn't trying to be funny."

"I hate it here. I can't take it anymore." The tears spilled out and she sobbed. She wiped her eyes with both hands. "I just can't take it anymore."

No one wants to see their spouse this way—reduced to hopelessness and tears. In the blink of an eye, Dale went from feeling horny, to feeling horrible. Compassionately, he said, "I know you hate it here, honey. I know. I'm sorry."

Struggling to get a grip on her emotions, she said, "Don't be sorry."

"Look, if it's any consolation, I hate it here too. It's just, I don't know what else we can do right now."

With a whisper she said, "I do."

"What? What can I do to make it better?"

"Let me go home. Stop fighting me on this, and just let me go home."

If only it were that easy. If only he didn't love her so much, both her and their son. If only he wasn't a fighter at heart with the soul of an eternal optimist. If only. "It is going to get better, Gina. Please. Hang in there."

"Not here," she whispered. "It's not going to get better here, and if we force this, then we'll end up hating each other and it will never, ever work."

There followed an extended moment of silence.

Gina rolled over toward him, wiped her eyes, and bucked up. "Dale. I can finish my nursing degree. Dad has ties to the university. He can get me in for spring semester. And mom, she said she'd watch Clint while I study and go to class. Dale. I want to do this. I *have* to do this."

He sat up and clicked on the lamp. He sighed and felt tears of his own coming on. Before, when she had mentioned how badly she wanted to go home, it seemed like nothing more than a fleeting notion. Now she seemed adamant, and strangely removed from their marriage. This worried him. He didn't want to lose her. He felt like pleading with her, begging. Instead, he said, "You have it all figured out, huh?"

She sat up with him, moved to her knees. She reached for his hand. "Dale, I have to do this, don't you see? I have to do this."

The thought of losing his wife and his son reduced him to tears. Jesus. He hadn't cried in forever. He felt like a blubbering idiot. "Spring semester, huh?"

"Yeah, only. . . ." her voice trailed off. She released his hand.

"Only what?"

"Dale. My flight leaves tomorrow, at two o'clock. Dad bought the ticket already."

"What?"

"My flight leaves tomorrow, Dale. At two o'clock."

"Tomorrow? Are you fucking serious?"

"Quiet. You're going to wake Clint."

He snatched the digital clock off the nightstand and did the math. His tears seemed hot, the blubbering idiot another person altogether, a fool. "That's . . . fifteen hours from now. You're giving me fifteen hours' notice? Are you crazy?"

Not backing down, in fact prepared for this, she said, "I've been telling you, Dale. I've been telling you this for weeks. But no, you don't listen to me. You grope at me and make stupid jokes and tell me over and over again that it's going to get better. Promises, promises. But it's not getting any better, is it, Dale? It's getting worse, isn't it? It's only getting worse!"

"What in the hell happened today? Did Mom say something? Dad?"

"No. Jesus. I mean, yes. Of course. Your mother says something hurtful and insensitive every day since we moved in, but that doesn't matter anymore. I'm over it. What matters is that tomorrow I'm mixing things up. Something has got to change, and I'm doing it. I'm changing it. That's it. I've had enough."

"You can't just up and leave me like this. It's not fair."

"Fair? Really, Dale? You want to talk about fair?"

"What? What did I do that's so horrible? I lost my job, okay? Fuck me. I did the only thing I could and moved us here, to a roof over our heads, and dinner. Don't you think I hate it here as well? I fucking hate it here. I hate how I feel here: like a damn loser. I hate it! And I hate the fact that you hate it here, but what the fuck else was I supposed to do?"

Silence. She turned away. "Please keep your voice down. You're going to wake Clint."

"You know, this is bullshit. I mean, seriously. I come home and find out that my wife is leaving me in fifteen hours, and I'm supposed to just shut up and like it? This is bullshit, Gina. Goddamn bullshit."

Shaking her head, assuming the tranquil nature that she so oftentimes assumed when things turned harsh and serious, she said, "I'm not leaving you, Dale. I'm leaving this situation. I never said it was over between us. We've talked about this. If you ever listened to me, you'd know that I'm not leaving *you*."

"Oh. Of course not. You're leaving me, but you're not leaving me. It makes perfect sense."

"Dale, I don't like you like this. You're scaring me."

"Really? Well, I don't like me like this either. I don't like being out of work like this and living unemployment check to unemployment check like this in the house I grew up in with Mom and Dad watching and critiquing my every fucking move like this. And I certainly don't like you not liking me like this and I don't like raising our son like this in an environment like this." He took a deep breath, ran a hand through his hair. "But I'm doing my best, Gina. I haven't given up. Unlike someone I know, and married."

"I'm not giving up." She turned to him. "Look, I can finish my degree, and here's an opportunity to do so. I can get a job, and we can get a place of our own. We, you and me and Clint, our family, we can start over again somewhere new. Dale, honey, it's not working here! And if we continue to stay here and try and make it work, we'll end up hating each other. Believe it or not, I'm doing this for us."

He laughed a disingenuous laugh. "Unilaterally. You're doing this for us, unilaterally."

"Something has to change, and now's the time."

"Now? Or two o'clock tomorrow afternoon?"

"Very funny. Look, you're mad. I get it. But this will all be for the best. Wait and see."

"No shit I'm mad."

She sighed and turned away. That was that. With or without his blessing, she was going to go home tomorrow at two. She crawled beneath the covers and pulled them up to her chin. She rolled away toward her son, who, miraculously enough, was still sound asleep in his crib.

"So that's it, huh?" Dale said. "End of discussion."

"That's it," she said. "Like you always say, there's a time to talk and there's a time to act. Good night, Dale."

"Yeah. Good night."

"Can you please turn out the light?"

"Oh! You bet. After all, you have a long day tomorrow, huh? You need your rest for the flight back home, don't you?"

"Thanks for understanding."

He clicked off the light. "How's that? Better? And how's the temp, dear? Good enough for you? Would you like me to set a wakeup call?"

"Eight o'clock would be nice." It came off sounding more sarcastic than she had hoped.

"Eight o'clock it is. Let me get that for you." He picked up the clock and threw it against the wall.

Clint started awake and immediately began to cry.

Gina threw off the covers. "Thanks. Asshole." She went to her son.

"You're welcome," he replied, throwing off the covers for his robe.

Downstairs, he grabbed the leftover sushi from the fridge along with two cold beers.

He went to the basement and clicked on *David Letterman*.

The sushi was fucking delicious, paired perfectly with ice cold Coors. He scarfed it all up and drained both beers.

When *Letterman* was over, he went upstairs and grabbed two more beers for the funny man who followed.

CHAPTER 19

The room was a first-floor box off of exit 25, thirty bucks a night plus tax.

The parking lot was nearly empty, which was good, not a lot of guests.

Sean Fitzsimmons pulled the Nissan as close to his room as possible.

Covered in glass from the bullet-shattered window, wincing, sweating buckets, he opened the car door and threw out his leg. He tried to put weight on it, but the damn thing wouldn't hold an ounce.

Standing on one leg in the snowfall, the temperature well below freezing, he was both extremely cold and extremely hot, add to that a dizzy spell as he slammed the car door and reached for his room.

He hobbled over, fumbled the key from his pocket, and opened up the motel door.

Inside, he slid the lock and caught his breath, his back against the door.

The sonofabitch shot him, twice in the same damn leg.

Goddamnit!

He made a desperate play for the bed, landed on top of the tacky, multi-colored comforter with a weighty bounce.

Okay. So he'd been shot. What was he going to do? Sit here and cry like a bitch, or man the fuck up?

He unbuckled his belt and unsnapped his jeans, his cheeks puffing in and out, sweating buckets. Carefully he wiggled free, pushing the jeans down over his shot-up thigh, the blood-wet fabric pulling away like a band-aid over hairy skin.

Tossing his jeans aside, he examined the gunshot wounds. The hole in his thigh was tiny compared to the pain. Farther down on his ankle he found another bullet hole, this time with an exit wound, the bullet having missed the bone. Regardless, his ankle throbbed, dangled as if tendons or something had been severed.

He wiped his eyes, grabbed a fistful of the comforter and blew his nose.

Mostly, his recollection of bygone events in his life was like fog. What was clear, however, were the old black-and-white westerns he used to watch on the television set as a kid. One scene in particular was a rowdy saloon with a vested pianist and a shady poker game, hookers in corsets. The good guy blew in after a long day's ride, sidled up to the bar, and downed a shot of whiskey. The bad guys didn't take kindly to his company, and it wasn't long before there was trouble. A dozen or more bad guys dropped before the good guy dashed away through the saloon's swinging doors; outside on a horse called Shirley. Just as he was about to steal away, however, one of the bad guys popped out and shot him clean in the arm. A dirty, rotten sonofabitch like that sonofabitch Eric Scholl, only Eric had shot him twice, and in the leg. And Sean never fancied himself a good guy, which hardly even mattered. What mattered is that the hero then rode out of town, up to a ridgeline where he dismounted Shirley and sat atop a boulder. From there he could keep a good eye on the trail he had ridden, as well as several others. From his satchel he pulled out a nine-inch hunting knife, a flask of whiskey, and some matches he used for his smokes. Uncapping the flask, he downed half the contents and set the rest aside for later. He rolled up his sleeve to expose the gunshot wound. He then fisted his knife, the sunlight glinting off of the blade. Shirley whinnied, danced her front hooves. A much-younger Sean could barely watch the rest of it, a painful, bloody spectacle that he would never in a million years forget.

Inspired, Sean hopped over to the dresser, where he snatched a six-pack of beer and placed it on the nightstand next to the bed.

He hopped over to the closet, dug around, and came back with a wire coat hanger, rusty with white paint chipping off.

He picked up the telephone and dialed 0 for the front desk.

"Hello? How can I assist you?" The voice was young and male.

Sean cleared his throat. "Yeah, I, uh, need a first aid kit in room 145."

"A first aid kit?"

"Yep. Cut myself shaving, prrrretty bad."

"Well. I'll see what I can find, mister."

"Mmmm. Thanks."

Hanging up, Sean picked up the coat hanger, uncoiled the ends, and bent it lengthwise. He inserted the tip between his teeth, bit down, and formed a tiny hook. In the process, he felt a tooth chip. Big whoop. He had much bigger cattle to brand. He collected the chips on his tongue and spit them out onto the floor.

Next, he pried the beer cans from the plastic casing, aligned them neatly on the nightstand. Fuck it, he thought, and drank one quickly.

Someone knocked.

Sean hopped over and poked his head outside.

"You asked for a first aid kit, mister?" Shivering in the dark was a young man, holding a kit that seemed a million years old, behind him the snow still falling.

"Yeah. Hand it over."

The kid held it back. "What happened to your forehead, mister?"

Sean edged the door closer to the jamb. He'd forgotten that he'd bloodied himself with the butt of his pistol. "Shaving. Like I said."

"You shave your forehead, mister?"

"Sure, when I ain't shaving my nut sack!" Sean snatched the kit and slammed the door, the windows rattling.

The young man called out: "Hey, that kit is gonna cost you twenty bucks, mister."

Sean yelled back: "Charge it to my room." *The nosy little prick!*

He hopped back to bed, where he examined the contents of the kit. The only items worthwhile were the gauze and the tape, everything else more or less useless. No disinfectant, no nothing! *Twenty bucks, my ass!*

From the front pocket of his jeans he pulled out a Zippo lighter.

On the nightstand, he arranged his items as neatly as he'd arranged his footlocker as an army recruit: coat hanger, cans of beer, Zippo, gauze, and tape.

He cracked another beer, slammed it, pulled out his pecker, and filled it back up again. Thinking nothing of this, he placed this can of piss back on the nightstand and then grabbed the remote control. He scrolled to some old sitcom with a laugh track, and then cranked up the volume.

He then pulled the leather belt free from the loops in his jeans, doubled up the band, stuffed this in his mouth, and chomped down hard.

Time to man the fuck up!

Over on the nightstand he cracked another beer and set it aside for later. Post-op, he would use this and the Zippo to disinfect the wound, just like that cowboy had done on TV. Beer, 100-proof whiskey, same difference, right?

Okay. You can do this, Sean. No problem!

Reverently, respectfully, he picked up the wire coat hanger, and my, how it trembled on the way toward his thigh, the tip with the makeshift hook positioned just above the gunshot wound.

He chomped down harder on the belt, slammed his eyes shut, psyched himself up, and then opened one eye just enough to see.

Ever so slowly, he lowered the hook, down inside his hot, pink flesh.

The tip disappeared, and at first he felt nothing.

For a moment he wondered if it was really going to be this painless.

The hook sank deeper, displacing blood and reddish-white pus, which oozed hot and thick.

Deeper he pushed the wire coat hanger, and then deeper still.

It hit without warning, a pain like white lightning, as if the coat hanger had touched a hot wire to complete the circuit. He convulsed, banged his head against the headboard, and nearly knocked himself unconscious.

When that initial shock was over, he pounded the mattress with his fists, screaming into the belt, crying, his neck bulging with veins.

When he opened his eyes, he found the tip of the coat hanger still deep in his thigh, the opposite end swaying rhythmically to and fro.

His cheeks puffing air, his body literally soaked in sweat, still chomping on the belt, veins everywhere—a massive one running along the top of his bald head—he re-gripped the hanger, and damn if he didn't go fishing again.

Damn if he didn't man the fuck up!

And despite the intense pain, *he . . . did . . . not . . . let . . . GOOOOO!*

His throat swelled bigger than ever, his head bouncing against the headboard, bouncing, bouncing.

Violently, his eyes rolled back in his head, and in the midst of all of this unthinkable pain he had a remarkably clear vision of himself as a child, over at a friend's house on the floor, playing the board game *Operation*.

It takes a steady hand.

Two kids laughing and plucking out hearts, femurs, funny bones, here, now, the street version of the game: plucking out bullets instead of bones.

Every red light was flashing, every buzzer buzzing.

But he did not let go!

And when the hook could go no deeper, he sensed something in there, quite possibly lead.

Christ Almighty he felt lead, he did, laughing mad—*pluck out that lead!*

It takes a steady hand!

He manipulated the instrument, brought it up and down, up and down, could hear his childhood friend encouraging him, telling him, *Yeah, you can do it, Sean. Get that bullet, buddy, and don't you worry about all of these buzzers buzzing, about your face blinking red, just go in there and pluck that sonofabitch out.*

In the street version of the game, it's okay if you get buzzed, just realize that you're connected to the game, to the circuitry, and when the buzzers buzz, you feel it. Boy, do you ever.

But God help him if it wasn't actually working. He could feel the foreign body tumbling up, away from the bone, tearing flesh toward the exit, dear God.

His friend was on his feet now, cheering, laughing his fucking ass off.

You can do it Sean! Holy shit!

And Sean was biting down so damn hard that it felt as though his jaw might snap off, like his neck might explode from the screams deep inside of there.

Don't give up now, Sean, you can do it!

And then . . . at last . . . the bullet popped out, mangled and bloody and coated with pus.

And then his friend disappeared, poof, but the pain remained, the buzzers still buzzing.

Yes, the game was over, with no clear winner, just a madman thrashing about in bed, pounding his fists into the mattress, thrashing his one good leg, babbling incoherently, making no sense whatsoever.

The street version of the game: where everyone is a loser, but thanks for playing anyway.

Deliriously, as if pummeled in a boxing match, he sat up and reached for the beer on the nightstand. He felt himself slipping. He had to be quick, or as quick as he could be.

Soaked in sweat, still chomping down on the belt, hastily, he doused the wound with beer.

Only, well, it didn't smell like beer, did it?

He brought the can up to his sweat-dripping nose, and sniffed.

Motherfucker!

The street version of the game: yeah, she's a bitch, with a few twists and turns!

He hurled the can against the wall. When it hit, the can exploded, urine splattering everywhere, the wall and the dresser drawers, even the ceiling. Christ, he could not believe that he had picked up the can that he had peed in. With the comforter, he attempted to clean up as much of the urine as possible.

He grabbed the other opened can and sniffed it. Satisfied that this can contained nothing but pure beer, he doused the wound he had doused with urine. He shook the can like a saltshaker until it was empty, tossed it with the rest of the garbage on the floor.

Next, he snatched the Zippo and expertly snapped a light.

The room was spinning, faster and faster, he had to be quick.

He kissed the flame to his urine- and beer-wet thigh.

Only, no *whhoomphfff!* like in that television show.

Desperately, crying tears of disbelief, he moved the flame up and down and left and right, singeing hairs, but no damn *whhoomphfff*.

He threw the Zippo, spit out the belt, and screamed out loud: "Ah, you *Mother FUCKERRRRRRRRSSSSSS!!!!!!*"

The closest occupant eight rooms down rolled over in bed and then covered his head with a pillow.

When the scream abated, Sean's body went slack as if a switch had been flipped. Awkwardly, he fell backward in bed, his head thumping one last time against the headboard.

The street version: it's all fun and games until somebody loses consciousness.

Meanwhile, on the television set, the credits rolled, and it was on to a rerun of *Seinfeld*.

CHAPTER 20

"**D**ale," Gina said. "Did you hear something?" She rolled over in bed and shook him.

"What's that?" he mumbled.

"I thought I heard something."

"Huh?"

"See. There it is again. Downstairs. Someone's knocking on the front door."

Dale found the digital clock on the nightstand. Gina must have replaced it after he threw it against the wall. He was surprised that it was still working. "It's six o'clock in the morning." He'd been in bed since 2:00 A.M., and yeah, he was tired. Perhaps even a bit hung over. How many beers did he have last night? His head was killing him.

"Go check," said Gina, nudging him.

Rubbing the muck from his eyes, he went to the window and squinted through the blinds. At the curb was a car with its headlights on. Otherwise, it was still dark out there, and still very cold.

Another knock echoed up the stairs.

"See," said Gina. "There it is again. Go see."

The argument the two had had the night before had kept his mind off the gunman. Not once, while watching late-night television and drinking beer, did he glance toward the basement window, searching for a gunman. Now, he threw on his robe and grabbed the baseball bat. Absurd to think that a gunman would knock on the front door, and ridiculous to bring a bat to a potential gunfight, but he felt safer with this in his hands. At least he had something.

At the front door he peered through the window.

He saw an elderly gent with a bald dome and fifty, sixty pounds of additional girth.

"Who is it?" Dale called through the door.

"Mecklenburg Police, sir. Detective Richard Polo."

Dale clicked on the porch light. The homicide detective pressed his cred pack to the glass.

Dale placed the baseball bat in the corner and unlocked the door. The cold rushed in.

"What's this about?"

"Are you Dale Riley?"

"Yes, sir."

"Do you mind if I come inside? It's freezing out here."

Dale thought for a moment. "Sure. Come on in." He opened the screen door, and then gestured toward the master suite. "My parents are still asleep, so please keep it down. C'mon. We'll go to the kitchen." There, Dale turned on the lights. "So, what's going on?"

"Mind if we sit?"

"No. Go right ahead."

The detective pulled up a chair at the table. "Please, won't you join me?"

Reluctantly, Dale joined him. "It's six o'clock on Sunday morning, sir. What in the hell is going on?"

"Your friend Eric Scholl asked me to come by."

"Eric?"

"He's, ah, he's in the hospital."

"Wait. What are you talking about?"

"He's been shot."

"Eric Scholl?"

"He's doing okay. No reason to panic, Mr. Riley. He's doing just fine."

"What's going on?" It was Gina, having sneaked downstairs.

Dale ran a hand through his hair. "Jesus. Honey. Eric's been shot." He looked to the detective. "Are you sure?"

"Yes. I'm sorry. But he's doing fine."

Gina, shaking her head to clear the cobwebs, said, "The guy you had dinner with last night?"

"Yeah," said Dale, finding it hard to digest the news. "What in the hell happened?"

Detective Polo said, "We're looking into that."

"Well . . . what do you know?"

"It's complicated. We're not sure. Anyway, they operated on him late last night. He's been in and out of consciousness. When he came to this morning, he asked me to come here to tell you."

To his wife, Dale said, "I have to go see him."

She nodded, collected her robe closer to her neck.

Detective Polo stood and pushed in the chair. "I'm heading there now. You can ride along, if you'd like, or follow."

Quietly, staring at the floor and seemingly lost in her own world, Gina said, "I have a flight this afternoon. At two o'clock. I still have a flight."

"I know," Dale said. "I know. Let me . . . I'll go see him, okay, and I'll get back as soon as possible."

"I just need a ride. To the airport."

"I know, babe." He was holding her now, rubbing her back.

She looked up at him, her eyes as serious as he'd ever seen them, intense and wet. "What's going on, Dale? Why are old friends of yours getting shot?"

He didn't know what to say, or even where to begin. "I don't know, honey. But I gotta go see him." He kissed her on the forehead. "I'll be back as soon as I can."

CHAPTER 21

The uncomfortable silence was but one of many reasons why Dale would have preferred his own wheels. That, and now he would have to rely on Detective Polo (by all counts a somewhat goofy gent with a stale, lingering odor) to return him to his home. Old Betsy remained in the driveway. He had asked Gina to excavate her from the snow so that, upon his return, he could drive them to the airport for that 2:00 P.M. departure. She didn't flinch when he asked this of her. Nothing. She nodded, and watched him go with Detective Polo. Dale hoped that upon his return, he would find Old Betsy still covered in snow, that Gina would have changed her mind about this nonsense of Wilmington.

"Everything okay over there?" asked Polo, glancing toward his passenger, his shoulders hiked up to his chin with both hands on the glove compartment.

"Everything is fine."

"It's just, I know marital trouble when I see it. Not that it's any of my business."

"You're right. It's none of your business."

"She said she's going home, huh? Isn't that what she said? Your wife?"

He wanted to reach over and crank up the radio. Detective Polo, however, might take this for what it was, a slight, which was not something he needed right now, as, again, he was depending on Polo for a ride home.

Dale sighed. "It's tough, huh? Marriage?"

Polo laughed. "It's a bitch, is what it is. But wha'cha gonna do?"

"Wha'cha gonna do."

Polo seemed satisfied with that. Dale left it alone.

At the hospital he followed Polo to Eric's room.

Inside, they were greeted by a heart monitor and bags of IV fluids, tubes coming and going.

Eric lay in bed looking sickly. Weakly, he waved Dale over. "Come on in." His voice came out listless and hoarse.

Dale walked over. Sitting bedside were two men in suits, neither of whom Dale recognized. He said, "Jesus, Eric. What in the hell happened?"

"The bastard shot me. Twice. Got me once in the side, right here,"— he winced when he tried to move—"and once in the left shoulder. The doctors said he missed the good stuff. Thank God. Right?"

"Christ."

"Dale, this is my partner, Lionel McCarthy. He flew in early this morning, just beat you in."

One of the suits stood, a tall and handsome man, strong and black and as serious as a heart attack. He extended a hand. "Special Agent Lionel McCarthy. Nice to meet you."

"Dale Riley, sir. Nice to meet you as well."

"And don't you worry, partner," Lionel said, retaking his seat. "We'll get that bastard. No one shoots a federal agent and gets away with it. No one."

Eric, the consummate host, said, "And that man sitting next to Lionel is Homicide Detective Jim Perry. He and Detective Polo are partners."

Politely, out of habit, Dale went to shake Perry's hand.

The detective, however, only snapped his newspaper. Absently, he said, "Nice to meet you, mister, but I ain't shaking that hand of yours." He gave Dale a quick inspection. "Don't know where the hell it's been." He went back to reading his newspaper.

Dale, not quite knowing what to make of this, shrugged and pocketed the handshake. He turned to Eric. "So, I mean, what in the hell happened?"

"He shot me, buddy."

"I know. But what *happened*?"

"The sonofabitch was tailing me. He got me in the parking lot of the hotel. I got him too, in the leg, I think. It was dark. I'm not sure."

"Did he get away?"

"Yeah."

"Jesus. You're lucky to be alive." What were the odds that within the span of a week both Alex Snead and Eric Scholl would be shot, one in a coffin, and the other in a hospital bed? He was about to bring this up, and then thought better of it. This wasn't the time or place, too many ears and untrustworthy characters.

A man entered holding two cups of coffee. He handed one to Lionel and sipped from the other.

Eric, coughing, wincing, said, "And Dale, this is Special Agent Roy Woodall. He's with the Charlotte folks here, the guy who lent me his car last night."

Roy didn't share Detective Perry's hangups. The two shook hands and exchanged hellos.

Checking his wristwatch, Dale turned to Eric. "Listen. I can't stay long. Sorry."

"What's up?"

"It's just, I got an important errand to run."

Polo, standing near the doorway, said, "His wife is leaving him. Said she's gotta be at the airport by two. A damn shame. Can't live with 'em, and can't kill 'em." He laughed.

What a big mouth, thought Dale, turning, shooting his ride home a dirty look.

Polo said, "Well, it's the truth, ain't it?"

Eric said, "So, she's leaving you, huh?"

"She's not leaving me. I mean, she is, but . . . remember what we talked about last night over dinner?"

Eric nodded. "Yeah."

"She's going to live with her parents for a while and finish her nursing degree. That's it. No big deal."

Eric offered a sympathetic nod. "You okay?"

"Absolutely. I'm fine."

Sipping coffee, Roy said, "That's what they all say at first, that they got to go live with mommy and daddy for a while, to better themselves. And then boom! Some shithead cop is serving you divorce papers." He looked to Polo, lifted his cup of coffee, and sipped.

Polo said, "What the hell is that supposed to mean?"

"I'm just saying that cops are shitheads. Present company excluded, of course."

Detective Perry, unmoved by any of this, set aside his newspaper. He looked at Lionel to his left. "So. You boys find a match to that fingerprint yet?"

Lionel took a sip of coffee. "Nope. Nothing yet."

"That's what I figured," said Perry. "You boys didn't find shit. You should have given that contact lens to us. We got a first-class lab right here in Charlotte. Hell, the killer would be in lockup by now."

Lionel said, "Right." To his partner, he said, "We did, however, find something else."

Eric lifted his head. "We did?"

Lionel looked to the one civilian in the room. "I probably shouldn't say. Perhaps later."

Eric said, "Why? Because of Dale here? Hell, Dale is a prior Marine with a Top Secret clearance. A lawyer. A hell of a good guy."

Lionel thought for a moment, sipped coffee, and then said, "You vouch for him?"

"Absolutely," Eric replied.

Dale said, "It's okay, guys. You can talk about it later, when I'm not around."

Eric said, "Don't be ridiculous. Lionel. What is it? What did we find?"

Under different circumstances, Lionel wouldn't have talked so freely in front of a civilian. But here we have two of Charlotte's finest, pieces of work the both of 'em, and intimately familiar with the case of the *SF Killer*. It seemed silly, then, to exclude a man who by every measure seemed intelligent and trustworthy. Not to mention that Eric had vouched for him, or that Dale was a prior Marine. Lionel said, "What we found is another dead body. Same M.O. Same killer."

Eric said, "What?"

"Yep. Down in San Antonio. The killer, he's on the move."

CHAPTER 22

The killer is on the move.
     Victim number three had hit the snooze button once too many times.

Inside the passenger terminal at LaGuardia International Airport, with her flight long gone, she noticed on the board that another was scheduled to depart for San Antonio in less than an hour.

In high heels, a Jovani dress, and a coat of mink, she hustled to this new gate and waited in line.

With a first-class ticket in hand she sighed, often, making sure that anyone within dynamite range was well aware of her frustrations.

When at last she was first in line, she set her purse upon the countertop. "Oh, pooh. I've had such a terrible morning. You would not believe it."

"And how may I assist you today, ma'am?" The gate agent—Trish, read the nametag—was young and eager to help.

"Well, Miss Trish, my nincompoop driver got lost on the way here. Can you believe it? Yes. Don't worry. He's fired. So I missed my earlier flight, but noticed on the board that there's another that leaves in thirty minutes. Perhaps—"

"Let me see what I can do, ma'am. Can I have your ticket?"

She handed this over. "There are just so many very important people counting on me. We have a very important dinner planned, lots of very rich donors for a very generous and very prestigious foundation."

"Well, it seems you're in luck, Mrs. Duckworth." Trish tore the old ticket in two and handed her a new one. "Have a good flight, ma'am."

Mrs. Duckworth studied this. Her moon face soon scrunched into a frown. "Oh, dear. This is terribly unfortunate."

"Excuse me, ma'am? Is there a problem?"

"Yes. See. Well, that ticket you tore up was for first-class service, Miss Trish. This one here is for coach."

"Yes, ma'am. This is a regional jet; there are no first-class seats. And you're lucky. I rebooked you in the very last seat."

"Oh, dear. It's just, well, that ticket cost over two thousand dollars. Can you imagine? Two thousand dollars for an airplane ticket?"

One of the pilots for the flight approached the counter and accessed the computer next to Trish. He printed off some paperwork and stood there and studied this.

Trish, giving him some room, said, "That is a lot of money, ma'am. I can certainly understand your concern."

"Can you?"

"Of course."

"Well then, maybe you could credit my card the difference. Oh, that would be just perfect, wouldn't it?"

"I'm sorry, ma'am. I can't do that. Our policy doesn't allow it."

"How about a voucher, then? For the difference? I'm sure we can work something out."

"Ma'am. Just to be clear, I was under no obligation to rebook you without an additional fee outside of a natural catastrophe. Your driver getting lost on the way to the airport doesn't count."

Seeing that she was getting nowhere, Mrs. Duckworth searched through her purse and pulled out a notepad and pen. It was time to play hardball. "I see. Now, Miss Trish, can I please have your full name?"

She pointed to her nametag. "Trish will do."

"Well, if you say so. And the phone number of your supervisor?"

"Please feel free to dial the 1-800 number for the airline and follow the prompts."

Putting her things back in her purse, she said, "Trish. Oh, dear Miss Trish. I hear McDonalds is hiring. You might wish to send in an application. Brush up on frying them fries and them burgers and whipping up those milkshakes, yes?"

From the paperwork, the pilot glanced from one to the other. "Trish, is everything okay?"

"Everything is perfect. Thanks." To Mrs. Duckworth she gritted her teeth and said, "Ma'am, we know you have your choice in airlines, and thank you so much for flying ours."

The flight arrived in San Antonio just past 6:00 P.M.

A limo was waiting on her.

In the back seat she dialed her husband's secretary. "Maria? Yes. Call my donors and reschedule for tomorrow evening at six. Oh, yes. It's been a terrible day. Don't ask. Mm. Okay. Bye-bye."

The limo entered the Riverwalk District. Mrs. Duckworth looked out the window, saw lovers and loners strolling the cobblestone banks where merchants peddled their wares, where restaurateurs served dinner and wine in the humid Texas air. It was all so vibrant and alive, and tomorrow night she would mingle among them. Tonight, however, she just wanted her room.

The driver pulled up to the Hotel Valencia. He hopped out and handed the passenger and her luggage to the bellhop.

The lobby was immaculate and trimmed with greenery and gold, marble floors echoing footsteps that were crisp and clean, with classical music playing lightly on well-hidden speakers. Like a big shot she made her way through, cutting line at the front desk, where she made her customary demands. The room had to be just so, nothing standard, king-sized bed, the cost reasonable, and on and on. She asked to see the manager, and then she asked to see the manager's manager. Her request to see the owner, however, was fruitless, as an acquisition group owned the hotel, the entire affair run by a board of trustees. In the end, however, she got her way, one of the nicest rooms on the property for about a quarter of the cost.

Inside her plush room, she watched as the bellhop hung her garment bag and set her suitcase atop the luggage rack.

"Anything else I can assist you with, ma'am?"

Her smile said, *yes, of course there is something else you can assist me with*. Why, she wasn't so old that she couldn't give this young buck a run for his money. With her eyes she undressed him. "Oh, I can think of a few things."

"If you think of anything specific, please call the front desk."

Playfully, she teased him with a twenty-dollar bill, offered it up, and pulled it back.

He smiled. This wasn't the first time he'd been hit on by a lady some thirty years his senior. They called these ladies cougars. He found her more of an insufferable hog.

At last she handed it over. "There's a lot more where that came from."

"Thank you, ma'am. And again, call the front desk if you need anything. Good night." Quickly he escaped. Down the hallway he laughed, couldn't wait to tell the guys on the staff.

Upon disrobing, she examined herself in the mirror. Sure, she was old and a bit overweight, but she still had some sugar down there, didn't she, some octane in them hips.

In the shower she washed off the day's stress.

She ordered room service. When it arrived, she devoured every bite and finished an entire bottle of burgundy wine.

Purring in the warmth of the bed's Egyptian-cotton linens, watching the flat-screen television, the telephone rang.

"Hello?"

"Mrs. Linda Duckworth?"

"Yes?" Perhaps it was the bellhop, hungry for a taste of that sugar. She purred.

"Ma'am, this is Mr. Curril at the front desk."

"Oh?"

"You might like to know, ma'am, that since you are such a valued customer, we'd like to offer a complimentary bottle of

Dom Perignon Champagne. We'd be happy to hold this upon your departure, or we could have a bellman bring it up straightaway."

"Dom Perignon? Why, yes. Bring it straight up."

"Very well, ma'am. Room 114. We'll be right there."

"Oh, no. Room 413. You must recheck your records."

"Oh, yes. I simply misread. Room 413. I'll send someone right this minute."

A few minutes later, a soft knock on her door pulled her out of bed. She threw on her robe.

Through the peephole she saw a man in a bellman's vest, older than the buck from before, his chin low, waving the bottle high.

She hesitated. Perhaps she sensed the evil; intuited the Grim Reaper.

"Ma'am, your champagne."

Sober, a tad less gluttonous, and she might not have opened the door. But she did open the door. She did. She opened the door, and smiled, and welcomed him in.

He was handsome, this man, and she wondered what in the world had ruffled her feathers so. She laughed a sigh of relief, accepted the bottle of champagne, and studied the label, smiling. She turned for her purse, feeling that a five-dollar tip was in order.

Yes, she turned for her purse.

She turned, and he stepped farther inside.

Quietly, he pulled a latex glove over the hand that once held the bottle. His left hand, already gloved, he'd hidden behind his back.

From his right front pocket he pulled out the scissors. He cupped these in his right hand to keep them well hidden, for now.

Before she reached her purse, she paused and turned around. "Haven't I seen you somewhere before?"

He smiled. "Yes, you have."

With his smile returned her fear. It was such an evil smile, so heartless, his eyes without love or hate but pooled with cool indifference.

It was the last smile that she would ever see.

That cold and wicked smile, and she never saw the scissors.

He was faster than she could have imagined. The scissors came in low and quick, and entered her just below her ribcage.

She dropped the bottle of champagne, which shattered when it hit the floor.

And my God, he was so strong, so strong that he lifted her up off her feet, the scissors sinking in deeper, deeper, his left hand clutching her robe for leverage.

Shock overcame her and she never fully screamed.

She gasped with wide eyes, amazed at how high he was lifting her by this single, excruciating point of entry.

Her chubby white feet kicked, kicked, above the shattered bottle.

With the scissor full hilt, he carried her toward the bed, smiling all the while, watching her eyes, enjoying her hot blood, how it burst from her heart and ran down his latex-gloved hand, down his wrist, his shirted elbow.

He tossed her on the bed, literally tossed her there, the scissors coming away with a slick-wet pucker, blood splattering everywhere. He tossed the scissors next to her. They'd come in handy later.

Savagely, he disrobed her.

He climbed in bed with her where he straddled her and came nose to nose with her. He wanted to feel her last push of hot air, to see her eyes when life as we know it escapes them.

A single tear rolled from her left eye, a scant, faint cry from her lips.

And then, just like that, the tension dissolved.

In her eyes he found nothing more than his own cruel reflection, a mask of evil incarnate. He saw power. He puckered his lips and kissed his own reflection in her wet, dead eye.

He reached for the scissors.

And the ritual soon began.

PART III

ALWAYS FAITHFUL

I'm not a butcher,
I'm not a yid,
But I'm your own,
Lighthearted friend!

—Yours truly,
Jack the Ripper!

CHAPTER 23

The cell phone woke him from a very deep, bizarre sleep, one riddled with many a wicked dream, the last of which had him sprinting through an arid canyon with a rabid band of coyotes giving chase; overhead, clouds of black vultures rolling in from the west. The Wild Wild West.

He had been out of federal prison a little over a week now, an ex-con who had served his time and who was eager now to catch up on what he had been missing. He had employment and seed money, a cell phone and a Ruger .45. Out back he had wheels that the cops might soon be interested in (the rental agreement had the car due back three days ago). He had one man in the bag, and three men yet to go. It should have been two. Hell, it should have been one.

And he had one hell of a fiery left leg.

The *William Tell* Overture played from the cell.

Hi Ho, fucking ranger!

He popped open an eye, found himself lying on a tacky, sweat-soaked comforter. He had on underwear and a t-shirt. Sunlight poured in through the split in the curtains.

He spotted the cell on the dresser, seemingly miles away. He reached for it; winced from the pain.

"Will you hold your fucking horses?" he muttered, his face mashed against the comforter.

The joint smelled like wash-off from a slaughterhouse.

No sooner had he sat up then he sprayed the bed with vomit.

"Ah, fuck me," he said, wiping his jaundiced face with the comforter.

When the cell stopped chirping, he thanked God above.

Dumbly, he glanced around. *What in the hell happened?*

Last he remembered, a zit-faced kid had handed him a first aid kit. That was it. He wasn't sure if the bullet was still in his thigh or not. He had no recollection of soaking his wound with urine and beer and then attempting to light it afire.

Again, his cell phone, as jaunty as ever.

He threw a pillow. "Shut the fuck up, would ya? Jesus. Give me some time to think."

The phone, however, insisted.

Trying to stand, his left leg was having none of it. He collapsed to the floor. He cursed and broke a fresh sweat. Grimacing, he crawled to the dresser. He snatched the phone. "What the fuck do you want?"

"I don't have a lot of time," the man replied. "So what I want is a progress report."

A progress report. This asshole wants a fucking progress report.

Sean Fitzsimmons actually laughed. "A progress report, huh?"

"A progress report."

"Give me just a sec, huh? Just one second." With the cell in hand, he crawled to the nightstand, pulled a smoke from the pack, and poked it between his lips. He rested against the bed, fisted the Zippo, and snapped a light. The smoke tasted delicious.

"Are you there? Hello? Is anyone there?"

"Yeah yeah, I'm here," said Sean. "I'm here."

"Quickly, a progress report."

He exhaled, watched the smoke rise. "Well, sir, you ain't gonna like it."

"What do you mean?"

"Three's dead, so I got that going for me, but the other three are still alive."

"Jesus, watch what you're saying."

"Yeah yeah, watch what I'm saying. Sure." He took a deep drag, coughed, and knuckled the snot from his nose. "It's just . . . I'm not thinking too clearly right about now, boss. Feeling a little woozy."

"Have you been drinking?"

A fit of pained laughter, followed closely by a snort, he said, "Yeah. I've had a few cold soda pops, last night, but that ain't the problem."

Silence. And then: "Well, tell me, what's the problem?"

"Well, sir, the problem, as I see it, are the two fucking holes in my left leg. That's the motherfucking problem . . . *sir!*" He took his first daylight gander at his thigh. Christ, what a mess. It looked like an ant hill or something, fat and purple and maybe ten inches around, pus oozing thick from the center, a thin red line of what looked like red ants crawling beneath the skin for the groin region, stretching for the heart. *And when they get there, when they reach the mother lode, well, it's game over, isn't it?* He cried out: "Fuck me running."

"Hello? Hello? Are you there? Hello?"

He took another drag, desperate and deep, coughed fitfully. "Yeah. I'm here."

"Are you able to complete the terms of our agreement?"

The terms of our agreement. What a fucking asshole!

"Sir, I ain't no pussy, sir. I'm all-Army, sir. Bad to the bone!" His sobs made him sound less convincing.

"Ex-Army."

"Still badass. I'll get the job done, sir. Don't you worry about that. I owe those motherfuckers."

"Very well. Now, if you're up for it, I'd like to tack on a little extra work."

"Extra work?"

"Two. He has a wife."

"And?"

"Enough said."

"How much?"

"Same as the others."

"Why stop there? Huh? How about the Pope? The fucking Dalai Lama? How about Mother Teresa? You want I should do her, too?"

"Mother Teresa, she isn't with us anymore. So do we have a deal, or not?"

"Deal," Sean said, and with that he hung up.

CHAPTER 24

hen Special Agent Lionel McCarthy was finished telling the group what little he knew of the crime scene down in San Antonio, it was not overlooked that Linda Duckworth didn't fit the profile. The first two victims' surnames were of Muslim descent, Khalil and Saleem. Linda Duckworth was American mutt, albeit a rich American mutt.

"It's not uncommon," Lionel began, when the opinions settled down some, "for a killer such as this to at first target a specific group, and then, once blood has been tasted, to branch out."

"That sonofabitch," said Detective Perry. "Not that them Muslims don't have it coming, 'cause they do, but to go after hardworking American citizens like that just ain't right."

Eric, growing increasingly weary of this, and in great need of some shuteye, said, "Khalil and Saleem were both American citizens, Perry. And as far as we know, *hardworking* American citizens."

"Yeah, but they wasn't born here, was they? Probably came on over with them terrorists."

Roy chimed in: "You're a dumbass, aren't you?"

Perry stood. "What the hell did you just say to me?"

"I asked a simple question," said Roy, confident, not backing down. "I mean, do you think you're a dumbass or not?"

"I call it like I see it," said Perry. "Open your damn eyes. Those two Muslims are dead 'cause of all the trouble they brought to the red, white, and blue. Serves 'em right."

Lionel, above the fray, ignored Perry and said to his partner, "This guy moves around quite a bit. Businessman, perhaps."

Eric replied, "Hotel management? Maybe he's going from one to another, auditing the books or something?"

"Maybe it's a cult," said Perry.

"A cult?" said Roy, incredulously. "Are you fucking kidding me?"

"You got a better idea, wiseass?"

To clarify things, Lionel said, "Serial killers tend to work alone."

"That's my point," said Perry. "Maybe it ain't no damn serial killer, but some religious cult or something."

Roy laughed. He looked toward Polo. "You responsible for this guy?"

Polo shrugged. He had pulled a package of peanuts from his pocket and was making quick work of them.

"Look," said Dale, "I really gotta get going. It's getting late."

Eric said, "Thanks for coming, man. I appreciate it."

"Yeah. So, you know, after I drop off Gina at the airport, maybe I can swing back by. Bring you a milkshake or something. A cheeseburger. Give you a hand job or something. Keep you nice and relaxed."

The hand job bit: that was Eric's joke. Eric smiled, his complexion ashen. "You'd do that for me? 'Cause I could sure use a hand job right about now." Weakly, he pointed toward the sink. "The lotion is over there."

Perry, with a shocked expression, said, "You two fucking homos or what?"

Roy, laughing, said, "Jesus Christ, Perry. Relax. If anyone needs a hand job around here, it's you."

Lionel, the voice of reason, said, "All right, gentlemen. It's time to go. Let's give Eric here some rest."

And with that, the room cleared, but not before Roy gestured toward the door and said to Perry, "Ladies first."

For Dale, the drive home was as pleasant as the drive to the hospital, a cold cabin and an over-chatty driver.

When Polo turned the corner for home, Dale found Old Betsy in the driveway, defrosted and ready to go. Gina hadn't changed her mind after all.

Polo pulled up. "Good luck with the marriage, Mr. Riley."

"Thanks," he said, and then quickly hopped out. Already Dale could hear the goddamn organ music from inside the house. It seemed to have an immediate effect on him now, like some Pavlovian dog, organ pipes deflating his spirit, sucking the life right out of him. Perhaps Gina was right after all. Getting the fuck out was the only way to salvage the marriage, if not their sanity.

Inside, staged near the doorway, was Gina's luggage. It wasn't the luggage he'd expected to see, either. Upstairs, in the closet, was a brand new Samsonite set that had been given to them at Christmastime. Yet here, near the doorway, was the tired old set that she had brought with her into the marriage, dragged up from the basement. Hers, and not theirs. Was this a prelude of things to come? Her CDs and his, photograph books this way and that way, an even split of their financial assets, which would amount to half of nothing plus interest? The only thing they owned of any real value was the Honda out front, and how might they divide that? He imagined a chainsaw and a dark night, sparks flying everywhere. He'd get the driver's side, and she'd get the glove box.

Most importantly, how might they split up Clint?

Dale knew a ton of divorced men—the divorce rate among Marines a tragic seventy-five percent, another sacrifice they make for their country—and each had been screwed over by the settlement.

Suddenly this all seemed tragically real.

"Is everything okay, honey?" It was Gina, holding Clint in her arms. "Is your friend okay?" She had on jeans and a sweater, tennis shoes, comfortable clothes for the airplane.

"I'm sorry. What was that?"

"Jesus, Dale. You look like hell. Are you okay?" Tenderly, she moved to test his forehead for a fever. In the end, however, she refrained. With barely enough resolve to see this through, the last thing she needed right now was to become soft. With a shy smile she brushed his cheek instead.

"I'm fine," he said, reaching up to hold her hand.

"How's your friend? Is he doing okay?"

Absently, he said, "He looks like hell."

Slowly, she pulled her hand from his. "Dale? Are you okay? You're acting funny."

"It's just . . . why didn't you pack the Samsonite? It was already upstairs in the closet. It's newer. It's nicer."

"Oh." She shrugged, as if to suggest that her choice of luggage was no big deal.

"Gina? Are you going to take half the Honda Civic? Is that what's going on here?"

"Are you sure you're okay?"

He paused, ran a hand through his hair. Truth was, he didn't *know* if he was okay. He didn't know anything anymore. He glanced toward the kitchen. "Do Mom and Dad know?"

"Do they know what, exactly?"

"That you're leaving me . . . for us?"

"I told them that I'm going home for a while, yes, to finish my nursing degree. We've already said our good-byes."

"How did that go?"

"Awkward, as usual." She glanced at her watch. "We really should get moving."

"Thanks for cleaning off the Honda."

She smiled, her lips thin.

He said, "Hope it starts."

"It started earlier. No problem."

"It always starts for you. Why is that?"

"A woman's touch. It's getting late, honey. We need to go."

"My parents, did they ask where I've been?"

"Yeah. I didn't tell them anything about your friend getting shot. Just told them you went to Starbucks with your friend from last night."

"Okay." He kissed his son on the forehead, walked to the kitchen. Gina followed.

At the kitchen table the newspapers were spread out as always, a crossword puzzle in dad's hands.

Dad set aside his reading glasses. "Everything okay?"

"Yeah," Dale said. "Listen, I have to take Gina to the airport. I shouldn't be long."

Mom glanced up from her knitting. "Are you sure everything is okay?"

"Everything is fine, Mom. Gina . . . she's going to finish her nursing degree. That's it."

The mood was peculiar, weird. Mom seemed genuinely pleased if not amused by this. She never used to be this way, so cruel. Dale wondered if she wasn't losing her marbles. Early onset senility.

Dad said, "Well, we're going to miss you around here, Gina, and you too, Clint."

Dale said, "It's all for the best, Dad. We've talked about it. We've thought it all through." In a show of solidarity, he put his arm around Gina.

Mom said, "It probably is all for the best." She looked to her husband. "Don't you think, dear? All for the best?"

Dad didn't answer.

No one said a word.

It was all too weird.

At last Dale said, "Listen, we have to go. The roads are terrible out there, and the drive is going to take a while."

"You go on, son," said dad. "And drive safe."

CHAPTER 25

nside the passenger terminal at Charlotte Douglas International, Dale hustled a gate pass from a ticketing agent, and then fed the x-ray machines with his wife. Air traffic was behind schedule, but at least the planes were moving. People were camped along the corridors, sleeping and playing cards, talking on cell phones, waiting their turn to board. Trash overflowed the bins. The place smelled of burnt coffee and day-old hotdogs, with the slight stink of rotten feet to round it out.

At the departure board, the flight to Wilmington was listed as thirty minutes late.

"It could be worse," said Gina, bouncing her son in her arms.

Could it be worse? Dale wondered, to which that little voice in his head replied: *Of course it could be worse, Mister Riley. Of course. It could be worse, and worse, and worse! Just you wait and see!*

Arriving at the departure gate, they found a few empty seats together and occupied them. The place was humming, crowded. Dale needed aspirin. He closed his eyes and massaged his temples. He inhaled to a count of five, exhaled to a count of ten, Zen in sixty seconds.

A minute later, his headache was stronger than ever.

When he opened his eyes, when the world came into focus again, that's when he saw it, the ghost.

Goosebumps ran the length of his flesh.

His jaw dropped.

In disbelief, he rubbed his eyes.

The ghost accessed a computer at the boarding counter nearest Gina's departure gate, doing so with a big smile and seemingly few worries.

The two had first met in the fall of 2001. This is when a fresh-faced Dale Riley, having successfully passed the North Carolina bar exam, traveled north to the Marine Corps training grounds, Quantico, Virginia. He would join the JAG Corps and do heroic things, he along with the other post-9/11 wannabe Marines. He'd retire after twenty and then land a lucrative gig with a prestigious law firm. He had it all figured out, the world by the balls.

First, however, he would have to graduate from Officer Candidate School, OCS.

The campus at Quantico was far different from the campus at Chapel Hill. There was a rugged edge here, life was hard and the talk was tough. A hundred or so young men from around the country had gathered to test their mettle, setting themselves up in rickety bunks, their sparse belongings stuffed inside wobbly metal wall lockers. Pit bulls roamed these squad bays with poisonous breath barking orders, climbing down throats and tearing new assholes. Each bad haircut followed another, their dignity stripped as the gaggle of would-be officers stood naked that first day for inspection (later, they would be allowed the dignity of their underwear). The pit bulls walked the line, informing these disgusting creatures in no uncertain terms how pathetic they were as human beings, barking at each and every one of them, taking note of those who flinched. And then all hell broke loose. *Move it! Move it! Move it!* the pit bulls shouted. And move it they did. For ten grueling weeks they did nothing but move it. They moved it until their toes blistered and ankles were broken. They moved it over rugged terrain both day and night with fifty-pound rucksacks on their backs, puking their guts out and holding each other up. They moved it on their bellies through mud and manure, tossing hand grenades and firing rifles and mortar rounds and artillery shells. They moved it into classrooms where they learned leadership skills and battlefield tactics and then moved it back into the woods for practical application. They moved it for ten grueling weeks of utter hell where a good seventy percent either called it quits or were sent home packing with a bad haircut because they couldn't quite move it fast enough or smart enough or with a strong enough sense of determination.

Dale's biggest fear was that he too would be sent home. What would he tell his family and friends, his uncle the Marine? *I failed. I tried, but I just couldn't cut it.* That was unacceptable. So he moved it harder than the next guy, doing his best to stay ahead of the pack. One morning, however, he committed a fatal error.

After only a few hours of sleep, the candidates were roused from their bunks and ordered to reconvene outside on the parade deck.

Exhausted, Dale found himself outside in the dark. It was four o'clock in the morning. Standing in formation, rubbing sleep from his eyes, it was here when he realized his error: he'd forgotten his rifle. He'd pulled it from the rifle rack at the back of the squad bay, set it on his bed to get dressed, and somehow forgot it there.

Sonofabitch!

If there were a Marine Corps ten commandments, leaving your weapon behind would be in the top three, right after every Marine is a rifleman, and kill. Kill, of course, would top the charts. In the Corps it's all about the kill. Ask a seasoned Marine how he's doing, and he might only reply with: kill! Ask about the weather, and the forecast might call for kill with a chance of kill.

Feeling as naked as that first day in formation, Candidate Dale Riley stood in the pre-dawn dew with dread washing over him.

It was over. Men had been washed out for far less-stupid errors. It was over.

And then from the dark someone tapped him on the shoulder.

"Hey. Thought you might need this." It was Mike Ruffers, aka Captain Mike Ruffers of the infamous Ruffers Court-Martial, only then he was merely a nasty, stinking sonofabitch candidate like

Dale. Unlike Dale, however, he was carrying a rifle; in fact, he was carrying two. He held one out. "Here."

"Holy shit," Dale said, eagerly taking possession and inspecting it in the dark. "Jesus, man, thanks. I thought I was toast."

"I saw you run out without it. Figured it might come in handy."

With the pit bulls closing in for inspection, Dale said, "I owe you, Mike. Big time."

"That's okay. Just, you know, kill, okay, and ooh rah, and Semper Fidelis."

So yeah, Mike Ruffers had saved Dale's bacon that morning. In the ensuing weeks, an opportunity never presented itself for Dale to repay the favor. The class graduated, thirty all told, whittled down from well over a hundred. Mike Ruffers went down to Pensacola, Florida, to attend Naval Aviation Flight School, and Dale Riley went north to Newport, Rhode Island, where lawyers bone up on military law. They kept in touch for possibly a year or so, and then life got in the way, and then ooh rah, and then there was kill.

One morning, years later, while sitting in his office, Captain Dale Riley got a curious phone call. Typically, he allowed voicemail to pick up. Bogged down with paperwork, he welcomed the diversion.

"Captain Riley. How can I help you, sir or ma'am?"

"Dale? Dale Riley?"

"Yes?"

"Holy smokes, Captain Dale Riley. How ya been, man? How's life been treating you these days?"

"Who is this?"

"It's me. Captain Mike Ruffers. Remember?"

"Mike Ruffers?"

"The one and only. How ya been, man? What have you been up to?"

"Practicing law, Mike. Nose to the grindstone. What about you?" Dale sensed that something was up. Acquaintances rarely call from out of the blue to ask how life is treating you.

"Well, funny you should ask," said Mike. "See, I'm in the brig. They locked me up, Dale. They said I willfully and without cause bombed a village in Afghanistan. Dale, I'm calling because I need a good defense attorney. I need your help, man. I'm in one hell of a jam."

Dale, as well as most everyone else in the Marine Corps, had heard about the bombing of the Sorubi village. A guy was being held in pretrial confinement, his name not yet released. Domestically, the news was picking up steam, would soon spread across the globe.

"You're the one? You're the accused?"

"I'm innocent, Dale. Innocent! I was hoping you could help me out."

Dale leaned back and drummed his fingers on his desktop. He thought for a moment. "Why me?"

"I trust you, man. I don't know many lawyers, and those I do know I wouldn't trust with my dog, let alone my life."

Dale gazed out the window. Representing the accused in this case held little, if any, appeal. The media outlets were painting this guy as a monster, a vendetta killing for 9/11. Did Dale really want to be associated with a monster? But was Ruffers really a monster? "This case is gonna require a lot of time and effort. To be honest, Mike, I just don't think I have the time to do right by you. I'm swamped." Not to mention that talk around the water cooler sustained the notion that the accused would hang from the gallows. The Afghanistan president, President Karzai, was calling for a head on a stick. Collateral damage had been heavy from the start of this conflict, and he and his cabinet had had enough, the bombing of the Sorubi village the final straw. The brass at Headquarters and the politicians in Washington seemed intent on appeasing him. Success in Afghanistan required political cooperation. So hang one man, satisfy the powers that be, and continue with the mission. What sane lawyer would wish to align himself with a dead man walking?

After a considerable break in the conversation, Mike cleared his throat: "I remember a morning at OCS, Dale, when you were standing in the dark with your dick in your hand instead of your M-16 rifle. I remember that morning as if it was yesterday. Do you remember that morning? How you said that you owed me, big time?"

"Mike, it's just—"

"Well, now's your chance. Here's your opportunity to repay that favor. I . . . need . . . help. I did not do this thing, Dale. I swear to God Almighty!"

Dale sighed. He wished he had never answered the phone. "Let me . . . I can't promise anything, okay? I'm swamped with work, but let me take a look at this. Give me some time to read the JAG investigation."

"You'd do that for me?"

"I'll take a look. I can't promise anything right now."

CHAPTER 26

S itting inside the passenger terminal, waiting for Gina and his son to board their flight to Wilmington, the last thing Dale wanted right now was for Mike Ruffers to look up from his paperwork and make eye contact. He wasn't in the mood. Not that he owed his current lot in life entirely to Mike, but certainly he'd cemented a good bit of the foundation, hadn't he?

Mike Ruffers, however, the ghost from Dale's past, glanced up from his paperwork and homed in on the man who sat watching him.

From across the way, the two held captive the other, a game of who would be the first to blink.

Mike gave in with a smile. With paperwork in hand, he ambled over.

"Dale Riley? Holy smokes, I can't believe it. How ya been?"

Although he'd seen better days, Dale stood and lied: "I'm doing great. And you?"

"Almost didn't recognize you, man. You've . . . changed." *You've put on weight, swallowed a cow.*

"Living the high life," said Dale, none too convincingly.

Mike, decked out in an airline pilot's uniform, trim as ever, smiled a devilishly handsome smile. "Geez, how long has it been, anyway?"

"Since the court-martial. Almost two years."

"Time flies, huh?"

Dale shrugged.

"And who is this, might I ask?"

Balancing Clint on her knee, Gina fished through the diaper bag. "This is my wife, and my son."

"Gina," Mike called to her, smiling. "How ya been?"

Confused, looking from one to the other, Dale said, "You . . . know my wife?"

Defensively, Gina quickly replied, "I don't know this guy." She looked at Mike and furrowed her brow. "Who are you again?"

Still smiling, Mike said, "Mike Ruffers, ma'am. Your husband and I go way back." He put his arm around Dale and squeezed his neck. It wasn't a particularly mean squeeze, although it was harder than what would be considered polite, if not borderline aggressive.

Dale pulled away, sensing an odd dynamic. "How did you know my wife's name?"

"I heard you say it, old buddy. I heard you call her Gina."

Had he called her Gina within earshot of Mike? Maybe, but Dale sure couldn't remember doing so.

Mike took a knee and grabbed the child's chubby hand. "And what's your name, little fella?"

"Clint," Dale said, still feeling uneasy. "His name is Clint."

"You want to be a pilot someday, little buddy? Fly the friendly skies?" Subtly, so that Dale wouldn't notice, Mike shot Gina a wink. "The chicks, they dig pilots. You'll be fighting them off with sticks."

Gina, her eyes everywhere but on Mike, wrapped the diaper bag around her shoulder. She stood. "He's hungry. Dale, we'll be over there near the window."

Mike stood with her, and the two watched her go.

Mike, with his hands on his hips, said, "That's a fine family you've got there, ole buddy. I thought about getting myself a wife like that, having a little dude just like that, settling down. But, you know, I just can't seem to commit. So many women, so little time."

Mike Ruffers: still the prick he used to be. Dale turned to face him. "You know, you never said thanks, Mike. After all I did for you, not one thanks."

"Come again?"

"My peers, they all thought I was crazy for taking your case, and maybe I was. They all thought that you should have hired a civilian attorney, but no. I did it. I took your case and put my career on the line. I did you a favor and lost everything. Everything, and you couldn't even track me down to thank me, could you?"

Mike actually seemed to be enjoying this. With an arrogant tone, he said, "You want thanks, huh?"

"No. In fact I don't."

"Well . . . what then?"

"I'd be content for you to go fuck yourself. That's all I really want, Mike. For you to go fuck yourself." Wow, it felt good to say that. To put Mike in his place even after all this time. Dale actually smiled a genuine smile, though he remained very serious.

Mike, taken off guard but quickly regaining his wits, said, "Currently I have to fly a jet to Wilmington, so how's about I go fuck myself later? Tomorrow, perhaps, or Wednesday, on my day off?" He smiled. "Would that suit you?"

No. It wouldn't suit him. Nothing about Mike suited him, in particular the part where Mike said he'd be piloting the jet to Wilmington. "You're flying the airplane to Wilmington?"

"Nonstop." Mike laughed. "Holy shit. Are you coming?"

Dale didn't answer.

"'Cause if so, it is my responsibility to inform you that I have the authority to deny hostile passengers. I'd hate to have to do such a thing, but your profanities might leave me little choice." Mike began to scan the passenger manifest that he held in his hands. "Ah yes, here we go: Gina Riley with a child under two. Seated in 8B." He regarded Dale with yet another sly smile. "I don't see your name on here, buddy. So you're not coming, eh? To Wilmington?"

Again, Dale didn't answer. At a loss for words, he watched his wife and son near the windows. He didn't like the vibe here, how everything seemed off.

Mike continued: "Well, regardless, you might wish to tell your lovely bride that seat 8A is empty. She'll have plenty of room to stretch out. Very lucky, I'd say. Normally this flight is booked solid."

"Not a soul in seat 8A, huh?" said Dale, doing his best to stay grounded. "That's really great news, Mike. I'll tell her that."

Mike smiled and folded his paperwork. "It's been great playing catch-up, but I have to preflight the jet." He gave Dale a once-over, from head to toe. "I hear Weight Watchers has a pretty good program, that or Jenny Craig. You might want to look into that."

"Fuck you, Mike."

Mike laughed, turned, took a step, and then turned around again. "And Semper Fidelis, ole buddy. Semper Fi." With that, he snaked his way through the waiting passengers and down along the jet bridge.

Dale watched him go, feeling like he'd been slimed or something. He shivered.

Over the intercom the call was made to begin boarding for non-stop service to Wilmington, North Carolina.

Dale approached his wife and son near the windows. He put his hand in the small of her back.

"You don't have to go, you know. It's not too late to change your mind." He wanted to mention that on top of everything else, Mike Ruffers was the pilot of that plane. But he just stood there, staring at his feet, unable to look Gina in the face.

Gently, Gina kissed him on the cheek. "I have to do this, Dale. As crazy as all this is, I have to go, and finish my degree. You know that, right?"

"Yeah," he woefully replied. "I know."

And with that, he kissed them good-bye.

CHAPTER 27

For a very long moment Dale stood at the windows, looking through the frosted glass, feeling the cold from outside. From here he could see inside the cockpit, watched as Mike Ruffers and the other pilot flipped switches, snowfall accumulating beyond upon the airfield. Farther inside the jet would be Gina and Clint, seated in 8B with nary a soul in 8A, her lucky day to stretch out.

Yes. Very lucky indeed.

Dale could still hear Mike's parting words, his disingenuous tone—*Semper Fidelis, ole buddy. Semper Fi.*

To a Marine (and Dale was still a Marine, make no mistake, for once a Marine, always a Marine), Semper Fidelis is the impetus of warfare, a battlefield cry, nothing remotely to be mocked or used lightly.

Semper Fidelis, a Latin phrase adopted by the Marine Corps, meant "always faithful." In the heat and in the chaos of battle, Marines rely upon one another with their lives, and therefore trust is paramount, faith, the shared belief in a common goal, a belief in one another as brothers and sisters in arms, defending and protecting the Constitution of the United States of America against all enemies, foreign and domestic. Semper Fidelis sums it up, and solidifies the bond, the trust, which, in turn, lifts morale and that can-do spirit, makes a sane man fierce, a force of feared Marines.

Semper Fidelis!

To mock this is to tarnish the very ethos of the Corps, an organization bent on doing our nation's dirty work, or cleaning up after others leave a mess, so that the common good can endure and thrive. Marines sacrifice so that others won't have to, and a Marine would have it no other way.

After Captain Riley reviewed the Ruffers JAG investigation oh, so many years ago after that fateful phone call, he took a ride to Camp Lejeune, North Carolina. At the brig the prison guards led him along through a dark and winding corridor, toward Mike's cell. There, he found Mike sitting crisscross in bed, reading a bible by a dim, yellow bulb overhead.

Rattling his keychain for the key specific, the guard said, "Prisoner Ruffers. You got company."

Mike, squinting toward the dark corridor, said, "Who is it?"

The guard opened the cell and brought in a chair. He said to Captain Riley, "You got ten minutes, sir."

Captain Riley entered. "Mike. It's Dale Riley."

Mike, wearing the standard blue jumpsuit, set aside the bible. He hopped to his feet and eagerly shook hands. "Holy shit. Does this mean you're my lawyer? That you're going to take the case?"

"Let's sit." Dale took the chair, crossed his legs, and smiled. "You look good. Aside from the getup and the living quarters."

Mike, sitting on his bed, pinched the top of his jumpsuit, and snapped it. "This? This is horseshit. I defend my country, and this is the thanks I get? Utter horseshit." He looked at Dale, the overhead bulb casting odd shadows. "So what's it going to be, buddy? You with me, or are you against me?"

"Well, to be perfectly honest, I haven't decided one way or the other. I thought I should drop by so we could talk." So that Dale could ask questions, and look Mike in the eyes. Should he find something disagreeable there, he'd cut the line and call for the guard. If, however, Mike seemed genuine with his proclamations of innocence (as he had sounded over the telephone), Dale might feel compelled to offer up his services. Because let's face it: the JAG investigation was a joke. Dale had read it one night after dinner, and was surprised that the convening authority at the Article 32 hearing had endorsed it for a court-martial. It didn't sit well with him that any man should be made a scapegoat for a crime that he hadn't committed, no matter what the geopolitical implications were. The question was: had Mike committed this crime or not? Barring a confession or video evidence, one can never be certain either way. However, Dale felt that he was a good judge of character and had a decent bullshit barometer. Whether or not he would take the case would depend mostly on what he saw in Mike's eyes.

Mike said, "But you're here, man. That's a start."

Dale settled in. "So, I read the JAG investigation."

"And?"

"I'll be honest, Mike. If the government had a rock-solid case, I probably wouldn't be here right now."

"Yeah?"

"The evidence is circumstantial. I'm surprised they didn't scratch this for another investigation, that they sent this off for a court-martial. I can only reason that they were in a hurry to get a conviction."

"That's what I've been saying. I didn't do a damn thing."

Dale opened his briefcase and pulled out the file. From this he pulled out a photograph. "So you're telling me that you didn't do this?"

The photograph was a panoramic shot taken in the early-morning hours after the bombing at the Sorubi village. The sunlight was reddish and soft, caressing the recently deceased that had been arranged side-by-side as if for inventory. Their bodies had been scorched, charred, a woman on her knees nearby, praying. In the background one could see the destruction of the village, adobe homes obliterated into ashen shadows. Farther beyond were the cold and snow-dusted mountains. Dale pulled out another photograph, this one of two kids, their charred heads pressed together, their skulls seeping blood and brain matter. Both photographs gave Dale the chills. He held them up for Mike to see. He watched Mike's eyes.

Mike leaned forward to get a better look. "I swear, buddy. I swear I didn't do that. I swear." Mike sounded sincere, his eyes unflinching and devout. Mike then snatched the photographs from Dale's hand. He took a closer look—examined one, and then the other—and seemed sickened by what he saw. He returned these photos to Dale. "Look at this sick shit. Not me. No way. Not in a million years could I ever do something this twisted and evil!"

Dale held open the file. "Mike, put the photographs back, please."

Reluctantly, Mike complied. "I didn't do it. I didn't bomb that village. I didn't kill all those people. I swear." As if to punctuate his innocence, he placed his hand upon the bible that lay next to him in bed. He lifted his other and pledged the following: "I swear to God I did not do that!" He looked heavenward. "Strike me dead if I am lying."

Dale, watching Mike closely, set the file inside the briefcase. He leaned back and crossed his legs. Wearing his camouflaged uniform, he adjusted the hem near his boot. Most liars are easy to spot. They squirm or they itch, they can't maintain eye contact, or they collapse like a house of cards and give it all away. Dale avoided the liars and cheats as much as possible. As a defense attorney, he preferred, if a man were in fact guilty, for this man to come clean and own the crime. Then they could rebuild for a plea from there. Dale could work with a man like that. He had no time for the liars and the cheats. The liars and the cheats coax you out onto a shallow island, and inevitably the tides come in and there you stand like an asshole getting soaked. Make no mistake, you're the asshole, 'cause a liar is what a liar is, a cheat is a cheat, and you should have known better than to dumbly follow along.

Dale watched for the signs, but they didn't come. Either Mike Ruffers was innocent, or the best liar he'd ever seen.

Mike, uncomfortable in the silence, said, "Come on, Dale. Semper Fidelis, right, always faithful. I had your back, and now's the time for you to have mine. It's us against the evildoers, Dale, and they would like nothing more than to see me hang for a crime that I didn't commit. Our government, they got it wrong this time, and we need to prove them wrong so that we can continue to fight the good fight in God's name. Now, are you going to cover my ass, or not?"

Truth be told, Dale was in a spectacularly good mood. The night before, he'd gone out to dinner with his then-girlfriend, Gina Finnigan. They went to the movies, and then back to his apartment for the night. They made love, twice, and in the afterglow she said I love you.

This was the first time either one had said the L-word. It felt wonderful to hear. He reached over and kissed her fully on the lips. Closely, he confessed the same.

For the third time that night they made love. In the morning he awoke in good spirits, the same spirits that had accompanied him to the brig, and then to Mike's cell. Dale could still smell her on his skin, and this made him smile.

"What is it?" Mike said, smiling with him. "What's so funny?"

"Nothing," Dale replied, fingering the hem of his trousers. "Tell you what, Mike. I'll do it. I'll take the case. Why not."

"Really?"

"Yeah. Really."

"Oh, man," said Mike, clapping once and rocking with glee. "Thanks, buddy. Holy shit!"

"We have a lot of work to do, Mike. I can't guarantee an acquittal."

"You can do this, Dale. I have faith." He held up the bible and smiled. "The Lord has faith."

Dale stood and sealed the Devil's deal with a handshake, one in it for love, and the other for his hide.

Now, through frosty windows, Dale watched as Mike flipped switches in the cockpit of a jet. He felt uneasy, and he wasn't exactly sure why. Again, he tried to remember if he'd spoken Gina's name while Mike was within earshot. He couldn't remember. And the way Mike looked at Gina, and the way she looked at him.

The entire interaction didn't sit well; something was amiss.

Because his wife and son were aboard—seated in 8B with nary a soul in 8A—he wished the flight well, to include his former client, the scumbag Mike Ruffers.

Reluctantly, he turned, and slowly walked away.

CHAPTER 28

Dale Riley, surrounded by weary travelers, felt more alone than he had in some time. Elbow to elbow, he ambled down the passenger terminal, in no particular hurry.

Thirsty, he stepped into a bar and pulled up an empty stool.

"What'll it be, bub?" the barkeep inquired, wiping the bar for a coaster.

"Sam Adams," Dale replied.

The barkeep tucked away the towel and plucked a frosty mug from the rack. "One Sam Adams coming up."

On the near wall was a widescreen television, airing a college basketball game—Georgetown vs. Syracuse—coach Boeheim pacing the sidelines. Upset, the demonstrative coach stormed a ref and motioned for a time out. The station cut to a commercial.

The barkeep placed the frosty mug of expertly poured beer.

"Thanks," said Dale, taking a sip, watching the commercial.

Arguably, the Marine Corps runs some of the best commercials in the nation, here a young kid in shorts with long hair, running through a desert with a faraway look in his eyes. The music had a primal beat, this sense of urgency. Now, the commercial cut to a gaggle of young recruits dressed in green, heads shaven, standing at attention with a pit bull barking orders. Dale loved these commercials. They reminded him of better, youthful days. Back to the lonely desert runner, determined but lost, running fast for nowhere. The men in green are running helter-skelter but in slow motion, mud flying everywhere, harried looks on hardened faces, deep through a vast pit of muck. The desert runner finds himself at the base of an extremely steep cliff, looking up, just as the men in green board a helicopter, the whop-whop-whop of the rotors in time with the beat of the music. The sun crests the cliff's edge, and the desert runner begins to climb. The helicopter turns, flies fast, and lands. The men in green disembark and fan out. Determinedly, hand over hand, the runner climbs, the beat intensifying, a hand slipping, hanging by the most tenuous of grips. A hand reaches over the cliff's edge and grasps the hand of the runner. This hand pulls him up, and up, and up, the hand of a freshly minted Marine. At last, the desert runner is at the cliff's edge with other like-minded souls, standing solid like rock, having found himself in the dress blues of a United States Marine. The music cuts, and two words are born from a white pinpoint and cover the screen from left to right. A baritone voiceover says, "If you have what it takes, call your recruiter today. The Few, the Proud, the Marines."

Those two words: *Semper Fidelis!*

A dark and final blink, the commercial was over.

Dale smiled, raised his glass as if to toast the Marines in the commercial. He drank.

The barkeep, who had been watching him while wiping down the countertop, said, "You a Marine?"

"Yep."

"Figured as much. Saw that look in your eye when that commercial aired."

"And you?"

"Six years. 3rd Battalion, 2nd Marines. Beer's on the house."

"Thanks," said Dale.

"No problem."

And as uplifting as the commercial had been, suddenly Dale felt heavy, recalling the recent confrontation he'd had with Mike Ruffers.

The interaction between Mike and Gina had been odd, to say the least, but it was more than that. It was something else.

It was Mike's sleazy nature, and the evil look in Mike's eye. It was the fact that Mike was an airline pilot, flying from city to city and state to state.

It was something else, though, wasn't it?

Dale drank, and thought.

Yeah, it was something else.

Something that Dale felt he had a grip on, but his mind slipped, and he hung there, thinking.

He drank beer and recalled the confrontation with Mike, the way he had looked up Gina's name, a memory that seemed to play in slow motion to the whop-whop-whop of the rotor blades, a memory overlaid with the commercial, with a lonely runner going nowhere, lost in the desert, the music a primal beat.

He reached for that ever-elusive thought, something just out of reach, hand over hand, and yet nothing reached out for him, no idea solidified.

Precariously, he hung there.

What the hell was it? What was bothering him so much?

When he went to take another sip of beer, the mug slipped from his hand, falling, and when it hit the floor it shattered, spread like the pinpoint from the commercial, which had filled the television screen from left to right with two words: Semper Fidelis.

Dale lost his breath, drunk with revelation.

"Are you okay, buddy?" It was the barkeep, 3rd Battalion, 2nd Marines, coming from behind the bar to help clean up.

"No. I'm not okay." His eyes were frantic, and he went to pick up the pieces.

The barkeep, kneeling with him, said, "What is it, man?"

"I . . . I gotta go. Holy shit, I really gotta go."

"Then go," said the barkeep. "I got the rest of this."

Dale looked at him, and thought about saying Semper Fi, but just couldn't bring himself to do it, the words thick on his tongue. Instead, he squeaked out, "Thanks." And with that, he ran off.

CHAPTER 29

From the passenger terminal, Dale bolted outside into the snow, across two lanes of traffic where he threw up his hands in a mad gesture for a van to stop and give way.

"Are you out of your mind?" the van driver yelled, slamming on the brakes and sliding mere inches from this madman. He rolled down the window. "I could have killed you, buster. Watch it."

Dale, having dodged certain death like a drunk matador, kept moving.

At his Honda he fished out his keys and fought with the lock.

Inside, he hadn't the patience to beg Old Betsy to start. He turned the key in the ignition, and pumped the gas pedal. "C'mon, goddamnit!"

Without protest she sputtered to life.

He probably should have given the engine a chance to warm up. Moreover, he probably should have taken into better consideration the weather. At the end of the row he misjudged the impact the ice would have on the stopping distance, and had just enough time to yell *"shit"* before the front end smashed into a retaining wall.

His forehead banged against the steering wheel, and fireworks exploded before his eyes.

Old Betsy ricocheted off the wall, spun, and came to a rest.

Dazed, Dale glanced around, outside, at the dented front end.

The engine was still running, no steam.

In the rearview mirror he found a gash in the middle of his forehead, the beginnings of what would become a good-sized bump. He touched this and winced.

He said to himself, "Okay. Calm down, buddy. Breathe, and calm down." He took a deep breath, Zen in sixty seconds.

Once again, he set off.

The drive uptown was met with nearly every red light the city had to offer, most of which he ran. The streets were cluttered with snow and abandoned vehicles. Some roads were impassable. He followed the ones well traveled.

It was such a crazy notion, wasn't it? And the more he thought about it, the crazier it seemed. But damn if it didn't make sense.

Uptown, he pulled into the parking deck at the Presbyterian Hospital, found an empty spot on the third level.

He zipped inside and up the stairs, taking them two, three at a time.

On the fifth floor a nurse yelled out after him: "Slow down, sir. You're going to hurt someone."

But he didn't slow down. He couldn't.

He turned a corner and burst inside the room.

He stood there breathing heavy, his cheeks flushed.

"Dale?" said Eric, puzzled, if not a bit startled, by this sudden entry into his room.

Catching his breath, Dale said, "We gotta talk."

Special Agent Lionel McCarthy entered next. "Mr. Riley. Visiting hours are not for a while yet."

Special Agent Roy Woodall entered behind him.

The two had been waiting in the lobby when Dale dashed by like the wind. They followed him in.

Enter, now, the head nurse, her hands on her hips, her chin defiant. Because all eyes were on Dale, she turned to him as well. "What in the hell is going on in here? Visiting hours aren't for another ninety minutes, sir. I'm going to have to ask you to leave."

Eric said, "Jesus, buddy. You're bleeding all over the place."

Dale touched his forehead. His fingers came away wet with blood.

"C'mon, Mr. Riley," said Lionel McCarthy. "Let's go outside." He grabbed Dale's elbow.

Dale yanked free. "Eric. Can you talk? I just need a minute." Eric looked better than he had this morning, had color in his cheeks, his eyes bright and clear.

Eric shrugged. "Actually, I'm feeling pretty good."

The nurse said, "I bet you are. That IV drip could take out a rhino." She returned he eyes to Dale. "Now, sir. Please. Before I call security."

Dale turned to face her. "Ma'am. Please. I have a wife. A son. They're in danger. At least, well, I think they're in danger. I don't know. I need to talk to Eric. Just for a minute, please."

She hesitated.

Dale added: "Do you have a family, ma'am? Children?"

What broke her wasn't the fact that indeed she had children. What broke her was the pleading tone in Dale's voice, and the look of desperation in his eyes, not to mention that gash in his forehead. She sighed and turned to Eric. "Are you sure you're feeling okay?"

"Yeah. I'm feeling pretty good."

"I bet you are." To Dale she said, "That gash is going to need stitches."

Again, he fingered his forehead.

She said, "When you're finished here you head down to the ER on the first floor. Promise me."

"Yes, ma'am. Promise."

"You have five minutes, sir, and then you'll have to go."

"Thank you so much."

With the nurse away, Eric said, "What in the hell is going on?"

With their arms crossed and wearing suits, Lionel and Roy had that stern look of authority, and in any other circumstance might have been intimidating.

Dale took a deep breath. "Okay. You're never going to guess who I just ran into at the airport."

Eric shrugged.

Roy said, "So you drove your wife to the airport, huh? She went through with it after all."

"Yeah. I drove her to the airport."

"Sorry, man. That sucks." He seemed to relax, uncrossed his arms and leaned against the foot of Eric's bed.

"You're right, Roy. It does suck."

Introspectively, Roy said, "Eh. You're better off without her."

In the company of men, a comment such as this is meant to convey sympathy. At the moment, however, Dale found this particularly annoying. He barked out, "Thanks, Roy, but I'm actually worse off without her."

Roy said, "Hey, I'm just saying, man."

Dale, not in the mood for this, turned to Eric. "Mike Ruffers. That's who I ran into at the airport."

"Really?" Eric said. "How's he doing?"

"I don't know. I don't care. Listen, what's important is what he said to me."

"What did he say?"

"He said Semper Fidelis. He turned to me, there inside the terminal, and he said Semper Fi."

Rubbing his chin thoughtfully, Lionel inquired, "That's a Marine Corps thing, right?"

"Yeah," said Eric. "It's Latin for always faithful."

Dale took a step toward Eric. "He was wearing a pilot's uniform."

"That makes sense," said Eric, wanting to shrug but knowing that pain would come with it. "He's a pilot, right?"

"He's an airline pilot now. Eric, listen to me: he's flying the two o'clock flight to Wilmington. Gina and Clint are on that airplane."

Clearly confused by this, Eric said, "I don't get it. What—"

Increasingly agitated, Dale said, "He looked her name up from the passenger manifest."

"I still don't get it."

Dale said, "He flies from city to city. He said Semper Fidelis. Don't you get it?"

"What in the hell are you talking about?" Eric said.

It was as if Dale didn't want to come out and say it. As if doing so might make it all true. He took a deep breath, exhaled, and shook his head. "I don't know. Maybe . . . maybe I'm not thinking too clearly right now. I've had a lot on my mind." He went to the sink and grabbed a tissue. In the mirror he dabbed the bloody knot on his forehead, saw fear in his eyes, worry. *Jesus. Mike flies around from city to city, had said Semper Fidelis.*

Dale closed his eyes and took another deep breath, Zen in sixty damn seconds.

CHAPTER 30

Special Agent Lionel McCarthy, rubbing his chin thoughtfully, said, "Mr. Riley—"

"Dale. Please. Call me Dale."

"Dale. Kindly explain who this Mike Ruffers fellow is, and why your encounter with him has you so worked up."

Holding the tissue against his forehead, Dale said, "Mike Ruffers. He was a client of mine back when Eric and I were in the Marine Corps. He was a combat pilot. He'd been accused of bombing a village in Afghanistan, of killing a lot of people."

"You were his attorney?" Lionel asked.

"Yes. Eric helped with the case, with research, strategy, interviewing witnesses and stuff."

In light of the recognition, Eric tipped his head and smiled. "The right-hand man himself."

"And now," Lionel said, "you're telling me that this Mike character is out of the Marine Corps, and that he's an airline pilot?"

"That's correct."

"So you got him off the hook?" said Lionel. "At the trial?"

"Yeah. Mike walked."

"And now he's flying your family to Wilmington?" said Lionel. "Your wife, who just left you, and your son?"

Dale nodded. A part of him wanted to argue that Gina hadn't left him. That it was only temporary so that she could finish her nursing degree, and that they were still in love and happily married.

They were, right? Still in love, and happily married?

Sure they were. You bet.

Roy, still leaning against the foot of Eric's bed, contemplatively said, without force or conviction: "My wife left me eight months ago. Trust me, I'm better off without her. You have no idea."

Even though Roy seemed an affable fellow, a guy's guy, Dale had had enough. "How do you know you're better off without her, Roy? How can you quantify something like that? That's just a stupid thing to say. I mean . . . do you feel better off without her?"

At first taken aback, Roy dismissed Dale with a wave of his hand. "Of course I'm better off without her. We're all better off without them."

"What if we're worse? You ever think of that? What if your wife hadn't left you, and what if you woke up this morning a better man than the man you are right now?"

"Ridiculous," Roy countered. "For one, I'm thinner without her. And that's quantifiable. What? Now you're going to tell me that fatter is better than thinner?"

Lionel, still rubbing his chin, having clearly tuned out Roy, said, "And this Mike fellow said Semper Fidelis, and this is what has you so worked up, correct?"

Dale, shaking his head, turning his attention to Lionel, said, "Look. Earlier this morning, when we were brainstorming about the *SF Killer*, someone said that perhaps he's a traveling businessman. Well, what if he's not? What if the *SF Killer* is an airline pilot? And what if this airline pilot is a former Marine? Semper Fidelis, right, SF. Mike, he's a bit of a religious nut, like the *SF Killer*. Mike's hateful, a bigot, a racist. Yeah. He got off the hook at the court-martial, but only because the evidence was circumstantial and the government failed to prove their case. At first, I wasn't sure if he was guilty or not, but later, well, my gut told me that he was, guilty as charged. Only, I didn't listen. Or perhaps I did. I'd been offered something in exchange for hanging Mike out to dry, and I seriously considered taking it. I entertained the idea longer than I should have, and maybe I did so because my gut was telling me that Mike was, in fact, guilty. He denied it, of course, but don't they all? In the end, however, it wasn't guilt or innocence that prevailed, but the law. I practiced the law, I did my job, and Mike walked. A lot of innocent people died that night in Afghanistan, and no one was held accountable. What if out of hatred he had killed all those people that night, and out of hatred he's killing others?"

Roy, in another world, in fact having heard not a word that Dale had spoken and seemingly engaged with his shoes, said, "I have more money now than I ever had with her, and more sex. Hello? Both quantifiable! And no one's nagging me to fix the kitchen sink or stop the runny toilet. Oh, let's paint the walls, dear, or let's go shopping. My God, the shopping alone is enough to know that I'm better off without her."

Thankfully, Lionel was listening to Dale and not Roy. Slowly, logically, he said, "So what you're saying is that perhaps this guy, this Mike Ruffers fellow, a former client of yours, a former Marine, an airline pilot now, is traveling from city to city, and killing women in their hotel rooms? That perhaps he is in fact the *SF Killer*?"

"That's exactly what I'm saying," said Dale. "So tell me I'm crazy, please. Tell me that I'm out of my mind, and that none of this makes sense."

Roy looked up from his shoes, and said to Dale: "You know what? You're fucking crazy."

Roy having disrupted the exchange of ideas, Lionel held up a hand for him to shut up. To Dale he said, "Actually, Mr. Riley, Dale, it does make sense. It's certainly worth looking into."

Feeling very tired now, drained, Dale looked to Eric. "He looked up Gina's name from the passenger manifest. What if he picks his victims from this list of passengers? What if he singles them out before they reach their destinations? What if he follows them to their hotel rooms? What if he follows them home? It may not always work out, but when it does, people die."

Eric, thinking this through with him, said, "That might explain the first two victims, Khalil and Saleem. He brought the war home with him, and sought out those whom he believed were Muslims. He saw their names on the passenger manifest and singled them out. And then something else triggered the killing of Linda Duckworth, some other deep-seated hatred." He looked to Dale and raised his eyebrows. "I hate to say this, but it fits. It makes sense."

Lionel confirmed this with a nod.

For Dale, there was little consolation in hearing that he wasn't quite crazy (even though Roy begged to differ). It fit, it made sense, and this filled him with dread. The bump on his forehead was nothing more now than a distant annoyance. Fear took center stage. Dale felt helpless and desperate. Why had he let them go to Wilmington? Why hadn't he stopped them in the terminal?

Lionel said, "Well. He's prior military, right?"

"Yeah," said Eric. "Marine Corps."

Lionel said, "So what we can do is get Mike Ruffers's fingerprints from the military database and run these against the fingerprint we found on the bloody contact lens. It might take a few days, but it's worth a shot."

Dale said, "He's flying my family to Wilmington. Right this second. We had a confrontation. I told him to go fuck himself. That's when he smiled at me and looked up my wife's name from the passenger manifest. Lionel. We don't have a few days."

Lionel said, "What would you like us to do?"

Holding pressure against the split in his forehead, Dale stood thinking. It wasn't easy. Fear clouded his mind, that and the throbbing from the bump.

Roy, talking to his shoes again, said, "She used to do this thing with her tongue, you know, and the sex. God. At times it was unbelievable."

The room fell silent, nothing but the steady beep from Eric's heart monitor.

What would you like us to do?

Dale stood thinking.

Currently, as far as he knew, his wife and son were safe and alive. That was the good news. Dale had to dismiss the fear, the worry. He had to think.

He said, "Can't you guys just meet the jet in Wilmington? Can't you dispatch some guys until we figure this out?"

Lionel shook his head. "It doesn't work that way. We have to have some probable cause, something more concrete than a hunch. I'm sorry."

"Of course," said Dale. Something more concrete like evidence. Something. Anything. Blotting his forehead, Dale stood thinking. There had to be something. Anything. In fact, he felt that there was. But what?

And then, by God, he had it.

Holy shit, he fucking had it. "Lionel. Agent McCarthy. You have to come with me. I think I have that something that could help."

"What is it?"

"Just . . . follow me, okay? I'll explain later."

Lionel turned to Eric. "You going to be okay?"

"Yeah," said Eric. "Go. Call, and let me know what's going on."

"Thanks," Dale said to Eric. To Lionel: "C'mon. Hurry."

On the way out the door, Lionel turned. "Roy. Are you coming?"

Lost in thought, Roy looked up. "Maybe I *am* better off with her."

"What are you talking about?"

He seemed sad, and serious. "Maybe Dale isn't such an asshole after all. Maybe I am better off with my ex-wife."

"Oh, for the love of God. Grab your shit, and let's go."

CHAPTER 31

From the encounter with the retaining wall at the airport, the headlight on the passenger's side of the Honda Civic dangled like an eyeball that had been popped clean from the skull, hanging only by the wires, the optic nerve. It banged against the fender the entire ride home. The chains on the left front wheel were clacking heavily against the wheel well, much more so than the right. But Dale didn't have time to tighten them up, or to tinker with the headlight. Maybe later. Rode hard and put up wet, Old Betsy was hanging in there.

He pulled into the driveway.

Behind him, the Grand Marquis pulled alongside the curb.

Lionel McCarthy, in the passenger's seat, talking on his cell, held up a finger for Dale to give him another minute or two.

Dale acknowledged this with a nod, and approached his parents' house alone. In the basement, he had something that he believed might confirm or deny the assumption that Mike Ruffers was the *SF Killer*, something that might mobilize the forces to Wilmington.

Dale moved quickly, unlocking the front door, entering.

In the foyer, Dale had a strange feeling that something was amiss. At first he wasn't sure what. He didn't rush down into the basement as planned. Instead, he stood there, looking around.

"Mom? Dad? Hello?"

He set his keys on the credenza and then peeled off his father's overcoat.

"Mom? Hello."

It was quiet in here; too quiet.

The organ music; where was the goddamn organ music?

"Mom?"

He smelled something rank and pungent, as if a wild animal had been let in.

"Hello?"

The intruder came by way of the kitchen, wearing a hunting jacket and tattered jeans, his head bald, dark bags beneath blood-shot eyes. He hobbled like a zombie or something, every move labored and creepy.

Dale's heart gave a heavy, sudden thump.

The intruder, leaning awkwardly to one side, nearly tilting over, said, "Mom and dad have been naughty. They're in timeout." His words came slurred from a voice both harsh and deep. His eyes, though bloodshot, were full of hate and as cold as the eyes of a Rottweiler.

"What do you mean they're in timeout?" Dale said. "Where are they?"

The intruder smiled, his teeth black and yellow and sprouting from grossly infected gums. Clumsily, he reached down inside the front of his jeans and pulled out a pistol. It was a slow, laborious move that Dale seemed helpless but to stand and watch. The intruder, the gunman (yes, the same gunman who had shot Alex and Eric, here, now, to shoot him, Dale managed to cobble together in his swimming brain), lifted the weapon and smiled. "Don't you worry about those old coots. They're fine. Now's the time to worry about your own ass, Mr. Dale Riley."

In the sights of the pistol, Dale raised his hands. "What do you want?"

The gunman's laugh was mean and sarcastic. "What do I want?"

Dale nodded.

"I want what's owed to me, is what I want. I want my fucking life back." With the pistol the gunman thumped himself in the chest. "I want the goddamn American dream: a condo on the beach and a fat bank account. But what do I get?" He took an awkward step closer, the pistol wild in his hand. "I'll tell you what I get: I get misery is what I get. I get my leg shot up is what I get. And I get orders from my dickhead boss. You're a military man, right?"

Again, Dale nodded.

"So you know that when your dickhead boss gives you an order, you obey it, right?"

Not always, Dale thought, deciding that now would not be the best time to debate the finer points of military etiquette.

"So what I want, what I need, is the whereabouts of your . . . bitch . . . *wife!*" He finished this sentence with a good bit of spittle, wiping his lips with a sleeve.

"My wife? You want to know where my wife is?"

"Did I fucking stutter? Where is she?"

"What does my wife have to do with any of this?"

"I'm the one asking the questions, tough guy. Now where is she?"

"I don't know."

The gunman took another step closer, steadied his aim. "Don't make me blast mom and dad, 'cause I will. I'm in a blast-mom-and-dad kinda mood." He took another step. "Now, where is she?"

"I swear, I don't know."

The gunman took another step closer, and then another.

CHAPTER 32

Special Agent Roy Woodall sat in the warmth of his sedan, texting his ex-wife, Sheila.

Enjoying the snow?

Immediately, she replied: *It's okay. Toby, however, is loving it.*

I miss him. How's he doing?

Fine.

I miss you, too.

Roy had to wait for the next one. Seated next to him was Lionel, talking on his cell with the boys up at Quantico.

Dale Riley had entered the home.

At last she texted back: *I guess I kinda miss you, too.*

Roy smiled. *So what are we going to do about it?*

I don't know.

How about coffee? On me.

Oooh. Big spender.

Dinner?

Let's start with coffee. But . . .

But what?

It's just . . . don't get your hopes up. I'm still hurting.

I know. I'm sorry. It'll never happen again. (The *it* he was referring to was the affair he'd had with a single mom down the street, busted by the very means he was currently employing to woo back his ex.)

167

It should have never happened in the first place.

I know. I'm sorry. I'm a dope.

A big dope.

The biggest. What time for coffee?

Lionel, finished with his call up to Quantico, clipped the cell to his belt. "What the hell is taking him so long? I'm going in. You coming?"

Roy looked up from his texts. "I'll catch up."

"No problem." Lionel stepped outside.

Roy read the following text: *Today's not good. The schools are closed. I don't want to bring Toby and get his hopes up.*

Okay. Let me know what works. I'm sorry. I'm such an idiot.

Coffee doesn't mean we're back together.

No, he thought, *but it's a good start.* He texted: *I know. You guys build that snowman yet?*

Lionel trekked through the snow, and up to the front door. On the stoop, kicking snow from his shoes, he glanced inside. In the foyer was Dale, his hands in the air, wearing a mask of fright and confusion. Peering farther in, Lionel spotted a man with a pistol. He thought about turning for Roy. Instinct took over, however, and he pulled his Sig Sauer.

Slowly, Lionel rolled the doorknob.

When he entered, his overcoat snapped like the cape of a Batman character.

Dale and the gunman started.

Lionel took aim. "Put it down."

Swiveling his pistol from one man to the other, the gunman said, "Who the fuck are you?"

"I'm Special Agent Lionel McCarthy, FBI. Now put down the weapon."

The gunman said, "FBI?" To Dale he said: "What the fuck is the FBI doing here?"

Lionel said, "I've got a better question: what are you doing pointing a gun at my friend?"

"Well, you're not going to stop me, Mr. FBI Man. Neither snow nor sleet nor bullets can stop me now, motherfucker." With his free hand he hiked up his shirt. "Not even these goddamn ants can stop me. I'm fucking Teflon Man, bitch!"

When Dale saw the trail of infection, he winced. "Jesus Christ."

Lionel, studying the gunman's torso, said, "Sir, you need a doctor. Put down the weapon, and we'll get you in to see a physician."

The ants, as they were, were marching toward the gunman's heart. Upon staking their claim, death would come hot and violent, Teflon Man or not.

"I don't need no goddamn snitch doctor, Mr. FBI Man. What I need is the wife of one Mister Dale Riley. And then I need the motherfucking man himself." Lowering his shirt he looked to Dale. "Tell me where she is and I'll kill you quick. Fuck with me a moment longer, and your pecker goes first."

Lionel, his aim as steady and as sure as his heartbeat, said, "No one's shooting off anyone's pecker. Now put down the gun."

A dense pall of surety settled in. The gunman said, "Well then, it looks like we have ourselves one of them good ole-fashioned Mexican standoffs, eh? I love them ole western movies, don't you?"

Lionel shrugged. "Who doesn't?"

"They're bullshit, you know? The stuff about sterilizing wounds with booze and a match is bull-fucking-shit."

Lionel stepped closer. "I wouldn't know."

"You wouldn't know, huh?" Rocking on his one good leg, with his free hand the gunman undid his belt buckle and dropped his jeans. "Well, I would know, and I'm here to tell you that it's bullshit."

When Dale saw the origin of the ant trail, he winced yet again. Oddly enough, he found himself feeling sorry for this guy, whose thigh seemed far worse than his torso, akin to a boiling volcano. It almost didn't look real, like some Hollywood makeup job for the horror flicks. Dale wondered how he could put even an ounce of weight on that leg.

"You need a hospital," Lionel said, pragmatically. "Put down the gun, and we'll get you to the emergency room."

The gunman, standing in his pee-stained underwear, teary-eyed, yelled: "And then what? Huh? And then what?"

"And then you get better."

"In jail! I get better in fucking prison. No, thanks. I've been there; I've done that. And I ain't going back."

"Okay," said Lionel. "Just put down the gun, and we'll figure this all out. We'll think of something else besides the emergency room."

The gunman, his emotions all over the map, smiled. "You put your gun down first."

"Not gonna happen, mister."

"My fucking sentiments exactly, amigo."

CHAPTER 33

Looking forward to coffee with his ex, Special Agent Roy Woodall was feeling pretty good about life. He missed Sheila, and he missed Toby. Yeah, he had screwed up big-time. The single mother down the street, Elise, hadn't been worth it. For whatever reason, she seemed to be working her way up and down the block, wrecking homes. He'd been stupid. But again, he believed that he could change.

He pocketed his cell and exited the Grand Marquis that he had recovered first thing that morning from the parking lot of the Doubletree Hotel. On his way to the house, he fingered a bullet hole in the rear panel. A company car, he'd have them fix it later. Hell, he might even trade it in for a newer model.

At the front stoop he didn't stop to kick snow from his shoes as Lionel had done just moments ago. Light on his feet, he opened the front door and entered the house.

The gunman freaked this time and pulled the trigger.

The report was deafening, the round high and to the right.

Unarmed, Dale hit the floor.

Roy, frightened to death, crouched and groped for his weapon.

Lionel, regretting that it had come down to this, squeezed the trigger.

The gunman got off another round—a wild one that punched a hole in the ceiling—and then collapsed like a marionette doll.

Lionel holstered his pistol. "Call 911. Hurry."

Dale went to the nearest phone and placed the call.

Roy, stunned by all of this, cautiously walked up to the gunman. "What in the hell just happened?"

Lionel, on his knees, was checking for a pulse. "He's dead. Damn it!"

"They're on the way," Dale called out, his ears still ringing from the gunfight.

Lionel stood and surveyed the room. "Is everyone okay?"

"Yeah," said Dale. "I think so."

Lionel looked to Roy. "What about you?"

"Other than the fact that I just shit my pants, I'm fine."

"Jesus," said Dale. "Mom and Dad." And with that, he took off to search the house for them.

CHAPTER 34

Dale found his parents on the stairwell that led down to the basement. They appeared so old, and so it was odd that they should also seem like frightened children.

"Oh, my God," Dale said as he immediately assisted his mother. "Are you okay?" He glanced at dad, whose head was bleeding. "Dad. I'm sorry."

His mother stepped into the kitchen. "That man hurt your father."

Rick, holding a dirty rag that he had found in the basement up to the wound on his head, said, "Stop it, Ellen. It's not so bad." Regardless, it seemed as though he might cry.

"Are you okay, Dad?"

Following the two into the kitchen, each step labored and slow, Rick said, "Twenty years ago, I would have beaten that man with my fists." He then rolled his arthritic fingers into a fist, which he shook awkwardly in the air, a tear now dropping from his eye.

Dale led his mother to her chair at the kitchen table. "I'm so sorry, Dad."

Rick sat with her, his right hand still in a fist.

Ellen, wiping her nose with a sheet of paper towel, said, "We heard shots."

"I'm fine, Mom."

"Where's that man?" Rick said, peering around the corner toward the living room, not daring to go in there.

"Don't worry about him, Dad. He's gone."

"He's gone?"

"He's dead."

"You shot that man?" asked Rick.

"No, Dad. Not me. The FBI. Special Agent McCarthy. Everything is okay."

Ellen, with a scared and trembling voice, said, "Son, what happened to your head?"

Dale touched his forehead. It had stopped bleeding, but the bump had grown bigger. "It's nothing, Mom. I'm fine."

Confused, Rick said, "He was asking about your wife. Why was he asking about Gina? What's going on?"

"I don't know. But he's dead now, and everything is going to be okay. Mom. Shush. Take it easy, okay?"

Respectfully, Special Agent Lionel McCarthy entered the kitchen. After introductions, he said, "Mr. Riley, could you come with me for a second?"

"Sure. Listen. Mom. Dad. I'll explain it all later, okay? Right now an ambulance is on the way. Just sit tight and take it easy." Walking away, he couldn't believe how old they appeared. It was sad. Yeah, Mom was being a pain in the ass these days, but that in no way negated his love for her. He loved them both, very much. After all, they were his parents, and Lord only knows how much they had put up with when Dale was just a kid. Hell, they were still putting up with him now. Dale wished he had killed the gunman himself.

In the living room, Roy was sitting on the sofa, sifting through the contents of the gunman's pockets.

From the coffee table Lionel picked up what appeared to be a photocopy. He held it up for Dale to see. "Recognize this fellow?"

Dale snatched the photocopy. Down in the basement with his boxes of things he had the original 5x7. This was his promotion photograph, snapped a week after he had pinned on captain. In it, he was wearing a short-sleeved khaki shirt with ribbons and medals and his shiny new insignia. Fit and trim, he was wearing the steely-eyed look of a Marine.

"This is a photocopy of my promotion photo," Dale said. "This was on the gunman?"

"Yep." Lionel handed Dale another photocopy. "What about this guy? Recognize him?"

Dale traded out. Here was Lieutenant Colonel Eric Scholl, wearing the same get-up, the same steely eyes. Dale looked at the gunman and stated the obvious: "That's the guy who shot Eric last night."

"Probably," Lionel said. "His weapon of choice was a .45, same caliber used on Eric. I'm certain ballistics will confirm this." Lionel held up a third photocopy. "Now. I don't have a clue who this gentleman is."

Dale took a look. "His name was Alex Snead. He's dead. Shot and killed a week ago. He was the prosecuting attorney at the court-martial of Mike Ruffers."

"Interesting," Lionel said. "And what about this guy?" Lionel held out the final photocopy. Here was a young man in a Marine aviator's flight suit, standing on the deck of an aircraft carrier with his right hand resting on a jet.

"That's Mike Ruffers," Dale said. "The guy I told you about."

"The pilot?"

"Yeah."

"The guy you saw at the airport today?"

"The one and only."

Lionel, furrowing his brow, said, "Any idea why this man here would want the four of you dead, and quite possibly your wife?"

"No clue." And yet he did have a clue. He did. However, the immediate threat had been . . . neutralized, so to speak. Thus, he could deal with this later. Foremost was the safety of his wife and his son. Regardless of the fact that Mike Ruffers's photograph accompanied his own in the pocket of a hitman, this didn't negate the theory that Mike might be the SF Killer. The dead guy on his parents' living room floor was about something else, something that could wait, no reason to subvert the resources of the FBI just yet. The safety of his wife and son, nothing else mattered.

Roy, going through the man's wallet now, said, "His name is Sean Fitzsimmons. He has an expired driver's license with an automatic extension from the Justice Department."

"Ex-con," Lionel said. "Anything else in there?"

Roy, still thumbing through the contents, said, "Some cash. A business card for a parole officer in Tennessee, and . . . wait, what's this?" He unfolded a small slip of paper and set it on the table. "Well well well, what do we have here?"

The three closed in, and studied the slip of paper.

On it were four names penned in black ink:

1. *Mike Ruffers*
2. *Dale Riley*
3. *Alex Snead*
4. *Eric Scholl*

Lionel said, "That's a hit list." He leaned back on his heels and crossed his arms. "I'm going to ask you once again, Dale: why would an ex-con want the four of you dead? Does this have something to do with that court-martial you were telling me about?"

"I don't know." Dale said, entirely unconvincing.

Roy pointed toward the dead gunman. "Who hired the goon, Dale?"

"I don't know. Seriously. I don't." He wondered if perhaps he didn't sound a bit too defensive, watched as Lionel and Roy exchanged a disbelieving look.

Outside, sirens pulled up in front of the house.

With weapons drawn, men in blue uniforms approached the front door.

There was a knock, followed by a warning.

Uninvited, they let themselves in.

CHAPTER 35

The medics loaded Rick onto a gurney and then wheeled him out into an ambulance. Ellen remained by his side, shivering in the cold and as confused as ever. On the way through the living room she couldn't help but notice that someone had used one of her favorite knitted comforters to drape over the dead body of the man who earlier had burst his way in through her back door. What kind of scoundrel does something like that? Bursts his way through a locked door, roughing up elderly people, pistol-whipping her husband, demanding she turn off her beloved music to allow him some peace to think? And now this: his blood soaking through one of her favorite comforters. She wept. In the ambulance, she held her husband's hand and begged for their son to join them.

Standing at the back of the ambulance, Dale said, "I have a few things I need to take care of, okay? You two will be safe. They'll take good care of you. And I'll call the hospital as soon as I can, find out how Dad is doing."

"I'm doing fine," Rick said, seemingly more annoyed now than anything else. He studied himself on the gurney. "Christ. This is overkill."

"You hush," said Ellen. "You let the medics decide what is and what is not overkill."

One last good-bye, and then the medic closed the door and hopped into the driver's seat.

Back inside the house it wasn't long until homicide detectives Polo and Perry entered to take ownership of the crime scene.

In the living room, Polo hiked up his slacks, took a knee, and pulled back the comforter. "Yep, he's dead, all right." He said this as though he were the final authority on such matters. "Who shot this man?"

"FBI," a uniformed cop replied, one of four inside the house. "He's in the kitchen, with the others."

"FBI, huh?"

"He's got a badge and everything."

Polo and Perry entered the kitchen. There, they found the trio seated at the table—Dale bookended by the two federal agents.

"What in the hell do we got here?" said Detective Perry. "The Three damn Stooges or what?"

Seated to Dale's left, Roy said, "Welcome to the party, ladies. What took you so long?"

Detective Polo pulled out a chair, flipped it, and took a load off. "You know, when we got the call I almost couldn't believe my ears. I mean, I was just here this morning, dragging Mr. Riley out of bed. His friend had been shot, a special agent with the FBI, and now we have reports of more gunfire, at this house. Mr. Riley, why don't you tell me what in the hell is going on so that we can get to the bottom of this. So, what is it? What in the hell is going on?"

"I don't know what's going on," said Dale, reaching up to finger the split in his forehead.

Detective Perry pulled the toothpick from his chops, placed his wet and dirty shoe upon a chair. "What the hell you mean you don't know what in the hell is going on? You know something, damn it. People are getting shot up, and you know something about it. What, you owe the mafia drug money? Is that it? You got gambling debts?"

Confused, Dale shook his head. "What?"

Perry leaned in. "You pimping whores, Mr. Riley? Is that what this is all about? You a pimp daddy?"

"Pimping whores?"

"Is it kiddy porn, you sick fucker?"

"Jesus. No. Are you out of your mind?"

Polo, pulling Perry back some, said, "You'll have to excuse my partner, gentlemen. It's just . . . neither one of us believes in coincidences, is all. Something is going on, Mr. Riley. So why don't you just tell us what it is that you know. Help us to get to the bottom of this."

Amused, Special Agent Lionel McCarthy watched this exchange as a pro would watch the amateurs. Soon, he would have to step in and take charge.

Dale said, "Look. I have something in the basement that I needed to give to Lionel and Roy, and so they followed me home from the hospital. When we got here, the gunman was already inside. He had locked my parents in the basement. He fired his weapon, and Lionel shot him. That's it. I don't know why he was here, or what he wanted. Perhaps he was here to rob the place. I don't know."

To his partner, but more so for the others to hear, Perry said, "I don't like it one damn bit. I say we haul 'em uptown and put 'em all under the lamp."

Polo, his forearms resting on the back of the chair, said, "We can't haul in the FBI, Jim. I only wish that we could."

Roy confirmed this: "Can't haul us in, Jim. A damn shame."

"Then let's take the civilian," said Perry, undeterred. "We'll put him under the lamp. Get to the bottom of this. I don't like it one damn bit."

"What lamp?" Dale inquired.

Perry smiled. "*Thee* lamp, you sick bastard."

"What did I do?"

Perry leaned in again. "Where should I freaking begin?"

Dale guffawed. "You're out of your mind."

Perry said, "Maybe, but I'm the fucking law around here, so pack your shit. You're coming with us."

Dale said, "I can't. I have something I have to give to the FBI, remember?"

"What is it?" asked Polo.

"It's none of your damn business."

"You playing hard to get?" said Perry. "Polo, I ever tell you how much I love it when they play hard to get? Makes my nipples hard."

Perplexed by all of this, and with a god-awful headache, Dale turned toward Lionel for a little help here.

Lionel said, "All right, Detective Perry. Calm down."

Detective Perry snapped back, "Look! This is our juris-damn-diction until the DA says otherwise. We got the mayor breathing down our necks 'cause people are all the sudden getting shot up in the better parts of town. You two might be immune 'cause you got badges and shit, but far as I know Mr. Riley here doesn't have that luxury. His ass is mine, you got that?"

Lionel, finding Perry's tone disagreeable (to say the least), said, "Okay. You made your point. So here's what we'll do—"

Perry interrupted: "I'll tell you what we are going to do. We are going to haul his ass in and put him under the lamp."

Lionel, a patient man, began again: "So, here's what we're going to do. Mr. Riley is going to give to us what it is he has to give to us, and then, of course, you can have him for questioning. After all, he's a material witness to a shooting, a law-abiding citizen, and I'm quite certain that he'd be more than happy to assist you with your investigation." He looked to Dale. "Wouldn't you be more than happy to assist these fine gentlemen with their investigation?"

"Of course," said Dale.

Detective Polo said, "All right. That sounds fair. That sound fair to you, Jim?"

Detective Perry shook his head. "Hell, no, that don't sound fair. Fair is handcuffs and a damn riot baton."

Polo laughed and shook his head amiably. "Mr. Riley, please make it quick."

Dale moved toward the stairwell off the kitchen.

The special agents followed.

Detective Perry shouted out: "Move your ass, Mr. Riley. We ain't got all damn day."

CHAPTER 36

Dad, too old for this bullshit, had leaked a good bit of blood on the steps. Seeing this made Dale furious. He had a fairly good idea who had hired the goon, and paybacks would certainly be in order. Mostly, however, he worried for the safety of his wife and son. The rest could wait.

Past the blood, he led the feds down the steps. In the basement, he clicked on the lights. He went to the boxes that lined the floorboards at the far wall. This is the stuff that Dale had packed when he lost his job and could no longer afford his apartment. His personal effects, his worldly possessions—there weren't many.

He pulled the biggest box from the pack and dragged it over to the poker table. He sat and cracked the lid. Lionel and Roy watched from over his shoulder. "This is where I keep my Marine Corps stuff. Ah, here it is." He pulled out a file and set it atop the poker table. "This is the file I kept of the Mike Ruffers Court-Martial." He opened the file and began flipping through the pages, stopped when he reached the photographs. Carefully, by the edges, he pulled two free from the others, set these gingerly atop the felt. "These are photographs of the Sorubi village in Afghanistan, the village Mike had been accused of bombing. A lot of people died that night." The first photograph captured orange light at first dawn, the atrocity of several dead bodies, a woman on her knees nearby, praying. The second photograph still made his stomach turn, even after all these years, snapped in the darkness, the stark-white light of a flash showing two children with charred heads pressed cozily together, blood and brain matter oozing from their skulls. "These had been submitted into evidence as part of the JAG investigation."

"Horrible," said Lionel. "But why are you showing these to us?"

"When I first showed these to Mike Ruffers before I took him on as a client, he snatched them from me. He held them, and swore his innocence. See? He held them in his hands. His fingerprints would be all over these."

Lionel lifted his eyebrows and thoughtfully nodded.

Dale said, "You pulled a good fingerprint from that bloody contact lens, right? So maybe we can run that fingerprint against the fingerprints on these photographs."

Lionel took a closer look. "What is that, matte or glossy?"

"It looks like matte," said Roy.

"That's good," said Lionel. "Glossy has a tendency to smear."

"So, here," said Dale. "You can have them. They're yours." He pulled out a blank sheet of paper and folded them in.

Lionel said, "When did Mike last handle these?"

"It's been almost two years," said Dale. "Man, two years."

Lionel said, "It's a long shot. We'll see what we can find, but there are no guarantees. Two years is a long time, and no doubt your fingerprints will be all over these as well, probably others."

Roy said, "We can run the prints right here in Charlotte, at the federal building uptown. Upload them to Quantico, see if any match the fingerprint on the bloody contact lens."

"Yeah?" said Dale.

Roy said, "Sure. Easy stuff."

"Thanks, guys. But . . . how long, do you think?"

"Depends," said Roy. "First, we gotta get uptown. The roads are a mess. And then a lot will depend on the quality of the prints."

"It's just, well, I was hoping you could get someone to meet the airplane in Wilmington. They should be landing soon. Would that be possible? Have someone meet the plane in Wilmington?"

"Again," said Lionel, "we can't do that unless we have probable cause. I'm sorry."

"You can't send someone to her parent's house?"

"We just don't have the resources for that."

"What about the local cops? Can't you place a call and see if they can swing by?"

"I can tell you from experience, today's included, that local cops aren't out to do the FBI any favors. And they'd want to know why, and what evidence we might have. In the end, they'll probably just tell us to swing by ourselves. I can place the call and ask, but certainly no guarantees."

"Right," said Dale, stuffing the contents back inside the box, closing the top. "Would you guys at least do me a favor, or two?"

Roy shrugged. "What do you have in mind?"

Dale asked his favors, which elicited smiles from the both of them.

CHAPTER 37

Special agents Roy Woodall and Lionel McCarthy sat at the poker table.

Roy shuffled a deck of playing cards and dealt five apiece.

Lionel studied his hand. "Does a full house beat a flush?"

"Where did you go to college?" said Roy, arranging the cards in such a manner as to suggest that he had been at this since birth.

"Colorado State. You?"

"Clemson. Majored in criminal justice. Minored in poker. What? They don't got cards west of the Mississippi?"

"Academic scholarship. Had to keep a 3.0."

"Which is why you should have played more poker. It's a gateway drug for academic excellence. To answer your question, a full house beats most flushes. A straight flush or a royal flush beats a full house."

"That's what I thought. I'll take two cards."

"That's what you thought. Please." Roy dealt Lionel two cards; took three for himself. "Okay, what you got?"

"Two pairs: queens and fours."

Roy threw his hand on the table. "Boom! Full house. Damn. I knew we should have wagered money."

From atop the stairwell the basement door creaked open.

Detective Perry called down: "Hey. Riley. Your time is up. Let's go. We got the lamp warming up for ya. Come on. Light a fire under your ass. You remind me of my wife."

"Just a second," Lionel called out.

"No more damn seconds," Perry yelled down. "Pull up your skirt, Riley, and let's get."

"Five more seconds," said Roy, collecting the cards to reshuffle.

Thundering down the stairwell they came, pieces of work, the both of 'em.

Seeing the card game in action, Polo said, "What the hell is going on down here?"

"A friendly game of poker," said Roy. "Want in?"

Detective Perry said, "Where the fuck is Riley?"

"Riley?" Roy repeated, shuffling the deck with a dealer's flair.

"Yeah," said Perry. "Riley. Where the fuck is he?" He checked the space between the sofa and the wall, tossed the cushions from the sofa.

"Oh," said Roy. "Riley. He said he had a dentist's appointment."

"A what?" Perry yelled.

Lionel replied, "A doctor's appointment, actually."

Roy, dealing a fresh set of five, said, "Doctor, dentist, either way he said he had to get going. Said he was sorry to be missing the lamp. Asked for a rain check."

Detective Perry stormed the poker table. "Don't bullshit me, Roy. Where the fuck is he?"

At the window, Polo stepped up onto the chair. "Jesus H. Christ. He snuck out the window? You have got to be shitting me."

Perry said, "He what?"

"He snuck out the damn window. See for yourself."

Perry could have very well had a coronary. He replaced Polo on the chair, where out through the window he saw the snow that Dale had plowed on his way out. He hopped down. "You assholes let that sonofabitch sneak out that damn window on his damn belly?"

Lionel, enjoying a rare moment of levity, said, "How else was he supposed to sneak out that damn window but on his damn belly? That's a small window."

Polo said, "You're a shithead, Roy. You know that?"

"As a matter of fact," said Roy, "I do know that. But I'm trying to be less of a shithead, you know, for my ex-wife and my son."

"Don't kid yourself," yelled Polo, moving toward the stairwell. "You'll always be a shithead, Roy. Shit's in your blood!"

On the way out, Perry dumped the poker table, cards and chips flying everywhere.

The two cops stormed up the stairwell.

Roy dusted off his hands. "Guess the game's over, huh?"

Lionel tapped his left breast pocket, the one with the photographs inside. "Yeah. Let's get uptown, see what we find on these."

PART IV

Lightning and Thunder!

"Be self-controlled and alert.
"Your enemy the devil prowls around.
"He's like a roaring lion.
"Looking for someone to devour!"

—Peter 5:8

CHAPTER 38

Interstate 40 was a snowy, icy mess, the snowfall heavier than ever.

There were times when it felt as though he were trapped inside of a snow globe, going nowhere.

Every now and again he spotted metal on the side of the road, the glint of an abandoned vehicle or semi-truck.

He worried that there might be people inside, freezing to death. Perhaps they'd been saved. Regardless, to stop and open random doors would jeopardize his own safety. Should he see signs of life, then of course he would pull over and offer assistance. Currently, it was enough to keep her between the lines.

If only he could see the lines.

It was crazy to be out here.

He'd passed the last set of headlights a good ten miles back.

In the basement, he had asked a few favors of the feds: one, that they turn a blind eye to an old high-school stunt; and two, he needed to borrow a cell phone.

With Roy's cell phone in hand, he got stuck about halfway out the basement window—a high school stunt not working out so well with his new adult physique. "A little help," he cried out, but not so loud that the homicide detectives would hear him from the kitchen.

Roy went up to his backside. "What about that blind eye we're supposed to turn?"

"Just a little nudge, would ya?"

So Roy took the left butt cheek, and Lionel took the right, and on the count of three they pushed.

Dale groped for purchase, clearing snow down to the dead and yellow grass, the earth as hard as a rock. He mashed his ample gut, tore his shirt, and at last wiggled free. He crouched and offered thanks, and then hustled around the corner to the front of the house.

He had no coat or jacket, was damn near freezing when he reached beneath his Honda and freed the magnet case with the spare key inside.

Three patrol cars lined the curb, along with two unmarked cruisers, one of which belonged to Roy, the other to the homicide detectives.

Everyone was still inside. The coast was clear.

He sneaked around to the driver's side and hopped in.

He pumped the gas, closed his eyes, and turned the key.

She turned once and idled weakly, sounded as if she had a cold, the flu, or pneumonia. He didn't need Old Betsy to live forever, however, needed one last run of approximately three hundred miles.

He hit the wipers to dust the recent snowfall and quietly stole away.

For several miles he watched the rearview mirror. Nothing followed but the snow.

He traveled Interstate 77 north to the intersection of Interstate 40, where he turned east for Wilmington. He had made this drive countless times before, a little over three hundred miles, or, in nicer weather, about five hours. However, the snowfall was getting worse, the speedometer hovering around thirty miles an hour. He did the math. At this rate he wouldn't arrive in Wilmington until two o'clock in the morning. So much for that five-hour drive.

Darkness fell quickly.

The right headlight, hanging by wires, illuminated snow at odd angles. Every now and again it caught the slipstream, clanked against the fender, and startled him from a concentration so intense that it bordered on meditation.

As the miles fell behind him, the snow chain on the left front wheel clanked louder against the wheel well (the snow chain on the right seemingly doing fine). He considered pulling over to tighten the thing, but there was nowhere safe to do so, at least that he could see.

Cautiously, he took his right hand off the wheel, felt around in the center console, and picked up the cell phone. He held it up high so that he could glance from the road to this, and back. No one had called, and for the first time he noticed that the life of the battery was down to ten percent.

10%? What the fuck, Roy? Ever hear of a charger?

Beggars couldn't be choosers, however.

To hell with it, he thought, and very carefully dialed the number for the Finnigan residence.

On the other end the phone rang, and then voicemail picked up: *Please leave your name and number at the tone, and we'll return your call at our earliest convenience.*

Frustrated, he hung up, squeezed the cell phone, and cried out, "aaahhhh . . . *SHIT!*" How in the world could he explain the situation over voicemail? It simply couldn't be done. For a very brief moment he felt like pounding The Bitch's steering wheel and throwing the cell phone at the windshield as hard as he could. Instead, he took a deep breath and achieved Zen in sixty goddamn seconds. Kindly, he placed the cell phone in the center console, wiped the sweat from his face, and reaffirmed his grip on the steering wheel.

The clock on the dash read 6:14 P.M.

The needle on the speedometer was now hovering around twenty-five mph.

Again, he did the math.

It wasn't looking good.

He double-checked the math, and then remembered something Einstein had said, that insanity is doing the same thing over again and expecting different results.

Five minutes passed, and then another five.

The math hadn't changed.

And that's when the visions materialized out in the snowfall ahead of him: a vision of Mike Ruffers sitting inside his prison cell in pretrial confinement, swearing on a holy bible that he was innocent of those atrocities in Afghanistan; a vision of the hotel room in Charlotte as described to him by Eric Scholl; another vision of the hotel room in San Antonio, Texas, all that blood and all that horror; and there before Dale in the snowfall tinted red was a vision of Mike Ruffers in the passenger terminal, looking up Gina's name from the manifest, telling him that she's seated in 8B with nary a soul in seat 8A, very lucky indeed, and Semper Fidelis, old pal, Semper Fi; and at last Dale saw Mike standing in a dark room with scissors in hand and an evil grin on his face, the SF Killer standing over Gina with scissors dripping blood, red drops falling like the snow, fat and wet only warm.

Blind to the panic, Dale leaned harder on the gas.

The needle climbed to thirty and then to thirty-five.

At forty the left chain tore apart and violently passed beneath the car.

It all happened so damn fast.

The front end lifted, the car seemed to be floating.

Dale panicked.

Old Betsy drifted off and away and he slammed on the brakes. He turned into the skid, suspended in this snow globe of blood-red snow, captured here and spinning.

CHAPTER 39

T he flight from Charlotte arrived much later than scheduled.
A severe weather system had settled over Charlotte and the
greater Piedmont area, and the folks in meteorology had fired
a warning across the wires.

Subsequently, air traffic control grounded all the flights until the
meteorologists deemed the air safe for flight.

The taxiways backed up with aircraft both big and small, engines
running, the passengers growing weary.

When at last the weather system moved on, one by one the jets
were cleared onto the runways, where they pushed up power and
lifted off into the clouds.

Here at the Wilmington International Airport, south of the
snowstorm but with a promise of rain, a regional jet touched down
smoothly on the active duty runway, slowed, and taxied to the gate.

When the fasten-seatbelt light extinguished with a ding, Gina
unbuckled her seatbelt and shot up in the aisle.

With her son in her arms, she collected her items from the overhead bin.

Waiting in the aisle to deplane, she thought of her parents, her
old bedroom, about college and old professors. She couldn't wait
to live such a lifestyle again, and for the first time in what seemed
like forever she beamed with a smile.

She kissed her son's temple, said, "You excited to see your grandma and grandpa? Well, they're excited to see you as well. They are. They told me so."

Earlier that day over the telephone, her mother had said that she would follow the flight on the Internet. When they were thirty minutes out, she and Gina's father would trek to the airport and wait for her at baggage claim. From there, her father intended to go out to dinner at his current favorite restaurant, an Italian joint that had opened up six months ago with apparently excellent seafood and a very nice selection of wine.

Gina couldn't wait to sit and dine at a nice restaurant, imagining a huge bowl of pasta in a spicy marinara paired with a big glass of red wine. *Yum!*

The jet door opened and the passengers began to shuffle forward.

At the galley, the young flight attendant stood bidding adieu with light fingertips and a phony corporate smile.

Next to her stood the pilot, Mike Ruffers, who, with a captive audience, had told far too many lame jokes over the airplane's intercom system while updating them on the weather. The guy was a first-class creep.

Glancing at him now, he seemed sick, somehow, jaundiced. But that wasn't entirely it, was it, because his skin had color and his eyes were ghostly white. Still, he seemed sick.

Walking up the aisle, she felt his eyes cast upon her, caught a glimpse of a twisted if not lascivious smirk.

When she was next in line to deplane, Mike reached out as if to smooth her son's hair. "And how are you two doing this fine evening?"

Awkwardly, she swiveled her son from Mike's outstretched hand, dropping her coat and her diaper bag, holding up the line behind her. Just as awkwardly, and nearly bonking heads with the flight attendant who had knelt down to help her, she retrieved her items quickly, and then hustled away up the jet bridge without so much as looking back.

In the terminal, she stood for a moment, obviously shaken.

She held her son tightly, kissed him, thought it best to keep moving, not wishing for Mike to catch up to them; to look at her again in that creepy, lustful way of his, to reach out again for her son.

At the luggage carousel she spotted her father, nearly ran to him, cried out, "Daddy."

They shared a warm embrace, Clint getting mashed in between them, smiling just the same.

Dad always smelled great, was still very handsome, wearing a winter's sweater, black slacks, and spit-polished shoes.

He kissed her on top of her head, said, "We missed you, Sweet Pea. Welcome home."

Mom, on the other hand, wasn't much of a hugger. She wore an expensive fur coat and was holding her purse with both hands. She offered her daughter one of those high-society pecks on the cheek, and then the other.

Examining her daughter, Payton said, "Oh, you look fabulous. Motherhood suits you."

Gina forced a thin smile. "Thanks." Now motherhood suits her. When Gina confessed her pregnancy, after the disappointed looks and the lectures, Payton said that the family had friends who could handle the matter discreetly. For Gina, this was out of the question, a non-starter. And although the groom was far from the ideal son-in-law, Payton was, at the very least, content that her daughter would marry before giving birth, making Payton, in the end, an honest grandmother. But when Gina and that man exchanged their wedding vows, and despite the best effort of one of the city's finest seamstresses, her daughter was still noticeably pregnant. People, of course, talked. Before Gina could be swept away for a not-so-ideal honeymoon at the family beach house at Hilton Head, Payton cornered her and told how embarrassed she was, devastated, in fact, by the entire sordid affair. And now this comment that motherhood suits her. Whatever.

Payton shook Clint's hand, offered a similar peck on his cheek. "And how is my grandson doing?"

On Clint's behalf, Gina said, "He's doing fine. I'm impressed, actually, considering the day that we've had." In spite of her marital woes and lack of money, she couldn't imagine her life without Clint. Indeed, motherhood suits her. She showered her son with more kisses.

The luggage carousel began with a jolt.

Gina pointed her luggage out to her father.

On the way outside, Payton said, "Your father, bless his heart, has been talking about *Pescadora* all day. Why, he didn't have any lunch to save himself for the occasion. Can you imagine?"

Pulling luggage behind them, Cole called out, "Clint. Little buddy. When you try the Chilean sea bass you are going to swear that you've died and gone to heaven. And the tiramisu? Bellissimo!"

Gina turned and smiled. "Yeah. Clint's eating a lot of sea bass these days, Dad. Tons of the stuff. He has a real discerning palate."

CHAPTER 40

Interstate 40 bends south just past Cary, North Carolina.

Although still overcast, the snow had finally stopped falling. *Thank God.*

The roads were wet and slippery with patches of melting snow, which kept the drivers (and there were many more now than before) on their toes but certainly didn't impede them.

Here, now, was Dale Riley in the hammer lane, hanging with the hotshots. The posted speed limit was seventy. Dale had the speedometer up to eighty-eight—as fast as she could go without the steering wheel shaking apart in his hand. He'd thought about pulling over a mile or so back, to undo the remaining snow chain, but that would only take time that he couldn't afford to waste. Farther back, when the left chain broke free, Dale thought that his life was over. It nearly was. A guardrail saved him, and when the front panel kissed it, Old Betsy spun and came to rest a good fifty yards down the road. She was still humming, however, and when Dale set off again he did so slowly, refusing to look at the speedometer, the clock, refusing to do the math. He prayed to a God that he hadn't prayed to since the funeral of Alex Snead, certain that it couldn't hurt.

When at last the snow relented, he opened her up to sixty, seventy, all the way up to eighty-eight, slowing only for those assholes who found leisure in the left-hand lane.

Farther south, when the traffic thinned, he grabbed the cell phone and hit redial. Again, he got this: *Please leave your name and number at the tone, and we'll return your call at our earliest convenience.*

"Fuck!"

Where in the hell are they?

Before kindly returning the cell phone to the center console again, it rang. Incredulously, he studied this, and then frantically searched for the TALK button. He found it, punched it, and said, "Hello? Gina? Hello?"

"Dale?"

No. Not Gina. A man's voice instead.

"Yes? Who is this?"

"It's Roy, with the FBI."

"Oh. Roy." Sick with worry, he had nearly forgotten about Roy.

A long pause followed, a deep hesitation, and then Roy said, "We, uh, were able to pull some readable fingerprints from the photographs you gave us."

"And?"

"We uploaded them to Quantico, to run against the fingerprint from the bloody contact lens."

"Yes? *And?*"

"And Special Agent Lionel McCarthy just got off the phone with Special Agent Reynolds up there, and, well, where exactly are you right now?"

"What?"

"I'm just wondering where you are."

"I'm on the fucking road, Roy. Driving to Wilmington. Remember?"

"You're still on the road to Wilmington?"

"Check the weather, Roy. It ain't exactly springtime."

"Maybe you should pull over for a second so we can talk."

"Pull over?"

"Just for a second. You seem really stressed out right now."

"Look. I'm not pulling over. This drive has taken long enough. Just tell me what the fuck they found."

"Dale—"

"Yes? Hello? Are you there? Hello? Roy? Talk to me, man? Hello?" He checked the cell phone. No lights, no nothing—the battery dead. *Dead!* Dead like Alex Snead. Dead like the dead gunman that Lionel had shot inside his parent's living room. Dead like the victims of the *SF Killer*, who travels from city to city, from one hotel to another . . . and who's to say that he only frequents hotels? That he won't come knocking on the door of the Finnigan residence, posing as a UPS man or something, special delivery.

He squeezed the dead cell phone, and then smashed the damn thing against *The Bitch's* steering wheel, doing so over and over again until the little numbers flew from the casing, until the wire guts were showing and nothing remained but bits of electronics, his hand bloody from several gashes.

I'm just wondering where you are. That maybe you should pull over for a second so we can talk.

Pull over.

You seem stressed out, so pull over. I have something to tell you.

And what was it that Roy was going to tell him?

What could be so wicked that Dale had to pull over lest the news send him careering off the Interstate?

We uploaded the prints to Quantico, and well, where are you right now?

Pull over.

We've got some news for you.

And you're not going to like it.

Mike had looked her name up on the passenger manifest.

Mike had singled her out.

Jesus Christ!

And once again a horrific vision bloomed before him in the darkness, Mike standing over Gina with scissors in hand dripping blood, and Clint was there as well. The dead eyes of his wife turned to Dale and asked him why, *why didn't you save us, why? And our son? God. Look at our son.* It was an impossible vision to see, to comprehend, the violent death of their son, a vision that Dale desperately wished would go away. But it wouldn't go away, it lingered, and so as if to outrun it Dale mashed on the gas, pressed as hard as he could, mashed the pedal to the floorboard.

Old Betsy screamed like his son, her one good light slicing a path in the vision up ahead.

At last the vision faded, broke free like the one remaining snow chain, which came undone and clanked beneath the undercarriage, littering the Interstate behind them.

CHAPTER 41

C lint would never know, but the Chilean sea bass had indeed been delicious. It came rubbed with sea salts and spritzed with fresh lemon, grilled to perfection. Cole relaxed with a second glass of wine.

Gina had the fruit de mer over linguini with a rich marinara, opting for water instead of wine. Fatigue had overcome her, quite certain that a glass of wine would put her to sleep before dessert.

Mother had settled on the swordfish steak in a light, buttery cream sauce with a modest helping of lightly grilled vegetables.

Everything was delicious.

It had been forever since Gina had been out to a decent restaurant. She enjoyed the ambiance and relished every bite.

Clint was next to her, strapped into a wooden high chair. He had a 2012 bottle of Mother's Breast Milk, not quite vintage but satisfying nonetheless. Remarkably, after a rather long and hectic day, he remained in good spirits.

For dessert, Cole ordered tiramisu with a cup of black coffee.

Mother opted for coffee as well, sweetened with cream, and with this she had an ample slice of questions—her first bite was this: "So, has he found work yet?"

The he in this particular question was Dale, as if saying his name might otherwise humanize him, his very existence, it seemed, something that Payton had not yet come to terms with. It was always *that man*, or *he* or *him*. Never Dale.

"No, Mother," Gina replied, forking in a bite of Key lime pie. "Dale hasn't found a job yet. Dale is looking, but it's a tough economy out there. It's difficult to find work. Even for the well educated like Dale. My husband. Dale."

"Yes," Payton agreed, "but any fool can paint a picture, can't they? The real genius lies with those who can sell them."

"What does that even mean?" Gina asked, chasing the pie with a sip of cool water.

"Well," Payton began, "it's just, your track record with boys isn't so great, is it? Remember Mark Adams?"

Of course Gina remembered Mark Adams; mom wouldn't let her forget him.

Payton said, "Oh, he was the perfect gentlemen, wasn't he? And then late one night we get a phone call from the police. He's driving you around drunk, of all things. And what about Tony Lee?"

"Tony was a jerk, Mom. Okay?"

"It's just . . . we have a pattern, don't we, and you had such a wonderful relationship with Simon Perkowitz?"

"Yuck." Simon Perkowitz was the unfortunate son of Doctor Marcus Perkowitz, an ER doctor who played golf with dad on Sundays. In her sophomore year at college, Simon, two years her senior, had at last found the nerve to ask her out on a date. To be nice, she said yes. They went out to dinner and a movie (Simon yet another original thinker), but the chemistry wasn't there. No sparks. Nothing. She spent the rest of her sophomore year avoiding him until at last he bought a clue.

"He's a dentist now, dear. He opened his own practice right out of dental school. He's very successful and lives in a beautiful new home."

"Simon is gross," Gina replied, quickly reverting back to an adolescent vocabulary as the mother-daughter pair resumed a decades-old argument.

Oblivious to this, Payton said, "He's such a fine young man. Some lucky lady is going to land him very soon, you wait and see, and live a very respectable life."

"So now my life isn't respectable?"

"But you have all the answers, don't you, dear?"

"No, Mother. I don't. What I have is a headache."

Cole, digging into his tiramisu, said, "Why don't you leave her alone? Let's enjoy our evening, our grandson."

Taking a sip of coffee, Payton said, "Isn't that the problem with these kids nowadays? Everyone wishes to be left alone. No one wants to roll up their sleeves anymore, and work. It's all a big party, isn't it, dear? I hear it in the lyrics of all your new music when I suffer the unfortunate occasion of happening upon a so-called 'hip' radio station."

"Mom. You never worked a day in your life." She pushed away her pie, half eaten.

"Why, I'll have you know that I had the toughest job in the world. I raised two lovely daughters and kept a very fine home."

"You're right, Mom. You win."

"It's not a matter of winning or losing, dear. I just want you to be happy. I want what's best for you."

"So do I."

"Yes. But does he?"

"Who?"

"The man whom you married."

"Dale? You mean Dale, right? You can say his name, Mother."

"Yes. Of course. So does he, or does he not?"

"Does Dale what, mother?"

"Does he want what's best for you?"

"Of course."

"Then why won't he let you go, dear? It seems as if he's holding on to you for dear life, and dragging you down with him."

Gina had her own concerns about the strength of her marriage, and of course she did wonder if the urge to defend her husband, *Dale*, was due in whole or in part to defying her mother, or whether or not she genuinely wished for her marriage to endure. Of course she still loved him, but did she love him enough? Not that she would ever confess this to her mother, but on the flight home she fantasized about what her life would be like as a single mother. She found some parts of this fantasy appealing. Dale had become insufferable and nearly impossible to live with. He had become self-loathing, and sad. He was drinking too much and eating too much and found doom and gloom around every corner, hardly the knight in shining armor that she'd married. But she also knew that he had it within him to be a better man, a better husband and father. He just had to snap out of his funk. She had coaxed him and urged him and told him to hang in there, but his solitary trips to the basement were becoming more and more frequent. At first she followed him down there, and tried her best to hang out with him, to just be with him. However, she quickly tired of the beer and the late-night television, finding it all so hopeless and depressing. She did not want to become that couple, that person. Something had to change. Yes, perhaps he had been bringing her down, but here was an opportunity for her to step it up and bring him up with her. Isn't that what marriage is all about? When one or the other falters, the other is there to pick them up and dust them off? So yeah, she had entertained the idea of what her life might be like without him, and loathed the idea in its entirety. She was married. She was the wife of Dale Riley. Together, they had a child. Currently, the times were tough. Sure. No denying. But they would get through this, survive and endure. Of this she was certain. She said to her mother, "Please, don't badmouth my husband."

"Well, I'm—"

She held up her hand. "Mom. Enough."

There wasn't much talk on the drive home. Gina sat in the back seat with her son, watching the scenery panel by, landmarks and memories of easier times. She missed this place, and yes, she missed her parents, to include her ofttimes persnickety mother. For what-ever peculiar reason, this is how Payton demonstrated her love, nitpicking at the tender aspects of her daughters' lives. Would it be better to have been ignored? In some regards: yes. In others: no. Gina never had any misgivings about her mother's love for her, even though there were times when this love came with a hearty dose of criticism. In time, they'd find a comfortable rhythm again. Between now and then, there's always aspirin.

The Finnigans lived in an exclusive community that had been developed along the rocky shores of the Intercoastal Waterway. Cole entered the neighborhood and drove along down to the second block, to a two-story brick home with three years left on the mortgage. He parked in the two-car garage and assisted his daughter with her things to her second-floor bedroom.

Inside her old bedroom little if anything had changed: same curtains, same comforter, and same carpet. The teenage posters, however, had been stripped clean and replaced with pieces of local artwork—paintings of conch shells, and black and white photographs of the ocean.

In the adjoining bathroom, Gina ran a warm tub. She stripped off her clothing. With Clint in her arms, she entered the waters. God. It felt exquisite. The stress sloughed off like ice. She very nearly felt like her old self again, happy and optimistic. She kissed her son and bathed him.

Dressed in warm pajamas, she carried him downstairs, where they said good night to their hosts. It had been a long day, and both mother and son were in need of some sleep.

Upstairs, she set her son in the nearby cradle and curled up in bed with a fashion magazine. On the nightstand was a telephone. She had yet to call her husband. Honestly, she did not wish to speak with him. For just one night she wanted to put it all behind her. However, that wouldn't be the right thing to do. She picked up the phone and dialed. Voicemail picked up, Dale's mother in her scratchy voice, a rude tone, and the typical spiel. Gina said, "Hey. It's me. We're here. Safe and sound. We're going to bed now, so I guess we'll talk tomorrow. Goodnight, honey."

She hung up, thought for a moment, and then took up again with her magazine.

For thirty minutes she read of love and celebrity, and then her eyes grew weary and she clicked off the lamp.

Softly, because he was already asleep, she said, "Good night, Clint."

She closed her eyes and fell fast asleep.

She dreamed pleasant dreams.

They wouldn't last.

CHAPTER 42

I t began to rain. It came in buckets, blasting Dale's windshield. The wipers couldn't keep up. Drivers were pulling over to wait this one out. Not Dale. He leaned forward until his chest was nearly pressed against the steering wheel. He focused on the Interstate and didn't so much as blink.

Up ahead he saw a sign, and slowed to get a better look.

Welcome to Wilmington, North Carolina
The Port City

He took the first off-ramp, traveling faster than conditions allowed.

He knew these streets by heart. Back when he and Gina were dating, there had been times when they would drive these streets for hours, listening to the radio. They'd sing and laugh, find quiet alleyways and hold hands and kiss.

That all seemed like an ancient memory.

The clock on the dash read 11:58 P.M., two minutes shy of the witching hour, much better time than at first he had calculated.

He tried not to think of Roy or of the lost phone call. He tried not to think of the vision, the one with dead eyes and haunting questions of why, of a screaming child, of scissors dripping blood.

When that unthinkable vision crept in, he shook his head and damn near slapped himself across the face.

He focused on the road signs, turning left and right, running these streets on memory, speeding by restaurants where he and Gina had shared cheeseburgers and milkshakes, parks where they had strolled hand in hand. Everything was dark now, soaked with rain and uninviting. This was hardly the time to reminisce.

He came upon the neighborhood and turned in.

Million-dollar homes lined the streets, fortresses to the tumult of rain.

At last he came upon the home.

He pulled along the curb and killed the engine. He patted Old Betsy on the dash. He thanked her. She had made it.

But had she made it in time?

He wanted to breathe a sigh of relief, but one of these homes was not like the others.

He glanced around the neighborhood, saw porch lights and lights on in windows. Streetlamps stood sentry like beacons at sea.

Here at the home of Doctor Cole Finnigan, however, he found only darkness.

A bolt of lightning flashed overhead, a thunderclap followed.

Dale felt fear and worry, but there was more than this, something deeper and much more powerful, as if there were shackles coming undone. Sidelined by unfortunate circumstances, he had become everything that he loathed, unhealthy, drunk, perpetually unemployed, a sorry old sack of an excuse for a life, all of that coming unshackled now. *Once a Marine, always a Marine.* He had joined the Corps to do heroic things, to be that superhero, and there were times when he'd been one, times when he'd been great. However, he had suffered setbacks. He had lost his way and had diverged ever further. But enough of that crap! Tonight, in these desperate hours of darkness and rain, he would find his way again. Fear, yes, it was real and very gritty, but resolve set in, an inner strength, that which compels a Marine into action. They travel the globe to stamp out tyranny and evil, to protect the innocent; warriors who were pissed the fuck off. Mike had looked up Gina's name from the passenger manifest, had flashed a sinister smile, and had said, "Semper Fidelis, old buddy. Semper Fi." Mike had tarnished the ethos of that which Dale and so many others who have ever worn the uniform hold sacred. Fuck Mike. God help Mike if he was in fact inside. God help Mike if he had so much as touched a single strand of hair on his wife or son or in-laws.

He exited the vehicle.

Perhaps it was only a power outage at this particular house, lightning somehow cutting off the juice.

But what were the odds that it would stand alone in the dark in this neighborhood?

Roy had phoned with news. First he wanted Dale to pull over. No one asks of another to pull over unless the news is dire. Good news can come in stride. Bad news? *Better pull over, Mister Riley, ole pal, I'm about to smack you right across the kisser.*

It was freezing outside, the rain pounding heavy, soaking through his torn shirt, his jeans.

He studied the home.

A frontal assault was out of the question. Every Marine worth his weight in gold knows that the element of surprise can weaken the most hardened of armies. Better to sneak around back, enter quietly, stealthily, and then wreak utter havoc.

Dale swept away toward the back of the home. Carrying those extra pounds, still he moved with ease.

Around back, he nearly tripped over the first confirmation of trouble.

He took a knee and examined the animal. "Are you okay?"

It was Taffy, the family dog, unresponsive, very likely dead. Dale petted the dog's coat, felt a patch of wetness that was still warm. *Blood.*

God help that sonofabitch if he has harmed my family!

He found the back sliding-glass door ajar and quietly entered.

He stood in the kitchen, dripping wet.

He stopped, held his breath, cocked his head, and listened.

The house was deathly quiet.

The refrigerator didn't hum and the clocks didn't tick. Neither was there light, no neon green from the kitchen appliances; no digital blinks of technology. The power had definitely been cut.

A bolt of lightning lit up the nighttime sky and flooded in through the windows.

There, by the island, he saw the body of Doctor Cole Finnigan.

Hustling over, it was suddenly dark again.

Dale fumbled around, felt Cole's body, his head, down to his neck in search of an artery. He felt a pulse. Thank God he was still alive, and now he could hear him breathing. Unconscious, but breathing.

From upstairs he heard a cry: his son, Clint, and not the cry of that horrific vision, thank God, not from fear or pain. This was Clint's hunger cry; as a father, Dale knew the difference.

And then he heard the light footsteps of Gina, up to retrieve their son, to take him back to bed with her, to breastfeed him there.

They were alive and unharmed.

Dale wanted to yell out to them, to tell them to lock the bedroom door and hide.

But he didn't. He kept quiet, stood, listened.

He believed that between here and the upstairs bedrooms was the killer, Mike Ruffers. In fact, he felt certain of this. What he wasn't certain of was Mike's specific location, if Mike was downstairs, or upstairs, perhaps on the stairwell. The dog's blood was warm, which meant that he wasn't far behind him. No, to call out now would be to give away the element of surprise, not entirely sure if he even had that anymore.

He listened.

He heard his wife's footsteps return to her bed, and then quiet.

As he had throughout the city, Dale began to navigate his way through the house, moving by memory, leaving a trail of rainwater behind him.

In the foyer he found himself at the stairwell that leads to the second-floor bedrooms. Again, he stopped and listened; it was still very quiet.

Slowly, determinedly, he began his ascent.

Outside, wind and rain rattled the massive two-story window that overlooked the street out in front of the house. Midway up the stairwell, Dale looked outside, could see Old Betsy through the rain. He had left the headlights on, the one on the left beaming weakly down the street, the one on the right still dangling, illuminating the ground and blowing in the wind. Soon, the lights would fade to darkness, and with the battery would go everything else. She'd given him her very last mile.

Dale continued up the stairwell.

Nearing the top, it seemed he felt a presence.

Jesus, it was so damn dark up here, freaky in a sense.

The hunter becoming the hunted . . . if only it was that easy.

Lightning struck near, white light flooded in, the thunderclap shaking the home to its foundation.

In that brief second, Dale observed as much as he could, and then it was dark again, disorienting.

He'd seen nothing telling, nothing so ominous as that terrible vision.

He reached the second-floor landing, stepping as quietly as he could, his shoes, however, squeaky with rainwater.

He removed his sneakers, his socks, wishing he had done so sooner.

To his left he heard a rustle. He turned to face this and thought he saw a shadow.

Another bolt of lightning lit up the night, illuminated the presence.

In the far corner he saw him, and never before had Dale been so afraid—this fear like white lightning, hot, powerful, and electric. He froze.

Darkness enveloped them, and from the corner he heard this: *"Semper Fidelis, ole buddy. Welcome to the party."*

CHAPTER 43

"Semper Fidelis, ole buddy. Welcome to the party."

Mike Ruffers stood naked in the corner, in his right hand a pair of scissors (a knot of dog hair in the bolt), in his left a holy bible. And Mike had the perfect passage in mind with plans to circle this later with the fresh, warm blood of Gina Riley, hers or the child's—an executive decision reserved for the heat of the moment.

Mike had come of age in a home of religious indifference, what his mother called agnosticism, his father atheism. Regardless, Mike always sensed something of a higher power, be it God or Buddha or whatever. In college, when he wasn't studying aeronautical engineering, he had his face in the books of theology. He searched for answers. He found one his senior year. Not in a book, but in the flames of the burning Twin Towers, in the massive plumes of gray and black smoke: the face, the image, of the Devil. On campus, the young minds discussed the meaning of this image, some, to include Mike, believing that the Muslim extremists possessed this evil spirit, embodied it, and delivered it to our homeland. Something had to be done. Because many of his peers at Clemson University affiliated themselves with the Southern Baptists, and because he himself was dating one, these are the like-minded souls with whom he prayed. His religious fervor flourished. Upon graduation, he did the only sensible, if not responsible, thing that a soldier of God would do: he aligned himself with the fiercest of God's warriors. He would fight the evildoers and deliver God's fury. To do otherwise would be a great sin.

In the Corps he played the game as well as the rest of them, if not better. He earned his wings, got orders to his first squadron, and eventually deployed overseas. Sadly, the business of air warfare was not what he imagined—far too many controlling agencies, everyone with their hands in the mix. The glory days of finding your own target, and bombing it to hell, were over. Ridiculous. Overseas for nearly six months, he had yet to bag himself an evildoer, a Muslim, what some of the guys in the squadron were calling ragheads. So, on the eighth anniversary of September 11, he took matters into his own hands. Over the hardscrabble land of Afghanistan, flying at twenty-five thousand feet, he radioed Major Duncan McGuire and fibbed about his fuel situation (a forgivable white lie when told on God's errand). He said that his tanks were desperately low and that he had to get back to the ship, ASAP. Having served with Major McGuire for several years now, Mike knew quite well that given the choice between accompanying a broken airplane back to the ship or sticking around a warzone with the possibility of entering the fray, that Major McGuire would opt for the latter every time. And that's precisely what Major McGuire did: he sent Captain Mike Ruffers, call sign Angel 12, back to the ship, alone. In an AV-8B Harrier jet and at twenty-five thousand feet, Mike spotted the dim glow of the village and delivered six "hellos" from God Almighty. Indeed, a village elder would say that Mike was the Devil that night, spreading his wings, sweeping in, and breathing fire down upon them. Mike, however, fancied himself an agent of God. An angel, if you will. What a shame that five Marines had to die that night, tsk tsk, but shouldn't every Marine have their affairs in order, wills and powers of attorney, and, most importantly, spiritual redemption from the Man upstairs? It's a dangerous gig, this business of warfare, so pack up your shit and be ready to go.

Sidetracked by those legal woes, Mike's next kill wouldn't come until several years later, in another life, another career. Saleem was her name, Eloise Saleem of Muslim descent. She occupied seat 21C on the flight from Akron, Ohio, to Indianapolis, Indiana. She wore a headscarf and a loose, flowing dress. On a different day, Mike believed that beneath this dress she would wear a vest of TNT. She would enter a crowded café, push a button, and kill innocent Christians. Unless, of course, Mike did something about this. For the duration of the flight, he imagined possible scenarios, how he might stop her from killing. Nor was this the first time that he had entertained such thoughts, his mind's eye envisioning where and how he might kill her and others of her ilk. The jet landed at Indianapolis. At the gate, Mike watched as she deplaned the jet. He smiled and said good-bye, silently wishing her dead. Later that evening, when he and the other crewmembers were checking into their hotel, he saw her standing in the registration line in front of him. He feigned interest in the newspapers that were stacked on the front desk, set aside his luggage, ambled up, and snapped one open. He listened as the clerk assigned her to a room on the fourth floor. When it was his turn in line, he kindly requested a room on the same floor. The clerk obliged. There, inside his room, he waited. He kept the door ajar and watched the hallway. He planned. He schemed. He thought it would be clever to leave with her a message from God, something profound; something that might motivate the Muslim extremists to cease and desist this nonsense of jihad. He pulled the hotel bible from a drawer, resumed his seat near the door, and searched the holy text. He found the perfect passage: *Do not fret the evildoers, or be envious of those who do wrong, for like the grass they will soon wither, like green grass they will soon die.* He liked this. It resonated.

Watching the halls, he saw her pass by wearing sweats and carrying a bottle of water. The headdress covered her head and veiled much of her face. Dressed for a workout, it was much too cold outside for a jog. Most likely she was heading to the workout room in the basement.

Quickly, he changed into his workout clothes. He stuffed the bible and some scissors in his backpack, along with a pair of latex gloves.

He rode the elevator down to the basement. In the workout room he found her on a treadmill. She had stripped off her sweats, her headdress, and was now wearing shorts and a rather thin top. She presented a modest, if not embarrassed, demeanor. She didn't make eye contact.

Most importantly, the two were alone.

Mike sat on the recumbent bike and pretended like he gave a shit about his cardiovascular wellbeing. He pedaled and sweated and flipped through the channels on the television. He checked his pulse. He made it believable.

In time, she stepped off the treadmill and entered the bathroom.

Mike waited a few seconds and then hopped off the bike. From his backpack, he pulled out the latex gloves and snapped them on. He smiled and thought of a sick joke that they used to say in the Corps: *The first kill is the toughest, no lie, but what's the toughest thing after that? Keeping count!* With seventy-eight Afghans and five United States Marines, Eloise Saleem would be number eighty-four, nothing too remarkable about that. Perhaps the one-hundredth victim will get a nice little parting gift, so to speak, confetti, balloons.

He grabbed the scissors and the backpack.

One last look around, finding no one and certainly no surveillance cameras, he entered the women's restroom. Moments later, he exited, his heart rate through the roof—all in all, a very successful workout.

Two nights later he had a similar encounter in Charlotte, North Carolina, another Muslim extremist by the name of Aalia Khalil. Foolishly, she had opened the door to her hotel room (he had knocked and had said that he was there to check the Internet connection).

Having had a taste of blood, he was finding evildoers around every corner. The bratty bitch in San Antonio, Texas, had it coming. Her sin? Being a bratty bitch.

When Mike happened upon Dale Riley and his family at the departure gate for Wilmington, he knew that Gina would be number eighty-seven. It was simply God's will.

Upon landing at Wilmington, he rode with the others in a van to their hotel room. His copilot asked if Mike wanted to go out to dinner. Mike begged off, said he was tired. He entered his hotel room and locked the door. At the desk he pulled out his computer, accessed the Wi-Fi connection, typed in a few names, and hit ENTER. In very little time, Google came up with this:

Dale Alan Riley and Gina Rene Finnigan were married June 2, 2011, at three o'clock in the afternoon. The marriage was held at the United Pentecostal Church in Wilmington, North Carolina, with Reverend Thomas B. Theriault officiating. A reception was held at the Coast Line Convention Center imme-diately following the ceremony.

The bride is the daughter of Doctor and Mrs. Cole Finnigan of Wilmington, and the granddaughter of Mr. and Mrs. Robert Finnigan, and Mr. and Mrs. Hildebran. Gina is a student at UNC Wilmington and working toward her bachelor's degree in nursing.

The groom is the son of Mr. and Mrs. Rick Riley of Char-lotte, North Carolina, and the grandson of the late Mr. and Mrs. Riley, and Mr. and Mrs. McCorkle. A graduate of UNC School of Law, Captain Riley is a staff judge advocate stationed at Cherry Point Marine Corps Air Station, North Carolina.

Captain Dale Riley *was* a staff judge advocate, Mike thought with a smile.

Another Google search came up with the physical address of Doctor Cole Finnigan.

He pulled up *Randmcnally.com* and plugged in point A and point B. His computer screen showed a map and reported a distance of 2.6 miles.

2.6 miles. A slow jog, and Mike could be there in less than thirty minutes.

He closed his computer and set it aside.

From the desk he pulled out the hotel bible and carried this with him to bed. He flipped through the pages and found something fitting, another passage that would resonate. He checked his wristwatch. It was still too early to execute his plans. He clicked off the light, closed his eyes, and napped.

At precisely 11:15 P.M., his eyes snapped open as if triggered by an internal alarm clock.

It was time to get moving.

From his suitcase he pulled out a jogging outfit and changed. He slipped on thermal gloves and a watch cap, his running shoes. In his backpack he stuffed the bible, a pair of scissors, a change of clothes, and the latex gloves. He thought about packing an extra set of contact lenses, but decided against it. Should he suffer a bloodbath like the one he had suffered in Charlotte, he'd simply flush the lenses down the toilet like before. His vision wasn't so bad that he couldn't operate without them.

Outside, the clouds had opened up. Rain was falling heavy and cold. It was a miserable night. In other words, it was perfect.

He set off down the road, jogging at a steady pace.

He kept off the beaten path. Should a cop pull up and ask questions, he'd smile and tell them that he's one of those exercise freaks who, despite the weather, can't get through a day without an adrenalin fix. What's an endorphin junky to do? If they inquired of the backpack, he'd tell them that he was carrying Gatorade and Powerbars, fuel to keep him going. He'd be happy to show them the contents, if they would like. And should they call his bluff, he'd beat feet and hide. His best bet, however, was to avoid the main thoroughfares and thus the cops.

Along the side streets a few cars passed by, spraying rainwater, but no one stopped.

He was a shadow in the darkness, keeping pace with the rhythm in his head.

He was an agent of God, an angel.

He was the Devil, spreading his wings.

Soon, he found himself in a high-end neighborhood. Here is where the rich folks lived, and where a woman and her child would die a most sensational death tonight.

The rainwater tasted saltier than before. Off to his right, he could hear the unsettled waters of the Intercoastal Waterway, how they pulsed with power, thrashed and whipped rocks, coiled for another assault. Within the clouds, lightning flashed like spiderwebs, and thunder rolled like bowling pins. God was angry. Yes. It was such a fine night for a kill.

He came upon the house, slowed, walked, and looked around. He saw no one, only lights. He stepped off the road and onto the lawn.

He stepped into the shadows.

On the western side of the home he found the utility box.

He set down his backpack and pulled out the scissors.

He popped the box and snipped the phone lines. Next, he'd kill the power.

But not so fast.

A canine came tearing around the corner, barking, growling; and Mike, with scissors still in hand, brought them down in a violent, deadly blow. The dog yelped, fell, limped away. Mike picked up his backpack and stalked the dog around to the back of the house. There, in the rain-soaked lawn, he ended the life of the beast. It was a satisfying kill, an appetizer before the entrée.

He wiped the blades clean of blood and stuffed the scissors back inside the backpack.

He found the glass-sliding door unlocked and unguarded. Quietly, eagerly, he let himself in. He was high as a kite now, anxious, could no more help being a killer than a man drawn to the priesthood. In other words, he was who he was, and he liked it. Most people can't stand themselves, and pity their lives. Not Mike. He relished every moment.

In the kitchen he heard someone coming.

He found refuge behind the island, squatted, and waited.

He watched as an old man approached the glass door.

The old man slid it open and called out: "Taffy? Here, boy. C'mon. It's freezing out there."

Taffy didn't come. Mike came instead. He came quickly and delivered a powerful blow to the old man's temple. The old man's arms flailed, and his knees tendered their resignation.

Mike caught him before he hit the floor. He had no intentions of killing anyone other than Gina and the child; so after dragging the old man behind the island, he patted him on the head and wished him good night.

Mike went back, closed the glass door, stood for a moment, and listened.

Glancing around, the house was immaculate and rich, expensively furnished with high-end appliances. More so, the house was silent. No one stirred.

From his backpack he pulled out a change of clothing, the bible, the scissors, and the latex gloves. As neatly as a surgeon, he arranged these items atop the granite countertop.

He stripped off his wet clothing, his boxers and socks, and stuffed these items deep inside the backpack. His shoes he set near the doorway for later.

His plans were to rape Gina, and then kill her. Naked would simplify the clean-up process, and so naked he remained.

Moving with sure and quiet steps, he searched for the circuit box. From off the kitchen he opened the door to the garage, and found it there on the eastern wall. He went to it, grabbed the master breaker, and pulled.

The house fell into darkness.

Rain pelted the brick outside, the windows, but all of this seemed distant, remote, like an undertone to the silence, if there were such a thing.

He worked his way back inside the kitchen and over to the countertop.

Lightning struck, illuminated Mike's naked body, strong with ropy muscles.

And again there was darkness.

He felt along the countertop, found the latex gloves, and snapped them on.

Next, he grabbed the scissors, put his thumb in one loop, and his middle finger in the other.

Then he grabbed the bible.

Moving cautiously, he went deeper inside the home, reaching out in front of him, feeling furniture and walls.

He was in no particular hurry.

Gina and the child were as good as dead; they just didn't know it yet. Soon they'd be stricken with horror. The child he'd take quickly, believing that he'd derive little pleasure from the screams of such a young and innocent life. The mother, however, well, he had some wonderful plans for the mother, hadn't he? Together they would bathe in the blood of the infant, the rape violent and red and flashed with white lightning. He'd claw at her flesh, her hair, and the more she screamed the harder he'd rape her. The climax would be supreme. Then, oh, and then, sweet Gina, let's see what toys we have to play with, shall we? He'd introduce the scissors; trace them slowly, seductively, down the length of her blood-soaked cheeks, down to her neck. At her breast, he would pause, perch the scissors on end, flex, and puncture her nipple. Ribs might crack, unless, of course, he found a sweet spot in between them. Wildly she'd scream, writhe, and, with any luck, fight back. Please, God, let her be a fighter. Eloise had accepted death so easily, as did the annoying old coot down in Texas. Aalia, however, fought like a marlin on the fishing hook, hitting him, kicking him, biting and scratching. He wrestled her to the ground, where she screamed and bucked her hips. He ripped off her pajama top, brought the scissors high, and savagely sunk them in, all the way down to the hilt.

Now, he imagined pushing them in slowly, past Gina's ribcage, holding the tip shy of her wildly beating heart. He'd kiss her one last time, and with his penis inside her, he'd push the scissors deeper, deeper, until he penetrated her heart and the blood gushed forth. God, how he longed to feel her last breath of life, to feel her muscles go slack. He wouldn't ejaculate inside her, although the thought held such wonderful appeal. An act such as this, however, would leave behind his DNA and make it far too easy for the feds to find him. No, he would pull out and masturbate to completion later, inside his hotel room with the scent of her death still on him. With her dead body sprawled out before him, he'd snip the letters S and F into her midriff. Semper Fidelis, always faithful—faithful to God and country, to upstanding Americans and United States Marines, and faithful to the cause, to this war not only on terror, but on evildoers as a whole. Lastly, Mike would locate the bible, open it up to the book of Isaiah, dip his finger in her belly, and circle the following passage in blood: *The offspring of the wicked will never be mentioned again. Prepare a place to slaughter his sons for the sins of their fathers.* It was a good plan, and it left him feeling through the darkness with a rather wicked smile.

The downstairs rooms were empty.

He found the stairwell and climbed.

At the second-floor landing and through the massive foyer window he noticed a car outside, traveling slowly down the road. The car stopped directly in front of the house. Mike lowered his chin and focused outside.

A man exited the vehicle, a streetlamp washing him in light, clouds dousing him with rain. The man seemed familiar. Lightning struck, and now Mike was certain. His smile grew wider, wickeder. The man out there was none other than attorney-at-law Dale Riley, Captain Fucking America, here to crash the party.

The more, the merrier.

Mike found his way over to a distant corner, crouched, got real small.

Patiently, he waited.

He heard the back door slide open, and the squish of wet sneaker.

From the room to his immediate left he heard an infant cry, a mother's light footsteps.

The natives were growing restless.

He listened as Dale made his way through the house, wet sneakers climbing the stairs, slowly.

Mike reaffirmed his grip on the bible, the scissors.

He stood.

Captain Fucking America reached the second-floor landing; lightning flashed, a white halo of light around him.

Mike smiled, stepped from the corner, and said, "Semper Fidelis, ole buddy. Welcome to the party."

CHAPTER 44

Indeed, Clint began to cry.

Gina awoke, rolled over, and checked the digital clock on the nightstand. It didn't appear to be working. She shook it. Still nothing. She tugged on the cord to see if it was still plugged in to the wall, which it was. Exhausted, she replaced it on the nightstand, wondering how many hours the two had been sleeping. Not many, judging by how groggy she felt.

She sighed. "Okay, buddy. You win."

She sat up in bed and clicked on the lamp. Only . . . that wasn't working either. She looked out the window. Lightning lit up the sky, followed by rolling thunder. Perhaps an errant bolt of lightning had zapped a neighborhood power transformer, or had taken something out farther up the line.

Again, she sighed.

She went toward the cradle and found it by stubbing her toe. "Oh, crap!" She hopped, reached down, and massaged it.

When the pain ebbed, she put weight on her foot again, not all of it, just enough to pull her son from his crib and return with him to bed. It was cold in here, and she threw on the covers. Of course, without electricity, there wouldn't be heat either. She wondered how long the power outage would last, and prayed that it wouldn't last for long.

She undid her pajama top and offered her son the milk from her breast.

She hummed, caressing his soft, furry head. Once she warmed up to it, regardless of the hour, she rather enjoyed the intimacy of breastfeeding.

Just then, from right outside her bedroom door, she heard a rustling noise, which stopped her from humming. She glanced there, waited, and heard nothing else. She figured that it was probably Taffy, roaming the hallways, searching for a warmer place to bed down for the remainder of the night. Perhaps, when she was finished breastfeeding her son, she would open the door and let him in. She began to hum again.

This time she heard a man's voice, which seemed to freeze her blood. Her skin broke out in goosebumps. Her nipple closed up, and Clint had little choice but to gnaw to get some milk. She winced and pulled him away.

And then she heard a scream.

Jesus Christ! What in the hell was that?

It came from just outside her bedroom door, a scream that was both primal and guttural.

And then she heard another, from another man, a bit farther from her door. A fight. Two men were out there fighting.

Fright overwhelmed her. She pulled her son in tightly.

For a very brief moment she wondered if she might not be dreaming. She wasn't, of course, for the pain in her toe felt real, the cold felt real, the terror felt too damn real. She was both amazed and ashamed how easy it would have been to succumb to this terror, to pull the covers up over her head, to close her eyes, and pray. That, or crawl beneath the bed. She might have done either of these two had she been without her child. That such an innocent life was depending on her sent her scrambling to her feet, where she returned Clint to his cradle, and then pushed the entire contraption into the bathroom. Desperately, she kissed him and said, "I'll be right back, okay? Sssshhh. Be quiet." She locked the bathroom door and slammed it closed from the bedroom, was prepared to defend her son to the bitter end. She was moving on instinct and nothing more. She had never in her life considered such a frightening scenario, had no grand scheme plotted out in her mind. All she knew, all that she felt, was that she had to save her son at whatever cost. That was it; that was everything.

Okay. Now what?

She hopped in place, shaking her hands, thinking.

The men continued to fight, were grunting and screaming, banging against walls and on the floor. It sounded brutal, because it was.

Okay. She was not going to freak out. She wondered if she had locked the bedroom door. She ran there to check.

Before she could reach it, however, the door blew open, the screams, the fighting much louder. Her own screams added to the chaos as she stumbled away toward the bookshelf. She grabbed a hardcover copy of Salman Rushdie's *Shalimar the Clown*, screamed "Go away," and then hurled the book toward the door. She missed. The book splashed against the wall and then dropped like a rock to the floor.

She grabbed another book.

She would not go easy.

And never would they get at her son!

CHAPTER 45

Dale could sense it in the darkness, an evil presence, waiting.
Reaching the second-floor landing, it was then that he realized that upon entering the home, he should have removed his wet sneakers. For that matter, he should have grabbed a butcher knife from the kitchen. Christ if he wasn't screwing this up. But Clint began to cry, and emotion got the better of reason. Now he needed to slow down, to be smarter.

He removed his sneakers, and then his socks. He considered turning back for that butcher knife, but then lightning flashed and he saw Mike Ruffers in the corner.

He couldn't believe his eyes. Not only was Mike naked, but he seemed so evil, so utterly wicked and cold, and far more muscular than he appeared in his pilot's uniform. Freakishly so. And those eyes, my God, how gleefully cruel, and the glint of the scissors in his hand, and the tenor of Mike's voice when he opened his mouth and said, "Semper Fidelis, ole buddy. Welcome to the party."

And then darkness consumed them, and all that remained was the image—frightening, shocking.

In the dark second that it took Dale to process all of this, the *SF Killer* was on him. Not Michael J. Ruffers, no, but the *SF Killer*, the scissors sinking deep into Dale's left shoulder, in nearly the exact same spot where two years ago Major McGuire had bit him on the floor in that dusty military courtroom.

Dale screamed and backed away. The scissors pulled clean from his flesh, the pain white and hot like lightning, his blood warm compared to the rain—his left arm dangled, and he was unable to lift it.

The killer came at him again.

The blades cut through his shirt and sank into his gut. The pain was excruciating, and again Dale screamed.

He grabbed the killer's wrist as the scissors sank deeper, until Dale threw a punch that connected. Encouraged, he swung again and again, his right fist coming in huge, arcing swings.

The killer backed away, and again the scissors pulled free from Dale's flesh.

In the darkness they fought, one with merely fists, the other with cold steel scissors, which neatly severed Dale's left ear as they came in high and violent, would have sunk deep into Dale's skull had they been directed an inch or two the other way.

The game wasn't over, and although bleeding profusely, Dale continued to punch. He was missing now, however, and growing tired.

From the darkness the scissors jabbed him in the chest, the arm, as Mike danced in and away, in and away like a fencer.

Dale had to switch tactics, recalled the advice of a great general who had said that after thirty-odd years in the Corps, his best advice was to improvise, improvise, improvise.

Instead of swinging, Dale lowered his shoulder and bum-rushed the killer, picked him up and slammed him into the ground. There, they wrestled, toward the top of the stairwell where together they went for a ride, tumbled down assholes and elbows, blood and grunts, and brutal, savage violence.

At the base of the steps Dale found himself free of the killer and quickly made a move for the kitchen, for the knives there by the sink. Unfortunately, a few things had changed since Dale's last visit. Payton had done some furniture shopping. For two grand she had purchased a European vanity table, which she had staged against the wall and decorated with knickknacks. Dale reduced this to kindling, lost his balance, and landed face down.

In a flash the killer was on him, stabbing him with rapid, painful jabs.

Dale squirmed, got to his back and fought, his left arm still useless.

Jesus Christ, the killer was just too damn strong.

God help him, Dale was losing, out of breath and out of strength.

The killer straddled his chest, and with his knees pinned Dale's arms—both good arm and bad arm.

With the heft of his weight on Dale's torso, the killer ran a hand through his hair, laughed, and said, "You're mine, you fat piece of shit. You're mine." The killer leaned in and whispered into Dale's good ear, "And then I'm going to kill your son, you fuck. And when I'm done with him, I'm going to rape that slutty little wife of yours, and kill her too, only slowwwwwwly." The killer sat up, laughed, and slapped Dale across his face.

CHAPTER 46

In the bedroom, Gina had grabbed another book, her arm cocked.

Whoever had come through her bedroom door screamed out: "Gina! It's your mother!"

"Mom?"

Payton shut the door behind her, locked it.

Gina dropped the book.

They found each other in the darkness, clasped hands, both of them shaking like leaves.

"What's going on?" cried Payton.

"I don't know."

"Where's your father?"

"Is that Dad out there? Oh my God, is that Dad?"

"I don't know. I can't find him. I don't think it's him, but . . . it's so dark, and, my God, what's going *on*?"

Never before had she heard her mother so panicked, which, oddly enough, somehow grounded her. "Mom. We have to think."

"And where's my grandson?"

"Clint. He's in the bathroom. He's okay."

Nearly hyperventilating, Payton said, "Okay. Okay. Gina. We need to find your father, Gina. I don't know where he is."

"Mom, we gotta call the cops. C'mon." She pulled her mother toward the nightstand, where she fumbled with the telephone. She couldn't see the numbers, no matter how close, so she felt her way around and dialed what she believed was 9-1-1.

"And where's Clint?" Payton asked, peering through the darkness.

Gina brought the phone up to her ear, listened, and said, "Mom. I told you. He's in the bathroom." She heard nothing on the line, not even a dial tone.

"Oh God. That's right. In the bathroom." People of her generation don't freak out. People with wealth don't panic. They have moments, and she was having one hell of a moment right now.

Gina dialed the number again, and again she heard nothing.

The realization hit her like lightning.

She held the phone out toward her mother. The tide of panic rushed in again, crashing to the shores. "They cut the phone lines. First they cut the electricity, and then they cut the phone lines. Oh my *GOD!*" Realizing that the intruder had been this calculating, she nearly lost it. No one goes through this much effort unless they harbor deadly intentions.

Payton grabbed the telephone and dialed the number herself. Like her daughter, she heard only silence. She too held out the telephone. "Oh, my God."

Fighting against the tide, Gina said, "We need to get your cell phone, Mom. Where is it?"

Payton, still clutching the phone, still very much confused by it all, replied, "What are we going to do?"

Gina grabbed her mother by her shoulders and shook her. "Mom! Where's your goddamn cell phone?"

Payton collected herself, said, "It's . . . it's in the kitchen, I think. Recharging."

"Is it in the kitchen? Are you sure?"

"Yes. I'm pretty sure."

"Okay. We need to get to your cell, Mom. We need to call for help." To get to the kitchen, however, they would have to circumnavigate the fight. "Mom. Dad has a gun, right? Where is it?"

"It's in our bedroom. In the nightstand drawer."

"Okay. Follow me."

Gina cracked the bedroom door, poked her head out just as the melee went tumbling down the stairwell.

"Hurry, Mom. Let's go."

The master bedroom was opposite the stairwell, and quickly they went there.

"Okay, Mother. Go get it." Gina stood watch near the doorway, prepared to jump inside and lock the door should the fight find its way up the stairwell again. "Hurry."

Payton went in, grabbed the flashlight off the dresser, clicked it on, and went to the nightstand. The bottom drawer had a combination lock, which she fumbled with.

"Hurry, mother. Hurry!"

At last mom returned with a pistol and a flashlight. Clueless, she held the pistol by the barrel. "I don't know how to shoot this thing."

Of course not. Growing up, how many times had she heard her mother complain about the pistol, about violence in society as a whole? One would never believe that her mother was a diehard Republican, given her stance on the Second Amendment. "Okay. Give it to me."

Payton handed it over but kept the flashlight, the beam pointing at the floor.

Gina gripped the pistol like her husband had taught her. Years ago at a gun range, before they married, he told her to treat every weapon with respect, as an equestrian would treat a horse. It's a symbiotic relationship that you're in command of, which is not to suggest that the horse can't rear up on his hind legs and throw you on your ass. Having grown up riding horses, it was an analogy that Gina could appreciate. Furthermore, he went on to say that she should grip the pistol as she does the reins, nothing too tight or aggressive. And when the time comes to squeeze the trigger, do so slowly but surely, and allow the explosion to happen. In other words, a nice, firm kick with the stirrups, and giddy the fuck up. Holding the pistol as sure and as comfortable as conditions allowed, she said, "Okay. Let's go."

Down the hallway they went, Gina leading the way, her mother close behind her.

One held light, the other eternal darkness.

At the precipice of the stairwell they began their descent.

With soft, bare feet Gina could feel the cold, wet rain on the stairs. She shivered, chilled to the bone. She nearly stepped on a wet sneaker, moved it aside with her sore toe, and then nearly stepped on an even wetter sock. She had no clue that these items belonged to her husband. Had she, she might not have been so collected. Not that she was truly collected. Still, compared to her mother, she was without doubt the calmer of the duo. She turned, and whispered to her mother, "Watch your step."

Downstairs, the fight continued.

She couldn't believe that they were moving toward such a fight. However, what were their options? She reset her grip on the pistol. It felt different than the one at the range, heavier and not as well balanced. She didn't even know if it was loaded, and wasn't entirely sure how to check to see if it was. But at least she had a weapon, hopeful that in the worst-case scenario it would work. She prayed it wouldn't come to that—the worse-case scenario—whatever that might be.

Nearing the base of the stairwell, Payton caught the tangle of bodies in the beam of the flashlight.

The two men (one straddling the other) froze like deer in the headlights.

Neither one had the gray hair of Gina's father.

And the one on top was naked.

Bizarre!

The path to the kitchen was unobstructed. Now was Payton's chance. She handed the flashlight to her daughter and dashed to where she believed her cell phone was, on the countertop, plugged into an outlet.

Gina held the flashlight in one hand and the pistol in the other. The cops would have cringed. She was doing everything all wrong. First, she should have reverse-gripped the flashlight. And then, she should have crossed her wrists with her shooting hand on top. This aligns the beam and the barrel, which significantly increases the accuracy of the weapon. Instead, she held them separately, both flashlight and pistol clumsily bobbing around in the night.

She took a step closer, not because she wanted to, but because the man on the bottom seemed familiar.

What the hell?

She took another step.

Is my mind playing tricks on me?

Is that . . . ?

Am I still asleep and dreaming? Is that what all of this is? A dream? A nightmare?

She heard herself say, "Dale?"

My god, is that Dale? Is that my husband?

He couldn't answer her, was breathing heavily and bleeding very badly. With his left ear missing, his face was literally awash with blood. She had missed it on her way from the master suite to the stairwell, this little pink piece of meat on the hardwood floor, missed stepping on it by inches. "Dale? Is that you?" Her voice was as unsteady as her aim.

The naked man on top smiled and patted Dale on the chest. With the flashlight in his eyes, he couldn't see the pistol, not that it would have mattered. God was on his side and would protect him. He said, "Yeah. Dale. Captain Fucking America. Look at this fat piece of shit." He then threw back his head and laughed a maniacal laugh. When he was finished, he said to her, "Now watch me fucking end him, honey. Watch me stick his heart, and then snip SF into his fat fucking gut." He then slapped Dale hard across the face, Dale's arms still pinned beneath Mike's knees. "Semper Fidelis, right, old buddy? Semper fucking Fi!" He then leveled the scissors at Gina and smiled his cruel and wicked smile. "And then you're next, bitch. You and your fucking brat kid."

CHAPTER 47

Dale lay bleeding badly.

The flashlight blinded him, and so, like Mike, he had no idea that Gina also held a pistol.

Mike seemed to weigh a ton.

Exhausted, spent, Dale felt like the ultimate failure.

He felt worse than the ultimate failure, because it's one thing to fail yourself, but quite another to fail the ones that you love. Yes, he'd failed his wife, and he'd failed his son. He had come here to save them, but had failed.

Jesus.

His mind was slipping from consciousness.

And as easy as it would have been to close his eyes and allow Mike to kill him, he didn't. He held strong, or as strong as he could.

Gina had called out his name, and then she had screamed it.

Dale wanted to tell her to run, to hide, but he could hardly breathe, let alone call out to her.

He could imagine no worse ending to life than this, that hell itself could not be any crueler.

Mike laughed, and then turned toward his wife and pointed the scissors.

You're next, bitch.

You and your fucking brat kid!

And with that Dale closed his eyes.

He didn't close them because he had decided to call it quits: he closed his eyes to dig deep, to search his fibers for every last bit of strength.

He closed his eyes and saw his son on the day that he was born, his wife, happy, holding him in her arms.

In his mind he heard laughter, his wife's, and the innocent laugh of their son.

Times were tough, sure, but there had been good times as well, intimacy and love. Desires, wants, and secrets shared. Happy walks holding hands. Tossing the little one up in the air. There had been joy, and somewhere along the line Dale had forgotten how to experience it. He used to be a protector of all things sacred, and when he wasn't anymore, he lost himself. But once a Marine, always a Marine, for the ethos wears no uniform.

So yes, he closed his eyes.

Mike leveled the scissors toward Gina, and in so doing shifted his weight. Not much, but perhaps just enough.

Dale opened his eyes, and shot free his arm.

He reached toward his chest, grabbed Mike's scrotum, and . . . he . . . *squeezed!*

He squeezed until he felt a pop, and then he squeezed a little harder.

Mike dropped the scissors and screamed a high soprano.

Dale wiggled free from beneath him, still squeezing, yelled out: "Gina and my son will NOT . . . be . . . *next!*"

Mike reached down, tried to free himself, and collapsed to the ground.

Dale got on top of him, the tables now turned.

He released Mike's scrotum and with his elbow delivered a blow to Mike's face.

He delivered another, and another.

He kept them coming, raining elbows.

Harder, as hard as he could, smashing Mike's face.

Harder, goddamn it, *harder!*

Dale's lungs caught fire. He gasped for air, kept raining elbows.

He spent everything he had, every last penny. He even spent on credit, Mike's blood splattering the floor, the wall.

Dale collapsed to the floor, sucking wind.

He began to cry and had no clue that Mike was unconscious.

Dale threw a slow, awkward, misdirected punch, void of any power. He reared back and threw another, what amounted to a pat on Mike's bloody face.

Gina rushed up to him; fell to her knees. "Dale. Shush. It's okay. It's okay." Crying and shaking, she dropped the pistol and then the flashlight. She grabbed his arms, his head, hugged him, rocked him, and kissed him so desperately. "It's okay, honey. It's gonna be okay." She kissed him over and over. "I love you, Dale. God. I love you so much." She ended this with a sob, crying, holding his head.

From the kitchen, Payton screamed out: "My God. Your father. He's hurt."

Gina screamed back: "Mom. Call 911. Hurry. Please!" She could hear her mother crying, fumbling around for her cell phone. Soon she heard her mother on the phone, taking deep breaths to calm herself down, trying her best to explain the situation, not that she even understood it. In the end she just told them to come, quickly, to just hurry up. She hung up and called out: "They are on the way. But your father. My God!"

"Stay with him, Mom. Just stay with him." To Dale she said, "They're coming. Everything is going to be okay, babe. Everything is going to be fine."

Dale had gathered some wind. Still, he felt extremely weak and dizzy. He turned his head and saw Mike, the *SF Killer*, there in the glow of the flashlight. Mike's eyes were closed. Dale wondered if soon they might not pop open, à la Michael Myers on Halloween. Also in the glow, nearer to him on the hardwood floor, Dale saw the pistol. He couldn't believe his eyes. A pistol. Somehow, Gina had come with a pistol. With his one good hand he groped for it. He watched as his fingers wrapped around the grip, these fingers oddly removed from his mind, as if governed by somebody else. He tried to lift it, but it was much too heavy. It may as well have weighed a ton.

Gina watched this, and no, she didn't stop him. She offered him another kiss, more love. "It's okay, Dale. The cops are coming. The ambulance. Everything is going to be okay." She sobbed when she said this, her conviction not quite there.

To Dale, her voice seemed distant, a faint echo. For that matter, reality seemed warped. He had mined his reserves of energy, had taken out a line of credit, and now was the time to pay up. He could feel himself slipping. His wife was telling him that everything was going to be okay. He just wasn't sure. He didn't know. What if he slipped away, and what if Michael Myers then opened his eyes?

With his fingers wrapped around the grip, he dragged the pistol across the hardwood floor, carving out a nice-sized gouge. He dragged it to a point just shy of the monster's head. To a Marine, a pistol is second nature, even one that you've never held before. More or less, they are all the same. Intimacy with one translates to another, kind of like lovers. Like lovers, you develop a great appreciation; you discover what works and what doesn't, where to touch her and where to kiss her. He thumbed the safety latch, foreplay. The trigger would be the climax. Some require more stimulation than others, and some were quite easy. Some carried blanks, or were empty of ammo. This one was loaded, however; he could tell by the weight.

He pressed the barrel against Mike's temple.

All he had to do now was squeeze the trigger, enjoy the climax, Mike's brains splattering the wall in a massive, wet orgasm.

The trigger, the G-spot, oh so blissful ecstasy.

And then he heard a cry.

It was far more distant than the voice of his wife; more like a whisper.

He heard a cry; faint, but very real.

His son. Clint. Crying from the upstairs bathroom.

To Dale, the cry sounded like that of an angel, sweet and melodic, however sorrowful.

Dale hitched, fought with his tears, did his best to remain strong.

"It's okay, baby," Gina said, caressing his face, herself crying. "It's going to be okay."

Is it going to be okay?

Dale didn't know. He grimaced, fought to maintain consciousness, and reset his grip on the pistol.

Lightning struck, white light flooded in through the windows, illuminated the horror on the floor, the blood, the brutality, a pistol at the monster's temple.

Darkness fell.

And then there was thunder.

PART V

IT'S GOING TO BE OKAY

"Upon this, one has to remark that men ought to be either treated well or crushed, because they can avenge themselves of lighter injuries, of more serious ones they cannot; therefore the injury that is to be done to a man ought to be of such a kind that one does not stand in fear of revenge."
—Machiavelli: *The Prince*

CHAPTER 48

18 July 2012.
Wednesday morning.
Raleigh, North Carolina.
United States District Court.
The Terry Sanford Federal Building, downtown.
Courtroom Number Four.
The Honorable Judge Barwick presiding.

A placard near the courtroom door read of a maximum capacity of two hundred people. Many more were crammed inside.

The best seats were reserved for the witnesses and those with ties to either side. The second tier hosted the family and friends, the reporters, a sketch artist. The cheap seats had acquaintances and those with too much free time and not enough hobbies.

Nearly everyone was seated, the atmosphere electric. Introduce a noose and some torches, and surely mob mentality would take hold.

A deputy sheriff walked the aisle. "Quiet down, please. If you folks don't keep it down I'm going to have to clear the courtroom."

They hushed, but it wouldn't last for long.

In the second tier sat the father of Aalia Khalil, Mahdi. Sitting alone, he had introduced himself to no one. Mahdi sat with his arms crossed and a scowl on his face. He had seen the monster in the newspapers and on TV. He wanted to see him in person. He wanted, needed, someone to hate for the loss of his daughter. How many sleepless nights had he imagined all of the horrible things that he would do to him? The image he revisited time and time again was one with Mike Ruffers hogtied in a bathtub. Mahdi would fill the tub with kerosene. With an ice pick, he'd poke the monster to see if he was human. What color would he bleed? Whatever the color, it would mix with the kerosene, doing so in sickly swirls and eddies. He imagined a lighter. He imagined flames and he imagined screams, but never could he imagine happiness, a sense of revenge perhaps, a sense of justice, but certainly not happiness. An Iranian immigrant, he didn't believe that the American justice system was all that just. Too many bleeding hearts and appeals. He prayed that Judge Barwick and the jury would prove him wrong.

Two rows behind Mahdi were the husband and the ten-year-old son of Eloise Saleem. The Khalil and Saleem families had not met, and never would. These were not social times. Ed Saleem had his arm around his son in a manner of distrust and protection, his worldview forever altered in the aftermath of his loss. He agreed with the roaming deputy: that everyone should shut the fuck up. A tough guy seated directly behind him was currently talking big about beating the pulp out of the accused, that if he ever saw him out on the streets he'd knock his lights out, no questions asked. The tough guy asked his date (and she must have been his date, for who in their right mind would marry such a fool) if she would ever be so damn stupid as to open the door to her hotel room and welcome inside a madman.

"Of course not," she replied. "Who would do such a dumb thing? There are sick fucks everywhere."

Perhaps a sick fuck was right in front of them, driven mad by the loss of his wife and the inane comments from the peanut gallery. Ed fumed and hugged his son even tighter.

Linda Duckworth had a delegation from Long Island, her husband and stepdaughter, the husband of said stepdaughter and their eight-year-old kid. They planned to stay for a day or two and then drive back north. The newspapers were reporting that this trial could last for several weeks if not months, and they could ill afford the time. They wanted to come, however, and lay their eyes upon the accused, to see the last man who had seen Linda alive, the man who had taken her life . . . allegedly. In the court of public opinion, however, the man was as guilty as hell. Information had been leaked. The government had physical evidence that tied the accused to one of the crime scenes. In other words, the man was guilty. Like most if not all of the folks here, they wanted to see him hang (or burned). They prayed that a day such as this would soon be forthcoming. For now, they sat in cold silence. They had said everything there was to say, and had cried all the tears.

The back door opened.

Heads turned.

Instead of the monster, there entered three men, each well dressed in suits.

The three walked down the aisle and took the row up front that had been reserved for the government witnesses.

No one in the courtroom had any clue that one of these men (the one with the Frankenstein ear) had not so long ago held a loaded nine-millimeter pistol to the head of the monster. All he had to do that stormy night was squeeze the trigger and save them all the trouble.

And he had intended to do just that.

He had flexed his trigger finger and had readied himself for the climax.

Next to him was his wife, on her knees, holding him, crying, and telling him that everything was going to be okay.

He'd believed that in a moment, with Mike's brains decorating Payton's walls, that everything would be okay, dandy, in fact.

And then he heard the cry of an infant, his son.

Honestly, it sounded like the cry of an angel.

He had joined the Corps to be a hero, to do heroic things. Would a hero shoot an unconscious man in the head? And if Dale did just that, would he be able to live with himself? Would such an act be the path toward redemption, to finding oneself? Would he truly be fighting the good fight? The just fight? The righteous fight?

The angel cried.

And the Marine, the hero inside of him, just couldn't do it. As much as he wanted to kill Mike, it wouldn't have been the right thing to do. He had to see him brought to justice for real this time around.

Lightning struck, and then thunder.

A knock on the door, an announcement: "The police. Open up."

No one opened up.

Gina called out to them, cried for them to hurry.

The cops kicked down the door.

Dale released the weapon.

Gina held him and once again told him that everything was going to be okay. To shush, that it's all going to be all right.

He prayed that it would be.

The cops swarmed the house.

Medics came and gurneyed them all away.

Outside, on his way toward an ambulance, Dale saw Old Betsy at the curb. Her headlights flickered, winked, and then forever went dim. In the days that followed and upon his release from the hospital, Doctor Cole Finnigan would try the ignition. He would charge the battery, have a mechanic give her a once-over. Sadly, Old Betsy was done. Dead. A few days later, a tow truck would take her away.

Dale had spent the entire month of March in the hospital. Surgeons repaired his shoulder and sewed his ear back on (a cop had found it upstairs, placed it smartly in a baggie with ice, and gave it to one of the medics). Dale had lost a lot of blood. For the first few days he was in and out of consciousness. Nothing seemed real. His entire life seemed as though he'd been living a dream. What was real, and what was not? He didn't know. He stopped trying to figure it out. He came and he went. He thought he heard someone say that he was lucky to be alive, probably a doctor or nurse. This made him smile inside, for perhaps his luck was turning for the better. Lately, if it hadn't been for bad luck, he'd have . . . well, everyone knows how that saying ends, don't they. But perhaps those days were over now, the bad-luck days behind him.

Doctor Cole Finnigan had been diagnosed with a severe concussion. After a brief stay in the hospital, his doctor told him to stay off his feet for a while, to relax and stay home. The day of his release, he was back to seeing patients. Already he was way behind schedule.

In Charlotte, having been diagnosed with a concussion of his own, Dale's father returned home the next day. He, on the other hand, had no qualms about staying off of his feet, at the kitchen table doing crossword puzzles, listening to that organ music. With his wife, they phoned the hospital in Wilmington, checked on the health of their son. Ellen could never quite get her head around the situation. It confused her to no end. She sat at the kitchen table and knitted.

One day, in a moment of lucidity, Dale opened his eyes and found Eric Scholl sitting bedside. They chatted for a while. Eric showed off his scars from the gunfight with Sean Fitzsimmons. Impressed, Dale attempted to show off his own. It wasn't so easy. Dale was still wrapped up pretty tightly. In the end, he decided to show them off later. With this they shared a laugh. When the chatter let up some, Eric pulled out an envelope.

"Go ahead. Open it up."

With his good right hand, Dale grabbed the envelope, attempted to tear it open.

"Need some help?"

"Thanks. But I got it." He wedged his thumb in and brutishly ran it along. He gripped the letter inside and shook off the envelope.

He unfolded it and read. When he was finished, he looked up. "Are you fucking with me?"

Eric laughed. "No. I'm not fucking with you."

Dale rested his head and damn near cried. Yes. Perhaps the bad-luck days were behind him now, once and for all. He set aside the letter and quickly gave his eyes a manly wipe. "When can I go?"

"As soon as you feel up to it. We can wait."

The letterhead was from the Federal Bureau of Investigation, Washington, D.C. The content was addressed to Mr. Dale Riley, and extended a personal invitation for an interview. Another paragraph thanked Dale for his service to his country. Lastly, the letter wished Dale luck, good health and a quick recovery. It was signed by the Deputy Director, Sid Henry.

Dale wanted to hug his guest. Hell, he wanted to kiss him. He wiped his eyes again and said "Thank you" instead.

"It wasn't just me," said Eric. "Lionel is the one who put a bug in Henry's ear. Lionel likes you. Don't ask me why." Eric smiled.

"When you see him, Lionel, tell him thanks." Dale took a deep breath and let it out. "Christ, I need to study. What if I fuck up the interview?"

"I have some materials you can borrow. Trust me, if I can pass the interview, you can pass the interview."

"Thanks." Dale looked out the window. Sunlight warmed the room. As crazy as it seemed, perhaps this was all meant to be. In God's infinite wisdom, perhaps everything that had happened had happened for a reason. Hard to believe, given the severity of his wounds, the family's brush with death, but who knows? Regardless, here was a unique opportunity. Dale was determined not to screw this up.

Later, when Gina came around with Clint in her arms, Dale showed her the letter.

She read it.

She wondered if it might be too soon.

He assured her that it was already too late.

"I have to do this. This is a tremendous opportunity for our family. We can start over again, like you said. We can get a place of our own."

She smiled a melancholy smile. Yes, she understood. Just as she had to finish her nursing degree, Dale had to do what Dale had to do.

"What if you pass the interview? What then?"

"*When* I pass the interview, then they send me to the Academy for a few months. It's perfect. This will give you the time you need to finish your nursing degree. We'll visit, on weekends, and this summer we'll reunite, as a family again. It's perfect, Gina. This was meant to be." He searched her eyes. "It's perfect, right?"

She nodded; bit her lower lip. Perfect, however, wasn't the word she would have used to describe their situation. Perfect would have been a rainy night in bed with dreams instead of a murderer. Perfect would be her husband free from these scars and these wounds. Perfect would have been a life opposite from the year that they had shared; and although the future seemed far brighter than the road that they had traveled, there were still shadows up ahead, and uncertainties.

Clint reached for his father.

She set him on the bed, where Clint grabbed the IV line and nearly tugged the needle free from his father's arm. She stopped her son just in time, and together—husband and wife—they shared a laugh. It wasn't a perfect laugh at perfect humor, but at least it was real, and there was happiness there, and promise, however imperfect.

Wounds healed.

Time moved on.

Newspapers were running stories on the suspected *SF Killer*, profiles of Mike Ruffers. No one in the general population had a clue what the S and F stood for. There were wild speculations, of course, but that was about all.

And while the cogs of justice turned, Dale went to Quantico and interviewed with the FBI. He passed with flying colors and was offered a class date in mid-April of that year. Without hesitation, he accepted.

His time in Quantico went quickly. On the weekends, when he could, he flew from Dulles to Wilmington, where at last it seemed he was a welcomed guest at the Finnigan residence, Payton actually calling him by his first name. She had yet to call him son, however, but everything in its own time. No one spoke of that night. The Justice Department was piecing together their case, and from time to time someone or another would phone and ask to speak with either Gina or her parents. There was a strong possibility that all three would be subpoenaed to testify in court. The thought filled Gina with dread.

One weekend, a Saturday night in bed with her husband and in the very room where she had not so long ago hurled a book toward her mother, she awoke with a start. Immediately she went to the cradle and checked on her son. Clint was fast asleep. Thank God. She crawled back in bed. She picked up the phone. She listened and heard the dial tone. The digital clock was working fine. The room was warm with heat. She said, "Honey. Are you awake?"

Dale rolled over. "Yeah. Everything okay?"

"I don't know."

"We're safe. He's locked up."

"Are we safe?"

"Yeah."

"Is the door locked?"

"Yeah."

"The back door, too?"

"Yeah."

"Can you double-check?"

"Sure."

In June, with Dale assigned to the Washington, D.C. Field Office, the family of three rented a furnished bungalow in Old Town Alexandria. It wasn't much, but it was theirs. Gina had finished her nursing degree and would keep this in her hip pocket in the event she might need it later for work. For now, both she and Dale agreed that it would be best if she stayed home to take care of their son while they got a feel for their new city.

Special Agent Dale Riley's first assignment would be to testify at the trial of the suspected *SF Killer*. Accompanying him would be special agents Lionel McCarthy and Eric Scholl, the two agents originally assigned to the case well before Dale's subsequent involvement.

The day before the trial, on the seventeenth of July, the three flew into the Raleigh-Durham International Airport. They had a car waiting. They rented rooms at a nearby hotel. In the morning, they ate the hotel's buffet breakfast and did so in silence. They hopped in the car and drove to the courthouse. They entered courtroom four and assumed their seats.

And like all the others, they waited on the monster.

CHAPTER 49

A t precisely 9:00 A.M., the jury entered the courtroom. They came single file from the door up front, seven women and five men. All were nicely dressed. None smiled or made eye contact with those in the audience. They took their seats in the jury box where, quietly, they waited.

Next to enter the courtroom was Sheila Manning, the prosecuting attorney. What she lacked in beauty she more than made up for in smarts and determination. She had joined the Justice Department fresh out of law school, and over the years had earned a reputation as a shark. She had sent countless criminals to federal prison, and had a drawer full of death threats. For motivation, she oftentimes read these. They scared the shit out of her. Infuriated her. And in a sense, inspired her. In fact, she'd read one just this morning with coffee, written by the hand of another serial killer, promising that should he ever find his freedom, she'd be his next victim. These letters came in handy with parole boards. And not to lump them all together, she believed that Mike Ruffers was guilty of the crimes he had been charged with. So yeah, she read this letter with coffee, and intended to take it all out on Mike.

Trailing behind was a young male assistant. He appeared book-smart and wet behind the ears. Dale figured him a year or two out of law school, eager like the others to earn a reputation.

At the prosecutor's table, the two took their seats and pulled documents from their briefcases. They arranged these neatly. They whispered to one another. They waited.

No need for a drum roll. No need for a circus barker, or a king's fool. The announcement of the monster came with a chill. The back doors opened, and this chill swept in. A man near the back door would later swear to his parents that when the monster entered the courtroom, the temperature inside dropped fifteen, twenty degrees.

Heads turned.

No one blinked.

Here was the *SF Killer*, escorted by his attorney, Billy Roth.

Billy Roth was a publicity whore. Billy Roth had countless cheesy television commercials, and twice as many billboards. His signature look was a white, toothy grin and an ill-fitting suit, flipping a gangster wad of cash in his hands. Money you deserve, just dial this number. Have you been wronged? Well, dial this number. Government owe you money, or do you have an annuity? Well, then, just pick up the phone and dial this number. Apparently, Mike Ruffers had dialed the number. In person, Billy was shorter and fatter, a comical comb-over and suspiciously white teeth. His eyes were beady and calculating, and darted from person to person. He wore a fat gold watch and cufflinks, and carried an expensive leather briefcase. What he possessed in material assets, he lacked in character. He had no conscience, and he had no friends (Billy, however, would argue that he had tons of friends, millions of them, in fact, friends named Benjamin and Cleveland). His record of acquittals was on par with Sheila's record of convictions, and for this he earned five hundred bucks an hour, plus expenses. His current hard-luck client had given him fifty thousand dollars on retainer, every penny of which he had already spent. Mike was now paying with credit cards. Billy intended for his client to max these out, each and every one of them, and then apply for more. When the trial was over and when Mike was free with his life, Billy would kindly give him the name and number of the best bankruptcy attorney in town.

As for the monster, he wore a dark blue suit and a burgundy tie. He presented a wholesome grin, was handsome and confident. Gone were those murderous eyes that Dale had happened upon on the second-floor landing of the Finnigan residence. Gone was that rabid sneer and Satan's eyebrows. Gone were the scissors and the bible that the cops had discovered after they put Dale's ear in a baggie with ice.

From the cheap seats, a lady called out: "You murderer. I hope you rot in hell."

A sheriff came and escorted her quickly away.

Billy Roth and his client walked down the aisle and took their seats opposite Sheila Manning.

Billy shot her a smile, one that she didn't acknowledge.

She turned and focused on her paperwork.

Watching all this, Dale didn't like the vibe. Mike and his attorney appeared far too confident. Perhaps it was a ploy. Perhaps not. He remembered the court-martial, a flashback with him at the defense table, Captain Ruffers to his left. He remembered how Colonel Thoms had called him in that morning and had, more or less, promised him a promotion. All Dale had to do was throw his client to the wolves. Sadly, Dale had entertained this offer. In the end, however, he just couldn't do it. The hero had approached the lectern and all but accused Major McGuire of bombing that village that night. Major McGuire didn't appreciate this, hopped the railing, and tackled Dale to the floor. All hell broke loose. And throughout all of this, there sat Captain Michael J. Ruffers, amused, a sinister grin from ear to ear. No one saw this but Dale, and that's when he knew that Mike was guilty. That Mike had bombed the village that night. Despite this, however, Dale had made up his mind. He would not parlay incompetence for promotion. Guilty or innocent, Dale had a job to do, a mission, to provide the best defense possible. Assassinating Major Duncan McGuire was just the beginning. There was more, a silver bullet: testimony that Dale believed would secure an acquittal, a bullet that would kill the government's case.

When Judge Alberts reconvened the court-martial, and when Major Alex Snead rested on behalf of the U.S. Government, Dale called to the witness stand Corporal Jerry Sanford, United States Marine Corps.

Corporal Sanford was young and bone-thin, his face heavily painted with zits.

At the lectern, Captain Riley said, "Corporal Sanford, where were you on the night of September 11, 2009, the night my client, Captain Mike Ruffers, was accused of bombing the Sorubi village?"

"Well, sir, our unit was deployed to Afghanistan. That night, we were in the field, south of our headquarters, Bagram."

Captain Riley walked to the easel, where he had tacked up a map. "Corporal, do you recognize this area?"

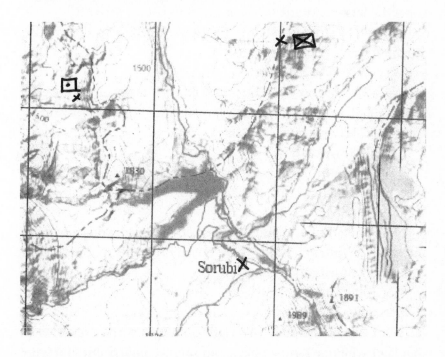

"Yes, sir. More or less, that was our area of responsibility."

"Can you please show the court where you were that night?"

The corporal approached the easel and pointed to the box with a dot in the center, the military symbol for field artillery. "We were right here, sir."

Back at the lectern, Captain Riley said, "And you're certain of this?"

"Yes, sir. We keep records of our locations."

"Corporal Sanford, how many artillery guns did you have in that position?"

"Six howitzers, sir."

"Can you please tell the court what happened that night?"

"Well, at first not much. It started off pretty quiet. But a little past midnight we got a radio call from the forward air controller, Striker. He's talking real fast, said he and his Marines were under heavy enemy fire. Said he needed artillery support."

"Okay. Now, before you go any farther, can you please show the court the lat/long of the target as given to you by Striker?"

Corporal Sanford pointed to the box with the X in the middle. "Right here, sir."

"Very well. Please continue."

"Well, we programmed our guns for the target. And then we waited for Striker to clear us hot. We can't fire until the forward air controller clears us hot."

"Did he clear you hot?"

"Yes, sir. About five minutes later, Striker radios and tells us to fire on the target. So that's what we did. All six guns. One volley. We fired."

"Now, according to your administrative record, you've been in the field of artillery for four years. Based on your experience, how would you classify the volley?"

"Not good, sir."

"And why's that?"

"Well, five of the guns was right on target. Striker testified to that later when he radioed back and said we nailed 'em. But what Striker didn't know, or anyone else outside our unit for that matter, is that we kind of screwed up."

"You screwed up?"

"Yes, sir. As a unit, we screwed up. See, one of our Marines, earlier that night, backed a 7-ton vehicle into the southernmost gun.

He'd been out in the field for nearly a month, and come midnight he and a few other Marines were given permission to go back to Bagram for a bit of a break. They have showers and decent chow at Bagram, so they were in a hurry. Later, he said he didn't realize what he'd done, that he'd backed into the gun and all."

"Didn't anyone notice this?"

"After the volley, yes, sir."

"Not before?"

"No, sir. It was dark."

"But the gunners programmed the lat/long of the target, didn't they? Surely someone must have noticed that the gun in question had been backed into?"

"No, sir. Prior to nightfall, we range the guns to fire on a specific point. When we get a target, we simply adjust off this point, and fire. We don't actually program the lat/long. Some howitzers have that capability, but not ours. The Marines on gun six simply adjusted their gun like everyone else, and on Striker's command they let her rip."

"And then what happened?"

"The gun nearly flipped over, sir. It's not supposed to do that. When the Marine backed into the gun, he dislodged the grounding spades. We're lucky no one got killed."

Dale let the irony pass. "Did anyone in your unit report this to higher headquarters?"

"No, sir. The gunny was afraid he'd get in trouble."

"So everyone kept quiet?"

"Yes, sir. The gunny said that the vast majority of terrain out there was unpopulated, and that the artillery round probably landed somewhere without doing any harm. He said it was not a big deal, sir."

"Corporal, why are you coming clean now?"

"I felt bad, sir. I wanted to say something, but I didn't know what to say, or whom to tell. When you called asking questions, I saw it as an opportunity to come clean. They've been calling me a traitor ever since, sir, the Marines in my unit."

"Don't you worry about them," said Dale. "You did the right thing. You may return to the witness box."

The corporal did as instructed.

Dale replaced him at the easel. He turned to the jury. "Ladies and gentlemen, do I need to point out the obvious? Look at this map. Look at the position of the target, its relationship to the artillery battery. And now look at the location of the Sorubi village. And there's something else you may wish to consider: the H-6 residue that the investigating officer discovered at this village is not only the primary compound in mark-82 bombs, but also the primary compound in the artillery shells that Corporal Sanford's unit employed in theater that night." Dale allowed the jury time to think. "I'm not saying that Echo battery willfully or inadvertently bombed the Sorubi village, nor do I honestly believe that Major Duncan McGuire bombed this village. All I'm saying, ladies and gentlemen, is that this was a war zone, a million different things going on, most of which were violent. What I'm saying is that no one can say with utmost certainty that my client bombed that village. We may never know who did this." He approached the jury, as close as custom allowed. "No one can prove that Captain Mike Ruffers, my client, bombed that village that night. No one." He stood and watched them think. He could see it in their eyes, the doubt. He turned to the bench. "That's all I have for this witness, your honor. Thanks."

Major Alex Snead did all that he could to discredit the testimony, to shoot holes in this theory, all to no avail. Dale Riley had introduced that silver bullet, and it was everything a silver bullet ought to be, deadly and accurate and taking everyone by surprise. The game, as they say, was over. The jury came back with an acquittal. Who knew then that the hell had just begun?

Special Agent Dale Riley sat inside courtroom four, eyeing the accused and his attorney. As confident as the two seemed, he wondered if Billy Roth had a silver bullet of his own. The thought scared the hell out of him. What if Mike walks . . . again? What then?

Are the doors locked?

Yeah.

The back door too?

Yeah.

Can you double-check?

Sure.

Last to enter was the Honorable Judge Barwick.

The bailiff called the courtroom to please rise.

Eric nudged Dale, leaned in, and whispered, "Time to rock and roll."

Yes. Time to rock and roll indeed.

CHAPTER 50

J udge Barwick was a thin and elderly gent with gaunt cheeks and a massive forehead. He moved with a rigid gait, his eyes cold and intimidating—eyes that had seen it all. He took his seat behind the bench and clacked his gavel. "Seats, everyone." He sipped from a coffee mug and then looked to the bailiff. "Let's begin, shall we?"

The bailiff read from the docket.

Judge Barwick addressed the accused and his attorney. "You and you, stand."

Billy Roth and his client stood.

Judge Barwick said, "You, Michael J. Ruffers, stand before this federal court accused of three counts of first-degree murder, and two counts of assault with intent. Do you understand these charges?"

Billy Roth said, "Yes, your honor. We do."

"Very well. Your plea?"

"Not guilty, your honor."

"It shall be noted. Take your seats." A quick shuffle of paperwork; another sip of coffee. "Ladies and gentlemen, this promises to be a rather emotional trial. This court demands proper decorum from all present, to include the attorneys from both corners. Any outbursts will be met with quick removal, and any inappropriate behavior from our attorneys will be met with even quicker contempt. There are to be no cameras or recording devices. If I hear a cell phone, you will be asked to leave immediately and will be hence banned." He looked from one attorney to the other. "Are there any further motions or findings?"

Both replied in the negative.

"Ms. Manning, are you prepared for opening statements?"

Sheila Manning stood. "I am, your honor."

"Very well. You have the floor."

In a dark pantsuit, she approached the members of the jury. She carried no notes. She knew exactly what it was that she was going to say, and she got right to it. "First off, let me thank you all for serving on this jury."

Billy Roth shot up. "Gratuitous, your honor."

Judge Barwick pointed his gavel at him. "Save it."

Having tested the waters, Billy resumed his seat. The judge would run a tight ship; one that Billy intended to sink, and to do so in very little time.

Sheila, undeterred, said, "Now, let me get straight to business. On the twelfth of February this year, in a hotel bathroom in Indianapolis, Indiana, a lady by the name of Eloise Saleem was heartlessly, cruelly, and viciously murdered. Later, you'll see the photographs. They won't be easy to look at. You'll see a stab wound to her chest, and you'll see two letters snipped into her abdomen, the letters S and F. There will be a bible covering the victim's face, with a passage circled in the victim's blood. Photographs will show a pair of bloody scissors that the killer left behind. We, the government of the United States of America, will show you records that prove that Eloise Saleem was a passenger aboard a flight from Akron, Ohio, to Indianapolis, Indiana, and that the pilot of this aircraft was the defendant, Mike Ruffers. We will show you hotel records that will prove that Mike Ruffers checked into the same hotel as Eloise a minute after she had checked in. We will introduce surveillance video of the defendant and the deceased, both standing at the registration desk, along with testimony from the clerk stating that Mike Ruffers asked for a room on the same floor as the victim, this so that he could watch her, follow her, and kill her. There were others. Again we will show you documented proof that the defendant flew victim number two from Newark to Charlotte International. Her name was Aalia Khalil. And yet again, the defendant stayed at the same hotel as she. He entered Aalia's room and killed her. It was a bloody, violent death. But here, unlike the previous crime scene, the defendant made a mistake. After murdering Aalia, the defendant was literally covered with her blood, some of which had spattered into his eyes. At the time, the defendant was wearing contact lenses. After he killed his victim, he went to the bathroom to clean up. He removed his latex gloves and then his contact lenses. He went to flush these lenses down the toilet. Only, one didn't flush. It stuck to the side of the toilet bowl, and was later discovered by federal agents investigating the crime scene. The contact lens was covered with Aalia's blood. Imprinted in the blood was the defendant's fingerprint." She pointed to the defendant. "His fingerprint. The match was perfect. Two days later he killed another in San Antonio, Texas. Her name was Linda Duckworth. Again, she was a passenger on the commercial airplane that the defendant piloted, traveling from New York to Texas. Make no mistake, the crime scene in San Antonio was his—a stab wound to Linda Duckworth's chest, the letters S and F snipped into her midsection, her face covered with a bible, a passage circled in her own blood. His M.O., to the T. His next stop was Wilmington, North Carolina, where his luck ran out. There, he invaded the home of another passenger aboard his aircraft. But in Wilmington he was stopped before he had a chance to kill again. On or near his person the police discovered a pair of scissors and a bible. Michael J. Ruffers was arrested and stands before you this day to face these charges and to be held accountable for his crimes. We the people will prove beyond a reasonable doubt that the defendant is guilty, that he heartlessly killed three women with intentions to kill others. The evidence is irrefutable. And we ask that you do your civic duty to your country and find him guilty of these charges. Thank you. Your honor, I'm finished." Sheila turned smartly on her heels and returned to her seat.

Judge Barwick said, "Okay. Mr. Roth, you're up."

Billy didn't approach the jury as Sheila had done. Instead he took the lectern. From here he could command not only the jury, but the entire courtroom. He had the presence to do so.

Dale watched him, impressed if not unsettled by Billy's confidence. Perhaps it was an act, this cocksure demeanor, or perhaps Billy had something up his sleeve. Perhaps Billy had a silver bullet of his own, testimony or evidence that would destroy the Justice Department's case against his client.

Did Billy have a silver bullet?

Did he?

Why, of course he did.

Locked and loaded, Billy stood at the lectern that fateful morning and pulled the trigger. He stunned the courtroom. He caught Sheila Manning completely off guard. He knocked the wind from Dale Riley; knocked the freshly minted special agent right on his ass.

Of course, Dale was outraged when he heard this, when the silver bullet caught him right between the eyes and blew his mind. In the spirit of Major Duncan McGuire, he felt like hopping the railing to pound the hell out of the scumbag defense attorney. He might have done so had Eric not been there to grab his wrist and hold him back.

Yes, slick Billy Roth took the lectern that fateful morning, and here is what he said.

CHAPTER 51

illy Roth shot his cuffs.

He seemed the type who might have then pulled out a comb to slick back his hair, but he didn't do that. Instead, he flashed a cheesy smile. He loved the lights, the attention, all of these wonderful people who had gathered here today to hear the truth, and they damn well would hear it.

He smiled at Sheila, said, "Well well, isn't that just a wonderful ole story? Wonderful!"

He then smiled to the audience. "Heck, if I didn't know any better, I'd throw the switch myself and watch my client die with an electric helmet on his head."

He then turned toward the jury. "But I do know better. See, I know the truth. Do you want to hear it? The truth?" A few in the jury nodded; most, however, did not. "There's no denying the deaths of those poor women. It's a terrible thing. Every night I pray for them and for their families. I hope that you all are doing the same."

Sheila fought the urge to roll her eyes; talk about gratuitous.

Billy continued: "And I pray that they catch the sonofabitch who killed those women, I do!" Billy pounded the lectern, and people jumped. "I swear to God Almighty that when they *do* catch the killer, I'll be there the day when he pays with his life. I'll come with popcorn and a soda pop and I will watch it like it's my favorite television show." He ran a hand through his hair, licked his lips. "Now. I can see how some of you have been looking at my client. You look at him, and you think he's guilty. Ms. Manning over there certainly thinks he's guilty. Hell, nearly every man, woman, and child in America thinks he's guilty. But he is not." Again he pounded the lectern. "You've all been fed a feast of lies, my friends, to include the Justice Department of these United States of America. Hell, Ms. Manning over there couldn't get enough of these lies, gorged herself on 'em."

Unamused, Sheila tossed her pen on the desk, folded her arms.

"But do you know what? That's okay. There is, in fact, the truth, and that's why we have all gathered here today: to hear it." He paused, drummed his fingers on the lectern. "Now. Allow me to introduce to you someone. Let me introduce to you another victim in this god-awful mess. Oh, he's a fine young man, he is. He's an honorable young man, and he has integrity. Faithfully he served his country in these United States Marine Corps, logged over one hundred combat sorties in both Afghanistan and Iraq. He put his neck on the line because he loves America, because he loves freedom, and because he loves each and every one of you." Pointing to the members in the jury, Billy said, "He would die for you, and for you, and for you, so that you can live a proper life and enjoy the freedoms that we all here today share. His name is Michael Joseph Ruffers, and like I said before, he's a fine young American. And all that he asks of you is that you listen to the testimony with an open mind and see the evidence that the Justice Department presents for what it is: misdirected and, yes, tainted. *Tainted!*" Billy looked to the audience, to special agents Dale Riley, Eric Scholl, and Lionel McCarthy. He smiled to all three of them, the silver bullet in its chamber. "So. Let's get to that truth, shall we? Now. While it is true that my client entered the home of Doctor Cole Finnigan on the second of March of this year, what is fabricated is that he went there to kill anyone. Ladies and gentlemen, he didn't go there with murderous hatred in his heart, he went there for love." He smiled, enjoyed the puzzled expressions in the audience, in the witness stand, on the mug of Sheila Manning. "That's right. He went there for love."

Dale stirred, this nonsense of love the last thing he had expected to hear. *For love? Really? Where in the hell is Billy going with this?*

Dale was about to find out.

Billy relished the moment. "You see, ladies and gentlemen, inside the house of Doctor Cole Finnigan was a young woman whom my client had been seeing for several years now. A married woman, I grant you, and therefore this is a relationship that could be classified as lascivious and immoral. Personally, when I first heard mention of this affair, I was sickened. Regardless, her name is Gina Riley, daughter of Doctor Cole Finnigan and then-estranged wife of FBI Special Agent Dale Riley. Yes. Michael Ruffers and Gina Riley were having an affair. There. I said it. The dirty truth is out there." When he saw Dale's reaction—the vacant eyes and dropped jaw—Billy tried not to smile. Next, denial would set in, and then anger. To watch the grieving process unfold on the face of a special agent was to Billy Roth deeply satisfying. "It's disgusting! I know. But certainly not so disgusting and so criminal as murder."

Eric grabbed Dale's wrist. He did so to calm him, to hold him back, to tacitly tell him to cool it. An outburst would discredit their later testimony, so relax and allow Billy his say. The truth will eventually come out.

"Now. This affair goes back several years, to when my client was an officer in the United States Marine Corps. Back then, it wasn't an affair, you see. The two were simply dating. The two were lovers. But there came a time, as with every relationship, when one or another wants more than something casual. Gina wanted a commitment. She gave Michael an ultimatum—marry me, or I'm gone. In the end, my client just couldn't commit. He wasn't ready. Sadly, the lovers parted ways. Who can say for certain when Gina Finnigan and Dale Riley began dating? A special agent now, back then Dale Riley was a captain in the Marine Corps, he and Michael Ruffers colleagues. Ultimately, Dale Riley did what Michael Ruffers couldn't: he committed to the beautiful Gina Finnigan, and the two were later married. Now. This is not to suggest that the passion between my client and Gina Riley was over. It wasn't. They continued to see one another. I know. Disgusting. They met in dirty hotel rooms and in the back seats of cars—sneaky, these sexual encounters, and terribly deceitful. Again, it is an act that I don't condone. And when at last Gina could no longer keep up with the charade, with the *farce* that was her marriage, she left her husband. It was over. She booked a flight from Charlotte to Wilmington. Her intentions were to live with her parents and finish school. Moreover, her intentions were to be with my client, Michael J. Ruffers. Knowing full well that my client would be piloting the jet to Wilmington, she bought a ticket on that very flight home. Now. When the aircraft landed in Wilmington, she invited Mike over to her parents' home. She told my client that her parents mustn't know of this affair, that he should go late at night, and that she'd let him in through the back door. Then they would sneak up to her room and have relations." Billy took a deep breath, watched the expressions—the bewilderment in the eyes of the jury, confusion in the audience, outrage on the face of Dale Riley, an outrage that would soon spread to his cohorts—special agents Scholl and McCarthy—for they were next in line for evisceration. "Dale Riley knew something was up. Whether he'd gotten his hands on an e-mail or eavesdropped on a phone conversation, he discovered that Gina and Michael were set to hook up in Wilmington. The day that Gina left him he got in his car, and through a terrible snowstorm he drove over three hundred miles from Charlotte to Wilmington. He sneaked in through the back door of the Finnigan house. The storm had taken out the lights. Doctor Finnigan heard something and confronted the home invader. Dale, outraged by all of this, indeed never caring much for Gina's parents in the first place, hit his own father in-law with his fists, knocking him out cold. On his way upstairs, he found a pair of scissors on a table and grabbed them. Full of hate and jealous rage, he entered Gina's bedroom and found the two lovers naked in bed."

Not a soul in the audience blinked, and hardly anyone breathed.

Billy continued: "Savagely, Special Agent Dale Riley attacked my client, stabbing him with the scissors. Of course my client fought back, and in the end both men lay bleeding, badly injured. Thank God that the matron of the house had the sense to phone the police department, who arrived just in time, as Special Agent Riley pointed a loaded gun at the head of my client. The police saved my client's life that night, and for that we are forever grateful." Billy took a dramatic pause, waited until he could hear a pin drop. "Here, now, is where it gets interesting."

CHAPTER 52

Billy Roth stood at the lectern, smiling beneath the surface, his eyes dancing with delight. He gave himself plenty of time before moving on to chapter two, for chapter one had been such a delight.

In the audience, Dale couldn't believe his ears. To suggest that Gina and Mike were having an affair was nothing short of despicable. It felt as if someone had dumped acid on him, his skin boiling hot. He struggled to remember that night. It wasn't always easy. He'd lost a lot of blood, had suffered severe trauma, and so no matter how many times he relived it, there were always missing pieces. Missing pieces like Dale sneaking in through the back door and punching Cole's lights out. That hadn't happened, of course, but it certainly seemed believable. Hell, Billy's entire theory seemed believable, that after knocking out Cole, Dale grabbed a pair of scissors and went upstairs. He found the lovers in bed, and isn't that why Mike was naked when the cops arrived? Because an outraged husband had dragged him from the arms of his wife, roughed him up, threw him down the stairs? And isn't that why Gina came with a flashlight and a pistol, yelling at Dale to leave her lover alone? Nonsense, of course, as the two had never been lovers. Ever. And yet . . . sitting here in the audience, listening to this outlandish theory, Dale remembered the interaction at the airport. Somehow Mike knew her name, and she wouldn't even look at him. Avoided him at all costs. Was terribly rude to a stranger. Only, was he a stranger? Was he? Or did they know one another? And had she, in fact, intentionally booked her flight on the jet that he would be piloting? Is that why she gave Dale such short notice that night, the night when she told her husband that she was going home, without him? And did she then invite Mike over? Sneak him in through the back door so that her parents wouldn't know?

Stop it, Dale said to himself. *None of that happened! I didn't intercept some e-mail or overhear some conversation, and I certainly didn't drive through a snowstorm to kill Mike Ruffers.*

Well, actually, he did drive through a snowstorm to kill Mike Ruffers, didn't he? He drove through one badass snowstorm to do just that. But he didn't do it because Mike was screwing Gina. He did it because Mike said Semper Fidelis, remember, and because all the pieces fit. He entered through the back door of the Finnigan house because Roy Woodall had phoned and had asked Dale to pull over. *Pull over, Mr. Riley, because what I have to tell you is gonna be a doozy.*

Okay. Fine. Let's all pretend for one moment that Billy is telling the truth. Fine. Dale knocked Cole's lights out, fine. Grabbed scissors and attacked Mike, who'd been invited over and was now screwing Gina. Whatever, but fine. How does any of this explain the bloody contact lens the feds found with Mike's fingerprint on it, discovered at an entirely different crime scene? Explain that one, Billy Roth. What'cha got?

And Billy would happily oblige.

It was time for chapter two, time for things to get *interesting.*

Billy said, "Now. Let me tell you all a little bit about Special Agent Dale Riley. For nearly ten years he was a JAG attorney in the United States Marine Corps. Most military officers in this position would put in another ten and call it a career, retire with a lifetime pension. Captain Dale Riley was no different, wished to retire like everyone else. Only, well, shucks, he just didn't have the goods, did he, wasn't that consummate Marine." Slowly, he walked back to his desk, grabbed a slip of paper, and waved this in the air on his way back to the lectern. "Ladies and gentlemen of the jury, I have here a copy of his very last fitness report, signed by his boss, Colonel Thoms. It's an ugly document that no professional would want on their permanent record. It speaks of disloyalty and a lack of good judgment. It's so bad, in fact, that Captain Dale Riley was passed over for promotion to major and unceremoniously forced to resign his commission. Disgraced, he left the Corps. He left nearly ten years of service. He left a steady paycheck, and he left good friends, one of whom goes by the name of Eric Scholl, Lieutenant Colonel Eric Scholl, ten years Dale's senior. The two were friends back then, and remain friends to this day. Lieutenant Colonel Eric Scholl did what Dale couldn't: he retired after twenty years of military service and took another government post, this one with the Federal Bureau of Investigation, where he is currently employed as a field agent." Drumming his fingers on the lectern, he smiled to the jury. "Guess where Dale Riley is currently employed? That's right: with the F-B-and-I. See, Eric, his good buddy, helped Dale get a job there, and a week or so ago Dale Riley graduated from the Academy. They are with us here today, ladies and gentlemen. We are blessed with their company, the company of special agents Eric Scholl and Dale Riley, accompanied by a much senior agent by the name of Lionel McCarthy. They are here with us today because before Dale Riley landed a gig with the FBI, Lionel McCarthy and Eric Scholl had been assigned to investigate the so-called *SF Killer*. It is my belief that one night over beers, Eric informed Dale of the specifics of this case. On or about this time is when a distraught Dale Riley, in turn, informed Eric of the affair that he had uncovered between his wife and Michael Ruffers. So yeah, there's a killer out there carving S and F into the bellies of his victims. Nice, but Dale didn't give a shit about that. Dale, you see, wanted nothing more than revenge. He was irate. He was ashamed. He wanted my client to pay. So, after commiserating, the best friends schemed. An idea was formulated, one that would promote a career and satiate the other's need for revenge. What if they could somehow pin these horrific killings on Mike Ruffers? How beautiful would that be, to frame the man who'd been having an affair with Dale's wife?"

To make this next part believable, Billy had filed a pretrial motion, granted by Judge Barwick. In light of Mike's acquittal of the bombing of the Sorubi village, there was to be no mention of this in court. Michael Joseph Ruffers had been found innocent of those charges. As such, any mention of this event might jeopardize Mr. Ruffers's right to a fair trial. With the granting of this motion, Billy's next point would be nearly impossible for Sheila to refute.

Billy said, "So what did Dale Riley, the cuckold husband, do? He fished through his wife's collectables and found a photograph that my client had given to Gina several years earlier. It was a photograph Mike had snapped of Gina during a trip the lovers had taken to western North Carolina, Gina smiling as they ascended to the top of Grandfather Mountain. On this photograph were Mike's fingerprints, perfectly preserved. Special Agent Eric Scholl then used his resources to transfer a print to a contact lens. At the crime scene in Charlotte he dipped this contact lens in the pool of the victim's blood and planted it in the toilet." Although Billy had been addressing the entire courtroom, now he focused on the jury. "Guess who discovered the key piece of physical evidence that the Justice Department is hinging nearly their entire case on? Guess who found this bloody contact lens with my client's fingerprint on it? That's right. Dale's bestest buddy in the whole wide world: Special Agent Eric Scholl of the FBI. How convenient."

Jesus. Dale could not believe what he was hearing, and judging by Eric's reaction, neither could he. They sat side by side in the first row of benches. They sat in cahoots. That's how it felt. Like the two were in cahoots. Like they had plotted and schemed to frame Mike Ruffers, and it must be true because it certainly felt like everyone believed it. There were no cries of disgust or dismissive waves of hands in the air. No one in the jury rolled their eyes in disbelief. The goddamn story seemed believable: sensational, yes, but believable just the same. Sheila glanced over her shoulder, looked at them, her eyes as wide as saucers. *Is any of this true?*

Christ. Even Sheila believes it.

Billy wrapped it up with this: "Ladies and gentlemen, my client was framed. Mike Ruffers was framed by Special Agent Eric Scholl, and attacked by Special Agent Dale Riley. That is the God's honest truth. And I ask Ms. Manning, as she sits before us this day, in light of these truths, to drop the charges against my client and pursue criminal charges against special agents Eric Scholl and Dale Riley. It's gonna be a tough pill for her to swallow, I know. But I pray that after the dust settles, after she has some time to think, she will realize that she'd been lied to, this feast of lies courtesy of the FBI. Your honor, thank you. Members of the jury, thank you very much. That is all."

CHAPTER 53

The courtroom sat in silence, even the seasoned old man behind the bench, Judge Barwick. After all, they had boarded a locomotive for a destination called *Guilty-On-All-Counts*. On the way there they expected to see pastures named *Terrible Misdeeds* and landscapes called *Murder*. The locomotive switched tracks, however, and here they found themselves in fields called *Collusion* and *Corruption*, the destination unknown. Some found this exciting and rather adventuresome, although many others were uncomfortable if not somewhat frightened.

The father of Aalia Khalil didn't know what to think. What he felt was that this wasn't right, that the defense attorney had led them astray down the wrong track. When the defendant first entered the courtroom, when the temperature dropped a good fifteen, twenty degrees, Mr. Khalil had looked the accused in the eyes. Mahdi knew in an instant that this was the man who had killed his only daughter. Don't ask him how he knew this, he just knew.

When Billy left the lectern, quietly Mahdi said, "Lies. It is all lies."

The man sitting next to him leaned in. "What's that, fella?"

"Lies. He is lying." This time he said it louder, and heads were turning.

Mahdi stood and pointed a finger. "Lies. You are a liar."

Judge Barwick clacked his gavel. "Sir. You are to leave this courtroom right this second."

"But he is lying, your honor." To Billy: "You are a liar, and your client is a murderer."

Judge Barwick ordered his bailiff into action.

Mahdi didn't fight it, the bailiff grabbing him by his arm, escorting him out. He had the anger, sure, but he just didn't have the strength. The tragic murder of his only daughter had stripped him of his moxie. Leaving the courtroom, he felt shame, and defeat. He believed that there would be no justice. On his way out the door he covered his face, and he cried.

Judge Barwick clacked his gavel. "Let's take a recess. Court will reconvene in thirty minutes." He looked at his wristwatch. "Let's make it forty-five. Back in your seats at 10:30."

The bailiff called the courtroom to order.

Judge Barwick vacated the bench.

In the audience, Dale excused his way out.

Eric called out after him, "Dale. Wait up."

But Dale didn't wait up. Quickly he moved through the courtroom, the courthouse, and then down the stairs to the lobby. He bolted outside.

The temperature was well into the eighties, would top ninety-five by noon.

Already sweating, he hopped down the stairs to the sidewalk, where he whipped out his cell phone. Walking briskly, traffic zipping by, he hit the speed dial for home.

Gina picked up. "Hello?"

He turned a corner, traffic coming and going, a few pedestrians along the way. "Gina?"

"Who else?"

"Yeah." He jaywalked the street.

She said, "So how's it going?"

Here on the other side, the sidewalk was shaded. "Oh, it's going."

"Is everything all right? You sound funny."

"Gina?"

"Yes?"

He found a lonely spot alongside a five-story building and stopped. "The, uh, the defense attorney, he said some pretty incredible things." A delivery truck sped by, spending exhaust. Dale turned to face the building, plugged his other ear.

A long pause, and then quietly she said, "Oh?"

"Gina?" He pressed his forehead against the stucco.

"Yeah?"

Her voice wavered, and he sensed that she might be crying.

"Did anything ever happen between you and Mike Ruffers?"

Yes, she was crying.

Dale looked up.

He didn't care that the sky was blue and that the day was otherwise beautiful.

Her tears had answered the question, and he wanted to smash his forehead against the building. He wanted to scream. The turmoil inside was sickening, and violent. He wanted to kill someone. He couldn't believe that he hadn't pulled the trigger that night. What a fuckup. He felt sadness and rage. In a controlled yet angry voice, he repeated himself: "Did anything ever happen between you and Mike Ruffers?"

She didn't answer. She only sobbed.

"When?" Dale said. "WHEN?" God, he should have known. Their interaction at the airport, the fact that he knew her name, and the way she had looked at him. How she had dismissed herself and nearly ran toward the windows. He should have known. What a fucking *idiot!*

"Dale?"

"WHEN, GODDAMNIT?"

"I'm s-s-s-o sorry."

"That night? Were you fucking him that night?"

She sniffed. "What?" She sounded confused.

"They said that you were with him that night. That you were fucking him that night. WERE YOU?"

"My God, no!"

"When, Gina? Jesus!" And now he too was crying. He felt betrayed, and alone in the world.

"It was . . . it was *years* ago. It was a stupid mistake. You and I, we got in a fight. I got drunk. My God. I'm sorry. I never thought—"

"WHEN?"

"Stop yelling at me."

"Stop yelling? Are you fucking serious? WHEN, GODDAMNIT? I NEED TO KNOW WHEN THIS FUCKING HAPPENED!" The people driving by were looking his way. He hardly cared.

"I don't remember."

In a seething voice, he said, "Do you have any idea what this means? Do you? They're saying that you invited him over that night. They're saying that you two were together that night, and that you've been together for years."

"Oh, my God. That's a lie."

A kaleidoscope of emotions, he turned again to rage. "How many times, Gina?"

"What?"

"You said you fucked him. How many times?"

"Just that once. I swear. I don't even remember it. It was stupid."

"WHEN?"

"It was December 2010. Okay. It was around Christmastime. Dale, you had just found out that they were going to kick you out of the Marine Corps. You were miserable. You were taking it out on me. We got into a fight."

So it was true. Jesus, it was true. They had slept together, fucking true. With the weight of the world on his shoulders, his legs nearly went out from under him. He sobbed. "You fucking cheated on me. You fucking bitch!" Even though they had married in June of 2011, they'd been exclusive for a year prior. December 2010 would have been a part of that year of exclusivity.

December 2010: as if that month hadn't been bad enough. Now this. That first week in December he'd gotten a letter from Headquarters Marine Corps. Surprise, surprise, he'd been passed over for promotion to major. His boss, Colonel Thoms, had written that damning fitness report, and even though Dale had contested it, still, it stuck. The fitness report stuck, and the promotion board had taken a pass. His career was over.

December 2010: a nightmare of thirty-one days.

December 2010.

"Wait. Did you say December of 2010?"

"I'm so sorry. You have no idea."

Dale did the math. "ARE YOU SURE?"

"Stop yelling. Please."

"ARE YOU FUCKING SURE, GODDAMNIT?"

"Yes." And because the thought had always lingered, she added: "Oh my God, Dale. I know what you're thinking. And no. The answer is no."

"Do you know what I'm thinking, Gina?"

"The answer is no, Dale. NO!"

"Do you know what I'm thinking? Do you? FUCKING DO *YOU?*"

CHAPTER 54

How many miles he walked that day, he'll never remember. He walked while his cell phone vibrated madly in his pocket. He walked in front of cars that honked angrily. In a jacket and tie he walked as the sun rolled west and then winked and disappeared. He walked until his legs were all gone and his tears were all gone, and then he walked another mile.

He sat on the corner of Somewhere and Something, and at last answered his cell phone. He didn't say hello, simply looked up at the street sign and informed the caller of his location. He hung up and leaned against the metal post that held the sign. At the very least, he was lucky to have found himself in a better part of town. Another mile east and they'd be asking for his wallet and his watch, and that fancy new cell phone that came as a perk with his new job.

Thirty minutes later, Eric rolled up in a black sedan. He reached over and opened the passenger's side door. "Get in."

Dale picked himself up and hopped in.

"Lionel is back at the hotel. He thought it might be best if I came alone. That you might be more comfortable, you know?"

Dale didn't answer, watched the lights flash by out the window.

"There's a steakhouse I passed on the way here. You hungry?"

Dale remained silent.

"Well, I'm starving."

In silence Eric drove to the steakhouse. In the parking lot he went around to the other side and opened the door. "Get out. Yeah. I know. It was a shitty day. Believe me, I know. But it's time to get your ass out of this car and join me for dinner. C'mon."

Reluctantly, Dale slumped out.

He followed Eric inside, where the smell of grilled meat did nothing to spark his appetite. It should have, as he hadn't eaten anything since breakfast. Mostly, however, he just felt sick to his stomach.

The hostess showed them to a table.

There, snapping a napkin to his lap, Eric said, "Jesus, man, you look like shit. Go to the bathroom and clean yourself up, would ya? And for the love of God, snap the fuck out of it."

Dale stood. He looked around dumbly.

Eric pointed toward the sign. "The bathroom is that way."

When Dale returned, there was a drink on the table waiting for him.

Eric said, "I got you a double rum and coke. Cheers."

Dale made a half-hearted gesture, drank up, and winced. It was good. Strong. He drank some more.

The waiter came and took their orders. Eric went with the ribeye, rare, and garlic-mashed potatoes. Dale went with a shrug.

Eric said, "Bring this fine gentleman the same. Thanks."

With the waiter away, Eric leaned in. "Jesus, man. You're fucking pathetic. You know that?"

Dale couldn't argue. He finished his drink. "I spoke with Gina."

"Figured as much. And?"

"It isn't good."

"What did she say?"

"What do you think she said?"

"No clue, buddy. Why don't you tell me?"

"She said she slept with him, okay?"

Eric nodded, leaned back, and exhaled. "Shit. So she slept with him, huh?"

A bit defensively, Dale said, "She said it happened years ago, okay, and that it only happened once." Slowly, Dale was coming back into himself.

Eric drank, set down his glass. "Well, that sucks, doesn't it?"

Dale flagged the waiter, pointed to his glass for another. "Yeah. Sucks."

"Sheila is not going to like hearing this. She's been on my ass all day. She wants to speak with you as soon as possible."

"I know. She's been calling my cell nonstop."

The waiter came with another double rum and coke, and Dale went straight to work.

"Go easy," said Eric.

When Dale set down the glass, it was nearly empty. "It sure went to hell, didn't it?"

"In a handbasket."

"And that part about you planting the bloody contact lens? Holy shit, man!"

"Yeah. Holy shit is right."

Dale took a deep breath, sighed. "You want to know the worst thing about all of this?"

"It gets worse?"

"She slept with Mike in December of 2010."

"Yeah? Okay."

"Clint was born in August of 2011."

"Clint?"

"My son."

"Oh. But what does that have to—" Eric stopped in mid-sentence. His face flushed with embarrassment. He shook his head. "No way."

Dale nodded and finished his second drink.

Eric, uneasy with this, glancing at the décor, the porcelain roosters and washboards, the horseshoes, said, "Well, get a paternity test."

Dale flagged the waiter for drink number three. "A paternity test. Right."

"What's wrong with that?"

"I love her. After all the shit we've been through, I love her now more than ever. And I love my son just as much. I'm not sure what difference a paternity test would make. Or that it might make all the difference in the world. I just don't know."

Eric, himself a husband and father, said, "Yeah. I guess you're right, huh?"

Dale shook his head. "Am I right? Who the fuck knows?"

"So now what?"

Dale looked around. He leaned in. His eyes were tired and bloodshot, dark bags underneath. However, there was also strength, determination. "I've been walking around all day, hurting like a sonofabitch from all of this, but I've also been thinking. And when it hit me, well, that's when I sat down and answered your call."

"When what hit you?"

"I think I have an idea how best to move forward."

Eric raised his eyebrows. "Yeah?"

"Yeah. So when we're done here, why don't we go and have that sit-down with Sheila?"

"And?"

"We'll listen to her rant and rave about how we fucked the case for her, and then I'll ask her for a favor."

"A favor?"

"And if her reputation is what we've heard it is, it's a favor she'll be more than willing to grant."

"What's this favor?"

"It's more of a solution to our current problem, really."

"Okay. Now I'm confused. What current problem are we talking about?"

"Eric. If this trial continues in this direction, Mike is a free man. We know he's guilty, but that jury . . . I think they actually believed Billy's bullshit today. We can't have that. It's time to mix things up a bit."

"And you have what you believe is a solution as to how we can change the direction of the trial. Is that right?"

Dale smiled. It was an exhausted smile punctuated with genuinely gleeful eyes. "I have something that would blow this fucking trial out of the water."

"What is it?"

The waiter arrived with Dale's third drink.

Dale raised his glass. "To blowing this trial out of the fucking water, my friend."

"Are you going to tell me what in the hell you're talking about?"

Dale smiled, and drank heartedly.

CHAPTER 55

Wednesday afternoon.

Two armed soldiers stood sentry by the main doors, another by the west-facing windows.

The room in which these soldiers were occupied was well lit with sunlight and fluorescent lighting overhead.

The walls were clean and painted yellow, the floor with white tile.

On the weekends, the twenty or so tables would seat family and friends. Today, however, the place was nearly empty.

Two feds sat at one of the tables, wearing suits and patiently waiting.

In time, two additional guards escorted the prisoner inside.

The prisoner wore handcuffs and a blue jumpsuit, his head clean-shaven, as well as his face, on his left outer forearm a noticeable, amateurish, prison tattoo.

As the prisoner neared the table, the two suits stood.

Dale couldn't help but notice the prison tattoo—a black circle divided into fours, with each space numbered one through four. The number three had been X'ed out. That would be Alex Snead, loving husband, caring father, god-fearing Baptist. Having read the hit list found in the pocket of Sean Fitzsimmons, Dale knew that he was number two, that Eric was number four, and that Mike Ruffers, the reason why they were here, was number one.

The guards led the prisoner over and then assumed a post near the vending machines. There, they rocked on their heels with the others.

Dale cleared his throat. "Good to see you, sir. How have you been?"

The prisoner lifted his hands, the shackles on his wrists clanking. "I'm inside a federal prison, Mr. Riley. Suffice it to say that I've seen some better days."

Better days like when Colonel Christopher Thoms was a God at Marine Corps Air Station, Cherry Point. Better days when he lorded over his JAG Corps and dined with general officers. When young men saluted him and offered a wide berth. When his opinion mattered, his authority well respected. Yes, he'd seen better days indeed.

In Dale's opinion, the colonel's fall from grace began with a misguided sense of invincibility. The colonel had a God complex. For years, if not decades, Colonel Thoms had given orders, and the men in his command obeyed these orders without question. Those who failed to do so lost their jobs and were transferred. The most serious offenders—Marines like Dale Riley—had their characters smeared by damning fitness reports, which would ultimately destroy any chance they might have for promotion.

But those better days were over now, weren't they, the last when for the second time that day the colonel summoned Dale inside his office. The Ruffers Court-Martial was under way. Dale had wrapped up the day's session with one hell of a cross-examination of Major Duncan McGuire. After the melee, when Dale returned to his desk where Mike sat with those cold, reptilian eyes of his, the colonel came up and handed Dale a note. It read: *My office, asap!* Christ! Dale was not in the mood for this. He'd just been physically assaulted by the witness, and based upon the conversation he'd had with Colonel Thoms earlier that morning—the fact that the colonel wanted Dale to throw his client to the wolves—Dale knew, more or less, that he was in for another whooping, albeit one of the verbal variety. No, he wasn't in the mood. He crumpled up the note and tossed it aside.

Judge Alberts adjourned court for the day, and slowly the court-room emptied.

The MPs came and took Mike away.

Dale set his briefcase on the desk and popped the lid. He hesitated, thought *what the hell*, and then pulled out an item. Holding this, he weighed his options. He felt trapped. Helpless, and cornered. In a sense, he believed that this would be his only way out. So he stuffed the item in the front pocket of his slacks, closed his briefcase, and exited the courtroom.

The colonel's office was in the same building and up on the second floor.

Dale climbed the stairs.

He was nervous, and still shaken from Major McGuire's blows and that bite to his shoulder.

He hated the fact that he'd been put in this position. Hated it. Regardless, it was time to fight back.

The colonel's secretary let him in.

Sitting behind his desk, smelling a Cuban cigar, Colonel Thoms said, "That was a very nice cross-examination of Major McGuire. Very impressive." The colonel's tone was sarcastic.

Dale stopped in front of the colonel's desk, stood at the position of attention, and answered in the same sarcastic tone: "Thank you, sir."

The colonel eyed him meanly, tossed the Cuban on the desk, and then rested his forearms there. "You're gonna have a nice shiner in the morning."

Indeed, come morning, Dale's left eye would be righteously black and royally blue. Dale shrugged. The bite to his shoulder hurt worse.

The colonel said, "Too bad he didn't fucking kill you."

Dale didn't answer.

Colonel Thoms said, "What in the hell did we talk about this morning?"

"We didn't talk about much, sir. You talked."

"Are you fucking with me, Captain Riley?"

"No, sir."

"Your client is guilty, and we agreed that it would be in everyone's best interests for you to go into that courtroom and allow the prosecuting attorney to do his job with little if any interference. We agreed to that."

"I'm not so sure that we did, sir."

The colonel shot up. He pointed a finger. "Fuck you! We agreed."

"No, sir. We did not."

Cocking his head, Colonel Thoms said, "Don't you get it? Are you that thick? Your client is guilty. *Guilty!* He bombed that village that night. He killed those people. He killed those *Marines!* And he should pay with . . . his . . . LIFE!" The colonel slammed his fist atop the desk. The cigar jumped, came to rest on top of the MacBook Pro.

Dale, however, didn't jump, stood firm at the position of attention.

The colonel lowered his voice. "You unfuck this. Do you understand me? You figure out a way for the jury to see what everyone else already knows. You got that, hotshot?"

"No, sir. I don't got that."

The colonel came from behind his desk. "What?"

Dale didn't look at him, kept his eyes straight ahead. "I don't got that, sir. I cannot do that. My client is entitled to a competent defense. I'm his attorney. And I will do my job to the best of my abilities."

Colonel Thoms came nose to nose with him, towered over him, had him by at least fifty pounds. "Oh, you naïve little fuck. This isn't about the law. This is about right and wrong. Don't tell me that you're so vapid that you don't know the goddamn difference."

"I do know the difference, sir. But right or wrong is for the jury to decide. They have their job to do"—at last Dale looked him in the eye—"and I have mine."

"You had."

"Excuse me?"

"You had a job to do. Past tense. You're fired, Marine. You're off this case."

"You can't do that. You don't have the authority to do that."

Pointing a finger a centimeter shy of Dale's eye, he said, "I'm your fucking boss. I have the authority to mop the goddamn floor with your face if I choose to do so. You got me, Marine?" He then pointed toward the door. "Now, you go and tell Judge Alberts that you're sick and that you will no longer be representing Captain Ruffers at his court-martial. Tell him that because you just got your ass beat by Major McGuire, you can no longer continue. Tell him that you're traumatized. Tell him that you're fucking brain-dead. Tell him whatever the fuck you want to tell him so long as come tomorrow morning you aren't sitting to the right of that criminal trying to get his ass back out there so that he can kill again."

Dale shook his head, his eyes unflinching. "I can't do that."

"You can do that, and you will do that!"

Shaking his head, Dale said, "I'm sorry, sir. I can't." He turned to leave, stopped, turned back around. "Allow me to continue. As his lawyer. Let me do my job. I'm giving you another chance."

The colonel laughed. "Another chance? You're giving *me* another chance? Are you out of your fucking mind?"

"Allow me to do my job, sir. That's all I'm asking here."

"Your job, huh?"

"Yes, sir."

Nodding his head, walking toward him, Colonel Thoms said, "Yeah. Sure. Your job. You bet. Come tomorrow morning, you are hereby reassigned to eating my shit! Come with a fork or a spoon, you fuck. Come with a goddamn appetite!"

"I'm sorry that it had to come down to this, sir. I really am." Dale turned and walked away.

Colonel Thoms called after him, "You get your ass back here; you hear me?"

Dale, however, kept walking, up to the fourth floor, to the office of Judge Alberts.

In the anteroom, a legal clerk looked up from her paperwork. "May I help you, sir?"

"I need to speak with Judge Alberts. Is he in?"

"Yes, sir. He is. Can I tell him what this is about?"

"It's just . . . tell him it's about the Ruffers trial."

"Okay. Wait right here, sir. I'll see if he has a moment." She popped into the judge's office. When she returned, she held the door open for him. "The judge will see you, sir."

"Thanks."

Dale entered.

Judge Alberts was seated behind a simple, clean desk, the top dusted lightly with paperwork. The rest of the office was neatly decorated with photographs and books and personal items.

Judge Alberts had his jacket off, was wearing a khaki shirt and tie. He pushed away from his desk, offered a sympathetic nod. "You feeling okay, young Marine?"

"Yes, sir."

"That was a mighty nasty brawl, huh?" Judge Alberts offered a sympathetic chuckle.

"Yes, sir."

"Normally, I rather enjoy a good brawl. Just not in my courtroom, and with one of my lawyers."

Dale tried to smile.

Judge Alberts said, "So. I'm kind of busy here, Marine. I was in the middle of drafting up an order assigning counsel to conduct a preliminary inquiry into Major McGuire's actions inside my courtroom. So what is it? Why are you here?"

Why was he here? Already, Dale was having second thoughts. Perhaps he should have given himself some time to cool off. Sadly, however, he believed that time was not on his side. That with time, Colonel Thoms would outmaneuver him, legally. He wasn't sure how, and this is what scared him. Colonel Thoms could be your best friend, and your worst enemy.

"Captain Riley, I haven't all day."

Later, Dale would regret his next move. Later, he would wonder if there might have been another way. If there was, it never occurred to him. The military handles matters via the chain of command, Dale's first course of action to report a willful violation of the UCMJ to Colonel Thoms, the very man who had willfully violated the code, which had set the two at odds. Should that fail, his next course of action would be to request mast, a lengthy affair wherein Dale submits his concerns to his boss's boss, General Warren. Colonel Thoms and General Warren were drinking buddies, played golf together on weekends, the two thick as thieves. Barring that, Dale could write his congressman, his senator, and then wait and see if they expressed any interest. Typically, however, a congressional inquiry refers the matter back to square one. In Dale's case, Colonel Thoms. Standing before Judge Alberts, he reached inside the front pocket of his slacks and pulled out the tape recorder. He set it on the judge's desk and hit PLAY.

The two listened to the recent conversation, the quality of the recording remarkably good.

When it was over, Judge Alberts leaned back and shook his head. "I take it that that was a conversation between you and Colonel Thoms?"

"Yes, sir."

"And when did this conversation take place?"

"Just now, sir."

Judge Alberts sighed. "This is one hell of a can of worms, Captain Riley."

"Yes, sir."

Confined by law, Judge Alberts said, "First, that tape recorder belongs to me."

"I figured as much, sir."

"Realize that there will be an Article 32 hearing."

"Yes, sir."

"And that you will be called to testify against your boss."

"I understand all of that, sir."

"He's a powerful man, with friends in high places."

"I know."

"You really put your neck on the line here, son."

Still having doubts, Dale said, "Do you think I did the right thing?"

Judge Alberts thought for a moment. "Well, what do you think?"

"Honestly, I don't know. What would you have done? If you were getting strong-armed into doing something that was not only illegal, but immoral?"

Judge Alberts spread his hands. "We do what we think is right at the time." He studied Dale with intelligent, avuncular eyes. "The law can be elusive, and morality is like religion. Both can get rather tricky. There are times when even the best of us justify amoral acts on the basis of the very morality we claim to uphold. Laws are mere impressions, snapshots of a society's current belief of what is and what is not moral and ethical. Thus, laws change and evolve over time."

It was a professor's answer, and it cleared up nothing.

Dale said, "So, do you think I did the right thing?"

"Only you can answer that question. Certainly, Colonel Thoms broke the law. Command influence of an ongoing court-martial is a crime. And, now that I'm aware of this crime, I am bound by my position, and by the law." He snatched the tape recorder. "Now, if you'll excuse me, I have a lot of work to do."

"Yes, sir. Thank you."

As Dale reached for the doorknob, Judge Alberts said, "Oh. And just to be clear: you are not dismissed as counsel for the defense. The Ruffers Court-Martial will reconvene tomorrow morning, 0900 hours sharp. Get a good night's rest, and we'll see you in the morning."

Dale nodded and exited the office.

After all was said and done, Colonel Thoms was found guilty of the crimes and sentenced to four years at Leavenworth Federal Prison, eligible for parole in two. Before the colonel went away, he sent that damning fitness report to Headquarters. He phoned his friends in high places. The traitor's career was over. Dale's own fall from grace had just begun.

Sitting inside the visitation room, shackled, Colonel Thoms said, "I've been reading the newspapers. They have those here, you know?"

"Yeah?" Dale said. "And?"

"Mike Ruffers. He killed those girls, didn't he? He did it. Their blood is on your hands, Mr. Riley. You set him free, at the court-martial. He should have hanged for his crimes in Afghanistan, but no, you did your job, right? So I'm wondering, Mr. Riley, how do you sleep at night?"

Not so well, he thought, thinking of the conversation he'd had with Gina, the one about checking the doors, both front and back. "I've made mistakes in life, sir. No doubt about it. I am, however, trying my best to be a better man."

Colonel Thoms clapped, twice. "I'm sure that the family of those who have lost their loved ones would be happy to hear you say that, about you trying your best to be a better man."

Dale didn't take the bait. "Sir. We've come here today to make you an offer."

"Oh? And on whose authority are you inclined to make offers, Mr. Riley?"

Both Dale and Eric pulled out their cred packs.

Dale said, "The authority of the United States Government."

Colonel Thoms studied these, as the names of the special agents associated with the *SF Killer* had yet to reach the newspapers. "The FBI. I'm surprised. I didn't think that the FBI employed men of such low moral fiber."

Again, neither agent took the bait.

They pocketed their cred packs.

Dale crossed his legs. Yes, the colonel was still full of piss and vinegar. This was good. Soon, Dale would pitch the offer; drop the bomb, so to speak. First, however, he had to prep the battlefield.

CHAPTER 56

Special Agent Dale Riley pulled a photocopy from the breast pocket of his jacket. He set this on the table. "We found this on the dead body of an ex-con named Sean Fitzsimmons."

Colonel Thoms picked up the photocopy. "Is that so?"

"Sean was shot and killed inside my parents' living room."

Having studied the photocopy, Colonel Thoms set it aside. "And what does any of this have to do with me?"

Eric said, "We figured that you'd might like to know about his death. Send flowers to his family or something, a card. After all, you two were cellmates here for nearly eight months. Right?"

The colonel smiled. "As far as I remember, he was an asshole. The news of his death doesn't move me in the least."

"What about the photocopy of the hit list?" Dale said. "Does that move you?" Dale pointed toward the tattoo on the colonel's forearm. "Does it upset you that only one of the names has been x'ed out, so to speak?"

"You think this tattoo has anything to do with that hit list?" The colonel laughed. "This prison tat, that's the lingo in here, by the way, prison tat, it represents the years of my confinement inside this fine institution. Four years, but with good behavior I'll be out in two. Thus, I intend on skipping years one and two, leaving me with one year down, year three here, x'ed out, and one to go."

Dale said, "That's a ridiculous lie, sir."

"Is it? Sounds plausible to me."

Eric said, "We spoke with the cab driver who picked Sean Fitzsimmons up on the day he was paroled. The cabbie drove Sean to the First Citizens Bank here in downtown Leavenworth. There, Sean accessed a safe deposit box. Guess what password Sean used to access the box?"

Colonel Thoms shrugged.

Eric flipped the photocopy to reveal the password. "Angel 12. The call sign that Captain Mike Ruffers used on the night of the bombing of the Sorubi village."

Dale said, "And that safe deposit box, it was registered to Amy Benter of Baltimore, Maryland. Funny thing is, Amy Benter doesn't exist. You're from Baltimore, Maryland, aren't you, sir?"

Again, the colonel shrugged.

"You still have family and friends there, right? Your mom and sister? Maybe an old high school buddy or two."

Colonel Thoms said, "If I were a judge at an Article 32 hearing, listening to you piece together this sham, I'd throw it out for lack of evidence."

Dale said, "And if I were a lawyer, presenting the case, I'd tell you that I'm not finished. Now. Tape from a surveillance camera inside that bank shows Sean collecting a sizeable amount of cash, along with the Ruger .45 that he used to shoot and kill Alex Snead." Again, Dale pointed toward the colonel's prison tattoo, the tat, as was the lingo. "The number three man there on the hit list, x'ed out while having dinner with his family. Sean then went after number four, Eric Scholl here, and was damn near successful."

Sarcastically, Eric rolled two fingers, bowed his head as royalty.

Dale continued: "The next day, Sean entered my parents' home." Dale paused for a moment, studied the colonel. "What I don't understand, sir, is why Sean wanted to know the whereabouts of my wife. What does my wife have to do with any of this?"

The colonel glanced away, at the shackles, the floor. It seemed Dale had hit a soft spot.

The room fell silent.

A guard cleared his throat.

Dale said, "Why, sir? I don't understand. You said so yourself, that you're eligible for parole with two years served. The court-martial left you with your rank and your retirement income, so why not just do your two years and get on with your life? That's what I don't understand. For the life of me, I just don't get it. Why jeopardize your future by hiring a hit man? I know you were pissed off at me, and that you think that I betrayed you, but to hold a grudge like this, it just doesn't make sense."

Yes, Dale had hit a soft spot. When the guards roused the colonel from his cell and informed him that he had visitors outside of regular visitation hours, he figured that something like this might be up. He bolstered up, entered the room with a chip on his shoulder. However, the intense hatred that had accompanied him to prison was waning day by day. Back then, he would have lit the world on fire just for the hell of it. Nowadays, there were times when he could douse such a fire with his tears. Yeah, a grown man crying himself to sleep at night, a Marine, nonetheless. Pathetic. Catch him in the act, and he just might snap your neck. He was still as strong as an ox. But yeah, he was tearful these days, sorrowful. Even water finds its way through stone, given enough time. He looked up from his shackles, and said to Agent Riley, "You got a tape recorder in your pocket?" His laughter was forced, his eyes wet with tears.

"No tape recorder, sir. Something much better than that. But first I need to know why. Why couldn't you let it go and move on?"

The colonel puzzled for a moment. "Something better than a tape recorder?"

"A proposition, sir. One that I think you'll like. But first I need to know why."

Again, Thoms examined his shackles, and quietly he said, "Either one of you have any children?"

Both men nodded; Dale glanced away.

Colonel Thoms sighed. He'd told no one this. No one. Should he open up, and get this off his chest, perhaps he could then let it go and move on. Perhaps. He looked from one agent to the other. "I was married for thirty years." He glanced away, out the window. "Thirty fucking years. Jesus." He then looked directly at Dale. "She left me, you know. Earlier this year, she left me. Said she couldn't take it anymore. Me being like this, in prison." He lifted his shackles, and then rested them again in his lap. "You know, I blamed you. When the prison guard delivered those fucking divorce papers, I blamed you, Mr. Riley." The colonel smiled, but it was conflicted, accented with a tear. "I figured that if I lost my wife because of all this, that it would only be fair if you lost yours."

Dale's blood ran cold. He remembered Sean Fitzsimmons, standing feverishly in his parent's living room, asking as to the whereabouts of Dale's wife, Gina. Dale shook his head, and said, "No!"

The colonel nodded, seemingly ashamed.

"You're a bastard," Dale said. "You know that?"

"I am many things, Mr. Riley, but it is my understanding that your wife is alive and well."

"Fuck you."

"Yes. Fuck me." He seemed to drift away. "We didn't have any children, my wife and I, but yes, there was a child. Years ago, you see, when I was a first lieutenant fresh out of law school, I had an affair. I cheated on my wife. It was stupid, I know. I regretted it deeply. Still do. She was a sergeant, the girl with whom I had my affair, my legal clerk." Again, he glanced away and out the windows. "She got orders overseas to Japan, and shipped away. All for the best, really, for it gave us the distance we needed to get back to our lives. In Japan, however, she gave birth. And yes, the child was mine. Still, I never knew him. My son. I never had the opportunity to hold him or to look him in the eyes. My wife and I tried to have a child of our own, but it wasn't meant to be. Throughout the years, I never told her about my son. She never knew him or the love that I had for him. To this day she has no clue." He wiped his face, his eyes. "The sergeant, she sent me pictures and letters and kept me up to date. For that, I was always grateful. I assisted with money, when I could, and was very careful not to get caught. With every postcard and picture, I grew to love him more. It . . . sounds crazy, I know. Perhaps if my wife and I had had children of our own, I would have felt differently. But I had just that one child, a son that I loved very deeply." He looked to Dale, wiped a tear. "Funny, huh? A tough guy like me, crying."

"No, sir." Dale said nothing further. The colonel was on a roll; let him talk.

And then, just like that, the colonel slammed both of his fists on the table, the shackles loud, clanking.

The guards reached for their weapons, advanced.

Dale and Eric started.

When Dale realized that the colonel had no intention of attacking anyone, he held up his hands to ward off the guards. "Hold on, gentlemen. Give us a minute, okay?"

Cautiously, the guards retreated.

The room remained tense.

The colonel's face was red with anger, his eyes bloodshot, still teary. "He was there that night in Afghanistan! My son was there! It was in his blood, see, and when he graduated from college he joined the Marine Corps. He was an intelligence officer on his first assignment overseas, and he was at the Sorubi village the night that Captain Ruffers bombed it. Don't you see? Captain Ruffers killed my only son. He killed him! And you assholes let him off the hook." Had this encounter gone down a few months earlier, the colonel might have said fuck it, and assaulted them both. Now, however, he lowered his head and sobbed. A broken man. It was probably one of the saddest things that Dale had ever seen.

Eric and Dale shared a look of wide-eyed disbelief. *Holy shit.* Not in a million years would they have seen this coming.

For what felt like forever, the colonel sobbed.

The guards remained on edge, keen to certain aspects of the conversation, ready to intervene if necessary.

Dale turned to Eric. "Can you give us a minute?"

"You bet." Eric got up, walked to the vending machines, and dropped a soda.

When the colonel collected himself, Dale leaned in so that the guards couldn't hear. "I'm sorry for your loss, sir. That's . . . well, that's horrible. I wish I had known. Why didn't you tell me earlier?"

The colonel wiped his face. "The conditions surrounding the existence of my son were not, as we say, conducive for good order and discipline."

"Right. Anyway, I have a son, sir, and I can't imagine."

The colonel nodded.

Dale said, "Look. Sir. I want this to be over between the two of us, for the sake of my son. I'm sure you can understand that. I don't want to spend another minute looking over my shoulder, peering into shadows. Now. In exchange for this peace of mind, I have something to offer you."

The colonel looked up and waited. Again he wiped his eyes.

Dale reached into a jacket, pulled out a pocket bible, and set this on the table.

The colonel picked it up. "This is it? This is what you have to offer me?"

"This is the cherry on top, sir. There's much more." Dale leaned in farther, whispered into the colonel's ear.

The guards watched as the colonel broke into a smile from ear to ear, his once-teary eyes now bright and merry with vengeance.

CHAPTER 57

Friday morning.
0200 hours.

A white government van traveled east on Interstate 40, the entire vehicle wrapped in bulletproof glass and paneling, rolling on run-flat tires.

Two soldiers sat up front, two more in the back, each packing some variant of heat.

There was a fifth man as well, in back with his wrists and his ankles cuffed, his waist shackled tightly to the seat, which was bolted to the floor. At this hour, he didn't sleep, and wouldn't anytime soon. There would be plenty of time to sleep when he was dead. He simply stared into the darkness and remembered his son: First Lieutenant Mark Tegee of the United States Marine Corps. Before all of this went down, when Mark was still alive, there were times when the colonel would hold his son's photograph, and wonder what it might be like to sit with him and talk. He wondered what his voice would sound like, or what he might see in his son's eyes. He imagined sharing a beer with him, and that someday, with familiarity, that his son might even call him Dad. A pipe dream, really, but dreams were all that he had of his only son.

And then his son was gone. Just like that, gone. The Devil spread his wings, descended from the heavens, and blew fire down upon them. That's how a village elder described the horrific scene that night, no truer words spoken than these.

A madman killed his son.

His son.

Mark would never grow old to become the man that the colonel was not. He would never rise through the ranks, to captain, and then major, lieutenant colonel and colonel. He would never pin on general. Mark would never know marriage, and thus would never be faithful to love, to have and care for children, to be an honorable husband and father, to be honest, to be that better man. It would have been one thing had his son died at the hands of the enemy. There is honor in that. But that another Marine had killed him, a sick, murderous prick who had employed his weapon illegally and amorally, well, this was nothing short of an outrage.

Mike Ruffers should have paid with his life.

With any luck, it wasn't too late.

His son was dead.

The Marine Corps had disowned him, sent him to Leavenworth.

His wife had left him.

All he had left in this life was revenge.

Free his wrists and ankles, unshackle him from this seat, and arm him with a pistol. He'd hold it to the head of the driver and demand that he take him where they were already taking him.

And step on it!

CHAPTER 58

Friday afternoon.
1600 hours.

T he first week of the trial was nearly over.

After opening statements, Sheila Manning had called to the witness stand Homicide Detective Chad Allen of the Indianapolis Police Department. Throughout his testimony, Sheila entered into evidence the scissors that the killer had left behind at the crime scene, the bible that had covered the victim's face, along with a myriad of photographs. She presented the coroner's report and the forensics report. She introduced records from the airline that showed that Mike Ruffers had piloted the jet from Akron to Indianapolis on the day on which Eloise had occupied seat 21C. She introduced hotel records that showed Mike checking in only moments after Eloise. Later, she would examine the hotel clerk, who would testify that the defendant had asked for a room on the same floor as Eloise. The entire testimony took nearly three days.

Friday afternoon, she put on the whiteboard the most graphic photograph among them: Eloise Saleem the way that John "Jonny" Royston had found her, bathed in blood, her guts hanging loose, the bible covering her face. She asked the jury to take a good hard look at this, and to imagine that it was their daughter up there, their wife, or their mother.

She finished her examination at precisely 4:00 P.M. She had planned it perfectly. Billy wouldn't have time to begin his cross, which meant that the jury would enter the weekend with that horrific image in mind. With any luck, they wouldn't sleep.

Judge Barwick checked his wristwatch. "Okay. Court will reconvene first thing Monday morning, 9:00 A.M. Let me remind the jury that you are to speak to no one about this case or your involvement with it, not family, not friends, and certainly not the media. You are also to avoid any news of this case. Should anyone approach you about this, you are to report this to the court immediately. That is all." He clacked his gavel. "Court is adjourned."

Judge Barwick exited the courtroom, followed by the jury.

State troopers came and handcuffed the defendant.

The audience began to file out.

Subtly, Sheila turned to the audience, to the first row, and shot Dale Riley a questioning look. Beside him were Eric Scholl and Lionel McCarthy.

Dale gave her a nod.

Since opening statements, Dale and Eric had been absent from the courtroom. Not that it was nice to see them again, but it was, in fact, nice to see that nod. It was a done deal, and now only a matter of time.

Sheila stuffed her briefcase and walked away. Her assistant followed.

Billy Roth adjusted his tie and slicked his hair with the palm of his hand. On the courthouse steps would be reporters with microphones and cameras, and he had to look his best. He'd smile and proclaim the innocence of his client, the fairness of our judicial system, certain to throw out the name of his firm, nothing wrong with a little free advertising. When his name first hit national news, his phone began to ring off the hook, and hadn't stopped. Business was good. Hell, he might have to hire another attorney. Maybe two, and pay 'em like crap. He grabbed his briefcase and followed Sheila toward the exit.

The state troopers were leading the defendant toward a side door that would take them to a private elevator. On the way, Mike spotted Dale in the audience. He shot Dale a wink, and licked the very lips that had been at Dale's wife. By now, Dale would know the truth, that indeed Mike and Gina had had sex. The encounter had happened not long after Mike had been acquitted of the charges at the court-martial. An innocent man, Mike should have been living the high life. Unfortunately, his commanding officer had said that he had lost faith in him, had Mike report to the squadron's flight surgeon. An MD, the flight surgeon diagnosed Mike with a personality disorder. As such, Mike was unfit to fly military jets, which nullified his contract. The Marine Corps gave him the standard six-month notice of termination, when, at such time, they would send him away with an honorable discharge. It just wasn't right. He was an innocent man. Outraged with this news, Mike got on the horn and dialed his attorney. With the help of Captain Riley, the two would once again kick ass and take names.

Captain Riley, however, bogged down with Colonel Thoms's Article 32 hearing, didn't have the time or desire to take Mike's calls. In fact, he was done with Mike, done! The court-martial was over, and he didn't need the headache.

Only, Mike wasn't done with Dale.

It was one thing to be cast aside by so-called authority figures—commanding officers and flight surgeons—and quite another to be cast aside by your peers, the one man whom Mike had entrusted with his life. That Dale refused to return his phone calls was insult to injury.

One Friday night, after a few too many drinks, Mike hopped inside his car. If Dale wouldn't answer the phone, perhaps he would answer the door.

He drove to Dale's apartment complex and arrived just in time to see Dale exit his unit and hop inside a blue Honda Civic.

Dale set off, and Mike followed. One way or another, they were going to have words.

They drove west to Wilmington, where Dale pulled up to an apartment complex and entered a unit.

Mike watched.

Minutes later, Dale came out with a girl on his arm. The two hopped inside the Civic.

Again, Mike followed.

They drove downtown and parked.

Careful not to be noticed, Mike followed as they entered a bar.

Mike ordered a beer and watched them from afar. At first happy, the couple now appeared to be arguing. A group of college-aged kids showed up, and the girl seemed relieved with company; Dale, however, seemed put off by them—friends of the girl's, no doubt. Moments later, Dale pulled her aside, where again they argued. It was about this time when Dale threw up his hands and stormed away, out the front door, with no indication that he would return.

Still intent on that confrontation, Mike drained his beer and followed. When he reached the door, however, he had another idea, something far more sinister.

Mike returned to the bar, where he ordered another beer. He watched the girl. She was obviously upset. To cheer her up, her friends were ordering her drinks and taking her out onto the dance floor.

The night grew old, and more and more people crammed the bar.

The girl excused herself to the restroom. Mike followed her there and waited outside. When she exited, he struck up a conversation. She was obviously drunk, and he was without doubt as charming as Ted Bundy. It didn't take much to get her to laugh, and she was happy to accept another drink. And another. When she had obviously had too much, slyly, he sneaked her away from her friends.

God, he couldn't have planned a better night.

He took her to his car and drove her back to her apartment.

Kindly, gentlemanly, he helped her inside.

He shut the door behind them, and locked it.

In the morning, he rolled over and asked her if she was ready for round two.

She opened her eyes. Frightfully, she pulled up the covers. "Who are you?"

"Jeez, you pick me up at the bar last night, and now you can't remember my name? I feel so cheap."

Confused, hung over beyond belief, she hopped out of bed and threw on a robe. She felt like she was going to vomit. "I don't know what . . . if that happened, that was a mistake." She tried to remember, but her head was throbbing. "Please. Just go."

Mike pulled on his jeans and his shirt. "Sure. Use me and abuse me."

She pointed toward the door. "Go!"

Pulling on his jacket, Mike smiled and said, "Oh. By the way. Tell your boyfriend, Dale, that I said hello."

As confused as ever, she said, "You know my boyfriend?"

"Yeah. He's my lawyer. My name is Mike Ruffers. Tell him hey for me, would ya?"

"You're Mike Ruffers?"

"You've heard of me? Why, I'm flattered."

Shaking her head, adamant now more than ever, she said, "Get out! Now! Before I call the police."

"Okay. No need to get testy. You weren't so grumpy last night, were you?" He made an obscene gesture.

"Goddamn it, get out!" She started to cry.

Delighted, Mike picked up his keys and left her apartment. He thought about driving by Dale's apartment to fill him in on all the sordid details. In the end, however, he went home. He had banged his lawyer's girl, and with that he felt wickedly satisfied. Besides, the airlines were calling him now, interested in Mike's services. Perhaps his dismissal from the Corps had been a blessing in disguise. And speaking of blessings in disguise: who would have thought that several years later this encounter would come in handy at a criminal trial? When Mike confessed this to his attorney, Billy was quick to spin the facts, and it was beautiful, man, fucking beautiful.

Now, inside courtroom four and on his way toward the side door, Mike smiled and licked his lips and blew Dale a kiss. He imagined that this would infuriate Dale, and so he searched his eyes for that fury.

Only, Dale didn't react as Mike had hoped. Instead, Dale smiled, and stood firm.

Mike spat at him and struggled against the guards. "You fucked up, man. I'll be free before you know it. I promise you that."

The state troopers wrestled him away out the door.

Behind Dale, an unfamiliar man said to him: "What in the hell was that all about?"

Dale looked at Eric, turned to the man, and said, "Mike Ruffers is going down. Deep down, he knows this, and he doesn't like it one bit."

CHAPTER 59

During the week, Mike had a holding cell in the basement of the courthouse. On the weekends, the feds kept him at the Butner Federal Correctional Institution, an hour or so drive from downtown Raleigh.

A guard waved the car through the gates.

The troopers rolled to a stop in front of the admin building.

Inside, the troopers signed Mike over, where he arranged his suit on a hanger and threw on the local fashion.

"That's my lucky suit," he said to the prison guard. "Don't fuck it up."

"Follow me, wiseass." The guard tossed the suit on a chair. He led Mike to a low-security prison block where he opened the heavy iron door and shoved Mike inside. "Too bad you missed dinner."

Mike had been here for months now, his cell courtesy of Billy Roth, who had successfully argued against one of the more hardened federal pens. Inside, the men were out from their cells and in the rec area. They chattered in corners and loitered at tables, where they played cards and board games. Mike hated the lot of them. Fat cats, mostly, doing time for white-collar crimes.

Mike entered as if he owned the joint, the alpha dog; the playground bully.

He walked up to Simon and Pete playing chess, and rested his shoe on a chair.

He said to Pete, "Take his queen, you queen."

Pete, concentrating on his next move, and uneasy now with Mike there beside him, said, "I can't take his queen."

"Then take his king, you queen."

Pete and Simon exchanged a look.

Pete said, "I can't take his king either."

In a mocking voice, Mike said, "I can't take his king either." He looked around and saw no guards. He popped Pete on the side of his head, hard, just above his ear.

"Ouch. That hurt."

"Shut your trap or I'll punch your fucking face in, you faggot." Mike then turned and walked away, toward his cell. Jesus, he fucking hated these guys, each and every one of them.

The cells lined the rec area; Mike's tucked away in a corner.

He clicked on the light bulb, which illuminated his shitter and his bed, and something else. He stopped, looked around, and yelled out: "Hey. Which one of you cocksuckers was inside my cell?"

Of the approximately fifty cocksuckers in the rec area, not a single one replied.

Mike poked his head out. "If I ever catch any of you fuckwads inside my cell, I will beat you brain dead, you got me? Mother-fuckers!" He slapped the wall and reentered his cell.

That was the problem with this whole "socialization" nonsense. The cell doors would open, all of them, and the goddamn criminals would come and go at their leisure. The gays would get together and fornicate, and the prissy little bitches like Pete and Simon would sit and play chess as though they were actually accomplishing something. Or else they would enter Mike's cell and leave a small book on his pillow. They had probably kicked up their feet on Mike's bed and made themselves at fucking home. Hell, they had probably even used Mike's shitter.

Mike picked up the book. He intended to throw it out into the rec area, but when he saw the title, he froze.

Pocket Holy Bible.

Poking out from the top was a bookmark. Curiously, Mike ran his fingers to it and cracked it open, the *Holy Bible.*

There, he saw a passage circled in red ink.

"What the fuck?"

He flashed back to what he had done to those girls, dipping his finger in their blood, circling a passage in a bible. He wanted to believe that someone was playing a sick joke on him, for indeed this sensational aspect of the killings had made the news. What he felt, however, was fear. He ran his finger to the beginning of the passage (the same finger he'd used to dip into their blood), his heart beating wildly, his lips dry and his eyes wide.

Here was some of King David's best work.

He glanced toward the door, and then back to the passage: the Old Testament, before the birth of baby Jesus, back when God wasn't so tolerant, when He was full of piss and vinegar.

Mike broke out in goosebumps.

Quietly, his dry lips trembling, he read:

"The lord is my shepherd, I shall not want;
"He maketh me lie down in green pastures;
"He leadeth me beside the still waters;
"He restoreth my soul;
"He leadeth me down the path of righteousness for His name's sake;
"Yea, though I walk through the valley of the shadow of death,
I will fear no evil."

He was crying now, his entire body shaking.

He sensed a powerful presence, a presence not unlike God, and never in his life had he been so afraid.

Yes, he sensed a presence, had heard the footsteps approach, coming from the rec area, coming for him slowly, how the men had parted a path toward Mike's cell, no guards out there, and thus no one to save him.

Slowly, frightfully, he turned around.

There are times when the fight-or-flight instinct is so powerful that the body does neither, simply freezes.

In a very small voice, Mike said, "Do I know you?"

Colonel Christopher Thoms, United States Marine Corps, didn't answer the question.

Colonel Christopher Thoms stepped farther inside Mike's cell, his meaty hands rolled into fists. "You didn't finish."

"I . . . I didn't finish what?"

"The passage. From the bible there. You didn't finish."

Mike glanced down at the bible, and then back up again.

Colonel Christopher Thoms said, "For thou art with me; Thy rod and thy staff, they comfort me."

Colonel Christopher Thoms stepped farther inside. "Thou preparest a table before me in the presence of *mine* enemies."

"No. Please!" Mike backed away, dropped the bible on the concrete floor.

Colonel Christopher Thoms stepped farther inside. "Thou anointest my head with oil; my cup runneth over." And yet farther inside. "Goodness and mercy shall follow me all the days of my life; and I will dwell in the house of the lord, forever." Farther inside. "But you're not going to the house of the lord, are you?"

"Please. God. No!"

Mike was strong, but this man was a monster, compelled by the loss of his son and thusly driven by fury.

In an instant Colonel Christopher Thoms was on him, painting these walls red, the concrete floor, the mattress, and yes, even Mike's shitter, red.

Michael J. Ruffers went quickly and wasn't nearly the fighter that Aalia Khalil had been. He went like the lady down in Texas, surprised and full of fear; barely able to scream once the colonel was upon him.

In the rec area, Pete moved his rook. He smiled to Simon and said, "Check and mate!"

EPILOGUE

When Dale Riley awoke, he rolled over and stared up at the ceiling. He felt . . . better. Not great, just better. He looked out the window. He had the day off, and the sun was shining. He yawned, stretched, and broke a soft smile.

He pulled on some shorts and a T-shirt, laced up his sneakers.

In Clint's room, he opened the blinds. Clint was already awake, had pulled himself up by the slats of the crib, the contents of which he'd emptied out onto the floor, the stuffed animals, the lining, and even the mattress.

"I like what you've done to the place," Dale said, laughing, picking things up. "You want to go for a walk with me? Yeah?"

Clint cooed and shoved his knuckles into his mouth.

Dale lifted his son and kissed him. "Is today the day you say Dad? I know you can say Mom, but how about Dad?"

Clint frowned and shook his head, continued to chew on his knuckles.

"Oh, well. Maybe soon, right?"

In the kitchen they ate their breakfast.

Dale found his camera and took a photograph of the front page of the *Washington Chronicle*. This he would put in Clint's scrapbook.

With the dishes in the sink, he strapped Clint into the stroller.

Outside, the air crisp and clean, perfect for a walk.

Pushing his son, Dale set off down the block.

Together, father and son, they walked the vibrant sidewalks of Old Town Alexandria, passing shops and restaurants, businessmen and -women in suits, joggers in shorts, the Irish pub on King Street where he and Eric would oftentimes meet for beer and to solve the world's problems.

They walked past a bakery that smelled like heaven dusted with cinnamon, and for a brief moment he considered popping inside and ordering up the entire window display. However, his diet was going well, his weight below the two-century mark with ten more pounds to go. Salivating, he kept walking.

They walked past a park with dogs catching Frisbees and college kids with books.

And even in these sunny hours they walked by dark alleyways where deep inside were even darker men.

Dale glanced down at his son and wondered about the future: would Clint grow up to be one of the good guys, or would he be more like . . . ?

Past the alleyway now, Dale dismissed the troubling thought. Of course Clint would be one of the good guys, of course. Hell, he might even join the Marine Corps, and do heroic things, so that someday, man to man, Marine to Marine, Clint might look to his old man and say, *Semper Fidelis, Dad. Semper Fi!*

Always faithful.

The media never did find out what the S and F of the *SF Killer* stood for. Dale knew, of course, and was intent on protecting this motto from blemish. Semper Fidelis means nothing of what Mike Ruffers stood for. Semper Fidelis is everything that Mike wasn't. To have the media drag this through the mud would have insulted the hero in each and every one of us. It would have been a black eye to the one institution in America where honor is king and where sacrifice is noble. Dale's untimely dismissal from the Corps in no way lessened his sentiments for the hearts and souls of the men and women who call themselves Marines. Semper Fidelis would go on unblemished and inspire like-minded souls to raise their hands and take the oath. The ethos of Semper Fidelis would live on to protect the greatest nation on earth. Some may find this corny, but Dale believed it, and he prayed that someday his son might believe it as well.

Sheila Manning had phoned him some Saturday past with news that Mike Ruffers had died in prison, that another inmate had murdered him, an inmate that the Justice Department had transferred from Leavenworth just that morning.

"Is he okay?" Dale asked her over the phone. "Colonel Thoms? Is he all right?"

"He's awaiting formal charges for the murder of Mike Ruffers, but. . . ."

"But what?"

"He isn't eating, and he's not doing well, physically. Currently, he's in the infirmary."

"He's going to be okay, though, right?"

"That's up to him."

Dale sighed and had to stop himself from wondering whether or not he'd done the right thing. He did what he had to do to protect his family, as well as the innocent people that might have crossed paths with Mike Ruffers had the jury set him free. He gave an old man his revenge, which served as a benefit to all parties involved, excluding, of course, the newly deceased. Certainly, Dale had manipulated the justice system, but mostly his conscience was clean. Mostly.

Sheila said, "Judge Barwick declared a mistrial. Billy Roth is currently pitching a fit, all but accusing me of arranging the confrontation between Thoms and Ruffers."

"We're good to go, though, right? I mean . . . the prison transfer was perfectly legal."

"One could certainly argue that we were complicit in all this, but Colonel Thoms isn't talking, to anyone. And once Billy realizes that there isn't any money in pursuing this, he'll move on to more lucrative projects. I wouldn't worry too much. No one seems to care. Mike had no family at the trial, no real character witnesses, and so aside from Billy, no one is going to push the issue."

Sheila was right. The only loose string here was Colonel Thoms, and so long as he remained silent, informed no one of the conversation that he and Dale had had at Leavenworth, that Dale had given him a pocket bible and a convenient prison transfer, then there was nothing to worry about.

"Okay," Dale said. "Thanks . . . for everything."

Sheila said, "Good-bye, Special Agent Riley. Take care."

That was it. It was over. At last it was over.

An hour later, Dale having worked up a sweat, they returned to the bungalow and enjoyed the special day.

That evening after supper, Dale pulled the cake out from the refrigerator. He punched a candle through the icing and lit it with a match.

When the song was over, Clint blew out the candle and with a swipe of his arm nearly tossed the cake onto the floor.

Quickly, Dale prevented this from happening. When he glanced at his son, he recognized that cool indifference in his son's blue eyes, the similarities. He had no choice but to laugh while the chills consumed him, a vision of Mike Ruffers at the court-martial, in the aftermath of the melee, just sitting there while everyone else fought and scrambled; Mike Ruffers, naked, just outside of Gina's bedroom, holding a pair of scissors and a bible. Dale laughed it all off and cut for his son a generous piece of birthday cake.

Clint proceeded to make a mess of himself, had icing and cake all over his face.

Dark thoughts would come and go, as they had throughout the day, the days since the revelation of the affair, but for now Dale grabbed his camera and took more photographs.

He leaned in and kissed his son, many times over. Yes. His son! He'd raise him right, teach him to be honorable and virtuous, and so of course he'd be one of the good guys, of course. Of course.

He put a loving arm around his beautiful wife, pulled her in, and kissed her as well.

Gina leaned into her husband, her head on his chest with her arms around his waist. Together, they watched their son with his first piece of birthday cake. She then flexed to the tips of her toes and returned to her husband a kiss.

Yes. Everything was at last going to be okay.

It was all going to be just dandy.

ACKNOWLEDGMENTS

Special thanks to Stephen Hillis, my high school journalism teacher, not because I remember much from the chalkboard, but because he believed in me at a time when I was utterly lost. In my life, a teacher has made all the difference. Thanks to the men and women with whom I served, to the Marines of VMGR-252 and VMGR-452, the Betio Bastards of 3rd Battalion 2nd Marines. Liza Fleissig and the brilliant gang at Liza Royce Agency, your insight and assistance with this project has been amazing, thank you so much. Lastly, I would like to thank Pegasus for taking a chance with a debut novelist, and to Jessica Case, senior editor, for the countless hours and phone calls.

Now that you've read this book, I would like to quote from my favorite teacher of all time: "It's time get off your ass and go do something with your life."